Romantic Times **praises Norah Hess, Winner of the Reviewers' Choice Award for Frontier Romance!**

STORM

"A charming story filled with warm, real, and likable characters."

SAGE

"Earthy, sincere, realistic, and heartwarming....Norah Hess continues to craft wonderful stories of the frontier!"

KENTUCKY WOMAN

"*Kentucky Woman* is an Americana love story with the grittiness of a frontier Western that brings readers straight into the lives and hearts of the characters."

MOUNTAIN ROSE

"Another delightful, tender, and heartwarming read from a special storyteller!"

KENTUCKY BRIDE

"Marvelous...a treasure for those who savor frontier love stories!"

HAWKE'S PRIDE

"Earthy and realistic....Bravo to Norah Hess!"

PASSION'S FLAME

Sate cautiously smoothed a hand down her side, onto a rounded hip, then over the shape of her long, smooth thigh. He was so conscious of the rounded breasts crushed against his chest, of stomachs and legs pressed against each other, that it came as a shock when he finally realized the rigid body had begun to relax.

She stirred and Sate stiffened, her soft flesh branding him like a hot iron. Suddenly smooth bare arms were thrown around his waist and hardened nipples burned against his chest. It would be a dastardly act to take what she was offering, he reminded himself as he sought to remove her arms.

"No!" the single word slipped fiercely through the soft lips. "You are not leaving me tonight, hungry and aching."

FOREVER THE FLAME

NORAH HESS

LOVE SPELL **NEW YORK CITY**

LOVE SPELL®

February 1995

Published by

Dorchester Publishing Co., Inc.
276 Fifth Avenue
New York, NY 10001

The name ''Love Spell'' and its logo are trademarks of Dorchester
Publishing Co., Inc.

Printed in the United States of America.

CHAPTER 1

The moon was full, its light reflected by the snow, so that the bare trees and dark pines stood out starkly on the softly rolling hillsides. On the topmost hill a lone wolf raised his head and sent a mournful cry to the yellow disk suspended in the empty black sky.

At the bottom of the hill a trapper, his lean muscular body driving into that of a young squaw squirming beneath him, raised his black shaggy head and growled, "Howl, you bastard."

The girl, taking his hard, fast thrusts, shifted uncomfortably. The frozen ground was cold on her bare buttocks and she sent a surreptitious glance over her shoulder, her black eyes searching for the half-empty jug of whiskey which she has previously sampled. A few more long draughts of the fiery liquid and she wouldn't care how long this half-wild trapper kept at her, even though a good half hour had already passed. Evidently this white man had been a long time without a woman, she thought, and she was almost regretting her venture into his camp. But she had been belly-twisting hungry and frozen to the bone. The aroma of his roasting supper and the hope of a warm spot before his fire had driven from her mind the thought that later she would have to pay for her meal.

The girl felt the trapper's sinewy frame tighten and braced herself for another release. She stoically accepted the stepped-up battering of her narrow hips, keeping her eyes on the moon as the man gave one last strong shove, then fell on top of her, shivering spasmodically. She lay quietly, hoping that he had at last been satiated and that he would permit her to sleep beside his fire.

But there is no warmth in this trapper who sprawls his weight upon me, she reminded herself, and he wouldn't hesitate to send me away without a thought.

She had suspected his coldness from the moment she had stood uncertain in the shadows surrounding his campfire. For even as his huge dog caught her scent and raised his hackles and bared his teeth in a warning growl, the broad shoulders hunched before the fire never stirred an inch. Finally, although her legs ached from the many miles she had trudged that day, she reluctantly turned to leave, hopeful that farther along the trail she would run into a man more friendly.

She had taken but a few steps, however, when a gruff voice ordered, "Come into the light, squaw, and let me have a look at you."

The girl pivoted on the balls of her moccasin-shod feet, coarse black hair swishing across her dirt-streaked face. "Would you please call off the dog?" she asked nervously, eyeing the snarling animal and wondering if she dare walk past him.

The rough voice grunted as the man tossed a stick of wood onto the fire. Then the arrogantly held head turned slowly and the squaw stared into the coldest eyes she had ever seen. Their blue iciness scanned her slender body in its worn doeskin shift, and the girl shivered, caught by the strong urge to turn and run. This man could be very cruel if the opportunity should arise. A squaw would have to be on her toes every minute with this one.

She relaxed a bit when the man spoke a low word to the dog and it settled down beside him. After a moment she moved cautiously into the circle of light and stood before the narrow-eyed, assessing trapper. "What are you called?" he asked so abruptly that she jumped. When she stammered that she was called Smiling Waters, he grunted, "I'll call you Doxy."

"Doxy?" The girl frowned. "I have never heard such a strange name."

"It fits you," the chisled lips pronounced.

"Yes, sir," the newly named girl mumbled, more interested in the rabbit roasting over the fire.

Sardonic amusement glinted in the man's knowing eyes as he watched her, and after a moment he hunkered his whip-lean body down beside the fire and pulled the meat from the greenwood spit. "Are you hungry?" he asked, tearing a crusted brown leg from the steaming carcass and placing it on a tin plate. At her eager nod he added a piece of cold pone and held it out to her. After she had almost snatched it from his hands, he turned and filled his own plate.

The meal was consumed in silence broken only by the soft soughing of the wind in the pines and the crackling and crunching of the bones tossed to the hound.

Doxy's eyes were busy, however, as she devoured the meat and bread, and for the first time she noted the sturdy log cabin that sat several feet to their right. It blended in with the pines that surrounded it, making the log structure almost invisible to the casual eye. Her bewildered gaze sought the trapper, wondering why they sat outside in the cold when warm quarters were available.

"Is there something wrong with your cabin?" she ventured when her stony-faced companion drew a handkerchief from his back pocket and wiped his mouth, signaling that he was finished eating.

"The cabin is fine." The trapper pulled a blackened coffee pot off the coals and filled two battered cups with steaming liquid. Handing the girl one of the pewter vessels, he added, "I prefer being outdoors as long as possible."

"As do my people." Doxy nodded understandingly.

"And who are your people?" The tone of the question was uninterested.

"I am of the Pennacook tribe, out of Canada."

"You're a long way from home, squaw." Hard eyes raked over the girl. "How did you end up in Pennsylvania country?"

"A redcoat soldier brought me to this territory." A pensive look slid into the thin features. "When peace came, he returned to England."

"And left you stranded." The words came flatly, an angry undertone to them.

Doxy continued to sip the hot, bitter brew, not bothering to make the obvious answer as the buckskin clad man studied her thoughtfully.

He was facing a long winter, Sate Margruder reminded himself, months of being without a woman. This one seemed healthy enough—no sign of disease, her eyes were clear, and beneath the dirt on her face he could see no sores. When she looked longingly from her empty cup to the coffee pot and then over at him, he nodded permission to help herself. When she sat back, savoring the dark drink, her eyes widened and glittered at the words casually tossed at her.

"I want you to take note that I like my coffee strong, and that I expect you to make it that way."

Doxy leaned forward, daring to hope that she had been accepted as squaw woman to this hard-faced man, at least for the time being. Reading the question in her eyes, the trapper scowled. "You're a useless-looking thing, and probably not worth the grub it will take to feed you."

Finally there was life in the voice that declared eagerly, "I am stronger than I look. I worked hard for my English soldier."

"Beneath him, no doubt." The words were spoken dryly.

"There, too," Doxy conceded, her head lifted proudly. "Always he wanted me. Always he kept me with him, even taking me during a battle."

Margruder's lips twisted in a half smile. "So that's how we beat the English so easily."

"I do not know what you mean." Doxy frowned.

"Forget it. I'm more interested in how hard you'll work under me."

The young squaw looked into the unemotional eyes and sighed inwardly. It was time to pay for her supper. She resignedly prepared to lay back, lift her shift up around her hips, and let him have at it. But as she gripped the hem of the garment, it appeared the trapper wasn't ready to collect yet, for he had reached behind the log he sat on and pulled from beneath it a jug of what must be whiskey. Her eyes gleamed as he uncorked the brown clay and lifted it to his lips. She had developed a strong liking for the white, fiery liquid at a young age. Sixteen, to be exact, and had drunk it every chance she got in the past two years.

When the jug was handed to her with the curt instructions, "Drink up, get some spirit in you," she snatched the whiskey out of his callused hands, and after a few deep swallows, her Indian blood began to boil. Before long she was taking the initiative, inching closer and closer to the masculine frame stretched indolently before the fire. Her black eyes glittering at him, she reached over and slid a caressing hand down the front of his buckskins. Feeling his long, rigid strength, she exclaimed drunkenly, "You sure got something there, white man. The biggest I've ever felt."

"Yeah, well," the words were thick, "grab up some snow and scrub yourself out, and I'll let you feel it somewhere else."

After sliding him an uncertain look, and reading the seriousness in his expression, Doxy shrugged at the white man's crazy notion and, rising, walked over to a clean drift of snow. She flinched at the coldness between her warm thighs, and was thoroughly chilled by the time the trapper was satisfied and motioned her back beside him.

Now, her eyes still on the moon, Doxy sensed from the limpness of the trapper's body that this last time had finally satisfied his hunger. As though to finalize it, the wolf on the hill gave one last yowl and grew silent as the man pulled himself from between her legs.

"A fitting end." Cold blue eyes shot a bitter glance at the hill before turning his attention to the lacing of his buckskins. When he had tied off the leather strings, he looked at the girl and nodded toward the cabin. "You'll find a bedroll inside."

Doxy pulled the shift down around her chilled thighs and legs and was halfway to the cabin when a growled order followed her. "Be sure you have my breakfast ready by dawn."

Margruder watched the door close, then with a heavy sigh settled his long frame before the fire that was slowly dying out. He reached for the pipe and leather pouch of tobacco lying beside the jug.

"God," he muttered, crumbling and tamping "long-green" into the clay bowl, "I'm tired of wandering whores and sassy sluts, their stench, their calculated stroking with never a trace of feeling or tenderness in their touching." What would it be like, he wondered morosely, to hold a decent woman in his arms, to caress clean, warm flesh, to feel her respond to him with honest, passionate feelings?

He sighed raggedly as he brought a glowing coal to lie against the tobacco. He was tired, thoroughly tired of it all; the wasted, unachieving years.

Margruder stared into the flames, puffs of smoke drifting from the pipe stem clenched between strong white teeth as his thoughts drifted back. Only occasionally was he moved to smile.

Even before that winter when influenza had claimed his

entire family, he had hated the dull, dead monotony of farm
life. When he found himself left alone at seventeen he had
yielded to the call of the wilderness and had packed up grub
and gear, saying good-bye to the old homestead in New York
State. With the blood singing in his veins, he headed for the
then unexplored regions of Pennsylvania.

He had felt immediately at home in the small village he had
stumbled onto. The friendly Indians and rough mountain men
had liked his wild-natured, impetuous ways and had taken
charge of him in an offhand manner. The red man had taught
him the secrets of the forest and streams, and the white man
had settled him in to a house of his own. Using broad axe and
adze they had built this sturdy one-room cabin, constructed a
well drawing fireplace, and laid a soft pine floor. There was
only one window, but it was good-sized and gave him a
spectacular view of the forest and valleys when the shutters
were pushed open.

The settler wives had taken over then, furnishing his new
home from their own sparsely decorated cabins. One had
spared him a bed and bedding, another a table and bench, and
old Granny Hawkins had parted with one of her rocking chairs.
His cooking utensils were few and battered, but he owned two
tin plates and two pewter cups. He was set, everything
sufficient to his needs, the women informed him.

Those same women then sat back, waiting to see which of
their daughters he would court and wed. Out of a sense of
obligation he visited each home and spent an hour or so with
their rather plain-faced, simpering daughters. The young
ladies' prim and proper ways had grated on his nerves, making
him anxious to get away from them. After six weeks of insipid
conversation that managed to become lively only when
marriage was somehow introduced, he had had enough.

A half smile twitched the corners of Margruder's firm lips.
He had been in no hurry to relinquish his new freedom to some
sharp-tongued female who would make him account for his
actions and whereabouts. He ate when he was hungry, hunted
and fished whenever the whim hit him. He stayed away from
home until he was ready to return, maybe a day, maybe a week.
When approached testily on his need of a woman, he'd grin
and change the subject. That particular need had been filled by
the whores at the village tavern.

He had lived in his cabin, trapping for a living until he was twenty-five, until the rumbling of war with England had become a fact in July of '76. When the French, German, and Swiss volunteers crossed in French vessels to support the American forces he, too, had answered the call for help. He had taken part in the defeat of Burgoyne at Saratoga, then joined General Washington at Valley Forge in the desperate winter of 1777.

In the beginning army life appealed to him. The life of peril in the open had seemed a natural way to live. Then had come the strenuous years of ceaseless fighting, long night marches, and the lonely scouting within the enemy's lines during which he had sustained a severe leg wound.

Moisture filled the lean man's eyes as he recalled 1783 when peace finally came about and with it the final parting of the battle-worn men who had become closer to him than brothers. He had started his long journey home then, the war having left its mark on both body and soul.

The hard eyes which had glimpsed hell softened slightly. He had been warmly welcomed home by the villagers, drinks pressed on him, whores fighting over who should take him into the back room first. Yes, the first few days home had been like old times; tramping through the woods, joining his friends at the tavern, escorting a whore to the back room. But as time passed and he continued to visit old haunts it became harder and harder to recapture the exhilaration they had once afforded him. And equally disappointing was the diminished wildlife in the forest. Its scarcity was proved to him again as he ran his trap line. Each day he brought home fewer and fewer pelts. In his seven-year absence the game had either been trapped out or had been driven farther into the wilderness.

His hound approached the fire and settled down close to his master, seeking the warmth of his body. Margruder absently scratched the animal's battle-scarred ears, remembering how he had come in possession of the rough fellow.

A few weeks back he had wandered into the tavern at loose ends. The large smoke-stained room was devoid of patrons with the exception of a man and this dog. He nodded to the stranger, then, when he reached down and patted the animal's head, he was asked, "Do you want him?"

He glanced at the rotund man, wondering if he was serious. "I don't know," he answered, recognizing in the small eyes that it was no idle question. "Why do you want to give him away? He looks like a good hunting hound."

"He is, that's why I'm tryin' to find him a good home. I'm travelin' a far piece, and I'd just as soon not be bothered with him."

"Where are you goin', if you don't mind my askin'?"

The man spit a stream of tobacco juice out the open door, rinsed his mouth with a swig of ale, then answered, "There's a new territory just been opened up in Kentucky country. They say you can go all winter and not see a soul. And that's what I like. It's gettin' too crowded around here. You run into somebody every day."

"Where about in Kentucky is this new land?" he'd asked after ordering a mug of rum.

"Round about a small village called Squaw Hollow," the man answered, then asked impatiently, "Do you want the hound?"

The tail-wagging canine chose that moment to shove its nose into his palm, and he found himself looking for reasons he should take the animal. This fat piece of flesh sitting next to him wouldn't hesitate to let the dog go hungry occasionally if there wasn't sufficent food to share; weakened from lack of nourishment the fine-looking animal might not make the trip.

"What's his name?" He lifted his gaze to the stranger.

The plump shoulders shrugged. "I just call him hound."

"I'll call him Hawser," he decided, making up his mind. Margruder looked down on the head that had inched its way onto his lap. "Maybe we'll make that trek to Kentucky someday, Hawser."

The moon moved slowly in its orbit, and the somber man sat on, listening to the muted sounds of the night. He loved the wild solitude of the forest, as the Indians did, but there were times lately when the silence seemed unbearable. Often, when he should have been sleeping, he paced slowly under the cold white stars, his mind seeking he knew not what.

Sardonic amusement flickered in the cold blue eyes. Hopefully the squaw would ease some of his unrest, put a stop to his aimless night wandering.

The heat in the coals continued to fade. Margruder knocked out his pipe and, standing up, scraped ashes over the almost spent fire with a foot, then entered the cabin. In the darkness he made out the darker shape of the squaw rolled up in blankets as he moved to the bed in a corner. Its mattress of carefully laid pine boughs creaked lightly as it took his weight, blending with the strangled snore that came from in front the dead fireplace as Doxy turned over in her sleep.

As the trapper drifted off, he wondered if the squaw would think to look on the mantel for the flint kept there for starting fires.

The sky was just turning pink in the east when Margruder awakened to the aroma of brewing coffee and frying meat. He turned his head and watched Doxy as she knelt in front of a crackling fire, turning slices of salt pork in an iron skillet. After a moment he slid out of bed, stretched in his woolen underwear, then walked outside. He stepped to the end of the small porch and stood a minute, staining the white snow yellow. When he returned inside Doxy glanced at him and, seeing the manhood that jutted long and hard through the open fly, silently removed the pan from the fire, then lay back down on her bedroll and hitched up her shift.

Without a word spoken between them, he entered her, a few quick thrusts followed, and the lean body shivered as she felt its weight press down on her. After a moment the morose man pushed himself off her and she scrambled to her feet to replace the pan over the fire.

Breakfast was another silent meal. After one attempt at conversation, receiving a glowering look for her trouble, Doxy didn't open her mouth again until Margruder stood up and she realized he was about to leave to run his traps. "Mister"—she smiled tentatively—"what is your name? What am I to call you?"

His voice matching the harsh planes of his face, the trapper answered shortly, "Mister will do, squaw."

Doxy nodded dumbly, and went on nodding as he ordered before stepping through the door, "Have my supper ready by dark."

When she could no longer hear his crunching footsteps, she jumped to her feet, her black eyes glowering. "Hateful man!" she muttered. "Never talks." Then the sudden remembrance of the whiskey jug erased her anger, bringing an avid gleam to her eyes. She flew across the floor, jerked open the door, and hurried to the log that had concealed it the night before. She rammed a hand beneath the rough exterior to find nothing but frozen, rotted leaves. She sat back on her heels, chewing thoughtfully on a thumb nail. After a moment she jumped to her feet and hurried back inside the cabin.

There were few hiding places inside the single room. Her fingers probed and felt through the thickness of the pine-bough mattress and found nothing. Nor did she find the jug in the wood box, or in another spot or corner.

That left a good-sized leather trunk pushed up against the wall opposite the fireplace. Doxy stood and stared at it. Did she dare? Yes, if she put everything back exactly as she had found it.

She lifted the lid eagerly; staring down, she saw a bar of yellow soap lying on a stack of white, corase towels, a comb, a brush, and a straight razor alongside them. She picked up the razor and giggled. "He hasn't used this lately. He looks like a shaggy bear."

Doxy lifted the items out and carefully laid them aside, swearing gutterally as she found only neatly folded buckskins, underwear, and shirts. Her previous eagerness replaced by dark sullenness, she replaced everything and slammed the lid shut. In her disappointment, for she could almost taste the "fire water," she stamped toward her bedroll, kicking the dog as she went past the animal sleeping before the fire. He lifted his head and growled warningly before she turned a grim look on him.

"Shut up, dog, or I'll put you in the stew tonight." As Hawser growled again, she placed more wood on the fire, then crawled back into the blankets. She drifted off to sleep, the trapper's harsh order about supper growing ever more faint in her thoughts.

Darkness was just settling over the forest when Doxy glanced through the window and saw Margruder's lean frame approach the camp from the cover of pines. She glanced nervously at the pot of meat bubbling on the fire. The blankets had been warm and she slept later than she intended, barely awakening in time to get the stew started. She noted the dozen or so soft furry bodies strung together and slung over one broad shoulder and thought that the gruff one had had a good day's run. Maybe this would soften him and his demeanor would be more pleasant than it had been so far.

She hurried to the steaming pot and, with a long-handled spoon, industriously stirred the chunks of venison spiced with wild herbs, her ears attuned to the step upon the porch, her mind's eye envisioning the pelts being hung out of reach of marauding animals until the trapper was ready to skin and stretch them.

Doxy watched the latch lift and held her breath as the door swung open and broad shoulders filled it. Would he want his "pleasurin'" before or after he ate supper? She searched the hard handsome face and sighed inwardly. It was as stony as always, without a hint of gentleness in it. Without a word or a look in her direction the trapper moved directly to the wooden water pail sitting on a high bench beneath the window.

The squaw's lips curved scornfully as she watched the big man lift a dipper of water to his lips and drink deeply, then fill a basin and scrub his hands and face with a bar of yellow lye soap. But after he dried his face on a rough homespun towel and growled as he stalked to the table, "Make sure there's a clean towel here every evening," all signs of derision fled her features. For though she had lost most of her fear of the trapper, she knew not to become overconfident that he wouldn't take a stick to her if she roused his anger.

She had discovered that his gruffness didn't extend to cruelty when he had shared his rabbit evenly with her, and had allowed her the last piece of corn bread. The fact that he had more feeling for the hound who had greeted him with waggling tail didn't bother her in the least. As long as he provided her with warm quarters, and shared his food and whiskey, she would willingly satisfy his other hunger and keep her thoughts to herself.

Supper was eaten swiftly, again in almost total silence. When the still-faced man wanted more stew, or his cup refilled, he grunted and pointed. Later as Doxy gathered the plates and cups he filled his pipe and puffed quietly as he stared into the flames of the fire. She shot sidelong glances at him, wondering what thoughts could make him look so . . . sad.

She had put everything in order and was about to sit down when the curt words cut the air. "Open up your bedroll."

As she dragged the rolled-up blankets from under the trapper's bed and spread them in front of the fire, Doxy hoped the white man wouldn't take as long to satiate his hunger as he had the night before. Unless, of course, she was fortified with the staying power of the clear, fiery liquid.

Sitting back on her heels she looked at the brooding man staring into the fire and whined, "Where is the whiskey jug?"

She felt the chill of his eyes. "Are you telling me, squaw, that you couldn't find it today?"

Doxy tossed her head and muttered, "I didn't look for it."

"Like hell you didn't. I bet I was barely out of sight before you were rummagin' around."

When there was no response beyond a sullen look at his charge, Margruder rose and left the cabin. He returned almost immediately and Doxy frowned; the untrusting one must carry the whiskey on him.

Her eyes glittered as the cork was pulled and the jug lifted to chiseled lips. She watched enviously as the strong columned throat worked, swallowing the grain alcohol.

"I've been thinkin'," she was told when the brown clay was lowered and passed to her, "that this English lover of yours must have taught you different ways to pleasure him."

Doxy nodded and lifted the jug, savoring its contents as it gurgled down her throat.

"Well, get yourself in the right frame of mind then," she was warned as the trapper rose and began peeling off his buckskins, "for I have walked many miles today and have no hankerin' to work for my pleasure tonight. So I'll just stretch out here on the blankets and you can get on with it."

In the two weeks that followed, Doxy learned that only one night varied the usual weekly pattern. On Saturday nights she must bring in from the porch the big wooden tub and heat enough water to half fill it. She had gaped, open-mouthed, the first time the trapper stripped off his clothes and stepped into the rising steam. She had watched, fascinated, as he rubbed the bar of soap over his throat, his shoulders, then down the muscled ribcage that sloped to his narrow hips. When he had stood up her gaze fastened on the manhood that even relaxed was still longer and larger than any she had ever seen fully aroused. She had often mentally compared him to his great stallion.

Her admiration of his magnificent male body had stopped when the dripping man left the tub and ordered her into it. She had let out a howl, insisting that she would freeze to death, that he was crazy in the head. Then, without warning, she was scooped up and plopped into the water, clothes and all.

"Scrub yourself," he grated. "You stink."

And so the pattern was set. Doxy knew what was expected of her, when and how. She also knew it was useless to search for the whiskey jug. She shrugged; so what. She could have all she wanted in the evenings. In fact, he made it hard to refuse.

CHAPTER 2

Juliana Roessler awakened and stretched lazily. At peace with herself for the moment, she curled her slender body under the warm covers, a hand tucked under her round chin, her thick lashes shadowing her smooth cheeks.

Then, as she became more fully awake, yesterday's events, and the two years leading up to them, came rushing in. Gloom, her constant companion for longer than she cared to remember, settled over her like a heavy cloak. As if it weren't enough that she had lost her husband to the war, today her in-laws were making her move from the house on Philadelphia's High Street where she and Tom had lived since the day they were married.

A ragged sigh escaped the nineteen-year-old widow. She turned her delicately featured face into the cloud of blond hair spread out on the pillow, letting the tears flow silently. She cried for all that had been, the good times, and then the bad times that had began in her sixteenth year.

She had been fourteen that cold winter morning when dear Papa had been run down by a run-away team and coach and died instantly of a broken neck. Her frail mama had grieved for some months, and then one night had passed quietly away in her sleep. There remained only brother John and herself.

Juliana's lips curved gently. She realized now that it hadn't been easy for a young man just turned twenty-four to take over the rearing of a young sister, in addition to holding down a job at the bank. But he had managed somehow until the young men began calling. At that point he had decided that his sister needed the guidance of a woman. She needed a mother.

Poor John, she reflected bitterly. Of all the women he could have picked, he had chosen the worst possible one. The cold-natured woman several years his senior he had married abhorred his free-spirited sister and had not bothered to hide the fact. From the day she and John moved into Iva's ugly and austere home, the woman had done nothing but find fault with her new relation.

"Juliana, don't slouch," she'd peeved; "Juliana, don't be so forward with the men"; "Juliana, you are laughing too loud."

Finally the sour-faced female declared that she was embarrassed by her sister-in-law's wild ways and that the girl must go.

John had resisted his wife's demands at first, but her nagging insistence had finally worn him down and he had sent a letter to their Aunt Amy, Mama's older sister.

Staring up at the peeling ceiling, Juliana recalled unhappily that silent ride from Trenton to their old maiden aunt's house in Philadelphia. John had stayed only long enough to greet Auntie and to bring in the few pieces of luggage. When he prepared to leave her in the dark and drafty parlor she could not keep her eyes from begging him not to abandon her in this gloomy old house. But he had avoided her beseeching gaze and, giving her a peck on the cheek, mumbled, "It's for the best, Juliana. I can't do anything about it now, but maybe someday . . ." When she would have persisted vocally, the hunted, guilty look on his handsome face made her choke back the words.

She had stood in the doorway and watched his drooping figure disappear down the street, bewildered, wondering in what way she had misbehaved so badly in Iva's eyes. Did her sister-in-law have legitimate grounds for her accusations? Tillie, the maid, had claimed there was nothing wrong with her behavior.

"That old prune is only jealous of your youth and beauty," she'd declared. "She'd flirt with the gentlemen, too, if they would look at her."

She had giggled along with Tillie, for it was true: her sister-in-law wasn't much to look at. Her face was long and angular, and the skimpy brown hair worn in a tight knot at the nape of her neck didn't relieve any of her plainness. She had often wondered how John could bring himself to make love to that long, scrawny body.

Others wondered about that, too, she knew; and she knew that they believed John married the unattractive woman for her wealth. She suspected Iva thought so also. Why else would she drive her husband so, holding her money over his head like a whip?

Juliana sighed and laid a flannel-covered arm over her eyes. Iva's practice of using her money as an inducement had speeded her departure to Philadelphia, she was almost sure.

Her thoughts went back to that evening when she and her sister-in-law had sat together in the gloomy, uncomfortable parlor, Iva doing her endless needlework, and she staring disconsolately into the fire. She had sensed Iva's speculative sidelong glances, and felt that the thin lips would soon open to chastise her about some shortcoming. She was surprised, and strangely a little alarmed, when Iva began to speak in almost pleasant tones.

"Juliana, you are old enough to start thinking of marriage. Find a young man to your liking and I'll settle a handsome dowry on you."

To hid her unaccountable unease at the surprising subject, Juliana picked up the emery board lying on the table next to her. Filing her nails with quick little jabs, she answered, "I haven't cared for any of the men I've met so far."

From the corners of her eyes she saw Iva stiffen and she hurried to explain as she replaced the file on the table, "They all seem so . . . so spineless. When I marry I want my husband to be strong, strong in all ways, not afraid to pull me off the high horse that I admit I occasionally mount." She sighed softly. "All the men I know melt when I become the least bit angry with them."

Dark annoyance swept across Iva's thin face. "You're being mighty picky for a young woman in your circumstances. If you're wise, you'll take the first man who asks you."

Iva had swept out of the room with that sharp retort, pushing Tillie rudely out of her way as they met at the door. "Phew! Talking of high horses"—the maid laughed softly, unloading her burden of teapot, cups, and sugar bowl on a low table— "that's a mighty tall one she's riding. And I'd better keep myself busy before I get a tongue-lashing, too."

Tillie placed a new log on the glowing coals of the fire. Dusting off her hands, she turned a half-amused, half-serious smile on the worried young girl. "Miss Juliana, I'm afraid the kind of man you're seeking is very scarce in this town." Her eyes twinkling teasingly, then she advised, "You should go after one of those buckskin clad trappers or long hunters we see on the streets occasionally. One of them would soon show you who's boss."

Juliana had laughed and, tossing a pillow at Tillie's head, she had exclaimed, "I didn't mean that I wanted a husband who would brutalize me." She shook her head with a silent dark smile. Of all the qualities she had told Iva she wanted in a husband, she had found only one in Tom Roessler. He had been very kind to her.

Poor gentle Tom. Juliana breathed a long sigh, watching her breath as it formed a tiny cloud in the cold room. She hoped that at least she had brought him some happiness in their short married life, for certainly he had given her little enough.

A month had dragged by at Aunt Amy's, with autumn's gray skies and spells of cold rain adding to the dull monotony of the days. Juliana had not been out of the large, musty house except for an occasional ride in the park with Aunt Amy when weather permitted. To help pass the long days she had slept as late as possible in the mornings, which wasn't too late, as the old lady frowned on lying in bed after nine o'clock. The balance of the slow-moving hours saw her pacing from window to window with many heavy sighs escaping her lips.

One morning she and her aunt were at the breakfast table, the elderly woman going through the mail while she gazed blankly out the window at the gray drizzle falling outside. Her stiffened, arthritic fingers came to a blue envelope with a gold seal. Aunt Amy scanned the contents, then tossed it onto the table with an irritated frown.

"We've been invited to the Governor's Ball."

Juliana's spoon dropped from her fingers, clattering in the saucer. Hardly daring to hope, sure that the answer would be *no,* she looked through her lowered lashes at the round, kindly face, searching for an expression that would prove her wrong. The smooth, scarcely wrinkled countenance gave nothing away and she was forced to ask, "Will we be going?"

Aunt Amy heard the yearning in the question and her small bejeweled hand lightly clasped her niece's slender one. "Oh, my dear, I'm afraid I've been remiss in not taking you about more." Her tiny mouth pursed thoughtfully, then with a sigh she smiled ruefully. "As much as I detest such socials, one doesn't refuse the Governor."

"Oh, yes, I'm sure," Juliana agreed, her eyes sparkling. "It must be the event of the year."

But when her aunt agreed, and went on to describe past balls, the important figures who attended, the fancy gowns and sparkling jewels, Juliana slowly deflated.

What in the world would she wear to such an important affair? In her mind's eye she saw the three evening gowns hanging in the closet upstairs. Plain, simple frocks designed *not* to draw attention to her slender curves and ripe breasts. She had tried to argue with Iva about them as the dressmaker fitted and pinned the material to her, pointing out their unattractive cut, the dull colors. But as she had known she would, she had lost the battle.

"I will not have you looking like one of those creatures down on River Street," Iva had snapped sourly.

As if reading the thoughts rioting through her mind, Aunt Amy's faded blue eyes studied Juliana kindly. "I hope you don't mind, dear, but I looked through your wardrobe one day. It was plain that tight-fisted Iva hasn't been overly generous in the clothes department."

"She certainly hasn't." Juliana snorted her indignation. "And what really angers me is that I had some truly lovely gowns when I went there. Would you believe that Iva gave them all to charity? She claimed they looked like get-ups a barmaid would wear."

Aunt Amy patted the angrily clenched fist lying on the table. "Don't upset yourself, dear. Tomorrow, if the weather permits, we will go shopping. You shall have the most beautiful gown available. One deserving of your beauty."

When the big day arrived, Juliana had spent most of it dressing her pale hair in different styles. That evening at the dinner table Aunt Amy admired the shiny curls piled loosely on top of her head, remarking that the style complemented her graceful throat and small ears. "I shall dress first," she went on, "then send Kitty to help you. You'll need assistance with all those buttons in the back of your frock." Juliana had smiled and nodded, thinking with pleasure of the deep brown velvet that made her amber eyes look like warm honey in the candlelight.

An hour later the young maid was holding the lovely creation for Juliana to step into. "Oh it's beautiful, Miss," Kitty enthused as she settled the daringly low-cut bodice over Juliana's full breasts and shook out the voluminous skirt with its pointed lace gores running from waist to hem.

As the girl's nimble fingers did up the tiny buttons, Juliana fastened a single strand of pearls around her throat, then fitted matching earrings into her lobes. Her aunt called up the stairs that their coach was waiting just as she wrapped a white velvet cape around her bare shoulders. She descended the stairs to bask in Aunt Amy's sincere compliments.

When the old woman and the young girl arrived at the mansion the grand ballroom was thick with Philadelphia's most prominent citizens. Juliana's heart beat excitedly as she moved among the jewelry, scents, and bright gowns. As in Trenton, the men were drawn to her as a moth is drawn to a flame. With reckless abandonment she flirted outrageously with every man who claimed her for a dance. She realized later that although it wasn't conscious, she had made up her mind to snag a husband that night. It seemed the only way to escape her prison, even though her keeper was very sweet.

Many men had asked permission to call on Juliana as they circled the dance floor in stately steps, but toward the end of the evening shy-mannered Tom Roessler had proposed. "I know that . . . that I'm rushing you," he stammered, his face blushing scarlet at daring to ask this exquisite creature to be his wife, "it's just," he struggled on, "I can't take a chance of some other man asking you first."

Juliana coyly batted her lashes at him and murmured, "I am honored, Tom, that you should ask for my hand. May I think it over tonight and give you my answer tomorrow?"

His hands dampening hers with nervous perspiration, Tom agreed eagerly. "May I call on you at two?"

She had agreed, and shortly she and Aunt Amy were rolling homeward.

And despite the elderly lady's warning that young Tom was weak, that his parents would never accept her, the Roessler–Nemeth wedding took place three weeks later.

It was a big affair, second only to the Governor's Ball. John Nemeth, happy for his young sister and more like his old carefree self, gave Juliana away. And Iva was all smiles and loving words now that her sister-in-law was no longer a responsibility.

Juliana wondered if her brother's wife had settled a dowry on her as promised, and if so if it was generous or a mere pittance. She would have liked to ask Tom, but didn't want to appear ill-bred. It was obvious from the cool treatment she received from her new in-laws that they had already formed that opinion of her.

Juliana pulled her chilled arms back under the covers. Her eyes shadowed as she recalled her wedding night, the first of many disappointments in her short-lived marriage.

When the dancing and well-wishing was over she and Tom rode the few blocks to their new home; a wedding gift from his parents. Her new husband helped her from the rented carriage, and she gazed at the building bathed in full moonlight. She couldn't keep the surprise and disappointment from showing on her face.

"I know it's not what you're used to," Tom faltered, following her gaze to the small one-story frame, "but it's all my father had vacant at the time."

Juliana patted his arm, feeling sorry at his red-faced discomfiture, knowing that he knew as well as she that the paint-peeling abode was an intentional slap in the face to her. "Don't worry about it, Tom. Some new paint and colorful flower beds next spring will make it lovely."

"Oh, Juliana." Tom's voice trembled with his relief. "You're a wonderful girl. I'll spend my whole life making you happy."

Juliana pushed back the wry thought, *this is not a good start, my husband,* as he ushered her into the cold dreary parlor of the boxlike house.

She stood quietly in the near darkness while Tom felt his way to a small table and fumbled a minute until the rasp of a flint brought a small oil lamp to life. Smiling shyly at her, he picked up the lamp and moved toward a closed door. Juliana followed him slowly, running a quick glance over the sparsely furnished room as she went. She shivered at the stark ugliness of her new home.

When she stepped past Tom into the bedroom, she found no improvement. The carpet beneath her feet was just as dull, just as thin. The room held only the bare necessities: a bed that sagged in the middle, a wardrobe with one handle missing, and a cloudy mirror hanging on the wall.

Tom looked around for a table; finding none, he set the lamp on the floor, mumbling that he'd scout up a table tomorrow.

"Don't worry about it," Juliana repeated, her words of a minute ago, feeling that she would speak them many more times in the future. "I'm sure Aunt Amy can spare us what we need." She was suddenly seeing that old lady's home in an entirely different light. Compared to this unlovely place, Auntie's house was a palace.

Tom nodded, his eyes on the floor. When Juliana laid the small case holding her nightclothes on the foot of the bed and began to unstrap it, he turned away, muttering, "I'll go have a pipe while you get ready for bed."

Goose bumps covered Juliana's flesh as she undressed in the cold room, but some were from excitement. Finally the grand mystery of what went on between a husband and wife could be clear to her. She hurriedly pulled a filmy white gown over her head and climbed into the ice-cold bed. She waited eagerly, if a little nervous, for Tom to come and tear the gown off her. For that was what Kitty had giggled to her as she folded the garment into the case this morning.

Now Juliana snorted a dry laugh as she recalled that first night with her husband. Her gown had not been torn off, it had barely been wrinkled when it was gently pushed above her waist.

She had watched Tom enter the room, watched him remove his shoes, his hose, then his shirt and tie, and finally his trousers. When he stood in his one-piece woolen underwear she waited with held breath for him to discard those, give her her first view of the naked male. Her eyes widened in disbelief when he folded back the covers and slid into bed, his body still a mystery to her.

"Aren't you going to take your woolens off?" she asked, leaning up on an elbow and peering at him as the wick sputtered and burned out. "They must be awfully uncomfortable."

There was a long silence, then Tom muttered, "I forgot to bring my nightshirt."

Juliana was ready to retort, "Why bother with clothes,"

when intuition held her tongue. God forbid, but if Tom was anything like his father he would think it ungentlemanly to let his wife see his nakedness . . . and for him to see hers.

I can live with that, she thought, waiting for Tom to take her in his arms. After all it's the love-making that counts, the prolonged kisses, the urgently caressing hands and lips.

The seconds ticked by. Tom lay stiffly beside Juliana. Should I make the first move, she wondered; is it expected to me? I will, she decided, and at that moment Tom rose to his knees, and lifting up her gown, gently pulled her legs apart. Shock immobilized her when he crawled between them and she felt a warm hardness jabbing awkwardly at her intimate parts. She realized with dismay that she was not to experience stroking hands or warm lips at her breasts. Had the maid Kitty made up all those wild things she had told her to expect?

Ready to cry anyway from disillusionment and frustration, a small cry of pain escaped her when Tom finally, ineptly, entered her. Unbelieving surprise widened her eyes when he immediately rolled off her, and as he begged her forgiveness for hurting her so, she wanted to shout, "What difference, fool? Sooner or later I must be broken."

Again instinct warned her to be silent, that her husband would think her unladylike to speak so, that to his mind no decent woman would have the sensations and desires that were ripping through her body.

It had taken three nights before the consummation of the marriage was accomplished. And only then because Juliana had held back her cries and kept Tom fastened to her with determined legs. But within moments she wondered why she had bothered. After a few quick thrusts her husband had collasped on top of her, his breathing harsh in her ears, his woolen underwear scratching the tender skin of her thighs. She couldn't believe it when he gently kissed her cheek, thanked her, then rolled over on his side and fell asleep.

Is that it? she wondered, confused, tense, and aching. Is only the man allowed release? What does the woman do throughout the years? Suffer in silence?

It was near morning before the clamoring desire between her thighs had eased enough for Juliana to fall into a restless sleep.

The days had dragged by, merging into weeks, then into months. Each night brought the same quick, unemotional coupling and Juliana lived in a perpetual state of ragged nerves. And after about a year, to worsen her unrest, a faceless man began to enter her fitful sleep. His hands and lips would roam over her body, doing all the things that Kitty had promised. But her lower regions continued to ache, for her dream lover never quite brought her complete relief.

As the weeks passed, all respect for Tom deserted Juliana. Besides being a disappointing lover, she had discovered he wasn't his own man. He stood in great fear of displeasing his parents. It was still a wonder to her that he had found the courage to stand up to them long enough to marry her.

She tried not to let it bother her that Mr. and Mrs. Roessler still hadn't accepted her, and never tried to hide the fact. She and Tom were never invited to any of their social functions, and twice his mother had passed her on the street and looked the other way. But what did rile her, however, was that her in-laws ignored her and Tom's financial plight.

The dowry Iva had settled on her had been small after all, and was soon gone. They now struggled by on his scant army pay, and only when the larder was bare was Tom able to wheedle a little money from his mother. But when he was away on duty, she was forced to make daily visits to Aunt Amy's in order to eat.

Juliana stared at the frost-covered window, a grim smile touching her features. All the past insults, the indignities visited on her by the Roesslers, were as nothing compared to the blow they had delivered yesterday.

Standing before her like an avenging devil Tom's mother informed her that they wanted possession of the house no later than four o'clock the following day. "What do . . . do you mean?" she'd stammered bewilderedly, "give up possession? As Tom's widow the house belongs to me."

Her eyes spitting hatred, Mrs. Roessler sneeringly queried, "How can it belong to you when it was never Tom's?"

"I don't understand," she faltered weakly, clutching the back of a chair.

"Well see if you can understand this." Triumph glittered in her mother-in-law's eyes. "We never signed the deed over to our son, thank God."

"But it was a wedding gift. Surely Tom insisted that you should."

"Oh, he asked us to once." Mrs. Roessler shrugged indifferently. "And we told him that we'd think about it. When he didn't bring it up again, neither did we. We knew he'd become wise to you and was planning on terminating the marriage. So"—the haughty woman swept to the door, her husband at her heels,—"be sure you're out of here tomorrow."

She had stared after the pair in stunned silence and kept on staring long after the door had slammed behind them. It took the singsong cry of a peddler out in the street to bring her out of her numbed state. Dear Lord, what was she to do, where was she to go? She couldn't stay in Philadelphia.

She sat down dejectedly. There was only John. Surely, as a widow with nowhere to go, Iva would allow him to take her in. Thinking of John and his wife, she wondered again why they hadn't attended Tom's funeral. She had posted John the message of his death in battle immediately on hearing the news from his company commander.

Juliana's eyes fell on her flat purse, and she laughed hysterically. She didn't even have coach fare. Maybe Aunt Amy . . .

Her feet were numb by the time she walked the eight blocks to her relative's home. But once there she was warmly welcomed and led into the parlor where a bright fire burned in the fireplace. After Kitty had served them tea and left the room after offering Juliana her condolences, Amy looked at her niece and asked kindly, "What has that awful Bea Roessler done to you now?"

The repressed tears of two years flooded Juliana's eyes and rolled down her cheeks. All her hurt and bitterness was sobbed into the warm, comforting shoulder offered her.

When the storm was spent, she was handed a dainty hanky and a soothing pat on her arm. "I knew that you weren't happy these past years, but I had no idea things were that bad."

"It's no more than I deserve, Auntie." Juliana dabbed at her eyes. "I didn't love Tom when I married him."

"I know, dear."

Juliana widened her eyes. "You do, Auntie?" When Amy nodded, Juliana stared into her tea, saying earnestly, "I tried my best to be a good wife and to never let Tom know that I felt nothing but affection for him."

"And you succeeded, dear. That boy shone like a star every time you came near him. I think that's what his mother couldn't forgive." After a slight pause she added softly, "It will be nice having you back again. I've missed you."

Juliana's lips curved wistfully. "I wish that could be, Auntie, but you know as well as I that the Roesslers wouldn't rest until they had driven me out of Philadelphia, one way or the other. But that wouldn't stop me if I wanted to stay. It's that Philadelphia holds nothing for me now but bad memories."

"Yes," Amy agreed, shaking her head sadly. "I understand. And that Bea Roessler does have a poisonous tongue. She would tear your reputation to shreds." She smiled wanly. "I guess it's back to John and Iva, then."

"I don't know where else I could go, Auntie." Her short laugh held no mirth. "Assuming Iva will let me stay. And, as you might expect, I don't have a cent to my name. I was going to beg from you the coach fare."

"You never have to beg me for anything, Juliana," Amy said, raising her portly figure and moving across the floor to a rosewood desk. "You are my only niece, my dear sister's daughter."

She stood at the desk a moment, then returned to her seat, handing Juliana an envelope. "There's enough there for your fare, plus some extra in case that stone-hearted Iva refuses to take you in."

When Juliana's eyes filled with tears again, Amy held up a plump hand. "No more tears, child. Just make me a promise. If things don't work out for you in Trenton, don't do anything rash like you did in marrying a man you didn't love. You come straight back to me."

Dear, sweet Aunt Amy, Juliana thought now, I'll repay her just as soon as I can. She sighed. But right now, it's time to brave the cold of this room and get ready to leave. The coach should be by within the hour. She had already said good-bye to her aunt the night before. All that was left was to ready herself.

Forty-five minutes later she had built a fire in the cast-iron stove, brewed a pot of tea, stripped off her gown, donned the petticoat she'd laid out the night before, and pulled a bright red woolen dress over her head. After doing up its row of buttons, she slid silk stockings over her slender legs and slipped her feet into fur-lined boots. It would be a cold ride to Trenton.

She dressed her hair next, then settled a black velvet bonnet on her fair head and tied the ribbons under her delicate jaw. She had just closed her two bags and fitted a cape that matched her bonnet around her shoulders when she heard the heavy rumble of coach wheels rattling over the cobblestoned street. She picked up the bags, and without looking back, walked through the front door for the last time.

CHAPTER 3

~~~~~~

Juliana stepped out onto the small stoop and grabbed at the railing when a blast of cold wind drove her back against the door. Protecting her face with a mittened hand, she peered through the white veil of snowflakes that whipped across her face.

"I had no idea it was snowing," she muttered in surprise, the freezing air stinging her eyes with tears.

She hefted a bag in each hand, and as she made a careful way down the three slippery steps she grimaced bitterly. "Wouldn't you know I'd be leaving Philadelphia in a blinding snowstorm. It's somehow so appropriate."

Juliana broke off her dark thoughts when the coach crunched to a halt in front of her, the team stamping their hooves against the cold. A thin, sixtyish, bundled-up man scrambled down from his high unprotected seat. He nodded to her shortly, swung open the coach door, and, after tossing her bags inside, took her elbow to help her in after them.

"Looks like we're in for a bad one," he complained petulantly before slamming the door shut.

The cumbersome vehicle swayed as the driver climbed back onto his perch and snapped a long whip. Juliana leaned back against the hard seat as the big wheels began to roll again. She was the only passenger, and was thankful for it. It would have been difficult for her to make small talk with strangers today, to speak of trivial subjects with the worries that hung over her head. She stared blankly at the opposite seat, pondering again

27

what kind of reception she would receive at the end of her chilly ride.

What if Iva refused to take her in? What would she do? How would she support herself, having no training for any sort of work? Would she, after all, end up back at Auntie's, right back where she started?

She bit her bottom lip, forcing back a misery of tears. If her sister-in-law did let her move back in, could she bear living with the woman? John's wife would make her life as hard as possible, of that she was sure.

Her mind weary from fretting over her future, Juliana pulled her feet up under her and squirmed in search of a more comfortable position. If she could nap, time would go faster. But the bumping and swaying wasn't conducive to sleep and after a half hour or so she gave up the effort. She rubbed the film of moisture from the window next to her and, peering outside, discovered two things.

They had left the city behind and were now traveling through forest, and the snowstorm had grown into a full-fledged blizzard. Frozen white particles whipping relentlessly from a leaden sky beat with clicking sounds against the window. She watched the drifting white veil until the clinging snow on the glass formed a curtain that shut out the wilderness.

Juliana sighed and sat back. "Poor old fellow," she murmured sympathetically, hearing faintly over the howling wind the driver shouting and cursing at the straining team. "How can he see to keep us on the road? He must be half frozen besides."

The spoken thought had barely left her lips when the coach came to a jolting halt, sliding her across the seat. As she struggled to straighten herself, the door was jerked open and the old man peered in at her. He had tied a scarf over his hat and across his nose and mouth, but snow and ice was thick on his head and shoulders, clinging even to his lashes and eyebrows.

He uncovered his mouth and looked at her gravely. "I don't know if I can make it through, Missy. We're midway to Trenton, so it's six of one and half dozen of the other as to what we do." He paused and wiped his nose with the back of a mittened hand. "To tell the truth I'm half afraid to try and turn around. If we got stuck in a snowdrift we could be in big trouble. I was wonderin' if you have a preference."

Juliana stared at the anxious face for several moments before realizing that for the first time in her life she was being asked for an important opinion. And what an opinion, she thought wildly before stammering, "I . . . I wouldn't know . . . know what to suggest. I would just as soon go on but I'd hate to make the wrong decision. Why don't you use your own judgment? You've made the trip before."

"That don't signify much," the old man muttered, shaking his head thoughtfully. "I ain't never been caught in a blizzard before." After rubbing his nose and wiping his eyes, the driver allowed that they might as well go on. "I don't know what's up ahead, but I sure know what's behind."

The coach swayed and complained once again as the thin figure climbed onto the seat and shook out the reins. The weary team moved on and Juliana sat back, relief in her expression. She wouldn't have to face unfriendly Philadelphia again.

Almost at a snail's pace the team plodded on for another two hours. The barely seen white glow of the sun moved well to the west, and the ferocity of the snow didn't let up. Juliana's stomach rumbled from hunger and she hoped that John and Iva wouldn't have had dinner before they arrived in Trenton. There would be nothing for her should she miss mealtime, she knew.

She was thinking longingly of the piece of fruitcake she had left in her bedroom that morning when suddenly the coach gave a shuddering lurch and the horses let loose a frightened scream. There was terror in the cracked voice that yelled as gnarled hands swung a whip at the struggling team.

Fear heavy in her breast, Juliana cautiously opened the door on her side, then gasped when the wind snatched it from her hand and slammed it back against the vehicle. The breath caught in her throat when she saw that they hung on the very edge of a deep ravine, one wheel spinning crazily in air.

The blood pounded in her head. She knew she must get out at once: at any moment they could go plunging down into the yawning chasm below. Barely breathing, she began slowly and carefully to inch along the seat to the other side. Her fingers closed on the door handle and twisted. It held. Fine perspiration broke out on her forehead as panic washed over her. She was locked in. She would be dashed on the rocks below.

In desperation Juliana jiggled the handle, fighting back the scream that rose in her throat. The door suddenly clicked open. Relief surged through her. In her first overwhelming fright she had turned the latch the wrong way.

It took all her strength to push open the heavy door against the gale force of the wind. But finally she was teetering in its opening, balancing herself, wondering which way to jump in that blinding white blanket that shrouded everything in sight.

But there was no time for decision making as the coach stirred, then began to move. Juliana closed her eyes tight and leaped out. She had barely cleared the door when the big wagon and team went toppling. As she landed in a drift between two trees, Juliana knew that if she lived to be a hundred, she would never forget the terrified screams of the horses and old man as they went plummeting downward.

"Grieve for him later," a small voice from inside sounded in her dazed mind. "Right now you must find help."

Pulling herself up with the aid of a snow-covered pine branch, Juliana stood rocking as everything seemed to spin around her. She waited until the dizziness settled down, then peered through the snow and gathering dusk. She could see no sign of a road. "The poor old fellow must have wandered off it," she murmured, then wondered frantically what to do. I'm so turned around, she thought, I don't even know in what direction to walk.

She knew that she must first climb out of the high drift and look more closely for the road, or at least the wheel tracks. But after she finally struggled through the heavy wet snow, only smooth whiteness and crowded forest met her gaze. I must be going in the wrong direction, she wailed inwardly, and veered to her right.

Juliana's head was hurting fiercely as she plodded on. Nearly blinded by the pain of it she almost missed the narrow trail that was barely discernible beneath its white cover. "Thank God," she panted, pausing to hold her side. "A path always leads somewhere."

She stepped onto the narrow trace that twisted off through the forest, thinking prayerfully: Now if I can only come to its end before dark.

She felt that she had been struggling along for hours, snow-laden branches brushing at her face, the sodden bottoms of her cape and gown slapping coldly at her legs. And always, nagging at her brain, the thought, "Hurry. Soon it will be dark. You must find someone before then."

All thoughts fled Juliana's mind when suddenly, off in the distance, a wolf howled. She stood frozen a moment, then, like a tight coil swiftly uncoiling, she was rushing madly through the deepening darkness, her heart feeling ready to burst. Once a low-hanging branch caught her across the forehead, sending her sprawling to the ground. She staggered to her feet at the same time the wolf howled again.

"Oh, God!" she whispered, then moaned when, not too far away, another answered the wild call. She ran blindly on, terror gripping her heart.

Total darkness had almost descended when the wolf howled again. This time it was alarmingly close, and Juliana's eyes searched desperately among the surrounding trees. Too exhausted to go on, she was ready to give in to the horrible fate that awaited her.

She thought that she was hallucinating when, without a sound, she saw the figure of a man trotting up the trail toward her. When he drew closer and she knew he was not a figment of her imagination, she gave a little sigh and tumbled to the ground, spinning blackness rising up to meet her.

Sate Margruder was awakened by the howl of the wind just before dawn. He leaned up on an elbow and, brushing back the tousled black hair hanging over his forehead, peered through the uncurtained window. The gray light showed no new snow.

Not yet, he thought grimly, listening to the low whistle that occasionally swept down the chimney. His gaze moved toward the sound of a sneeze and a cough. Doxy knelt in front of the fire, waving her hand at a fine cloud of ashes stirred up by the wind and threatening to settle over the skillet and the salt pork frying inside. He shook his head when the girl wiped at her tearing eyes. Empty-headed squaw, don't know enough to put a lid on the meat. He could almost taste the bitter taste in his mouth already.

Sate lay back down and stared up at the smoke-darkened ceiling. It was going to take some doing, enduring this Indian for a whole winter. He had learned quickly that she couldn't hold an intelligent conversation. And as for cooking, hell, she couldn't do that worth shucks, and the cabin looked like a boar's nest. All she knew, or enjoyed, was to tilt the jug and spread her legs.

Speaking of which, his hand snaked beneath the covers. Did he want it brought to life this morning, he debated, fondling the inert manhood against his muscular thigh. Time enough tonight, he decided, flinging back the blankets and sitting up. If it snowed today, and it looked like it would, he'd need all his strength to fight it.

The threat of snow was more than a possibility a short time later when Sate left the cabin to run his traps. A northern wind struck him in the face, catching his breath and flinging it away. "Damn!" he muttered as an ice-laden tree came crashing down uncomfortably close by. "We're gonna have one hell of a blizzard."

He had been running his line for about an hour when the first snow began soundlessly, small flakes dancing in the wind. Soon, however, flakes the size of his thumbnail were swirling around him. In no time a new inch of the white stuff was covering his tracks.

As Sate moved from trap to trap, finding an animal in most of them, the wind blew harder, sometimes at a steady roar. By noon he was plodding through snow up to his knees. With tears running down his cheeks to freeze in his beard, he wondered if he should give it up for the day and return to the warmth of the cabin.

The thought was short-lived. If he didn't break trail to the traps now, it would be twice as hard tomorrow. By the time he visited the last trap, taking from it a thick-furred beaver, his shadow had begun to lengthen. He fastened a chunk of apple on the bare trigger and reset it. Then, with a shoulder weighed down with his catch, he breathed a tired sigh of relief and turned homeward.

Sate had just arrived at a fork in the trail, the left branch of which led home, when the distant cry of a wolf split the cold, sharp air. While he stood listening, peering through the white blanket, the trailing cry sounded again, then was carried off by the moan of the wind. "He's runnin' prey," he muttered and started down the left fork.

The sun had just passed the timberline and Sate was only a half mile from home when the howl came again, quickly answered by another. "Them bastards aren't far away." Sate took a tighter grip on his rifle. "I wonder if maybe they've got some man cornered."

He let the string of furs slide off his shoulder, and as he stood trying to determine the true direction of the yowls—wind could play tricks with sound—a faint scream reached him above the noise of the storm. "Good Lord, that sounded like a woman," he muttered, his muscles going tight.

It seemed an eternity to Sate as he cut through the forest, leaping over drifts, fighting his way through those too high to clear. His breath was coming in gasps and his body was damp with sweat by the time he was back on the main trail where he could lengthen his stride.

It was just as he rounded a large pine that he saw the slender figure of a woman. In the shadowed darkness of the forest he saw her sway, then crumple slowly into the snow. "God!" he swore hardly, breaking into a run. "What's she doing out here alone in a blizzard?"

The deep powdery snow rising in miniature clouds around his feet, Sate reached the limp, unconscious body. He took the narrow shoulders in his hands and gently turned her over, then caught his breath at the sight of the beautiful face exposed to the wind and snow. Not even in his wildest dreams had he ever conjured up such loveliness.

He bent his broad shoulders over the woman to protect her from the worst of the weather. As he pulled down the cuff of her mitten and found the pulse in the dainty wrist, the thought flashed briefly through his mind that he could easily snap it in two with his fingers. The beat was weak, but steady. Another glance at the waxen face warned him to get her to shelter as soon as possible.

He bunched his shoulders to pick up the slight form, then froze. He heard, off through the trees, a low, threatening growl. He swiveled slowly on the balls of his feet, his gaze piercing the snow and darkness. Just a few yards away he spotted a shadowy form, its hackles raised and it eyes twin spots of red. Keeping his eyes on the animal, he reached to jerk the rifle sling off his shoulders. It held fast. He gave the leather strap an impatient yank. It only gave an inch. Damn! It was caught on a tree branch at his back where he couldn't get at it.

It wasn't until he had stiffened his muscles, gathered his strength to do battle, that he thought, *Use your knife, fool.* He whipped the broad-bladed knife from his belt, thinking that for the first time in his life he had panicked. Had this helpless woman taken away his power to think straight?

The wolf began to move forward, fangs bared and stiff-legged. With one last desperate heave of his shoulder the stubborn limb gave a splintering crack, and Sate was free.

When the animal sprang he flipped his wrist and the keen piece
of steel went whizzing into the snarling throat. The shaggy
body dropped at his feet, shuddering a moment before lying
still. Sate raised his eyes to watch its mate dart off through the
trees, yipping and growling. He drew a sleeve across his
sweating face, his arm trembling slightly.

"Whew, that was close," he muttered, retrieving the knife
and wiping it clean of blood in the snow. He adjusted the rifle
on his shoulder, then scooped the woman into his arms.

Sate had not gone far when the soft body clasped to his
breast began to shake violently. She had gone into shock. His
arms tightened about her, and he turned her face into the
warmth of his chest as he tried to walk faster through the ever-
deepening snow.

In the darkness that had settled thickly by now, he kept the
trail mostly by instinct, keeping his direction by the sweep of
the wind. It seemed like hours had passed before he came to
the cluster of pine that sheltered his cabin.

A warm glow of light shone through the window, and Sate
thanked God that the squaw had a good fire going. When he
wrested the door open with a bang, Doxy jumped to her feet,
exclaiming, "What you got there, mister?"

Sate moved quickly across the floor, ignoring the stunned
question. As he gently laid the unconscious body on his bed,
he snapped at Doxy who was leaning curiously over his
shoulder, "Bundle up some hot rocks—this woman is damn
near frozen. I've got to get the blood movin' through her
veins."

Doxy lingered beside the bed, watching Sate's fingers work
feverishly at buttons and ribbons, and it took but a moment for
the cape to be removed and tossed to the floor. The soaked
bonnet came next, and when the pale hair spilled over the
pillow, the trapper drew in a sharp breath. Doxy's glittering
eyes darted to him and her heavy lids narrowed at the
undisguised wonder in his eyes as he gazed at the beautiful
woman.

She suddenly knew what his look meant. The trapper was hit
hard by the pale-face, and she would probably be sent packing.
Her face blank of the resentment boiling inside her, she stated
flatly, "Too late for hot rocks. She too far gone—she will die.
Do not waste your time."

The squaw flinched as hostile eyes were turned on her.

"Don't you say that! Don't even think it! Now get those rocks before I throw you out in the storm."

Doxy jumped. Looking as willing as possible, she hurried to the fireplace. While she poked and dug beneath the red coals with a fire iron, Sate bent over the still form once again.

Tiny buttons popped and spilled to the floor in his haste to strip away the wet clothing. The red dress was thrown to the floor: now he was confronted with the silk petticoat and underdrawers. Did he dare strip away these last articles? Yes, common sense answered him. If the girl was ever to become warm again, the wet garments had to come off.

Sate tried to avert his gaze from his hands as he removed the last piece of concealing fabric. But as his fingers brushed against smooth, silky flesh he was helpless not to look at what he touched.

His breathing shallow, he gazed at the perfectly shaped body, feasting his eyes on the full, pink-tipped breasts and the smooth, flat stomach. When his gaze was drawn downward to the gently flaring hips and the blonde hair curling between silken thighs, there grew a pressure in his loins the like of which he had never known before.

The slender form shivered, and Sate shook himself as though from a trance. He carefully lifted the light weight just high enough to pull back the covers, then gently slid her beneath them. Tucking the blankets tightly around the delicate shoulders, he looked impatiently toward the fireplace.

"Damn it, Doxy, hurry up with those stones."

Doxy knew from his tone that she had dallied as long as she could. Grabbing up a woolen shirt of his, she spread it out on the hearth, and with a pair of fire tongs lifted the hot stones onto its wide back. When she had folded the sides over and tied the sleeves together, she rose and carried them to the bed.

Sate grabbed the warm bundle from the squaw and, reaching under the covers, placed it beneath the white-cold feet that hadn't stirred. He hesitated but a moment before he began to rub her ankles briskly, slowly working upward.

He patiently rubbed and massaged for half an hour, all amorous thoughts gone as the body remained cold and unresponsive. His face revealing his anxiety, he stood up and ran distracted fingers through his hair. Anger and disgust twisted his features when Doxy tugged at his arm.

"Why don't you rest a while," she whined, "have a cup of coffee . . . maybe with some whiskey."

The trapper turned on her so fiercely that she took a step backwards. "You unfeeling bitch!" he rasped. "Even when a human being's life is hangin' on the edge of death you can only think of guzzlin' your damned fire-water. Well, let me tell you—"

He broke off in midsentence, slapping himself in the forehead. Why hadn't he thought of whiskey's warming capacity before? Its fiery heat was often the only lifeline of hunters and trappers caught out in winter storms.

Before Doxy's pop-eyed stare, he reached under the bed and dragged out the jug. The one place she had never looked. She hurried to bring Sate a cup and as he splashed some of the spirits into the pewter, he shook his head bemusedly. Once again this woman had caused him to lose his ability to think straight.

He lifted the blond head to lie on his shoulder and placed the cup's rim against her lips. When they didn't stir, he gently pressed his thumb against the lower one until both had parted. Slowly and carefully, he trickled the liquid into her mouth.

The woman jerked, her slender throat convulsed, and, turning her head, a choking cough was smothered in Sate's shirt front. As he held his breath, amber eyes opened slowly, a glaze of delirium in them. When a toneless, rambling mumble drifted through the pale lips, he laid the girl back down and stood up. Then, with desperation in his eyes, he shocked the squaw who had watched his ministrations closely. Before her gaping stare, he stripped off his clothes and slid in beside the girl. When he pulled the covers up over their heads, Doxy stamped over to the fire and flung herself into a chair.

Sate simply lay for a long moment, shocked by the temerity of his action. What if she should come out of shock? Would finding herself in bed with a stranger send her into one far worse? His lips firmed. He had to chance it. Nothing he had tried so far had worked. Maybe his own body heat would spark some warmth in her. Otherwise . . . He couldn't bring himself to finish the thought.

Carefully and gently, his hands shaking, he drew the slim body into his arms and aligned it against his own lean length. Hardly breathing, he tentatively ran a palm down the stone coldness of the narrow back, warning himself sternly not to let

desire creep into his body and mind. I am only trying to save
her life, he pointed out to himself as he cautiously smoothed a
hand down her side, onto a rounded hip, then over the shape of
her long, smooth thigh. I would do the same for anybody.

As the minutes passed, and he continued to massage her
flesh, there rose from her body and the hair tucked under his
chin the scent of wild roses. And though he fought it, railed at
himself for being a no-good bastard, it was no longer a clinical
movement he performed on the body clasped in his arms. As
though they had a will of their own, his hands were now
sensuously caressing.

Sate was so conscious of the rounded breasts crushed against
his chest, of stomachs and legs pressed against each other, that
it came as a shock when he finally realized the rigid body had
begun to relax; that the chill trapped in the blankets had been
dispelled. With hope flaring, he touched the woman's cheek,
feeling for some warmth. His fervent wish was encouraged
when her lips, pressed against the rapidly racing pulse in his
throat, issued a faint moan.

She stirred and he eased himself away from her, to make her
more comfortable. He groaned when, fussily, like a child, she
snuggled back against him. Sate stiffened, her soft flesh
branding him like a hot iron. His gaze rested on her red lips
and, for the first time in his life, he wanted to place his own on
a woman's. He had never given that tenderness to anyone.

Sate's gaze slid down to the hands curled under the round
chin, and he suddenly knew a disappointment so sharp that he
closed his eyes in denial. On the third finger was a wide, gold
wedding ring.

Fool! he groaned inwardly. Did you think that a woman like
this wouldn't belong to some man?

He raised himself on an elbow and looked down at the
woman who was so beyond him for a last time, and prepared to
leave her. She would be all right now, for already her skin was
taking on a rosy tinge. He pushed the blankets he had pulled
down in order to scan the woman's face and started to swing a
foot to the floor. Suddenly smooth bare arms were thrown
around his waist, pulling him back. His breath was a rasping
sound as hardened nipples burned against his chest like two hot
coals.

"Oh, Lord," he whispered in anguish when she threw a leg
over his, the soft triangle of hair between her thighs brushing
his hip. How long could he fight his fragile control?

It would be a dastardly act to take what she was offering, he reminded himself grimly as he reached up to remove the arms that clung around his neck. Not only was she another man's wife, she didn't know what she was doing.

"No!" The single word slipped fiercely through the soft lips. "You are not leaving me tonight, hungry and aching." While Sate lay stunned, with one swift movement, the woman was on top of him, the swollen warmth of his manhood sheathed inside her. "I want you so much," she whispered raggedly as she began to move up and down on him.

The rapid bucking of narrow hips on his, the velvet slide of her femininty stroking him, spelled the final end of his last remnant of control. He had tried, God knew he had tried. He wrapped his arms around her waist and, with an easy twist, she lay beneath him.

The girl made a soft sound of pleasure and raised her chin, seeking his mouth. His lips met hers, deepening the kiss as she arched her body against his.

"Oh God," he moaned, his hands kneading her breasts, "so sweet, just like I knew you would be."

Knowing subconsciously that the squaw watched them, Sate pulled the covers back over their heads before sliding his hands under the small buttocks to lift them up. Holding her close, supporting her, the woman eagerly accepted the demands of his powerful body.

Her black eyes glittering with resentment, Doxy knew the exact moment the hidden pair shuddered together, then lay still. There was malice in the glower she trained on the bed.

Sate braced himself on his elbows, taking most of his weight off the delicate body. He tossed back the covers, then smoothed the damp tangled curls from the woman's forehead, wondering what sort of man would leave such a beauty unsatisfied. Her almost wanton behavior in his arms told him that she had hungered for a long while, that perhaps tonight she had experienced a sexual release for the first time.

He lay a finger on the pulse beat at her throat, and found it slow and regular. She has slipped into a normal sleep, he thought, and slowly withdrew himself from the sweet tightness that had stroked him to incredible heights; heights he never expected to know again.

His body glistening with sweat, Sate sat up and reached for his soft leather trousers. Doxy watched him climb into them and lace them up. She scowled darkly when he approached the fire and growled, "Rustle me up some grub."

The young squaw darted a glance at the sleeping form on the bed and said recklessly, "The pale-haired one just took care of your man hunger. Let her take care of your belly hunger, too."

It grew onimously quiet in the room, the only sound that of sap dripping from the logs and hissing as it hit the coals. Doxy grew apprehensive; darting a glance at the trapper, she knew she had gone too far. She remembered thinking once that this man could be cruel if the need arose and she scrambled up from the chair. But she acted too late, too slowly. His arm snaked out and his fingers fastened in her hair.

His face inches from hers, anger throbbing in his voice, Margruder warned tightly, "Don't *ever* tell *anyone* I slept with that girl." With a push that sent the squaw stumbling backward, he added in the same menacing tone, "That goes for the girl, too. If you so much as hint it to her, you're a dead squaw."

Well out of the trapper's reach, and rubbing her smarting scalp, Doxy sneered, "Are you trying to say she didn't know you used her?"

Sate's face flushed guiltily, but his tone showed no such emotion as he answered shortly, "That's right."

Doxy moved away with a dry snort, its sounds scoffing at the white man's claim. As she resignedly swung the stew back over the hot coals, Sate lowered himself into the rocker and stretched his long legs to the fire. Shadows of deep thought crossed his eyes as he stared unseeing into the flames.

The wild emotional storm that had blinded him to all else was gone and now he faced cold facts. The woman who now slept a natural sleep would never have willingly made love with someone like himself. She was from a world of men so different from his ilk that it was like pitting a small lap dog against a wild, rangy wolf. In a conscious state he would probably scare the wits out of her.

But Doxy's remark that he had used the girl was entirely wrong. He had not used the delicate body. For the first time in his life he had made love to a woman. He had restrained his own need and waited until the tremors that shook her slim frame told him that she was ready to ride that exploding crest with him.

His fingers tightened convulsively on the chair arm. She

would remember none of it when she awakened. That wonderful time would belong only to him.

Sate started when Doxy announced sullenly that his supper was ready. He rose and, jerking his thumb toward the pile of feminine apparel lying on the floor, growled, "Hang those before the fire to dry. You'll find some buttons on the floor. Sew them back on."

Against her will, but afraid to refuse, Doxy gathered up the dress, underthings, petticoat, bonnet, and cape. She fingered their softness a moment, her lips curling in a sneer even as envy clouded her eyes. White woman, she thought darkly, pampered and spoiled, no fit mate for trapper.

But would he realize that? Doxy studied the weather-darkened face bent over a bowl of stew. He was besotted of the beautiful face and soft white body. Right now he couldn't think beyond the gnawing in his loins every time his gaze drifted to the bed in the corner. It wouldn't occur to him that such a woman would be useless in other ways. She could not cook his meals, help stretch his pelts when he came in from running his line. And her puny body—it could never endure the battering he would give it every night.

She waited until Sate had finished eating, checked the girl who continued to sleep quietly, then resumed his seat in front of the fire. After sending him a slidelong glance, she asked, "Will you send me away now?"

Sate sat back in the creaking chair and folded his hands behind his head. "Why should I do that? Someone has to look after her while I run my traps."

Doxy flashed him a sly look. "Then you will pleasure us both?"

Fury glinted in the cold blue eyes. Sate shot a glance over his shoulder, and didn't relax until the regular rise and fall of the girl's chest assured him that she slept on. Then, snapping his head forward, he grabbed Doxy's wrist with punishing fingers. "Don't come near me while she's here," he snarled. His grip tightened for emphasis. "You tell her that you only work for me, understand?" Doxy nodded and he released her. "Now heat me a pan of water," he grunted. "I'm gonna shave."

Juliana Roessler awakened slowly, her body languid and relaxed in a way she had never experienced before. All the tense knots were gone, and her whole body felt infused with a warmth and contentment that could only come from a complete release.

Her kiss-swollen lips parted in a half smile. Her dream lover had visited her again, and this time he had stayed; stayed and let his muscular body fulfill its promise.

A warmth grew between her legs as she remembered him there, his lean hips lifting, then driving back into her, all the time his hands supporting her as she took his pulsating strength. How glorious it had been. She sighed happily. Why couldn't Tom have given me the same wonderful feeling?

She giggled inwardly. She had finally seen the man's face, although in a kind of blur, and he wore a beard. Imagine fastidious Juliana Roessler putting a beard on her imagined lover.

A snapping, thudding sound penetrated Juliana's dreamy indolence; a noise like a log burning through and falling into itself. She opened heavy eyelids. Puzzlement creased her forehead as she gazed at a rough raftered ceiling instead of a smooth plastered one. What . . . where . . . ?

Soft, scuffing footsteps made her turn her head to the right, and her eyes widened in alarm. A man, a stranger, looked down at her cautiously. She drew a hand across her eyes. Was she still dreaming? He looked remarkably like the man in her dream, although he was cleanly shaved.

She lay very still, her gaze passing over the black curly hair sprinkled with gray to the firm yet sensual lips, moving down the muscular throat to where an unlaced fringed shirt revealed more crisp black hair.

Her eyes fastened on the knife in his belt, and she wondered crazily if he was one of those wild wilderness men that Tillie had jokingly advised her to marry.

Her eyes lifted back to the strong face and, noting the tense lines around the mouth, she wondered at how swiftly they faded away when she faltered, "Where . . . where am I? Who . . . are you?"

She thought no more about it when a deep rich voice said warmly, "My name is Margruder. Sate Margruder. This is my cabin." He waited for her to take in his words, understand them, then continued in a soothing tone, "I found you unconscious and half frozen about a mile from here." He watched her closely when he asked, "Don't you remember it, my carryin' you here?"

"No." Juliana shook her head, her finely arched brows furrowed in confusion. "It's all rather fuzzy. I remember wolves howling, and that I was terribly frightened. Then I saw a man coming toward me . . . my mind is blank after that."

Careful not to sound his relief, Margruder said, "I was that man, of course. I heard the howling and came to investigate . . . thank God."

"Yes, thank God," Juliana echoed with a shudder. "I can never thank you enough for saving my life."

Strong white teeth flashed in the lean brown face. "I can never stop being thankful that I was there to help you."

Margruder studied the blushing face framed by his pillow. He lowered his gaze to the pulse that beat slowly in the slender throat. Was she, he wondered, strong enough to be questioned, forced to recall what had sent her out into a blizzard, alone in the wilderness?

His eyes lingered on the strong lines of her jaw and round chin, and he came to a decision. Though this one looked fragile, he knew she possessed a strength of mind that was far from being tenuous. He hunkered down beside the bed and asked gently, "Can you remember what happened before that?"

Juliana stared at the wide shoulders, feeling strangely stirred, but not knowing why. She pressed slim fingers to her temples and tried to organize her thoughts.

There had been a steady slash of wind and snow against a window. What window? It had been small, and dirty, and it had rattled in the storm. She had bounced violently up and down on a hard seat when she gazed through the misty pane, and she had—

Juliana's features crumpled when painful remembrance gripped her. Her eyes jumped to Sate's, growing wider and wider with the look of horror in them. With a wailing cry she covered her face with her hands, and hard sobs shook her body. And Sate, who had never comforted a woman in his life, wanted to take this one into his arms and let her head lie on his shoulder until the tears ran dry.

But he could only find the nerve to hold her hands as she related to him, in a trembling voice with many pauses, everything that had happened. He let her continue to cry then, knowing that she must. When only shuddering sobs escaped her throat, he asked softly, "Why were you traveling alone? Where is your husband?"

Juliana withdrew her hands from Sate's warm grip and gazed down dispassionately at the gold ring on her finger. "I'm a widow," she said tonelessly. "My husband was killed in the last days of the war. I was on my way to my brother's home in Trenton."

A flare of joy filled Sate's eyes, and he quickly lowered his lids to hide it. It was only by force of will that he managed to convey sympathy in his voice when he murmured, "That's a shame."

"Yes, it was a shame," Juliana said flatly. "Poor fellow, he was only twenty-three."

Her tone, and the soft regret in her eyes, told Sate everything he wanted to know. The girl had been unhappy in her marriage. She felt pity for her young husband, but there was no love in the voice that spoke of the man. He wondered in what way the dead soldier had disappointed his wife.

He ignored the voice that sneered inside him: "Fool, so what if she's not grieving for a lost love? It's of no significance to you," and from the corners of his eyes he watched the lissome body stretch like a lazy cat, then draw her arms back under the warmth of the covers. He was about to inquire if she was hungry when her body stiffened and the amber eyes glittered up at him.

"Who disrobed me?"

Sate forced himself to look into the accusing eyes, but it took him a befuddled minute before he could think up, and say, "Doxy done it."

"And who is Doxy?" The cool tone expressed doubt that there was such a person.

"The squaw over there by the fire." Sate threw a warning look at Doxy.

Clutching the blankets under her chin, Juliana raised herself up and looked toward the fireplace. She was met by a steady stare from the figure in the rocking chair and was held for a second by the hostile glitter in a pair of black eyes. So that's how it is. Her lips sneered slightly as she ran a quick glance over the black hair hanging down a slender back, the gentle curves beneath a doeskin shift: The girl is afraid she'll lose her man.

With a twist of her lips, she murmured, "I see," and lay
back down.

Sate's face went red at the scorn in the two words that
branded him a squaw-man. He had never considered himself
that. He only lived with one during the trapping season, then
sent her away when spring arrived. Hell, he had spent equal
winters with white women, some whore who wanted a rest.

His voice was unnecessarily loud and belligerent when he
said, "She approached my fire a week or so back, and said she
was hungry, and that she was looking for work."

The mocking laughter in the wide eyes didn't escape him
when Juliana retorted smoothly, "And of course you hired
her."

Sate scowled down at the floor, then, pressing a hand to the
back of his neck, muttered, "I said that I might find a few
chores for her to do." The dog padded up to him, and he added
weakly, "She keeps the hound company while I run my traps."

Surprising herself, Juliana wanted to believe the trapper. She
was attracted to the rugged individual in a manner she had
never before felt for another man. It's his uniqueness that
appeals to my senses, she mused, and the way his eyes are cold
one minute, making me shiver deliciously, then so warmly
caressing that my blood flows like hot liquid. And now, seeing
him embarrassed, I want to put my arms around him as though
he were a little boy.

She sighed, half regretfully. It's none of my business who he
sleeps with. Once I leave here I'll never see him again.

Sate's relief was visible when she said softly, "What is your
dog's name?"

"Hawser," Sate answered promptly, relieved to have the
subject changed. He shoved the large animal closer to the bed
and commanded, "Shake hands with the lady, boy."

Juliana took the offered paw, then smiled up at the lean face
watching her anxiously. "My name is Juliana Roessler. After
saving my life, I think you could call me something more
personal than 'lady.' "

A grin tugged at Sate's chisled lips. He wanted to say, "I did
more than save your life, Juliana Roessler. You don't know it,
but I made your blood sing."

He only murmured, "Are you hungry, Juliana? I can have
the squaw bring you something to eat."

"That sounds good." She nodded eagerly. "It seems forever since I've last eaten."

"That's a good sign that you're gonna be all right." Sate flashed his white smile. "And while you're havin' your late supper, I'll go tend to my catch." He stood up, and Juliana found herself disappointed when he said, "You'll probably be asleep by the time I finish, so I'll say good night now."

Juliana nodded and smiled, then watched him walk over to the young squaw. He moves as gracefully as a woman, she thought. She could not discern what he was saying in a low voice directed at Doxy, but from the dour look on her face, she knew the girl was averse to waiting on the white woman. The squaw is jealous of me, she mused, and wondered again about the woman's relationship with the trapper.

It was ridiculous, but she hoped against hope there wasn't anything between the pair, Juliana realized as she watched Sate shrug his muscular body into a heavy coat, swing open the door, and disappear into the darkness. The thought of the Indian girl in his arms almost blinded her for a moment. By the time Doxy slouched over to her, a heaped tin plate in her hand, Juliana's dislike for the girl was equal to that shining from the black eyes to her.

"Here." The word was grunted as the plate of stew was thrust into Juliana's hands. She looked down at the thick chunks of meat lying in a bed of grease, then up at the face that made no effort to hide its animosity. She strove to hide her own dislike, telling herself that she was above verbal conflict with an ignorant Indian. She jabbed her fork into a piece of meat and, lifting it toward her mouth, lost her appetite completely when her glance fell on the girl's dirt-rimmed fingernails. Her stomach turned. She could not eat anything touched by those grimy hands.

She pushed the plate away and, speaking more sharply than she intended, asked for a cup of coffee. It appeared for a moment the squaw would refuse the request shot at her. When Juliana added, "If you please," she ambled over to the fire and picked up the steaming, battered coffee pot.

Surprisingly, the coffee was just as Juliana liked it, strong and fragrant. As she sipped it slowly, she tried to think of something to say to the brooding-eyed squaw who watched her closely. Finally she said, "I am very grateful to my host."

A few silent seconds ticked by, then shortly: "What is a host?"

Juliana sighed impatiently. "The man living here. Sate Margruder."

"Oh, the trapper." Cunning slid into Doxy's black eyes. Watching Juliana narrowly, she said in chastising tones, "He would not like you calling him by his name. You must call him mister."

Juliana's tickled laughter rang through the room. "Why shouldn't I call him by his name?" She wiped tears from the corners of her eyes.

"Because he say so," Doxy snapped, angry at the white woman's jeering laughter. "All his women call him mister."

Juliana read the spite in the words, the jealousy in the tone. Was the squaw being devious, intending her to believe something that had no foundation?

Her expression inscrutable, she asked casually, "Is that what you call him?"

"Yes." Doxy smirked and looked coyly to the floor.

Juliana flinched. The confirmation of her suspicions formed a tight knot in her chest. She struck back with words equally hurtful: "Don't you mind that the trapper uses you, that he doesn't even have affection for you?"

Doxy's red skin darkened with rage as she remembered how caringly the trapper had made love to this sneering white woman. He had never kissed *her*, never caressed her breasts, put his mouth on them. He had never waited, making sure that she had a release, too.

Well, this pale-faced bitch would never know any of this. She lifted her head proudly and spoke, eyes flashing: "Although I call him mister, *I* am not one of his women."

"Well, damn it, neither am I," Juliana snapped angrily, understanding the sneered innuendo.

A mocking look in her black eyes was Doxy's only response, and she repeated with clenched fists, "I am not one of his women! For heaven's sake I only just met the man."

Doxy shrugged. "Often one meeting is enough to become a man's woman." With a lifted eyebrow, she walked away, a taunting laugh floating behind her.

Juliana glared after her, then swept the plate of stew to the floor. She gave the pillow a whack and, scooting down under the covers, berated herself for letting the girl get under her skin. What did she care what went on between the trapper and the squaw? Another week from now neither one would be even a memory.

But as sleep claimed her a man with hard, blue eyes climbed in beside her. In her dreams they made wild, intense love.

CHAPTER 4

Sate Margruder lay quietly in the first light of dawn, listening to Juliana's even breathing. His lips curved in pleased satisfaction. He had been right: she was tough and healthy.

The familiar sound of crackling fire and sizzling meat brought his amused glance to Doxy, who was in the process of lifting a pot of coffee off the hot coals. The squaw was taking no chance's of displeasing him now, what with their beautiful guest installed in his bed.

He watched the girl's thrown shadow dance on the ceiling. "I don't trust her, though," he muttered to himself, flinging back the cover of the bedroll, "and I wish I didn't have to leave Juliana with her. God only knows what the spiteful bitch might tell her."

But there were traps to be run, and the coach accident to be looked into. He knew the ravine where the coach had gone over and he was satisfied in his mind that neither team nor the driver had survived the long plunge. Still, wilderness integrity dictated that he search out the spot and handle what he found. If the man was alive, he'd tend him: if dead, he'd bury him.

Sate stretched stiff muscles, thinking that the bare earth was more comfortable to a man's body than an unyielding wooden floor. He sat up and looked at the slight figure in his large, soft bed and wished that he could slide in beside it.

He grinned ruefully as he stood up. In her conscious state, Juliana Roessler wouldn't be as welcoming.

"It must have snowed all night," Sate mumbled as the drift of snow piled against the cabin door gave slowly to the push of

48

his powerful shoulders. He stepped outside and, closing the door behind him, gazed out over the silent, white world. He frowned suddenly. His encompassing study of the area had picked up the paw prints of wolves. They were uncomfortably close to the cabin, and ran right up to the door of the shed where his stallion was housed. Jake must have been mighty uncomfortable last night.

"The bastards are hungry," he growled, unlacing his buckskins and moving to his usual spot at the end of the porch. Ready to relieve himself, he hesitated, then stepped off into the snow and waded to the back of the cabin. A finer feeling that he was unaware of possessing rejected the possibility of Juliana seeing his yellow stain in the pristine whiteness.

Doxy wordlessly served Sate his breakfast, then lurked in the background, knowing intuitively that he wouldn't want her sitting with him now. As he continued to ignore her presence she sent many venomous glances to the sleeping form, still surprised that Margruder hadn't shared the bed again with the white woman. The black eyes narrowed in thought. Was he aware that the slim body could only take his riding it once a night? He would soon grow tired of that. She hid a pleased smile. The trapper liked his pleasuring long and often. The proud, delicate beauty would be useless to him within a week.

When Sate finally spoke to Doxy he had already shrugged into his coat and picked up his rifle. Not bothering to look in her direction, he said, "I'll probably be gone longer than usual." He glanced at Juliana's form outlined beneath the covers, and his expression softened. "When she wakes up, take her something to eat. See to her other needs, too."

He missed the angry narrowing of Doxy's eyes as she nodded acquiescence.

Sate stood outside a moment, his gaze lifted to the majesty of the pine-covered hills. Frosty night mists still shrouded the treetops, but the rising sun would rapidly disperse them. As he filled his lungs with the fresh, tangy air, his wandering gaze caught the high, effortless wheeling of two buzzards in the cloudless sky. He stepped off the porch, his lips tightened grimly. Somewhere beneath their ceaseless circling he would find the old man.

It took Sate longer than he had expected to run the trapline. For long stretches, his footprints of yesterday were completely obliterated by the newly drifted snow. It was only by landmark

alone he was able to find some of the traps, and occasionally
tiny tracks led him to others.

It was a couple of hours to sunset when he was finally
finished and arrived at the spot where he had found Juliana.

Most of her prints were snow-covered, but enough showed
through that he could track them easily. And though Juliana
would have sworn she had covered miles in that driving
blizzard, she had, in fact, walked in a circle. It was a simple
matter to bisect her path and come to the place where the
vehicle had gone over.

He stood on the rim of the ravine and peered down. At first
he could see nothing but a jumble of boulders on the snow-
covered floor. Then, from the corner of his eye, he caught a
glint of the western sun reflecting from metal. Leaning forward
and straining his eyes, he made out the coach. It lay smashed,
lodged between two stunted pines. His glance moved to the left
of the wreck to the team. They lay sprawled stiffly in a tangle
of reins and harness.

But Sate saw no trace of the driver. He eased himself over
the rough cliff edge, and with the help of the shrubby brush
growing in the gravelly wall started down. He was halfway to
the bottom when the growth gave way to sheer rock. "Damn!"
he grumbled, then, gritting his teeth, he descended the rest of
the way in a scrambling, sliding run.

He landed on his rump, his rifle held high. He picked
himself up and, glancing around, swore softly. Hidden from his
view above, he had missed the wolf pack that milled around
just above the coach. The blood-curdling sound of snapping
and snarling could only mean one thing. He would be lucky if
he found the driver's clothes. Taking a deep breath, every nerve
alert, Sate started toward the animals. They were so engrossed
with the bulk they worried with paws and teeth, he was able to
come within feet of them. He stepped behind a tall, wide
boulder and lifted the rifle to his shoulder. Laying his cheek
against its stock, he took slow, careful aim.

The shot smashed between a pair of fierce eyes. The wolf
dropped, and the others, startled by the sudden boom, took off
down the ravine, snarling and yapping wildly.

Sate stepped over the dead wolf, then stiffened, pushing
back the bile that rose in his throat. He stood a minute,
breathing deeply, then reminded himself that he had a job to do;
this was no time to turn squeamish. He walked over to a maple

sapling and snapped off a frozen branch about two feet long and half as big around as his wrist. Moving along the edge of the floor, still keeping an eye out for the wolves, began to pry rocks out of the ravine wall.

He was sweating freely by the time he had gathered material suffcent to his need. Keeping his eyes averted from the mangled piece of humanity, he walked to the coach. He used the stick again, this time prying open the dented door. He gave a satisfied grunt when he peered inside. As he had expected, a heavy lap rug lay crumpled on the floor. He jerked it toward him and a leather bag came tumbling in its wake. He grinned and thought, "Juliana will be glad to see this."

Sate spread the heavy cover over the old man's remains and tucked it in tightly. He stood up, removed his hat, and, folding it under his arm, looked down at the slight mound. A prayer should be said over the old fellow. He stared blankly at the ground, trying to recall some of his mother's long-ago lessons.

He shook his head; too much time had passed. He remembered watching a priest blessing a group of kneeling Indians a year or so ago. He thought a minute, recalling the gestures of the religious man, then hesitantly he made an awkward sign of the cross.

"I don't know your religion, old man," he said softly, turning to the pile of rock and stone, "but I guess they're all the same."

When the last stone was laid in place, Sate stood up and studied the above-ground tomb. "That's the best I can do, old-timer. At least the varmints won't get to you again. Come spring, when the ground thaws, you can be buried."

As Sate picked up his rifle and hefted the bag, he was startled by a cry for help ringing out on the still air. Before its echo could die away, he once again heard the chilling sound of snarling wolves. "Damn!" he swore, dropping the bag. He hurriedly checked the priming on the firearm, then headed down the rocky slope in a loping run.

A slight turn to the left brought him almost on top of four wolves intent on reaching a pair of feet that dangled from the top of a high, narrow ledge. The animals were oblivious to his approach, and he quickly moved to the shadow of a sturdy young pine; one he could scale if necessary.

He raised the rifle to his shoulder. Fire and smoke erupted, and amid the startled yapping that followed, one lean body leaped into the air, then lay thrashing in the snow. Seeing their comrade felled, the others disappeared down the ravine like shadowy gray ghosts.

Sate looked at the still smoking long barrel of his rifle, then to the man on his perilous perch. As he reloaded, he commented dryly, "Got yourself treed, did you?"

"Just in time, too," came the relieved answer as the stranger dropped to the ground. "I barely made it. I could feel those bastards' breath on my heels." He held out a hand. "Chad Madison is the name. I thank you for savin' my hide. Any way you'd slice it, I was done for. I'd have frozen to death before tomorrow mornin'."

Sate took the proffered hand, thinking: this is no hill man. He doesn't toe-in as he walks. Probably a city fellow who's gonna try his luck at trappin'.

His gaze flicked over the slender body, the weak, handsome face. If that's the case, he thought, he'll never make it. I've seen his kind in the army. They spent more time in a whore's bed than they did on a battlefield.

Sate gave his name and dropped the smooth-palmed hand. "What are you doin' down here? Are you lost?"

"Yes, I'm embarrassed to admit." Madison laughed easily. "I'm headed for Squaw Hollow and, in that blizzard yesterday, I got turned around. I was followin' a set of wagon wheels, figuring' they'd lead me somewhere, when suddenly they disappeared over the edge of this damn hole. I was starin' down to see if I could see anything, or anybody, when I lost my balance and slid all the way down on my rump."

His lips twisted wryly. "I landed almost on top of them devils. But before they knew what was happenin', I was on my feet and runnin'."

"If you never have any more luck in your life, you had your share today," Sate remarked, turning back toward the wrecked coach.

"Yeah, that's a fact," Madison agreed, following at Sate's heels, "although I'm hopin' to have some more when I reach my destination. I've decided to try my hand at trappin'. I hear tell that in Kentucky country the streams and forest are teemin' with every kind of fur you can think of."

Sate gave the man a curious look. Where are his traps and gear? he wondered. "Where are you from, Madison?" he asked.

"Originally Philadelphia. But with the war and all, I could claim most anywhere as home."

They reached where Sate had dropped the bag and, picking it up again, he said, "Let's get out of here. It's comin' on dark."

As the pair scrambled upward, grabbing at shrubby growth or anything that came handy, Madison panted, "Do you live close by, Margruder?"

"Yeah, about a mile away."

"A warm fire sure sounds good," Madison hinted, taking the last step that put him on the level ground of the snow-covered road.

Damnit, Sate thought as he led the way down the narrow path. I don't want him around Juliana. He's too smooth, too good lookin'. He's the sort who makes a habit of charmin' the ladies. He knows the right words to say to a lady, all the flowery compliments.

He frowned darkly when Madison said slyly, "I expect you have a squaw in your cabin. I can tell that a man like you needs his regular pleasurin'.

"There is an Indian girl at my place," Sate answered stiffly, then startled himself by adding, "She helps out my wife."

"Your wife? Is she white?"

"She is."

"I don't bother much with white wimmen," Madison said scornfully. "They got no stayin' power. After three or four good humpins' they're whinin' that they're tired. But you take a squaw, especially a young one, give her a belt of whiskey ever once in a while, and hell, she'll let you ride her all night without a word of complaint."

Sate stopped abruptly and swung around to face the man whom he was beginning to dislike intensely. "I'm glad to hear you say that white women don't appeal to you, Madison, because I don't want you botherin' my wife. She's just been through a bad experience and she's recuperatin' now. Maybe she'll be up, and maybe she won't. But that won't make no difference to you, one way or the other. The important thing is she's mine, and if you make one move toward her, either by look or action, I'll put my knife through your heart."

Madison's startled gaze followed the quick movement of Sate's hand, and he stepped back when the trapper grasped the smooth wooden hilt of the knife stuck in his wide belt. He laughed nervously. "Don't worry on that point, man. I never go after another man's property."

The grim line of Sate's lips said that he had his doubts about that, but he let the matter drop. They commenced walking again, and several minutes passed before Madison ventured, "The squaw, would you mind if she keeps my blanket warm tonight?"

Sate was tempted to retort, "Who invited you to stay the night, mister?" but he knew that he wouldn't. It was unheard of to deny a traveler a spot in front of your fire. Instead, he said tightly, "That will be up to the squaw. But mind, my wife won't like it if you use the girl harshly."

"I got your warnin'." Chad Madison laughed good-naturedly. "Don't get fussed about it."

Doxy gave the pot of bubbling beans a half-hearted stir with the long-handled spoon, then she flopped back into the rocker. She stared moodily into the fire. When was the white woman going to leave. There would be no whiskey until she did, nor would the harsh one approach her to fulfill his need as long as she was here.

The pace of the creaking rocker increased. The trapper had to be hurting by now. Maybe tonight he would take her to the shed in back of the cabin, along with the whiskey jug.

The sound of voices and scraping feet brought Doxy to her feet. More company? A man this time, she hoped. When the door swung open, her curious gaze swept past Sate to his companion. Her eyes widened. A fair-haired man, like her English lover.

Her avid study of the smiling stranger was cut off when Sate, his frowning gaze on the feminine clothes still hung before the fire asked sharply, "Didn't Juliana get up today?"

Doxy shrugged indifferently. "No. She sleep most of the time."

"You did give her something to eat? You saw to her needs?"

"I offered her stew, and she threw it on the floor. She lifted her nose at it."

Sate's lips tensed in a straight line. "Your cookin' would lift anybody's nose. You can't make a meal worth spit." He picked up the candle, reached for Juliana's bag, and moved to the bed. Chad Madison went to join Doxy at the fire.

The smoothness of a bare shoulder and a cloud of blond hair

shortened Sate's breath. He reached out a hand to stroke the shiny tresses, then drew it back. The amber eyes had fluttered open and were staring at him sleepily. When recognition grew in them and the red lips smiled a welcome, weakness washed over him. Never had a woman smiled at him so naturally, so sweetly. He hurriedly placed the candleholder on the floor so that she couldn't read his eyes.

"How are you feeling?" he asked in a voice rough with desire.

Juliana leaned up on an elbow, the blankets slipping down to expose the snowy flesh of the top of her breasts. "I feel fine," —she smiled—"except for some stiffness and soreness."

A guilty flush colored Sate's face, and he ducked his head to hide it. He was responsible for some of her discomfort, he knew, and worried now if his hungry devouring had left any marks on her. She would certainly become suspicious of their source. He reminded himself that it was a little late to worry about the traces of his lovemaking, and suggested, "Maybe you should get up for a while. You'll feel better if you move around a little."

"I hate to think of putting that dress on again." Juliana sighed. "It must look a sight."

Sate grinned and lifted the brown leather bag from the floor. "Look what I found today."

"Oh, Sate, you've found my clothes," she exclaimed happily, then in the next breath the gladness faded. "And the old man," she whispered, "did you find him?"

Sate waited only a fraction of a second before answering gently, "Yes, I found him. I buried him in the ravine for the time being. Later, when it warms up, and if anybody cares, he can have a proper burial."

"Oh, I'm sure there'll be somebody who cares." Juliana's concerned gaze wanted him to agree. "A wife maybe; children?"

Sate shrugged. "Probably." He glanced down at Juliana and wondered at the teasing gleam in her eyes.

"Forgive me"—she smiled—"but I forgot that I'm not supposed to call you by your given name."

"Why not?" Sate frowned. "I like to hear you say my name."

"Well, according to Doxy, I must call you mister. That all your women do."

Sate shifted uneasily and, shooting a dangerous look at the squaw who was lapping up Madison's smooth flattery, said tightly, "She just wanted to needle you. I hope you didn't believe her."

"Not at all." Juliana laughed lightly. "I told her that I wasn't one of your women, therefore I'd continue to call you Sate."

"And what did she say to that?" Sate held his breath, wondering how much the squaw had revealed.

"She just gave that laugh of hers. I don't think she believed me."

"I'll ram that laugh down her throat one of these days," Sate muttered under his breath, throwing a dark look toward the fireplace. Louder, he said, "I'd send her packin' right now if I didn't need her to look after you while I'm out runnin' my traps. She's a useless thing. I can even cook better than her."

To her amazement, Juliana suddenly found herself wildly wishing to exclaim, "Send her away. I can look after myself. And, my wild trapper, I bet I can cook better than you." Her eyes flew to the masculine profile. Had she spoken aloud?

She gave a whisper of relief. His attention, pointed and intense, was fixed on the floor. "God," she thought, "what put such ideas in my head? I must have gotten a worse whack than I thought when I jumped from the coach, for this backwoodsman and I share nothing in common." She stole a glance at the rough, lean face. No, a man like this would never seriously entertain desire for a woman like herself. The kind of woman who would attract and hold his interest wouldn't panic and become lost in a snowstorm . . . wouldn't faint from fear.

"And you?" a voice sneered inside Juliana, "How long could the trapper hold *your* interest? Would it be strong enough to overcome having to live in the wilderness, in a small cabin; no parties or dances, nowhere to wear your pretty gowns?"

"Oh, shut up," she rejoined silently. "I'm sure I'll never have to make that decision." When she announced a moment later that she would get up, there was nothing in her tone that gave away the conflict in her mind.

Sate's wide smile approved her decision and he unbuckled the two straps on the bag and lifted back the lid. Colorful, fluffy petticoats and gowns and robes spilled over the sides, and he gazed at them, marveling. He had no idea that such finery existed. Never before had he seen such.

He breathed deeply of the flower scent that drifted from the feminine articles, and watched with rapt interest as Juliana picked up and lay aside a brush, a bar of scented soap, and a soft washcloth. He gave a start when she said softly, "Now if I can please have a basin of warm water."

Sate nodded and called across the room, "Doxy, fetch me a pan of warm water." A few moments later when the surly-faced girl handed him a steaming basin, he ordered curtly, "Hold a blanket in front of her while she washes and gets dressed."

Juliana felt Doxy's black stare as she lathered her face, then her throat, shoulders, and arms. My white body must look weak and useless to her, she fumed, pulling a thin lawn gown over her head, then brushing her long, pale hair. Well, I bet I'm just as strong as she is, she continued in the same vein, shrugging into the bright red, wooly robe.

When she slid off the bed, straightened the gown, and pulled the robe's belt tightly around her small waist, Doxy dropped the blanket and returned to the fire, resuming her seat beside Madison. She knew when Juliana joined them, for she sensed the tremor that went through the stranger's body. Hot jealousy whipping at her, she leaned toward him and whispered warningly, "Touch his woman, and the trapper will kill you."

It showed in the nervous flicker of Madison's eyes that for a moment the statuesque beauty had made him forget Margruder's dire warning. He directed his attention to the fire, but in his peripheral vision he watched the big man's deferential handling of his "wife": draping a blanket over the rocker, helping her into it, then folding the wool's thickness around her shoulders. He picked up her slender bare feet, glanced up at her as he stroked them, then rose and brought her a pair of his woolen socks. They exchanged amused smiles as he slid them over her toes and heels, an excess of about four inches hanging loosely.

"A perfect fit." The girl laughed throatily, smiling into the blue eyes that looked deeply into hers.

Assured that Juliana was warm and comfortable, Sate finally nodded his head toward their guest. "Juliana, meet Chad Madison," he said shortly.

Having this permission to look openly at the woman, Madison hurried to take advantage of it. Standing up and bowing slightly, he murmured. "I'm happy to meet you, ma'am."

When he would have gone on, Juliana said coolly, "I'm pleased to meet you, Mr. Madison," and turned back to Sate.

While her coolness brought irritated confusion to Madison, it brought a broad grin to Sate's face. He wanted to lift her out of the chair and hug her. Madison hadn't fooled her for a minute. She had seen beyond his handsome features and smooth tongue.

Nevertheless, after the meal of poorly prepared stew was eaten, Sate took Madison with him when he went outside to dress out the day's catch. He had faith in Juliana, but not a whit in Madison. And though the Philadelphia man was more hinderance than help, whether by intent or ineptness, he swallowed his impatience, not about to send him back inside.

The last skin was finally pegged to the cabin wall. When the two men walked through the door, Sate's gaze went straight to Juliana. Doxy noted how his face softened and his eyes lost their hardness, and her own black ones flashed hatred at the object of his attention. In the hour and a half spent alone, no word had passed between the two women. Juliana's cool aloofness said that to her the squaw wasn't even in the room, while Doxy contented herself with thinking of ways to torture the white bitch.

Doxy's dark eyes quickly sparkled and danced, however, when Madison turned his charm on her. Sate watched the seduction, sardonic amusement lifting the corners of his mouth. He wasn't surprised when shortly, after glancing at the ladder leading to the loft, Madison stood up, pulling Doxy with him.

"I suppose you'd like some privacy." He smiled unpleasantly. "Me and Doxy will spread our blankets up there." He jerked his head over his shoulder. Not waiting for a response, the plainly aroused man hustled the giggling squaw up the rungs of the rough-hewn ladder.

Juliana stared after them, speechless with surprise and disgust. When she turned her startled gaze on Sate, he shrugged helplessly.

"She's perfectly willin'. If she wasn't, I'd intervene."

He had hardly finished speaking when the boards above them began a squeaking protest at the heavy, rapid thud of a driving body. Juliana's face went crimson, and Sate's voice was thick with embarrassed anger as he said while half rising, "Should I send them outside?"

Juliana's eyes widened. Surely he wasn't serious . . . but his grim face said that he was. She looked away, amazed that he would actually make the pair sleep outside if she was disconcerted at the sounds over their heads. She smiled inwardly: so rough in appearance and manner, he still possessed a thoughtfullness that was more gentlemanly than that of any man of breeding she had ever known.

She was saved a decision when, as suddenly as the telltale noise upstairs started, it ceased. She and Sate shot each other a relieved look, then grew silent.

The fire snapped and cracked, and Juliana gazed musingly into it. This man sitting at her feet, his arms clasped around his drawn-up knees, was beginning to stir emotions inside her that were better put to rest. For, as she had reminded herself before, Sate Margruder could never return those feelings. And though for the first time in a long time she felt secure, at home in this small cabin, she must, for her own peace of mind, remove herself from the trapper's disturbing presence.

She took a deep breath and said quietly, "Sate, the snow has settled so I should resume my journey tomorrow."

Juliana watched the big body stiffen, heard the sharply indrawn breath, and she wondered. Was Sate as disappointed as it appeared? She couldn't see his face, read what lay in those dark blue eyes. Neither could she read much from his voice when he spoke.

"Are you sure you're up to travelin' so soon? You still look pretty weak to me."

She forced herself to laugh lightly. "I always look this way. Don't let my frail appearance fool you. Actually, I'm pretty strong."

Sate turned around then and smiled at her, a smile so gentle and admiring, she felt she would melt from its warmth. He picked up one of her small hands and held it in his large one. His tone amused, he said, "I can't see much strength in these little fingers, but I know you have a man's courage. Most women, having experienced what you did, would still be in bed, whimperin' and shiverin'."

Juliana pulled her hand away, afraid its sudden trembling would alert Sate to what was happening inside her. "I take that as a compliment, Sate," she murmured unsteadily. "But if my brother John should come looking for me in Philadelphia and find me gone, he'd be beside himself with worry."

Sate turned back to the fire, saying brusquely, "Yes, of course you must go."

Silence grew between them again, Sate thinking that in a short period of time he had grown to feel for this woman as he never had for another, and wondered how he could bear never to see her again. Juliana mourned the fact that she would never experience the warmth of his arms, feel the touch of his lips or know the hard caress of his body.

Juliana stirred and sighed deeply. "Do you know when the coach passes by?"

Sate's answer was slow in coming. Finally, "Yes. It passes every Thursday afternoon."

"What day is tomorrow?" Juliana asked softly.

There was another short silence. "Thursday."

Juliana rose, gazed down at the dark head, and, toying with the ends of the robe's belt, said as calmly as she could, "I would appreciate it if you'd take me to meet it."

The rhythmic thudding resumed overhead, and his hands knotted angrily. Sate said hurriedly that of course he would.

Juliana murmured, "Good night, Sate." Her eyes shimmering with tears, and her mind cursing the vulgur noise that had spoiled their last minutes together, she crossed the floor and crawled into bed.

CHAPTER 5

Outside, the forest was still and shadowed when Sate awakened, only a faint pink light in the east revealing that dawn was approaching. He lay staring at the pale light through the window, his eyes gritty from too little sleep, a gloom such as he had never known filling his mind.

He sat up and peered at the dim outline of the figure curled in his bed, and lost all interest in the years that stretched ahead. Until now he had led his life mainly within himself, needing no one else. Now, after having made love to this woman, he felt he would never be complete again. The cabin would hold her image, carry her scent, and he would find it pure hell to live inside its four walls.

Repressing a ragged sigh, Sate swept back the covers and stood up. It would take all his willpower not to lock her up and refuse to let her go. To aid him in that struggle he must not deviate from his usual daily routine. Only in familiar repetition could he, perhaps, keep his mind off her leaving.

The morning's customary procedure was broken almost immediately. There was no Doxy squatting in front of a fire, preparing breakfast. In fact, there was no fire.

Sate stared down at the pile of dead ashes, then upward to the loft. Swearing under his breath, he strode to the ladder, scaled it in two long steps, then peered through the half-darkness at an empty floor.

"That damn fool squaw has gone off with that womanizing bastard," he muttered, and climbed back down to hunker in front of the fireplace.

It's no great loss to me, he thought, raking aside the spent ashes and carefully laying a pile of small kindling; I couldn't bring myself to touch her anymore. He shook fine granules of gunpowder over some shavings. Compared to Juliana's passionate response, the squaw's stolid acceptance of my body can only be considered an animal liaison.

Sate struck a flint across a stone and the flying sparks ignited the powder with a little *whoosh*. When the small pieces of bark and splinters had caught fire to his satisfaction, he added larger pieces of wood and, finally, some short split logs.

He watched the fire burn a minute, warming his hands over the flames. Then, picking up the coffee pot and a pan, Hawser at his heels, he went out into the chill of the morning. The snow crunched coldly beneath his feet as he followed the path, the new one since Juliana's arrival, to the back of the cabin. Relieved, he returned to the front and busied himself packing clean snow into the two vessels.

Sate went back inside, closing the cabin door quietly behind him, and placed the containers on the coals to melt and heat their contents. A few minutes later, while salt pork sizzled in a skillet and coffee brewed, he shaved his face and brushed his hair.

Should I wake her up? He gazed down at Juliana who slept deeply, a hand curled under her chin. And though he hated to lose one precious minute of her company, her strained features told him she needed her rest. He would leave the meat and coffee close to the coals, keeping them warm until she got up.

The sun was high, slanting through the shutters in bright, strong rays, when Juliana awakened. It was not the sun that had roused her, though. It was Hawser's moist nose shoved into her hand. It was quiet in the room as she leaned over the bed and rubbed the hound's smooth head.

"And how are you this morning?" She scratched behind a long ear. "I'm going to miss you, you old jugger-head. And him." Her eyes grew wistful. "Especially him."

She sat up and swung her feet to the floor, giggling at the sight of the oversized woolen socks which had kept her feet warm all night.

"How thoughtful," she said to the tail-wagging dog as she moved across the room and spotted the breakfast left close to the fire. "But the fire is almost out."

Where is the squaw this morning? she wondered as she added two logs to the glowing red coals. And the stranger, Madison? Were they with Sate?

Her lips curved in a soft smile. She had realized last night, when Sate had taken their visitor outside with him, that he didn't trust the man. He had probably made Madison go with him today to run the traps, and Doxy, obviously smitten with their guest, had tagged along.

While Juliana ate the crisp meat, sharing a bit or two with Hawser, she surveyed the cabin. Doxy was indolent, careless, and the large room reflected her laziness. Dust lay heavy on everything, and dust balls blew about with each stirring of air.

Sate's little home could be so attractive with a little care, she thought wistfully. She held out the last piece of meat to the hound. "I'm going to give this place a good cleaning, fellow. It will be my 'thank you' to him.

"And I'll make his supper, too," she added a few minutes later as she pulled the gown over her head, then put on the red dress.

It took but minutes to wash her face and brush the tangles out of her hair, and less time to pack her nightclothes in the bag and strap it tightly, ready to go.

Juliana became so immersed in making the bed and dusting the furniture, she forgot momentarily that in a matter of a few hours she would be leaving the place, never to set eyes on it again.

It was after she had swept the floor and was washing the window that her mood became cheerless again. She gazed out the shiny bright window, at the snow glistening white beneath the green of cedar and pine, and realized that she could grow to love this wild, beautiful, lonely land.

She pushed from her mind all the wishful thinking of things that might have been and went back to check on the venison roasting in the dutch oven. She had just replaced the lid when she heard Sate step upon the small porch. Already she could distinguish his step from any other.

The door opened and he stepped inside, bringing the scent of the outdoors with him. Juliana had to force herself not to fly across the room and fling herself into his arms. They gazed at each other for what seemed an eternity to her, then Sate broke away and swept his gaze around the room.

"You certainly have been busy." The lines at the corners of

his eyes deepened. "You've discovered that the squaw doesn't exactly excel at housekeeping."

"Where is Doxy and her . . . *friend*?" Juliana glanced up from the coffee she was pouring into two pewter cups.

"She and Madison took off sometime before I got up this mornin'," Sate answered, gratefully taking the cup she held out to him.

"Wasn't that foolish of her?" Juliana asked after he had eased his big frame into the rocker. "I mean . . . it's plain he's not a caring sort of man."

"Evidently it wasn't very plain to her," Sate said between appreciative sips of the strong fragrant coffee. "The squaw didn't look beyond his sugar-coated words. God knows where she'll end up after he finishes with her."

"Will you miss her?" Juliana asked, watching him closely through narrowed eyes.

Her heart leaped joyfully when he looked at her in surprise, then threw back his head and laughed scornfully. "What's to miss with that one? If ever I saw a useless female, that Pennacook Indian takes first place. Truth be known, I'm glad to be rid of her." He paused, then added, "I do wish, though, that she'd gone off with someone half decent."

Sate smiled suddenly at Juliana and changed the subject. "Something sure smells good."

"I made a roast for your supper." She wanted to add, "I wish I could be here to eat it with you."

Sate looked at Juliana, longing and pain in his eyes. But her lids were lowered so that he couldn't read her thoughts. By the time she willed her face to show nothing, she looked at him to find his face blank.

They lapsed into an awkward silence, and by the time they finished the coffee, it was time to leave for the coach. Sate picked up her bag and left to saddle his horse, while Juliana, her shoulders drooping, settled her cape around herself and pulled up its hood. The red velvet bonnet had disappeared. Doxy had taken it, she suspected. Several times she had seen the girl eyeing it.

She stood in the middle of the room, turning slowly, impressing it all on her mind. No matter where life led her, what man she might marry some day, she would never forget this rustic cabin, or the roughly handsome trapper who owned it.

With a long, ragged sigh, and unshed tears burning in her eyes, she quickly walked outside.

"This is Jake," Sate said of the magnificent black stallion stamping his hooves against the cold. "He's never felt a woman's long skirts before," he added, fastening the bag behind the saddle, "but I think he'll be all right."

Saying no more, he climbed into the saddle, leaned down, put his lean hands to Juliana's small waist, and lifted her effortlessly to sit in front of him. Jake gave a rumbling grunt, sidled about a moment, then, accepting the full skirts and a pair of dangling feet on his right side, calmed down. He pranced forward at the light pressure of Sate's heels.

Juliana peered around the muscular arm that held her steady in the saddle, and gazed back at the small cabin until a bend in the trail hid it from sight. She sighed, but softly, so that the stony-faced man who stared straight ahead wouldn't hear.

The sun was well to the west when Sate brought the stallion to a halt. Juliana stirred herself from the warm cocoon of his arms and looked around. "Is this the place?" she asked weakly.

"Yes," Sate answered, the first word he had uttered since they started out. "If the coach is on time it should be here directly."

I don't want to leave him, Juliana wailed silently to herself. I feel so safe and content with him. She peeked up through her lashes at his face, but saw none of the emotions that were raging in her like a storm. A bleakness overcame her, and suddenly she had to get out of those warm arms holding her so securely. The longer she knew their comfort, the harder it would be for her to leave them.

"Can we get down and move around a bit?" she asked slowly. "My legs are stiff."

Sate nodded and swung to the ground. He reached up and, grasping her waist, lifted her out of the saddle. But instead of placing her directly on the ground, he slid her slowly down the long length of his body as though he were unable to let her go.

Juliana felt the lean body tremble, and in the charged silence she ventured a peek at his face. The drawn features, the regret in the blue eyes, set her heart racing with hope. He looks the way I feel, she thought. Not fighting the urge that gripped her, she whispered softly, "I shall miss you, trapper. Will I ever see you again?"

The lean fingers on her waist bit into her flesh, but she was hardly aware of it as she watched the joy that shot into the blue eyes. "Do you want to see me again?"

"Yes! Oh, yes!" The answer was barely whispered.

His eyes rested on the curved fullness of her lips. Before his mouth came down on hers he whispered hoarsely, "I couldn't bear it, never to see you again."

Juliana pressed her body into his, echoing his moan of pleasure. "When? When will I see you again?"

Sate pushed the hood from her head and ran his hand over her smooth hair as his eyes drank in her lovely, delicate features. "Not until the spring, I'm afraid," he said regretfully. "When the snow is gone and I can bring in my traps."

"So long a time, Sate?" Juliana's eyes clouded with disappointment. "It will seem like forever."

"I know—for me, too." Sate claimed her lips again, hotly, hungrily. And Juliana, lost to everything around her, claimed by the sensations she had known only in dreams, missed entirely the distant rumble of approaching wheels. In a daze she felt Sate's lips leave hers, sensed that he was helping her inside the coach.

"Where in Trenton does your brother live?" Sate's voice jarred her back to the present.

She fumbled in the bag at her wrist and brought out a pencil and piece of paper. "It's easy to find." Her smile was tremulous as a moment later she handed him the address.

"I'll find it." Sate drew a thumb across her trembling lips. "To find you, I'd search the entire wilderness."

His lips pressed hers in one last kiss before motioning the driver on. The man cracked his long whip and the coach began to lumber away. Juliana kept her gaze on Sate until he faded from sight. She sat back then, her face a mixture of sadness and radiance. She had never dreamed a person could fall in love so quickly.

Iva's big, square, two-storied house stood in front of Juliana, and she couldn't help musing how like her sister-in-law it looked—a no-nonsense structure without shutters or trim to soften its austere lines. Sighing, her bag clenched tightly in her hand, she climbed the two steps to the narrow front door.

She lifted the heavy rocker and let it drop, hearing its loud clap resound down the gloomy hall inside. Within seconds she recognized the hurrying footsteps of the maid tapping on the stone-tiled floor.

The door swung open and a harried-looking Tillie gaped at her. "Oh, it's you, miss," she faltered, visibly ill at ease.

"Hello, Tillie." Juliana smiled warmly, sincerely happy to see the only person in this house who had treated her kindly. "Is John in?"

Tillie threw an uneasy glance over her shoulder, then half whispered, "Mistress Nemeth is in, but she's in a bad mood, Miss Juliana."

"When isn't she?" Juliana snorted bitterly.

After a slight hesitation, Tillie moved aside so that Juliana could enter. "I'll go tell her you're here," she said nervously.

Juliana watched the maid walk away, frowing in perplexed curiosity. Why was the woman acting so strangely? Had she listened at a keyhole, overheard some some remark of Iva's that boded no good for her young sister in-law?

She had no time to dwell further on Tillie's actions, for almost immediately Iva came sweeping down the stairs. Watching John's wife approach, listening to the starched petticoats rustle in that curiously cold manner, Juliana thought that she had never seen the woman look more unattractive.

Strands of Iva's thin hair had escaped its skinny knot to stick out in wisps around her ears and neck, not unlike the sparse down on a baby gosling, Juliana thought in grim amusement. When the thin, angular woman drew nearer, she noted that the pale brown eyes looked red and puffed, as though she had been weeping. Having never known this proud, cold woman to cry, she advanced toward her.

"I'm sorry to barge in on you like this, Iva," she began, her hand held out in greeting, an uncertain smile on her face, "but . . ." Her words died as a look of black hostility was shot at her.

Disregarding the offered hand and faltering words, Iva Nemeth asked icily, "What are you doing here?"

The question was so full of hate and barely suppressed rage that Juliana took a step backward. "Why, I thought . . . thought to say . . . hello to you and John," she stammered, afraid now to mention that she wanted to stay with them until spring.

Iva's eyes grew wild. As Juliana gazed back at her fearfully, she hissed, "Do you and your brother think that I'm a complete idiot? Do you think that I don't know he's sent you here to wheedle money out of me?"

"What in the world are you talking about, Iva?" Juliana gasped, falling back further at the enraged onslaught. "Isn't John here?"

Holding her side, panting slightly, Iva peered narrowly into Juliana's bewildered eyes. Then, apparently convinced that the white-faced girl was ignorant of past events, she collasped into a tall-backed chair against the wall. Her features slowly became composed, but her voice shook with indignation as she said harshly, "Your dear brother has left me."

Juliana stared at her sister-in-law with a mixture of disbelief and exultation. Was it possible that John had finally had enough of his shrewish wife and left her? It sounded too good to be true. It occurred to her that her own marriage had set her brother free. For hadn't he married Iva for her benefit in the first place?

And though she hoped devoutly that he wouldn't, Juliana said soothingly, "I'm sure he'll return, Iva."

"He won't be back," Iva answered with bitter conviction. "He's run off with a whore who worked in a tavern down on River Street."

"What?" The words erupted incredulously. "You must be mistaken. John never had any use for that kind of woman."

Iva's eyes flashes so heatedly that for a moment their pale color was almost brilliant. "I'm not mistaken," she hissed. "They were seen riding off together in the middle of the night." Her clenched fists pressed her bony knees. "I hope they never reached Kentucky. I hope the Indians caught them and, before they tortured them to death, scalped that fancy bitch's yellow hair."

The irate woman had risen as she raved and, alarmed, Juliana grabbed up her bag and began backing toward the door. Iva had gone mad. Feeling the door handle beneath her fingers, she muttered, "Good-bye, Iva," and slipped outside.

She stood on the small stoop, hearing through the heavy door the woman inside still yielding to the rage that boiled inside her. Iva was hurt, she knew, but only from smarting pride. How just, considering the many prides that Iva had trampled on during her lifetime, she smiled grimly.

But what's to become of me? Juliana's slim shoulders

sagged. John off to some wild place called Kentucky, and whereabout there she had no idea. She could not believe that he had gone with a tavern wench. That was entirely out of character. And how was she to find him?

And Sate? Tears stung her eyes as she walked down the steps. It was impossible to believe that she would ever see him again, ever again feel his arms around her, lose herself in his kisses. She was a fool to have ever thought that anything so perfect, so right, could ever happen to her. Her past life was proof of that, wasn't it?

The tears ran freely down Juliana's checks and her thoughts were in such turmoil she almost missed the loud hiss originating from the corner of the house. Throwing a curious look in that direction she saw Tillie standing in the shadows, a finger to her lips as she motioned her forward. She stepped quickly to the maid's side, her eyes questioning.

Speaking quietly and rapidly, Tillie said, "Mister John has gone to a settlement called Squaw Hollow. The poor fellow couldn't stand Missus any longer. Nobody faults him for leaving her."

Juliana gently squeezed the maid's trembling hand. "Thank you, Tillie." She paused. "Do you think John took a woman with him?"

Tillie looked uncomfortably at the ground for a moment, then, raising her head, answered frankly, "Yes, he did, Miss Juliana. But not a whore, like *she* claims, but a decent, hard-working young woman. Molly Anderson never set foot in the room where the spirits are served. She stayed in the kitchen of the Black Rooster Tavern, where she was the cook."

Tillie jerked her thumb toward the house. "She's so different from that one in there. She's young and pretty, a happy, laughing woman, a balm that poor Mister John needs."

Juliana nodded agreement. "I'm so glad he's found someone to love him, give him back his pride. I bless her."

Tillie grinned. "Thank you, miss. Molly is my niece. Mister John met her when she used to come visiting me."

Juliana returned the grin. "I see."

"Will you try to find your brother, miss?"

"Oh, yes. Just as soon as I can hire someone to take me to this Squaw Hollow. Do you have any idea how I should go about finding someone?"

Tillie frowned in thought, staring at the ground. She started to speak, then hesitated. "Trappers go to the Black Rooster a lot," she said finally, still frowning, "and if you'd speak to the owner he'd put you in touch with someone trustworthy who would guide you there. But the tavern is no proper place for a lady to visit."

Juliana gave an impatient wave of a hand. "Never mind that, Tillie, it's unimportant. The important thing is finding my way to John. How will I know this tavern owner? What does he look like?"

"Well, if you're determined, he's a big man with a black curly beard."

"Thank you, Tillie. And if you'd do me one other favor?" Tillie nodded. "In the spring, after the snow is gone, a man will come asking for me. Will you please explain to him what has happened, and where I've gone? Tell him to ask where John Nemeth lives, and that's where I'll be."

"I'll send him right on." Tillie smiled fondly.

Juliana leaned forward and brushed her lips across the lined cheek. "Bless you, Tillie, for everything." As she turned to leave her misty-eyed friend she caught a movement at the slightly parted drapes in the window just above her head. Had Iva been eavesdropping on their conversation? She shrugged. What if she had? The spiteful woman couldn't hurt her anymore.

The sun was dropping behind the chimney as Juliana walked into the main part of Trenton. Darkness would soon arrive and she had much to do before then. Her stomach gave an empty rumble. It was imperative that she find supper, and a place to spend the night. Tomorrow, early, she would visit the Black Rooster.

Now, to arranging quarters for the night. The hotels wouldn't take in single women, and if there were any rooming houses in town she's wasn't aware of them. Her soft lips firmed. That left only a room over some tavern. And how did one go about engaging a room in such a place? she wondered.

Juliana walked along the cobblestone street that was lined with shops on either side. She wasn't surprised that it was mostly men creating what noise and bustle there was on the long, narrow wooden sidewalk. At this hour the women were home, preparing supper.

An old man moved ahead of her, lighting the lanterns that hung at every intersection. Slowly lights began to appear in the shops, and, uncomfortably aware of the curious and appraising looks cast her way, Juliana fixed her eyes straight ahead. Only whores appeared on the streets at night.

She reached the lower section of town and a nervous sweat moistened the palms of her hands. She was in the squalor of the city now, where taverns, bawdy houses, and the dregs of Trenton were pushed together in a two-block area. Her gaze moved from one dimly lit tavern to the next. Her spirits dropped lower and lower. They all looked so dirty . . . so evil, somehow.

Juliana was nearing the end of the last street when she saw the building. It was larger than the others, and more respectable-looking, she thought, if only because the windows were clean. She stood undecided for a moment, then, firming her jaw, she walked across the frozen, rutted street.

A loud, ribald confusion of sound greeted her through the thin paneling of the door and she took a step back. She could not face the battery of eyes that would be turned upon her. There had to be something else. She turned to go, then froze. Coming up the sidewalk toward her were two men, swaying and holding on to each other as they loudly sang a salty song about a maid and her lover. She hurriedly tried to shrink into the shadow of the building but was too late. One of he men had spotted her. When he lurched toward her, instinct warned her to avoid him at all risk and she blindly swung open the tavern door.

Juliana blinked her eyes rapidly. The big room was crowded and hazy with tobacco smoke. The acrid smell of spilled rum and ale made her empty stomach nauseous.

No one seemed to notice her, and she took heart. Choosing the kindest-looking bartender behind the long bar, she started across the sawdust-covered floor, her chin high although her legs trembled. She was almost to her destination when a rough hand snaked out and grabbed hold of her arm.

"What have we here, now?" a leering voice drawled thickly.

Juliana gasped and tugged to free her arm. The man, buckskin-garbed, bewhiskered, tightened his hold and grinned at her blazing eyes. "Let me go, you dirty lout," she hissed fiercely.

Her demand only tickled the man, and he laughed gleefully as he staggered to his feet. "We have a little spitfire here, men," he called, pulling her so tightly up against him she felt the imprint of the knife stuck in his belt. "Do you think I can tame her?"

A circle of grinning, leering faces gathered around them, cheering the man on, calling out advice. Caught up in a blinding rage that she should be manhandled her in such a fashion, Juliana reacted instinctively. Her clawing fingers grabbed a handful of hair above each ear of her tormentor and, holding on tightly, she brought up a quick, sharp knee between his spread legs. With a yowl of pain the man released her and stumbled away doubled over in agony. Juliana turned to dart to the door, but another male figure stood in her way.

"Come on, pretty thing," a new voice taunted, "try that on me."

Thoroughly frightened now, and weak from her last struggle, panic crept into Juliana's mind as she tried to move around the large bulk blocking her path. She felt sure she was near to fainting; she frantically commanded herself not to. There was no doubt of the consequences if she should drop senseless to the floor.

Juliana felt her backside come up against a table. Without her realizing it, the man had backed her into a corner. In desperation she reached behind her, her fingers blindly searching the table's surface. If I can only get my hands on something, she cried inwardly, a bottle, a candlestick, anything to ward off this ugly face bearing down on me.

Her questing fingers brushed against a thick, heavy mug, then curled around it. She took a firm grip, then fast as lightening swung it around and out. The mug, liquid and all, smacked flat between red-rimmed eyes.

The watching patrons howled with laughter as the man stared owlishly at Juliana, buttered rum running down his face and seeping into his beard. He still, however, had enough presence of mind to hang onto his prey, and though Juliana's mind commanded her to fight on, her body was unable to respond. But as she leaned weakly against the table, her stance was at odds with the light of battle in her amber eyes. Admiration for her fiery spirit crept into the watching men's eyes. One stepped forward and lay warning hand on the hunter's arm, then was startled into immobility when a blood-curdling yell pierced the air.

They all turned and stared open-mouthed as an elderly Indian moved across the floor with amazing alacrity. Before the stunned audience could move he had Juliana's tormentor's arm up between his shoulders, and the point of a long blade laid against his throat.

A hush fell over the room and the men, who had only wanted to see the little wildcat tame the two big hunters, looked at each other ashamedly. Although each one there would have stopped the two from going too far, a red man—an old one at that—had stepped in and brought a halt to what they should have stopped from the beginning. Almost as one, the men began to explain in a rush of voices. But the cool aloofness of the faces of the old brave and the beautiful woman brought them to a faltering halt.

With his knife still on the heavily sweating hunter, and a hand on Juliana's arm, the elderly warrior began backing toward the door. Juliana lifted the latch and swung it open. The three stood there for a second, then, with a hard push in the small of his back, the white-faced hunter reeled into the grouped bunch of staring men. In the blink of an eye, man and woman were gone. When the men rushed outside, the street was empty. The oddly matched pair had disappeared.

Inside the tavern the bartender, whom Juliana had tried to reach, spotted the leather bag where she had dropped it. He picked it up and placed it behind the bar. If he wasn't mistaken, he grinned, sometime tonight, after the place was closed, the old Indian would return for it.

CHAPTER 6

Juliana rushed headlong behind her aged rescuer who sprinted down a narrow alley. She glanced nervously over her shoulder when he paused as though confused by the shadows thrown by the buildings that bordered them on each side. She listened intently. Were they being followed by the men, surely more savage than the man at her side? She heard nothing but the distant bark of a dog.

A low whinny sounded from the next alley and again they were pounding on. The dim outline of a small horse emerged from between two buildings and with a satisfied grunt the old man sprang onto its back, then reached a hand down to Juliana. She grabbed it and flung herself behind his wiry form. He jabbed his heel into the shaggy flank and the rangy little mount lunged away with such a burst of speed that Juliana barely had time to grasp the lean shoulders and hang on.

The pony dashed across three street intersections and they were at the edge of town. When the lights of Trenton grew dim, then disappeared, the mount was drawn to a walk. "No need to run now," the Indian spoke for the first time. "They too drunk to follow in forest."

An apprehension Juliana hadn't realized she'd carried eased away. The old brave spoke English. He seemed less savage, somehow. Her lips twisted wryly. The men in the tavern had spoken her language, but she had not been safe with them.

She withdrew her arms from the red shoulders and tugged at her skirt which rode past her knees. "I could have gladly shot them all," she gritted through her teeth.

"Don't waste energy in anger." The old man steered the pony among the trees that stood ghostlike in the cold moonlight. "I no think real harm come to you. The men watching, it big laugh to them; see small woman fight big hunters."

"If you thought that"—Juliana frowned—"why did you come to my defense?"

"I see fear in your eyes, white man see only anger on your face. He did not know what happen inside you."

Juliana shook her head in bemused silence. A red savage, yet so wise, so compassionate. "What is your name?" she asked softly.

"I am called Nemus."

"I am very happy to know you, Nemus." A pause, then: "My name is Juliana Roessler."

The Indian grunted, then made a startling statement. "One time called Juliana Nemeth."

Juliana was held speechless for a moment. "How do you know this?" she was finally able to ask.

"I recognize you."

"But that's not possible. We've never met before."

"Your face same like John's."

Juliana's eyes widened in disbelief. It was too far-fetched that this old Indian would know her brother. Afraid to hope, she asked breathlessly, "Do you mean John Nemeth?"

"Yes. My friend John."

Her thoughts racing with the unlikeliness of her planned search for her brother coinciding with meeting an old Indian who actually knew him, Juliana was only vaguely aware that the pony had been reined to a halt and that her companion had slid to the ground. It took an impatient grunt and a sharp whack to her leg to loosen her tongue. When Nemus cupped his hands to receive her foot, she besieged him with questions.

"How did you meet my brother? Have you known him long? Do you know where he is now?"

"First we gather wood, make fire, and eat," Nemus grunted. "Then we talk of John."

"But," Juliana began with barely concealed annoyance, "I . . ." She faltered when steady black eyes compelled her to obey.

"We eat first. A long story to be told. Not made short for impatient woman."

Juliana reluctantly accepted the fact that not one word about
her brother would escape those thin lips until their owner was
ready to do so. She followed him among the trees, searching
out pieces of dry wood. When Nemus was satisfied that enough
fuel had been gathered—enough for a week, Juliana thought
grumpily—she brushed the snow off a fallen tree and sat down.
Bunching her skirts around her legs, she watched the construc-
tion of the fire.

In a short time, but seeming forever to Juliana, a hot,
smokeless fire burned brightly. She gratefully held her feet to
its warmth and munched hungrily on the pemmican Nemus
handed her.

She sat forward eagerly when, finally, after he had lighted a
long-stemmed clay pipe, Nemus folded his legs in front of him
and began his story with slow gravity.

"One evening, six moons ago, I made careless campfire. I
was tired and cold and in haste for heat, I use fast-burning
cedar to make fire." A flicker of embarrassment shadowed his
face as he added, "Even youngest brave knows cedar sends a
strong scent in its heavy smoke." The thin chest heaved once,
and he continued on. "So, thinking only to warm my old
bones, I no hear two white men slipping up on me. When I
look in their cold eyes, I read their evil intent.

"They tie me to tree and pile brush around my feet. I know
my end is near and I begin to chant prayer to the Great Father,
asking that I meet my fiery death with courage and dignity. The
men laugh at my prayer, then one take a flaming branch from
my foolish fire and walk toward me. But when he lean down to
shove it under brush a shot is fired and he fall at my feet. When
other one move quick, he too hit by bullet.

"For long time nothing more happen and I said to myself
that maybe the shooter of rifle was as cruel as the two he had
saved me from; that he make me stay tied and slowly starve to
death. Then, as I accept this fate, two riders come from the
forest."

Nemus looked across at Juliana, his leathery face stirring in
a half smile. "That is how I meet your brother and his yellow-
haired woman."

Juliana's withheld breath rushed through her teeth. Leaning
forward, her eyes agleam, she asked eagerly, "Do you know
what happened to John after that?"

Again the old man wouldn't be rushed. He lay more wood

on the fire, and took a few puffs on his pipe before continuing. "John and his woman spread blankets beside my fire that night. As we talk I know John is new to the wilderness and its ways. When he say he was going to Squaw Hollow, I know I must go with him. In all Kentucky, that settlement is the roughest.

"I take him and his woman to the area, and John found man who want to sell his place and return to Boston with wife and children. He was a Quaker man and could not live with such sin and lawlessness as all around."

Juliana wrapped her arms around her drawn-up knees, trying to imagine her brother working on a farm. To her knowledge, John wouldn't know what a plow looked like, let alone how to use one. She spoke her thoughts aloud: "I just can't see my brother on a farm. He's completely ignorant of that kind of life."

"John's woman knows. She show him how."

Juliana recalled that Molly was Tillie's niece, and had most likely grown up on a farm, as had her aunt. She glanced at the stoic face across from her. Would he, she wondered, think it beneath him to guide a white woman to Squaw Hollow? She had heard of the red woman's stamina, her competence in erecting teepees and setting up camp, her ability to walk all day.

She sighed dispiritedly. She was so useless in this new land. When Nemus knocked the ashes out of his pipe and laid it aside, it took all her courage to voice her request: "Nemus, would . . . would you take me to my brother?"

The Indian was so long in answering that hope died inside Juliana. She had been right. He wasn't about to saddle himself with a helpless white woman.

She jumped when Nemus asked abruptly, "Does John's sister have money?"

Juliana's eyes registered her disillusionment. This red man, whom she was beginning to think so highly of, was, after all, as mercenary as the white man. "I have some," she answered stiffly. "Why?"

"Trip take three, four days, depending on you. I have extra pony, but will need food and blankets."

A deep flush stained Juliana's cheeks. Ashamed of the unflattering thought that had jumped to her mind, she hastily dug into the bag at her wrist. Handing over the money Aunt

Amy had given her she smiled and asked wistfully, "Do you think you might buy a little coffee?"

A gleam of humor flashed in Nemus's eyes. Then, remarking that he would soon return, he jumped onto the little mount's back, calling over his shoulder as he dashed away, "Keep fire fed."

The hoofbeats had no sooner faded away than the forest seemed to move in on Juliana. She shivered and drew closer to the fire, her glance darting constantly through the trees that now threw long shadows on the snow-covered floor of the woodland. She began to hear strange night sounds and her heartbeat quickened. When the wide-winged shadow of an owl swooped over her head, she squealed and ducked. She no sooner calmed her nerves a bit, even laughed a little at her fright, when directly across from the fire there appeared two small green circles of light, gleaming like needlepoints in the darkness.

She scrambled to her feet, terrified: a wolf. She tremblingly sank back down when a bushy-tailed fox darted past the campfire. When Nemus returned an hour later, she was a mass of jangled nerves. When he swung to the ground, she could have hugged him in her relief.

She repressed her expression of thanks until she spied the leather bag strapped to the extra pony Nemus had promised. As he tossed it to the ground along with a fustian bag of supplies, she exclaimed, "My bag! How did you ever get it, Nemus?"

Busily sorting out provisions, setting aside blankets and those foods that would supply tomorrow's breakfast, the old man grunted, "I wait until place closes, then go through window and pick it up."

"I deeply appreciate all you've done for me, Nemus," Juliana ventured a few minutes later after the old man had cleared away the snow close to the fire, then handed her two blankets.

Her thanks was received with a grave nod of the white head. "We go to bed now. Start early for Squaw Hollow tomorrow morning."

Juliana curled into the blankets, meaning to dwell a while on her memories of Sate and their thrilling good-bye. But her day had been draining. She fell asleep before Nemus finished laying out his own bed across the fire from her.

• • •

When Juliana awakened the next morning she thought for a moment that she was still asleep and dreaming as she gazed up at the canopy of snow-dappled foliage spreading overhead. She turned her head at the slipping sound of moccasin-shod feet and became fully aware of her whereabouts—and the reason. She looked beyond the campfire and could just make out Nemus, standing a few feet away in the morning grayness. The limp body of a rabbit dangled from his hand.

She leaned up on an elbow and called out cheerily, "Good morning." When she received a short grunt in return, she grinned. Evidently the white man didn't have a monopoly on morning grumpiness. Strangely desirous of the old brave's esteem, she rose from the blankets and rolled them into a neat bundle. When she joined Nemus at the fire he motioned his head at a pan of water sitting close to the fire.

"I melt snow for you wash face in. You make coffee while rabbit cook. Nemus no good at making coffee."

It was an hour past daybreak when Juliana was boosted onto the back of her own little pony, and the trip began.

By the end of the first day on the trail, Juliana was so sore and stiff that Nemus had to help her dismount. But she grew used to the daylong rides as they traveled the heavily timbered countryside with its many valleys and hills. Nemus was very accurate with his bow and arrow, and every evening they enjoyed fresh meat or fish.

On the fourth day, shortly before sunset, Nemus drew his little mount to a halt and motioned Juliana to do the same. "Squaw Hollow," he explained, staring down into a snow-covered valley.

Juliana leaned forward and squinted her eyes against the setting sun, making out four log buildings, each good-sized, two on each side of a wide, rut-frozen road. She lifted her gaze several yards up the valley's slopes and counted fifteen cabins scattered about in the forest of dark green pine and cedar.

So this was to be her new home—at least for while. It would depend on whether or not Sate would be content here. She hoped so. It would be good to live near John.

Her gaze dropped back to the floor of the valley. Of the small grouping of business places, only two showed any signs of life. Their doors opened often as men came and went. One was a tavern, she imagined, then frowned thoughtfully at the one next to it. This place was already brightly lit, including a lantern hanging on its porch.

"What place is that?" She turned to Nemus when from inside the building there erupted the faint strains of male and female laughter.

"That place!" The old man shook his head disapprovingly. "Bad women live in there."

Juliana hid her amused smile from the indignant Indian, although she was surprised to find a house of ill-repute so deep in the wilderness. "Which of the cabins up there belong to John?" she asked, changing the subject.

"John not have his woman living in the settlement." Nemus's eyes flashed scorn for the place below. "His cabin three miles from here."

Juliana's shoulders drooped wearily. Another three miles. Nemus had pushed hard today, and she was hungry and longed to get off her small mount. But when the old man lifted the hackamore and urged the pony down the gentle incline, she sighed and followed behind him.

No word passed between Juliana and Nemus until they drew opposite the building next to the tavern. When a burst of hilarity sounded from inside, Juliana leaned forward in the saddle to peer curiously through the window. She had time for only the briefest glance: at her first sign of interest, Nemus whacked her pony across the rump. As it lunged into a rocking canter, she had her hands full merely trying to stay on its back, much less controlling the animal. When she finally managed to rein it in, she shouted back at the scowling Indian: "Why did you do that? I could have fallen and broken my neck!"

"You no look in that sinful place," Nemus grunted, riding up beside her. "Bad things go on in there. Worse than in Trenton."

"Oh, for goodness' sake, Nemus, it wouldn't hurt me to look."

"You look on trail," Nemus grunted, kicking his pony on.

When they had covered almost the length of the long valley, Nemus pointed a long finger and said proudly, "John's place."

"Relax," Juliana commanded her racing pulses as she gazed at the small log house, now in semidarkness, nestled snugly before its backdrop of tall cedars that swept up the hill behind it. "He's my brother. Of course he'll be happy to see me."

A thin line of smoke rose from a stone chimney, and soft light glimmered through a shiny, clean window. Juliana guessed that there was only one room, and grimaced. They would be under each others' feet all the time. Would she really be welcome? Unease gripped her again.

As she and Nemus drew nearer she could make out a larger building looming behind the little home. Closer still, she could see it was a barn. Its wide doors opened as she studied it, and a man carrying a lantern stepped outside.

She peered at the slender masculine figure a moment, then her heart beat joyfully as she slid to the ground, crying out, "John! John!"

Juliana covered half the distance between them before John Nemeth reentered his senses from the stunned disbelief that had gripped him. He loped eagerly toward her, exclaiming, "Juliana? Is that you, sis?"

"Yes, yes!" Juliana laughed and threw herself into his outstretched arms.

"Where in the world did you come from?" John laughed happily, his arms tightening in a bear hug. "Is Tom with you?" He gazed over her head to where Nemus held the two mounts.

"No, I came alone," Juliana answered quietly, watching her brother's face, alert to see if he was displeased. Still holding his gaze, she explained, "Tom was killed in the last days of the war. I sent you a notice, but I know now why you never acknowledged it." She added after John's start of surprise, "His parents made me move out of our house, so . . so here I am, a weight around your neck again."

"Don't say that." John held her away from him. "You're my little sister. You belong with me."

"What if . . . Molly . . . doesn't want me?"

There was a tinge of embarrassment in John's short laugh. "I see you've been talking to dear Iva." Juliana nodded and he gently stroked the worried lines on her forehead. "Don't fret about Molly," he said softly. "She'll welcome you, and love you.

"And now," he said, turning her around and walking her toward the old brave, "tell me how you came to meet my old friend Nemus."

Their arms around each other's waists, Juliana related her unhappy experience with Iva, the scene in the tavern, and Nemus's rescue of her.

The two men shook hands, John's eyes gravely thanking his friend for his services to his sister. All three turned around when the cabin door swung open, spilling out a shaft of light. A shapely figure was silhouetted in its glow, and glancing up at her brother, Juliana saw the adoration that shone in his eyes.

"Who are you talkin' to, John?" a lilting voice called. "Do we have company?"

John took Juliana's arm and led her up to the porch. "We sure do have company, Molly, and you'll never in the world guess who."

The pretty golden-haired woman stared a moment, then let out a delighted laugh. "Your sister Juliana!"

"How did you know?" brother and sister demanded in unison.

While Nemus nodded his understanding, Molly answered as she bounded down the steps, "You're as alike as two peas in a pod. Welcome, sister." She smiled and kissed Juliana on the cheek.

Juliana tried to speak, to express her thanks. But only choked sobs escaped her throat. "Oh, John, she's worn out," Molly exclaimed, jumping to take Juliana's other arm. "Let's hurry her inside.

"Please don't be upset, Molly," Juliana managed as John helped her into a rocker before a blazing fire. "I'm not that tired." She grasped a hand of each. "It's just relief at being welcomed. It's been worrying me all the way here."

"Oh, Juliana." Molly sat down beside her. "Such as it is, you're more than welcome in our little home."

Juliana glanced around the large room, at the table and four chairs, the wall cabinet and dry sink at one end, large bed and dresser at the other end, then back to the two rockers and bench grouped in front of the fireplace. The curtains of bright red and yellow matched the cloth on the table and picked up the colors in the wide hand-loomed rug in the middle of the floor giving an allover appearance of warmth and coziness.

"I love your little home, Molly." Juliana reached over and squeezed a work-worn hand. "But aren't we going to be a little crowded?"

Molly's bright laughter pealed out. "Will you listen to her, John?" John grinned, and she continued, "Juliana, honey, do you know that there are families with as many as five younguns livin' in cabins that are smaller than ours?"

"You don't meant it!" Incredulity showed on Juliana's face. "Where do they all sleep? What about the parents' privacy when they . . . when they . . . She blushed, unable to finish her question.

Molly's lips twisted wryly. "Privacy means very little to most of the bunch livin' 'round here. They just up and do what they want when they want. Usually there's at least one youngun in bed with them at the time." She shook her head. "There ain't much them little beggars haven't seen."

At Juliana's increasingly shocked look, John said, after glancing at her heated cheeks, "The majority of people in Squaw Hollow are a different breed from what you're used to, sis. You're going to have to learn to take it all in stride."

"Indeed, yes," Molly broke in. "Like one of our neighbors using both his wife and her younger sister. Each spring without fail they both come up with big bellies." When Juliana was too stunned to respond, she continued, "When the preacher approached him about laying with his sister-in-law, who, by the way, is only fourteen, the farmer answered that, although it was none of the preacher's business what went on in his home, he was in a hurry to have some sons who would in time help him work the land. And that further more it had been the girl's idea that, in his words, he should plow her any time he wanted to."

Molly's lips curved in a sardonic grin. "Of the nine children crowded in that shack of his, only three are boys."

Juliana's scandalized gasp exploded in the room. "Why does the wife put up with it? Surely it must hurt her to see her husband in bed with her sister."

"It wouldn't do her any good to complain, if she did." Molly snorted. "She'd probably get a fist in the mouth for her trouble. Most likely, though, she doesn't care. Most likely she's glad to have him pester her sister; it gives her a rest. The winter nights are long, so it's early to bed."

Juliana blushed at Molly's frank talk, and wondered if she spoke from experience.

"But that's not to say that there ain't any decent folk in Squaw Hollow," Molly said, rising to her feet and bending over a large black kettle hanging from a pot hook. "We have several families who are law-abiding, and regular church-goers." As she stirred the steaming ingredients in the pot, she continued, "They work hard at their homesteads, and will eventually be the backbone of the community. They will gradually push the trash farther into the wilderness."

"Yeah," John said, pulling his long legs out of Molly's way as she moved between fire and table, preparing supper, "Nemus said it always happens that way. And that old Indian has seen the beginning of many settlements."

"Where is he, by the way?" Juliana asked. "Won't he be eating with us?"

John grinned. "Nemus doesn't set much store by white men's food. He prefers eating deer stew with some of his tribe camped down by the river. He does have a sweet tooth, though. When Molly bakes pies he eats with us."

"He was supposed to have joined us for Christmas dinner." He smiled at Juliana. "You put a stop to that."

"Oh, my goodness." Juliana's hands flew to her cheeks. "I completely forgot about the holiday. What's today's date?"

"The twenty-eighth," Molly answered, then: "Supper's on the table."

Juliana and John caught up with their separate news as everyone hungrily helped themselves to ham and beans served with golden cornbread. Juliana told briefly of Tom's death, and her harsh treatment from his parents, and John touched lightly on his leaving Iva. He reached a hand to cover Molly's. "She'll never give me a divorce. But me and Molly have agreed that, with the exception of Nemus, as far as anyone around here knows, she is Mrs. Nemeth. And if ever I am free, we'll have a quiet ceremony and nobody will ever be the wiser." John squeezed Molly's hand and gazed into her eyes. "Molly," he whispered tenderly, "I thank God every night that you love me enough to live with me, although I'm not yet able to properly ask for your hand in marriage."

Molly made no response, but her eyes smiling into John's spoke clearly of the love she held for him.

The hearty meal was topped off with flaky dried-apple pie that Molly had spooned dollops of cream over. By the time the dishes were washed and put away, Juliana was past trying to hide her wide yawns. Molly smiled at her sympathetically and walked across the room to her bed. Turning back the covers, she said, "Get into your gown and crawl in here. You look beat."

"But, Molly, I can't use your bed," Juliana protested, rising to her feet. "I'll be fine on a pallet. I grew used to it on the trail."

"John and I also prefer the floor," Molly answered firmly. "The folk we bought the place from left a thick feather mattress up in the loft. John and I will be quite comfortable there."

"Then let *me* sleep there."

Molly placed both palms on the bed and bounced them up and down. When a loud creaking of slats resulted she cocked a rougish grin at Juliana.

"Ohh, I see," Juliana stammered, her face turning crimson.

Molly kissed her cheek and said softly, "It's hard to believe that you've been married. I've never seen anyone blush as easily as you do."

Juliana disrobed in the shadows and, taking a nightgown from the bag, pulled it over her head. It will feel good not sleeping in my clothes anymore, she thought, climbing into bed.

Curled on her side, she conjured up the image of Sate's face. Why hadn't she mentioned him to John and Molly? she wondered. Then her lips curved in a dreamy smile. There was no mystery about it. This love she and Sate shared was too precious to talk about yet. She wanted to hold the sweet secret of it in her heart for a little while longer. Later, she thought; later. Her eyelids dropped in sleep.

CHAPTER 7

Sate Margruder watched the coach fade from sight, its iron-rimmed wheels cutting into the snow. When he could no longer hear the squeal of the ungreased axles he mounted the stallion and turned him back down the trail. And though he already missed the girl with the cloud of blond hair, his heart was light. He would see her again come spring. It still seemed like a miracle to him that one so beautiful, so ladylike, could return his feelings.

He let the reins lay loosely on Jake's neck, letting the animal choose his own pace as his master made plans for the future. A one-room cabin wasn't the kind of home Juliana Roessler was used to, and although he couldn't provide her with a two-story brick like those in Philadelphia and Trenton, he could add a kitchen and a bedroom to his cabin.

He would make them large, he dreamed, with windows on each side. And she must have one of those new-fangled cook stoves he'd seen at the village store. Then there was Mister Simpson who made furniture; real good-looking pieces. And he could get old Granny Hawkins to weave him some rugs on her loom.

I'll have to set out more traps, he thought; it's gonna take a good bit of money to do all that.

Sate started and focused his eyes in surprise when Jake stopped suddenly and pawed at the earth. The shed door stood before them. They were home; he had no recollection of getting there.

"You're hungry, huh, old fellow," he grunted, swinging to

the ground and leading the stallion inside his quarters. He stripped the saddle from the wide back and climbed under the slanted eaves of the loft to pitch down some forkfuls of hay. Climbing back down, the pitchfork still in his hands, he broke up the inch of ice covering the water in the trough. Then, with an affectionate pat on the broad rump, he took the beaten path to the cabin.

Hawser loped across the floor, wagging his tail rapidly at Sate, then slipped through the open door. Sate grinned as he leaned the rifle against the wall and removed his moccasins.

The cabin had never seemed emptier, Sate thought as he scraped away the dead ashes in the fireplace, down to where the live coals lay buried. Nor will I ever feel lonelier, he mused, coaxing flames with dry kindling. Nor will a winter ever seem so long. . . . His lean fingers edged the roast that Juliana had prepared closer to the flames to reheat. He hefted the coffee pot, found it half full, and placed it near the heat as well.

A short time later, after having eaten ravenously of the delicious, tender meat and finishing off the coffee, Sate sought his bed. He did not fall asleep immediately, however. Juliana's scent among the covers and pillow rose strong in his nostrils, and clear images of her came to mind. He relived the night they had made love and could almost feel her smooth body receiving his thrusting one. God, never had he felt such complete fulfillment.

Finally, the long exhausting day took its toll and he fell asleep with aching loins.

Sate's step was as light as his heart when he entered the forest the next morning and followed the well-defined paths in the snow. As he moved from trap to trap, the weight of the furry bodies growing on the rawhide strip slung across his shoulders, he paused often to lay new traps. Altogether thirty new ones were set and baited. Because of the extra time taken, night fell before he was finished. He was forced to light the wick in the lantern he always carried, and by its feeble light he ran the remaining traps.

He was bone-tired by the time he hung his catch on the cabin wall and stamped the snow off his feet.

Five days had passed since Sate had extended his line, adding three additional miles to be traversed. Every night the moon was well up in the sky by the time he was able to sink into bed.

But it's worth it, he'd console himself when his legs would ache and his feet were numb with the cold. He was working toward a prize that was worth much more suffering.

The aroma of freshly brewed coffee reached Sate first, warning him that someone was in his cabin. He began to walk faster, fuming that some bastard had dared enter his home and make free with his grub. He banged the cabin door open, then stopped short, his expression growing darker.

Doxy sat close to the fire, her slumped shoulders draped with a dirty shawl. Even from where he stood in the doorway he could see her battered face, the despair in her eyes. She stood up slowly and silently watched him close the door, then move to the fire and reach for the coffee pot. As he filled a cup, still without a word, she fidgeted nervously with a glossy braid, wondering if he would beat her. She knew the tales of squaws being beaten to death by drunken white men were true, and she unconsciously soothed a hand over a bruised cheek.

She started and gave a low whimper when Sate barked suddenly, "What are you doin' back here, squaw? Didn't you find Madison to your liking?"

Refusing to meet the hard, cold eyes, Doxy stared into the fire and muttered, "He went off and left me in Philadelphia."

Sate sighed disgustedly. "You idiot, didn't you know he would do that?" When Doxy shook her head, he sighed again, this time more sympathetically. "You surely didn't think that a man his type would keep you with him, provide for you."

"He said that he would," Doxy whined. "He said that I would have a pretty house and fancy clothes."

"I'm surprised he even bothered to tell you such tales." Sate grunted dryly.

Doxy squatted down before the fire. Holding her hands out to its heat, she said, "But that's why I went with him, because he promised me all those things."

"I still don't understand why he took you in the first place." Sate poured himself another cup of coffee.

The young squaw shot Sate a surprised look. "Doxy no good in bed?"

Sate was silent, keeping his thoughts to himself.

Doxy continued staring into the flames and several seconds

passed before she muttered, "That's not the reason he took me, anyhow."

Sate raised a questioning eyebrow. "Why did he take you?"

"He needed money to buy gear and traps."

The slow understanding that crept into Sate's eyes grew to anger as he listened to Doxy's story.

"When we arrived in Philadelphia, Madison took me to a room up over a tavern. It was so small only a little bed and stool would fit inside it. There was no bedding, only a straw mattress, dirtier than the ground outside. I didn't want to stay, but Madison said not to worry about its condition, that we were only staying overnight. I agreed to stay when he said he was going downstairs to get some blankets.

"I wait for him to return, when the door behind me open slowly. I turn around expecting to see Madison, but instead a huge, fat man stood there. I open my mouth to tell him he had the wrong room, but before I could get the words out he close the door and lock it.

"There was no way I could get away from him in that small room. In two steps he reach me and throw me on the bed. I told him that I would scream for my man, and he laughed and told me that he had just paid my man to be able to lay with me."

Doxy shuddered. "The terrible things that fat man did to me." She shook her head as though to shake away the memory. "Finally Madison called from outside, 'Your time is up, mister.'

"But before the big man was hardly off me, another was there to take his place. I ran into the hall and begged Madison not to do this terrible thing to me." She touched her battered face gingerly. "That is when he beat me."

Her voice breaking at times, Doxy continued on. "They came steadily all night, sometimes two at a time. I think I finally fainted, for the next thing I knew it was daylight and I was alone. I was afraid that Madison would return with more men, so I gather strength to slip out of the room and drag myself to the stables behind the tavern. I crawl into a pile of hay and stay there all that day and the next night. The next morning before daybreak I slip into the woods and make my way here."

Doxy's voice died away and Sate gazed down at her bent head, his fists unconsciously clenching and unclenching. He patted her shoulder awkwardly. "Get some stew in you and then roll up in your blankets. A good night's sleep and you'll feel your old self in the mornin'."

It was the first time Sate had ever spoken this kindly to Doxy and the young squaw read promise in his tone. Encouraged, as she unrolled her bedding, she asked the question that had niggled at her mind since returning to the cabin.

"Has your white woman left you, mister?"

Sate turned his head, giving a knowing, amused look at her question. "Only for a short time. Come spring, I'm joinin' her in Trenton."

Doxy's quickly shuttered eyes hid her expression as she rolled herself in the blankets, but the impatient jerks she gave the rough woolen material revealed her true reactions to Sate's answer. He had risen and started toward the door when her double-edged remark followed him.

"There are many long nights between now and spring."

Sate paused, his hand on the latch. "Yes. My waiting will be long."

"When I am mended"—Doxy leaned up on an elbow and smiled coyly—"I will make evenings go quickly for you."

Sate regarded her steadily, his lips curved faintly. "I'll wait for the woman I love." He opened the door and stepped outside.

Doxy laid back down and stared into the fire, not at all concerned with Sate's firm refusal of her offer. The big trapper liked his manhood tended to every night. She'd give him a couple of days. By then he'd be so loaded it would take half the night to free him of his juices. She fell asleep, a satisfied smile on her lips.

Sate returned from tending his chores, not sparing a glance for the figure rolled in blankets as he reached for the coffee pot and drained the last of its contents into a cup. Sipping it slowly, he stared into the dying fire. What was Juliana doing now? Probably in bed, asleep.

The memory of her slender, gently rounded body slipped into his mind and his body felt a tingle of longing. Involuntarily his glance took in the sleeping squaw.

"No!" he whispered fiercely. "I can wait."

The days slipped into weeks and two months went by. Two weeks later Sate was awakened in the middle of the night by the sound of rain pattering on the roof. The next morning when he stepped outside the cabin and unlaced the buckskins, his previous yellow stains had been washed away. He smiled widely. Before long he would hold Juliana in his arms again.

The ice in the river groaned and cracked throughout the shortening nights, and only isolated patches of snow remained in shaded spots. When the barren trees began to bud and put on new green growth, Sate began bringing home traps along with his haul. Doxy observed this uneasily. She knew that the trapper was preparing to leave. She had reconciled herself to the fact that he would eventually go to Trenton, for not once since her return had he lain with her.

One evening after Sate had scraped and stretched the hides of the day, she said as they sat before the fire, "I'm wondering if you plan to go to your white woman soon."

"You're wonderin' right." Sate dug a split log from the firebox and laid it on the fire. "In fact, I'm leavin' for Trenton tomorrow mornin'."

Doxy picked at the fringe on the hem of her shift. "And what about me?" she asked sullenly. "What am I to do?"

"Hell, I don't know." Sate stood up and brushed pieces of bark from his hands. "Go back to your people, I guess. Winter is over. There'll be food in your camp now that spring is here." He sat down and pulled out his pipe. "I'll leave you some grub and money."

"And whiskey, too?" Doxy sat forward in the rocker.

Sate nodded impatiently. "A jug of whiskey, too."

The next morning Doxy leaned against the doorway and watched Sate ride away, the stallion eager to run, the little pack horse that followed not as anxious. He was heavily burdened with hides and camp gear. Hawser ran ahead, sniffing the ground, trying to make up his mind which scent to follow.

"Not even a look or a word of good-bye," the young squaw muttered. There gathered a malicious determination in her black eyes. Someday, somehow, she would bring the trapper and his proud lady to their knees.

In the meantime, she consoled herself, the promised money and jug of whiskey lay on the table, and in the dried gourds lined against the wall were plenty of supplies. She had fared far worse when parting with some white men, she recalled. Some had sneaked away in the night, leaving her nothing, while others had simply never returned to their cabins.

Doxy turned back inside, moving to the table. She uncorked

the jug. I'll stay here a few days, then find my tribe. She tilted the whiskey to her lips and let its rawness burn down her throat.

It was late afternoon, three days later, when Sate entered the business district of Trenton. He stopped the first man he met and inquired where he could buy a bath and shave. He was directed to a Chinaman's bathhouse at the end of the same street. Half an hour later when he left the place all trace of his days on the trail had been cleansed and shaven away. He mounted the stallion and called to his dog. Lifting the reins, he headed for the lower part of town, prepared to do business with the tight-fisted Scotchman he had dealt with before.

It was getting close to sunset when Sate walked out of the trading post. He had dickered for over an hour with the fur trader, but a satisfied smile rode his lips as he climbed back into the saddle. This time he had remained firm on the worth of his furs. They were all prime pelts and for the first time in his life money was important to him. He was about to acquire a wife, one who should have more than a one-room cabin and a few sticks of furniture.

He patted the roll of bills in his pocket, thinking of the two rooms he would add to his log cabin, the window with real glass each addition would have, the oven he would build next to the fireplace. Visions of other things that he would do for Juliana's comfort filled his head as he set out in search of her.

Sate found the street he sought in a residential section at the edge of town. He turned Jake onto its narrow way, feeling that the red brick houses lining it on either side were moving in on him. He shook his head. How could people live, breathe, so closely packed together?

He spotted the house number midway in the string of buildings. Picketing the stallion to a sturdy hitching post at the edge of the cobblestone pavement, he smoothed his buckskins and moved up the brick wall leading to the large front door. His hand shook a little as he lifted the knocker and let it fall. Soon now he would see her. He heard the loud clap resounding inside, then caught the sound of quick footsteps. His heart raced. Were they Juliana's?

The door swung open and a tall, thin woman stared at him coldly. He snatched the fur cap off his head and said hurriedly, "Good afternoon, ma'am."

Pale brown eyes ran disdainfully over his buckskin garb, then shifted back to his face.

"Yes? What do you want?" thin lips snapped ungraciously.

Sate shifted his feet, confused by the woman's attitude. "I'm . . . is . . . does Juliana Roessler live here?" he stammered.

He was studied more closely now, and he wondered if he was mistaken in thinking that a sly look flickered across the sharp-angled face. That thought, along with everything else, was washed from his mind at the woman's tart response.

"Not anymore, she don't. That ungrateful witch has left my good and decent home."

A sick feeling settled in the pit of Sate's stomach, as though an ominous warning of things to come. Unconsciously flexing his fingers, he asked politely, "Do you know where she is now?"

"In hell maybe." The woman laughed shortly, contemptuously. "She left here with some fancy gentleman she'd met on the coach."

Stunned, feeling like he'd been kicked, Sate could only stand and stare at Juliana's sister-in-law. A fancy gentleman? His numb mind couldn't conceive it. Who? Surely not Madison. A nasal voice broke in on his abject wondering:

"We're glad to be rid of her, actually. She's man-crazy. She gave us no end of trouble."

Hurting to his very marrow, Sate muttered some incoherent word and turned away. If that ugly mouth uttered one more word, he might smash it with his fist.

He moved heavily down the walk, only vaguely hearing the door slam behind him. Swinging onto Jake's back he paid no attention to the urgent tapping on an upstairs window, missed seeing the anxious features of the maid, Tillie. As if in a trance, he rode down the street, his pain growing into anger. Anger directed at himself.

Fool! Fool! he raged inwardly. Thinking that a woman like Juliana Roessler could truly love a rough backwoodsman. She was only amusing herself with me until some fancy man came along.

His chin dropped to his chest. And he, poor blind idiot, had loved her with a fierceness that equaled the blizzards that tore at the hills.

The firm chin came up and the blue eyes turned glassy. But

no more, by God. The muscles along his jawline knotted. Now he hated her. Hated her with the same strength he had loved her.

In his black rage Sate had been unaware where the stallion was taking him. His mind cleared when he discovered they had traveled to the far end of town. He spotted a tavern and pulled the mount in. Whiskey was what he needed now; to pour it down his throat until he could no longer think or feel.

He pushed open the tavern door and stepped into a smoke-filled, spirit-reeking barroom. He stood a moment running his eyes over the crowd, then started pushing his way to the bar, ignoring the angry glances that followed him. Jostling two men aside, pushing between them, he called loudly for whiskey. Frowning, the bartender placed a bottle and cup before him and moved away. This big trapper was spoiling for a fight and he didn't want to be close when he started swinging.

Steadily and silently, Sate poured and drank until the bottle was half empty. His brain was nearly numb, only a small part of it still whispering that the beautiful Juliana had played him for a fool.

He shook his head fuzzily and swung around. Hooking his elbows on the bar, he stared bleary-eyed at the laughing men around him, and resentment grew in his breast. Why should they be so happy, he so miserable?

In a voice loud and belligerent, he called out, "I can whip any bastard in this room. I can whip you all at the same time."

A low murmur, thick and menacing, rose from the crowd. As he continued to bait them, allowing that they were all cowards, that they all wore yellow streaks down their backs, the murmur turned into a roar. The angry men surged to their feet, hurling insults back at him. When in one body they began to move in on him, there was a glint of savage glee in Sate's eyes when he charged to meet them.

He fought fiercely, but futilely. By sheer weight alone he was carried to the floor where hard fists pummeled his head and body. He had the sensation of flying, cold air hitting him in the face, then nothing.

Hawser's wet nose nudging him in the face brought Sate around. He lay a moment, not knowing where he was. Then the cold mud against one cheek brought the painful memories flooding back. Juliana's deception. A deliberately provoked fight.

He sat up, then reached for his aching head. When the spinning stopped, he opened his eyes. He sat in front of the tavern out of which he'd been tossed. He glanced around: the town was dead. Picking up his cap lying beside him, he clapped it on his head and, grabbing the dangling reins, pulled himself to his feet. A hundred throbbing pains moved through his body as he struggled into the saddle. He grinned crookedly. "Them bastards sure gave me a working over," he muttered as he nudged Jake in the flank and headed out of town, Hawser trotting along behind him.

Two miles out of Trenton, Sate came to a river. He reined in and swung to the ground. Kneeling on its bank he sloshed the cold water over his battered face. Then, staking Jake in a patch of new tender grass, he scrounged around, gathering twigs and wood. But later, when he sat before warm, dancing flames, a lovely face formed in the red coals and despair settled over him again, despair that was much heavier in these early hours before dawn.

He got to his feet and paced a while, then wearily rolled himself in the blanket he had spread in front of the fire. He lay in the forest stillness, struggling for the oblivion of sleep. Then the slap of an oar on water saw him flinging aside the blanket and instinctively rolling for cover beneath the ground-hugging branches of a large cedar. With infinite caution, he raised himself up and peered through the thick foliage.

Shortly, without a sound, a tall young brave came trotting from the river. In the moonlight Sate saw that the lad was darkly handsome and bore a red feather stuck in his scalplock. The Indian was bound to see his fire, Sate knew, debating what he should do. Some tribes were friendly to the whites, many of them living in proximity to and harmony with white men's settlements. But was this young man one of them?

While he waited, gripping his rifle tightly, the brave approached the fire. Squatting down, holding out his hands to its warmth, his head turned slowly to the rumpled blanket, then to the cedar. "You can come out, pale-face," he said gruffly. "I bear you no ill will."

His lips twisted in a wry grin, Sate parted the branches and stepped out. "It isn't only the red man I'm cautious of, Indian. A bunch of whites beat hell out of me tonight."

Steady black eyes took in his swollen face. "I see this." The corners of the firm lips twitched slightly.

"Not that I didn't have it comin'," Sate hastened to add. "I asked for it, and I got it."

"How so?" The brave pushed a smoldering log up against the others.

Sate shrugged. "I was crazy mad, and got all lickered up at a tavern. When I started a fight with every man there, they let me have it good."

His visitor's gleaming eyes studied his battered face once more, then he smiled. "I think you enjoy a good fight."

Sate grinned sheepishly. "I expect I do, sometimes."

"You should go to Squaw Hollow, then. There you could fight all day, and all night. It's a mean bunch living there."

Recollection sparked in Sate's eyes. Hawser's former owner had been on his way to Kentucky, all excited about the wildlife there. He hunkered down beside the Indian. "Besides the people, what kind of place is it?"

"It's a place of wild beauty," the young brave said solemnly. "Its forests run thick with animals, and its soil is so rich it will grow anything that is dropped into it."

Sate found his spirits rising as he listened to the description of the new territory. What better place than the deep wilderness to lose the thoughts and remembrances that were tearing him apart? He couldn't bear to go back to the cabin; see in his mind *her* walking about its one room, sitting in front of its fireplace, and lying in the bed. The deceiving wench had ruined his home for him, too. He looked across to the teenager. "How do I find this place, Squaw Hollow?"

"Stay on this trail for three days. Soon after you will need to start heading south. But by that time you will begin to see an occasional settler or homestead. Anyone can direct you from there." The young man rose to his feet and said gravely, "I wish you Godspeed in your journey, and His help in all your undertakings."

"My same thoughts go with you, friend," Sate answered sincerely.

After a grave nod, the brave turned, taking only three steps before a bundle of bristling hair and bared fangs charged toward him, arresting his progress.

"Down, Hawser!" Sate roared, bringing the snarling hound to a quick stop. "I'm sorry," He turned and apologized. "I forgot the dog was out there. I lost him a mile or so back, and he's just now catchin' up."

Unshaken, the Indian commented, "He's a fine-looking animal. Strong and brave. It would be wise to keep him near you as you travel. The forest is full of red brothers who are not friendly to the white man."

"I'm aware of that." Sate reached down and grabbed Hawser by the ruff. "And I'll certainly take your advice." Abruptly, then, his visitor disappeared in the direction from which he had come. A short time later there came the sound of a dipping oar and Sate wondered where the young man traveled on his lonely journey.

Dismissing the thought, he sought his blankets again. But this time Sate was more at peace with himself as he pulled the hound down beside him. He had made a decision. It was his first small triumph in the battle he knew he must fight, and win.

CHAPTER 8

~~~~

Juliana turned over on her back and watched her brother as he coaxed the fire to life under the carefully stacked pieces of wood in the fireplace. It was an event she had observed every morning for over two months.

When the fire caught and flamed up the chimney, she transferred her gaze to the small window where the rising sun reflected brightly off the glass panes.

Watching a sunrise was only one of the many changes that had taken place in her new life. Her new way of life was rough, but a kind that had quickly appealed to her. Her lips twisted wryly. How Iva would laugh if she could see her milking the cow, Molly's most prized possession. And how it would please the hateful woman to see her lugging water from the river in order to scrub the family laundry on a board, a bar of yellow soap gripped by her roughened hands.

"I spit in your eye, Iva," she muttered into the blankets, "and you must know by now what you can do with your money. Poor as it is, there is more love and contentment in this one room than there is in all your big cold rooms put together. And Molly has more compassion in her little finger than you have in your entire skinny body, she thought, watching John climb back up the ladder to Molly.

Molly, Juliana mused, her eyes softening. The laughing, carefree woman had become the sister she had always wanted. A half-smothered giggle from the loft made her smile gently. She knew the morning routine of the pair above her quite well. For twenty minutes or so they would engage in lovemaking,

John groaning his passion, Molly crying hers out. The ladder would creak a few moments later as John descended it, then there would follow the thud of falling kindling as he built up the wood in the fireplace. By the time the fire's warmth reached her bed in the corner, Molly would be up and preparing breakfast.

And there would be no embarrassment or shifting of the eyes when they met at the table now; not like that first morning after she had heard John and Molly making love.

In her discomfort, she had remained in bed until John had gone to the barn before rising and joining Molly in front of the fire. Unable to look at her directly she had watched the young woman through her lashes, trying to find a similarity between the apparently wanton woman of a short time ago and the one who now calmly and efficiently performed the mundane task of frying bacon and eggs.

Several seconds passed before she realized that Molly was returning her scrutiny, the faintest amusement in her blue eyes. Her face flamed when the pretty woman said frankly, "You might as well get used to hearing me and John. You've been married—you must know about passion and need."

Juliana remembered how she had tried to mask her reaction to the straightforward words, but the wise eyes studying her didn't miss the look of confusion that swept over her face. The slight annoyance faded from Molly's eyes as she moved swiftly to sit down beside her.

"Juliana, dear," she exclaimed softly, "you don't know the first thing about the joys of the marriage bed, do you?"

Tears of humiliation slipped down Juliana's checks and she was gathered into warm, comforting arms. By the time she had sobbed out her story, Molly was shaking her head in disbelief at Tom Roessler's miguided, or misinformed, idea of intimacy between husband and wife.

"That poor foolish young man," she said after a while, putting Juliana away and pressing a handkerchief into her hand. "His staid ideas robbed him of so much." She grinned impishly at Juliana. "Make sure your next husband knows enough to leave his gentlemanly ways outside the bedroom door."

How she had blushed then, Juliana recalled, for Molly's warning had made her think of Sate. He would be gentle, she was sure, but there would be nothing of the gentleman in his lovemaking, she knew.

Feeling her nipples tighten at her thought of Sate's lovemaking, Juliana forced him from her mind and, rolling over onto her back, made herself think of other things.

She stared up at the ceiling, absently watching the dancing shadows thrown by the leaping flames in the fireplace. A smile curved her lips. She liked to think that through an idea of hers she had been able to repay John and Molly a little for their ready willingness to share their home with her.

One morning soon after she arrived she had been making up the bed, and Molly had been rolling out dough for a dried-apple pie. "Why do you bake so many?" she'd asked. "You end up giving them to Nemus's people."

Molly shrugged. "Mainly to pass the time, I guess. Besides, Nemus has been awfully good to me and John."

Juliana nodded inattentively, a sudden thoughtful glint in her eyes as she finished the bed, then moved to straighten up the cabin. Molly looked up at her when she pulled out a chair from the table and sat down.

"Did you ever give any thought to selling your pies, Molly? They're delicious. I bet they'd sell faster than you could make them."

Molly snorted impatiently, her eyes on the circle of dough she had just laid over an apple-filled pan. "Juliana, you're not living in Philadelphia or Trenton now. Like I've told you a dozen times, no one has any money in these parts. Anyhow, the wives do their own baking."

"What about the men who have no wives?" Juliana pointed out stubbornly, watching as Molly supported the tin in one spread hand, the other wielding a knife, slicing off the excess dough. "The trappers, for instance. I'll bet they're just starving for something sweet."

Molly turned startled eyes on Juliana, the pastry suspended in midair. "You know, Juliana"—she placed the pan on the table and sat down—"I completely forgot about them. They have money, and the tavern gets most of it." Her eyes sparkled. "Why shouldn't we get our share? And my pies won't make them sick the way that poison does at the tavern."

"And?" Juliana scooted closer to the cluttered table. "What do you think?"

"Well, that Quaker woman left a barrel of dried apples up there in the loft," Molly said, thinking out loud, "enough, I think, to feed all of Squaw Hollow. I have plenty of lard, rendered from the two hogs we butchered last fall. And there's enough sugar until the sap runs in the maples this spring, so the only thing we'd need to buy is flour."

"Do you have the wherewith?" Juliana asked anxiously.

"Foolish girl, of course not," Molly answered ruefully. "But I'm pretty sure I can get credit at the Post."

"Well, then, we're in business." Juliana grabbed a flour-covered hand and squeezed it.

"Oh, Juliana, I don't know." Molly's excitement had suddenly turned to anixety. "How would we go about it? How many pies should we bake? And how are we gonna let the men know we've got them?"

"Well . . ." Juliana played with a strand of her hair, staring thoughtfully down at the table. "What if, while we're at the Post, we put up a sign advertising them?" She lifted her eyes to Molly and giggled. "I expect some of them can read."

Molly's eyes sparkled back at her. "And they can tell the ones who can't. I wish we could take some orders, though," she added on a serious note. "I'd feel like a fool if we spent the whole day baking and no one showed up."

"They'll be here," Juliana said firmly as she rose to her feet. "Now let's clear the table and get on down to the village."

Her eyes blazing with purpose, Molly jumped to her feet and reached for the heavy shawl hanging on a peg. "Never mind the table," she ordered, wrapping the warm woolen over her head and shoulders. "Get your cape and we'll go right now. I can't wait to get started, to make some money for John. He's got so many plans for this place—more stock, and a nice house built out of boards."

When the two young women stepped outside, they saw that the sun shone so brightly they decided to walk instead of saddling their mounts and riding down to the Post. Moving down the packed mud trail, Molly continued telling Juliana the history of the surrounding homesteads, as she did whenever they walked together. Juliana noted with an inward smile that there were few Molly had a good word for.

When they approached a dilapidated shack standing only feet from the narrow trail, she was told in hushed tones, "That's where the Smiths live. You know, the man who breeds his wife, *and* his sister-in-law."

As Juliana glanced curiously at the building a brood of thin, dirty children bunched in the doorway to watch them pass.

Through a dirt-streaked window the haggard face of a woman peered out at them. "Poor thing," Juliana thought out loud, "what an awful exsistence she must lead."

"Yes," Molly agreed soberly. "She and the majority of the women living in the hills. Even the squaws." She indicated with a nod of her head the man and woman coming up the trail toward them.

The man, a thin, bewhiskered hillman, led the way, a gaunt, scantily dressed squaw trudging along several feet behind him. Indignation sparked in Juliana's eyes. The woman was bent almost double from the weight of the gear and supplies strapped to her back. They were almost abreast of the pair when the man stepped off the trail, muttering some word to his companion. She looked up at him dumbly, and swearing viciously he swung an arm across her narrow chest. She staggered to one knee. While Juliana gasped in outrage, the woman frantically grabbed hold of a bush and pulled herself upright. At another low growl, she stepped aside into the deep mud so that the white women could pass.

Juliana and Molly came to an uncertain halt, their eyes showing their angry revulsion at the man's cruel action. When he doffed his cap and bowed slightly, Molly jerked up her chin disdainfully and almost snarling, said, "Come along, Juliana. Comfort yourself with the hope that she'll put a knife in his heart some night while he's asleep."

Juliana felt the man's searching gaze pass over her as she went past him, and, repressing a desire to slap his face, she contented herself with throwing him a look of loathsome contempt. His coarse features reddened and his narrow eyes dropped at her scorn.

She and Molly had gone but a few steps when an anguished cry rang out. They spun around to see the brutish man draw back his booted foot and savagely kick the squaw repeatedly on her bare legs. Tears smarted Juliana's eyes. The woman was being punished for the look *she* had given the man. How many times, she wondered, had the hapless squaw been the recipient of his anger and frustration?

"Why does she put up with it?" she cried angrily. "Why are men like that allowed to get away with such cruelty? Can't something be done for women like her?"

"Honey"—Molly glanced at her angry and confused face— "it's unlikely the squaw, and others like her, would appreciate any interference on their behalf. Unfortunately they've developed a dependency on whiskey and will accept any hardship, any indecencies, if they know that in the end they can guzzle the rot-gut that is slowly killing them."

An image of another squaw flashed before Juliana, younger and more attractive than the one who had now passed out of sight. Had Doxy been sleeping with Sate before she came along? And if she had been his squaw, had he treated her badly?

She gave her head a small shake. No. Sate was not a brutal man. She had felt a gentleness in him. He could be brusque and unfeeling with a squaw, no doubt, but he would never strike one.

"Oh, Sate." The cry was inward sigh. "Please hurry to me."

Their thoughts occupied with the unpleasant event back on the trail, Molly and Juliana trudged the rest of the way to the Post in silence.

"Well, here goes." Molly smiled nervously, her fingers crossed as they mounted the two steps of the low building and stepped onto the porch.

Molly pushed open the door and they moved inside. She closed it quietly behind them and they stood to one side, accustoming their eyes to the darkness of the room. Its only light came from the flames in a fireplace and from one good-sized window whose oil-paper panes muted the rays of the sun.

An assortment of scents assailed Juliana's senses as she stood there; the pleasant odor of spices, leather, and yard-goods, as well as the offensive stench of untanned furs and hides. As objects began to take shape around her, her eyes were drawn to the group of men crowded around the warmth of the fire. By their garb she recognized trapper, hunter, and homesteader.

One roughly dressed individual stood with his back to the fire holding the men's attention as he angrily ranted about a new excise law on liquor that had recently been passed. When there came a sudden cessation of voices, Juliana knew that the presence of the two women had been noted.

"Let's get it over with." Molly nudged her with an elbow. Juliana nodded and drew back the hood of her cape as she followed her.

Her light blond hair tumbled freely about her shoulders, and the beauty of her face was revealed as she stepped into the dim light. A sharp intake of breath came in unison from the watching men. She paid no attention to this flattering tribute to her looks. Since she was fifteen men had been staggered by her beauty. How she looked was none of her doing, and she took no pride in it.

Molly nodded to a few acquantances who politely acknowledged the silent greeting as she and Juliana made their way to the middle-aged man standing behind a wide counter. Under the curious and interested eyes of the men, Molly quietly stated her business. When she finished her earnest request, a wide smile spread over the man's broken teeth.

"That's a right smart idea, Miz Nemeth." His loud voice carried to every corner of the room. "And I'll be one of your best customers." Molly later told Juliana that the storekeeper was a squaw man, and that his Indian didn't know how to bake a pie.

The men pressed closer, their interest in the women all the more whetted. When their eyes ran over the shapely figures, Molly winked at Juliana and whispered, "They think we're selling ourselves."

Juliana went scarlet, and sighed her relief when Pete, the storekeeper, also knowing what was in the men's minds, needlessly pounded on the table to get their attention.

"Listen up, you fellers," his loud voice boomed out, "especially you men without wives. How would you like to be able to buy fresh-baked apple pie every day?"

It took a moment for the rough men's licentious disappointment to pass. But when it did, there was a burst of applause. "Well, these two young women are gonna have them," Pete continued when the noise died down. "Starting tomorrow you can pick them up at Miz Nemeth's place. If you want to put your order in now, belly up to the counter."

In the pushing, shoving melee that followed, a thin, short man reached Pete first. "Let me be the first to get my name down," he exclaimed. "I ain't had no pie since my ma used to bake them."

"Like hell you're the first," another yelled, shoving aside the smaller figure and grabbing up the stub of pencil.

Juliana and Molly were jostled about as the others crowded around to laboriously print their names on the piece of paper supplied by the storekeeper; and after a while Juliana became suspicious of the gentle pushing and nudging. She was almost sure that the seemingly innocent touching was done on purpose. When a young hunter's arm rubbed slowly against the side of her breast she shot a look at his face. The soft dreamy look in his eyes told her the awkward caress was intentional.

She decided to give the man the benefit of her slight doubt, however. She took a step backward. So did the hunter, his arm still pressing into her. When she took another step and he was still with her, she snapped sharply, "Would you mind putting your arm somewhere else?"

Her angry ejaculation brought inquiring looks to the pair. The hunter turned smiling eyes on her face and when she would have moved again, his arm dropped down to her waist. "What about if I put it here?" He grinned.

Bitter rage flashed in Juliana. Was she to be subjected to the same treatment accorded her in the Trenton tavern? Well, then, this lout would learn the same lesson those two had. Her hand flew up and the smart smack of her fingers across his smirking face sent the hunter staggering back into the crowd.

Molly stared wide-eyed, but all the men were convulsed with laughter. And then, to her surprise, the man who carried Juliana's fingerprints on his cheek was laughing as loudly as the others. When the keeper of the Post could finally speak, he gasped, "By god, you men ain't used to a female standin' up to you, huh? The womenfolk around here ought to take a lesson from this little lady."

He held out a large hand toward Juliana. "Let me shake your hand, little heller. You sure put that big bad man in his place." The name was instantly taken up.

"I'll shake your hand, too, Heller," others choroused, crowding around, making sure they touched only her hand.

The last to approach her was the one who had started it all. "I'm sorry about that, Heller," he apologized. "It's just that we ain't used to seein' a woman like you in these parts." He grinned and amended, "In any parts."

"I'm sorry I hit you so hard." Juliana smiled back. "I didn't know I had so much power." The young man grinned again, fingering the red patch on his cheek.

The single men continued to hang around, their eyes never leaving Juliana's person as Molly took care of business.

Besides the flour, pie tins were bought. They had orders for sixteen pies and there were only four pie plates in the cabin.

Finally, all was assembled on the counter, and when Molly explained that John would pick up everything later, there were loud offers to carry her purchases. When she and Juliana left the store, eight males accompanied them. The boyishly eager men plowed through mud almost to their ankles in order to walk at Juliana's side. In the pushing and shoving, one bag of flour was dropped and spilled, and three rolling pie tins had to be chased down. When finally the cabin was reached and everything placed on the table, Molly shooed her helpers off, then leaned weakly on the door.

"Did you ever see such a bunch?" she gasped.

Juliana collapsed in a chair, laughing. "No, never."

"You've got every man at the Post lusting after you, Heller," Molly teased.

"Now, Molly, don't you go calling me that, too," Juliana protested.

"I won't, but you can bet the rest of the settlement will. You might as well get used to it."

"Oh, dear, do you really think so? It sounds so . . . so wild like."

"That's what a heller is," Molly explained with a grin. "A mean, wild cat."

A troubled frown creased Juliana's forehead. "Do you think John will be angry about it?"

"No." Molly shook her head. "He'll think it's funny." She paused before adding, "John ain't what he used to pretend to be, Juliana. That awful Iva made him do and say things he didn't mean."

Juliana sighed softly. The trappers today had reminded her of Sate with their buckskins and shy manners. She jumped to her feet and started clearing the table. Keeping herself busy was the only way she could keep him out of her mind. She vaguely heard Molly mutter, "I think I'll bake a few extra, just in case."

She could never forget that first day when the men came for their pies, Juliana thought now, her lips twitching in remembrance. Or how she and Molly had worked through the morning; Molly kneading and rolling out the dough, and she preparing the sweet syrup that would be poured over the apples.

The hands on the clock showed three by the time the last pastry was baked and joined the others that were lined up neatly on the table. Molly sniffed their sweet, spicy aroma, then stood off to survey the pies critically.

"Well, Juliana, what do you think?"

"I think they look marvelous." Juliana flopped down into a chair, rubbing her aching arms. "The men will go after them like a pack of hungry wolves."

Molly sighed. "I wish I'd told John."

"He would have objected, Molly, just like you thought. I can hear him now: 'That's a crazy idea, honey—you'll only be wasting your time and apples.'"

"And maybe he'd have been right," Molly grunted, moving to the window and gazing down the trail toward the settlement. "Shouldn't they be coming by now?"

"Molly," Juliana scolded, "they'll be here. Now go put on a clean apron."

Fifteen minutes later the men began to arrive, a steady stream, pushing and shoving, tracking mud and pine needles onto Molly's clean floor. They paid their money and the two women, smiling graciously, handed them the sweets.

"Don't forget to return the tins," each man was reminded. "Without them there can be no more pies."

Most of the tins were emptied right outside the door, then handed back in. A few of the men attempted to eat theirs inside the cabin, but Juliana reminded them sternly that the cabin was their home, and not an inn.

John missed the "thundering herd," as Molly had dubbed their customers, by half an hour. He knew the pair were pleased with themselves by the smug looks on their faces. When they were ready they'd tell him what they'd been up to. Stubbornness was one thing the pair had in common.

But after supper was eaten and Molly plunked a pile of notes in front of him and quipped, "Go buy yourself some more stock, John," he couldn't have questioned them about anything. The breath had stopped in his throat.

Their words tripping over each other's, both women talking at once, John's stunned look turned to one of incredulity when at last he sorted out what they were telling him.

Before the fire was banked and the candle blown out that night, a couple of hours were spent discussing what the new source of revenue could do for the betterment of the homestead. Whether or not the mattress in the loft rustled later on, an exhausted Juliana had no idea. She was asleep almost immediately and didn't awaken until Molly shook her shoulder the next morning.

From then on she and Molly were busy from dawn until late afternoon. The days passed swiftly for Juliana, occupied as she was, but Sate slipped into her mind often. Lately he was her constant companion during her waking hours for, two weeks ago, the ice in the river had broken up, and a few days later it had started to rain. All traces of snow were washed away now, and there was a gentleness in the air. Her eyes grew soft and dreamy. Even this very minute Sate could be on his way to Trenton. Wouldn't he be surprised when Tillie sent him to Squaw Hollow?

"Juliana, are you gonna sleep all day?" Molly's teasing query made Juliana sit up in bed. "Or maybe you're daydreamin' about that last customer we had yesterday."

An unbidden warmth swept over Juliana as she remembered the man Molly referred to.

He had been the last one to step through the door. She glanced up at him, a polite, impersonal smile on her lips and was frozen by a pair of slate-gray eyes. He is the most attractive man I've ever seen, she thought, instinctively taking in his strong-featured, clean-shaven face.

Her eyes swept over the heavy growth of curly brown hair, liberally sprinkled with gray, on to a pair of wide shoulders straining at his blue woolen shirt and then down to narrow hips. His trim, lean body looks much younger than his face, she thought; around forty years old.

"I would like to buy one of your pies, please," he said in a husky, deep voice.

Juliana blushed fiercely, for she had just caught herself wondering what it would be like to be held in this man's arms and had decided that to experience his brand of lovemaking would be something out of the ordinary.

The stranger must have sensed her discomfort for he teased gently, "Since it's your last one, maybe you were savin' it for yourself."

She gazed into his smiling eyes and relaxed. "To tell you the truth"—she flashed a wide smile—"I'm sick to death of apple pie." She picked up the flaky delicacy, but suddenly paused. To Molly's surprise she asked impulsively, "Would you like to sit down and eat it here . . . maybe have a cup of coffee?"

"I'd like that fine," the answer came eagerly. "I can't remember the last time I've had the pleasure of a white lady's company."

Flushed, and strangely excited, Juliana placed a plate, knife, and fork before the handsome man, then poured three cups of coffee. Taking a seat across from him she offered, "My name is Juliana Roessler and this is . . . my sister-in-law, Molly Nemeth."

"I'm very pleased to meet you, Juliana Roessler," he replied quietly, eyes intent on her face. Molly gave a small cough and the gaze moved away. "And you, too, Miz Nemeth."

The man returned his attention to Juliana. "My name is Roth Adams. I have a place about twenty miles from here."

"Oh, so far away?" Molly questioned. "Have you come in for supplies?"

Roth Adams nodded as he sliced into the pie. "Yes, and I just about stop breathing when I think how close I came to not makin' the trip."

Her chin propped on the heel of a palm, watching his firm lips move as he talked, Juliana asked huskily, "How so, Mr. Adams?"

For several seconds his deep gray eyes held her amber-flecked ones with a look almost of regret shadowing them. Then the spell was broken when the clock began to strike and Roth pulled his lips into a teasing smile.

"If I'd stayed home, I'd have missed meeting the most beautiful woman in the world."

Over Juliana's answering soft laughter, Molly added, "And missed eatin' the best apple pie in the world."

"That, too," Roth agreed. Leaning back in his chair he remarked, "I can't remember when I had pie last."

"I take it you're not married," Molly said.

A moment of waiting silence followed the question. Then, shooting Juliana a look that seemed apologetic, Roth answered quietly, "Yes, I'm married."

Juliana asked herself why the stranger's answer should

bother her so. She was deeply in love with Sate, and would marry him soon. Still, those three words had sent a charge of feeling through her that definitely sprang from disappointment. As from a distance she heard Molly exclaim, "She don't bake you pies? That's mighty odd."

"Not really, Miz Nemeth," Roth answered quietly. "Zoe knows nothin' about bakin' pies or cakes. She's an Indian woman."

Molly mouthed a surprised "Oh," and the subsequent silence was strained.

Roth rose, breaking it. Smiling down at the pair, he said, "I'll stop by for more pie the next time I come in."

"Please do." Molly smiled at him.

"It probably won't be for a while," he added, walking toward the door. "I only come in about three times a year."

With the latch in his hand, he turned to say good-bye, and Juliana interrupted him by standing up and hurrying toward him. As though someone else put the words in her mouth, she found herself saying, "I'll walk you outside, Mr. Adams."

His startled look turned to one of pleasure, and he handed her a shawl hanging beside the door.

The sun was sliding behind the timberline when Juliana and Roth stepped outside and silently walked toward the white stallion tied to a tree. The animal whinnied at their approach and Juliana rubbed its head and its velvet nose. She wasn't surprised when large hands settled on her shoulders and turned her around. Roth gazed down at her, a yearning in his eyes. His voice was thick and shaky when he murmured, "Oh, Juliana, I wish . . . I wish . . ."

Suddenly she was swept into his arms with such a fierceness she smothered a gasp of pain. With a deep groan his warm firm lips captured hers, and against her will her softness molded itself to his hard body.

She was released as suddenly as she had been embraced. His breath ragged, Roth cried, "Oh, God, Juliana, if only I could have met you three years ago." He swung into the saddle, gazed down at her a moment, then, jabbing his mount with a heel, the animal shot away, disappearing down the trail.

Juliana stared after him, her fingers on her swollen lips. Was there something wrong with her? She questioned her conscience. Had her sister-in-law Iva been right about her all along? How could she love Sate so deeply and still be drawn to another man?

It was plain old physical need, Juliana now told herself disgustedly as she swung her feet to the floor and reached for her robe. "Hurry to me, Sate," she whispered as she felt for her slippers.

CHAPTER 9

~~~~~

The first two days on the trail Sate followed the old Philadelphia road, with recognizable landmarks to guide him. But from the very beginning of the third day when he entered land new to him, it seemed to tease and taunt with trails that crossed and recrossed.

It was wild and rugged terrain, abounding in tall hills and deep valleys. Many times he came upon stone cliffs that ran for miles and, and at some points, towered hundreds of feet in the air. High boulders, taller and wider than some town houses, were a common sight, and interwoven among them were ravines, some small, others quite wide and very deep. Twice he took a wrong trail, losing hours of daylight time retracing his steps.

Still, with all its unpredictability, Sate found himself attuned to this land. Its harshness and ruggedness appealed to him, made him feel at home. He felt that if he was to find contentment anywhere, it would be in these hills.

Just at sunset on the fourth day, Sate came to a large clearing and spotted the cabin sitting in its center. It was small, but sturdily built. And so was the barn and the three other outbuildings. Their neat, kept-up appearance showed pride. Whoever lived here meant to stay.

Sate shook his head. The damn fool. A hundred miles from nowhere and half the Indian tribes still on the warpath.

Smoke rose from the tight, compact chimney and he felt a pang of hunger. It was supper time and the owner of this place was sure to set a good table.

Riding Jake up to the log building, he swung down and looped the reins over the railing that ran around the edge of the wide porch. Then, brushing down his trail-worn buckskins, he stepped upon the broad planks and knocked on the door.

No sound came from within. Disappointment clouded his eyes. It looked like another supper of pemmican and parched corn. And worse, another night of shivering in his blankets. He didn't know how much more sleeping out in the cold, damp weather he could stand.

Reluctant to give up so easily, he bade Hawoor wait beside Jake, then followed a beaten path that led to the back of the cabin. At the corner he stopped and grinned. A young squaw, very pretty, was loading her arms with wood from a stack of logs against the cabin wall.

Her arms full, the girl straightened up, then gave a startled cry when she saw the stranger. Sate ran his eyes over her shapely figure and desire whipped through him. He had been a long time without a woman.

But something warned him to push back his need, that this was no common squaw. He swept his eyes over the clean, shiny hair hanging down the slender back, took in the clear healthy tint of her skin and the neat deerskin shift that hung just below her knees. No, this one was treated kindly by some white man.

He smiled and said quietly, "I'm sorry I frightened you. Is your man around?"

The girl's black eyes studied him for a long moment, then, as though she was satisfied with her scrutiny, she nodded and pointed. "You'll find him in the barn."

Sate answered, "Thank you, ma'am," and cut across a small, newly budding orchard to the large building.

He passed up the huge double doors that would accommodate the passage of a team and wagon. From the smooth expanse of unmarred ground, there had been no traffic there since winter set in. But a well-trodden path led to a small side door, and this one he pushed open.

Familiar sounds and odors greeted him. His lips formed a half smile. It had been a long time since he had been inside such a structure. Over the fluttering and cooing of pigeons in the loft there came the crunch of hay and corn between grinding teeth and the soft sound of milk streaming into a wooden pail.

Clearing his throat, Sate called out, "Anybody here?"

The foaming sound ceased and a gruff voice demanded, "Who are you? What do you want?"

This one doesn't greet visitors with open arms, Sate thought ruefully, and it's just as well he doesn't. I'd be careful, too, if I had a squaw like that one in my cabin.

He stood quietly, adjusting his gaze to the gloom, then moved a little farther into the barn. "My name is Sate Margruder," he called out clearly. "Your squaw said you were out here."

There was a moment of silence, then: "Zoe is not my squaw. She's my legal wife."

"I'm sorry. I meant no disrespect. She's a good-lookin' woman."

A figure nearly as tall as himself emerged from a stall and walked toward him. In the dim light from the lantern hanging on a peg, Sate couldn't make out the man's features very clearly, but from the firm grip of the hand he shook, a quiet strength pulsated.

"Glad to know you, Margruder." The words were spoken gravely. "I'm Roth Adams. If I sounded unfriendly at first it's because a man can't be too careful, livin' so far from civilization."

"I'd be the same. There's a lot of trash movin' 'round these days—red and white."

"I don't worry about the red man. Zoe's father is a Pennacook chief, and we're not bothered by them. But many a white man would do murder to get his hands on a woman like Zoe."

Sate nodded agreement, and Adams said, "Supper will be ready pretty soon. Why don't you bring in your horse and tend to him."

By the time Jake was fed and rubbed down, and Hawser had lapped up a pan of scraps, night had fallen. The two men stepped outside the barn; the lantern, swinging in Roth's hand, lit their way to the candle burning in the cabin window.

Inside, it was warm and neat as Sate had known it would be. When he shrugged out of his coat and handed it to Roth, he was surprised at the man's age. Although rugged and virile-looking in body, the leathery face and world-wise eyes marked him as around forty.

Adam caught his surprised look and grinned. "I take care of her needs quite adequately," he said quietly.

A guilty flush spread over Sate's face. He had been wondering just that. "I'm . . . I'm sure you do," he stammered.

Amusement flickered in Roth's eyes, then, turning to his wife, he laid an arm across her shoulders. "Zoe, meet Sate Margruder."

The girl unconsciously pressed against her husband, and Sate smiled inwardly. There was no doubt that Adams was handling that department quite well.

His thought was all the more confirmed when all through the meal Zoe's eyes strayed constantly to her husband, the hunger in her eyes carefully concealed. And later, as he and the big man sat smoking and talking before the fire, she came and sat at Roth's feet. Leaning her head against his knee, her slim fingers stole up his pants leg and stroked his calf. Roth smiled down on her as her father would smile at a favored child begging some favor.

That's how he thinks of her, Sate thought in surprise. He looks on her as a beautiful child who begs for the strength of his loins. He doesn't love her as a woman, only as a toy who drains and relaxes him every night.

When the clock on the mantel struck ten, Roth, directing a sly grin at Zoe, remarked, "I think it's time I take this one to bed." Sate was envious of the older man. His red-skinned wife would love him all through the night.

A short time later, rolled up in his blankets before the fire, Sate listened to the rustling noises and was reminded of Juliana. She had responded to him just as Zoe was reacting to Roth. He sighed raggedly and turned his back to the fire and, to the accompaniment of squeaking bed slats, fell asleep.

The next morning after breakfast Sate went along with Roth to the barn. Climbing to the loft, Roth pitched down piles of hay to the animals below. Between swings of the long-tined fork, he remarked in feigned innocence, "I hope me and Zoe didn't keep you awake last night."

The look Sate shot up at Roth was just as artless. "Now why should all that gruntin' and whackin' keep me awake?" he growled. "After all, I'm only a poor human."

Roth chuckled. "I just thought I'd ask. Zoe gets carried away sometimes. Makes an uncommon amount of noise."

Sate didn't respond to the bantering right away. He waited until the big man lifted the fork with another load of hay before responding out loud, "Zoe doesn't always make noise, I noticed. Like this mornin'. She was awfully quiet just before you two got up. I couldn't hear anything but pantin' and snortin'. I thought for a minute a bear had crawled in bed with you."

Roth's loud, ringing guffaws startled the roosting pigeons and sent a tomcat scooting for cover. "By God!" he gasped, "you don't miss much. The truth is, I'm too lazy in the mornin's to work for my pleasure."

"How long you been married, Roth? Zoe looks kinda young."

Roth climbed back down the ladder. "She's older than she looks. She was sixteen when I bought her from the chief, and we've been married a little over three years."

"Three years! You mean to tell me that you've been carrying on like last night for three years and you're not down in your back yet?"

Roth responded to the teasing with a wicked smile. "You damn well know it. I come from a long line of lusty men. I always outlast Zoe."

"Then why in the hell don't you have a passel of younguns?"

Roth's smile faded. "Zoe can't have babies, Sate. Some kind of accident when she was young crippled her insides. That's why her father was willin' for me to marry her."

"I'm sorry to hear that, Roth."

Roth leaned on the fork handle, a yearning in his eyes. "Sometimes it bothers me. Every man would like to have a son, I guess. You know, his own flesh and blood, someone to carry on after he's gone." He straightened up and added, "I never mention it to Zoe, though. She feels ashamed that she can't give me children."

Because he didn't know what to say to Roth, Sate changed the subject. "What can you tell me about this Kentucky territory? Have you ever been in them parts? Have you ever heard of a place called Squaw Hollow?"

Startled surprise jumped into his companion's eyes. "Strange you should ask me that," Roth said. "I just came from Squaw Hollow three days ago."

"The hell you say. What can you tell me about it? I've heard some tall tales about the place, and I'd like to get the straight of it."

"Well, the first thing I can tell you for a fact," Roth said with a grin, "I had me the best apple pie there, and saw me the most beautiful woman in the world. They call her Heller. If I didn't already have Zoe I'd sure try for that one. She had me droolin' at the mouth, and—"

"I'm not interested in beautiful women," Sate interrupted shortly. "What about the settlement? Is it large? What kind of people live there?"

"Probably everything you've heard about the Hollow is true," Roth said, leaning back against a stall. "There's a mixture of people livin'there. Some good, but mostly bad. They steal, kill, raise hell in general.

"There's a lot of hunters and trappers; a lot of game around there. There are Indians, of course, some decent and some nothin' more than vermin lookin' for a swig of whiskey. Then naturally, like anywhere else, you've got your whores. Most of them look like they'd cut your throat for a copper piece."

Sate gave a short, humorless laugh. "You don't paint a very pretty picture, friend. Sounds like a man takes his life in his hands when he ventures in there."

"I'll tell you one thing: no faint heart had better wander in there. He sure as hell won't last long."

"Well, I've got a pretty strong heart so I think I'll just go and look the place over," Sate remarked and began to saddle the stallion.

"I thought you would." Roth laughed dryly. "And I know there's no use tellin' you to be careful." He stuck out his hand. "So I'll just say that I've enjoyed your company and that the next time I'm in Squaw Hollow I'll look you up, see how you're farin'."

"You do that, Roth." Sate inserted a moccasined foot in a stirrup. "I'll be glad of the chance to repay your hospitality."

Roth Adams stood a moment, watching the trio until they moved out of sight. "A strange cuss," he muttered, "and won't have any problem holding his own in the Hollow."

It was late in the day, almost dusk, when through the leafless trees Sate spotted a party of six braves. Their faces were painted with vermilion, visages that made him shiver. "A war party," he grunted to himself. "I wonder where they've been and where they're goin' now."

He reined Jake behind a wide spreading cedar and signaled Hawser to lay down, and not to bark. Are they renegades? he mused, watching the small party ride past his hiding place, their guttural voices raised in jubilant tones. Many young, angry braves had broken away from their tribes and come together since the war: attacking isolated homesteads, lone travelers, keeping alive an unease between the red man and the white.

When Sate could no longer hear the Indians, he nudged Jake lightly with his heels and moved back on the trail. As he rode along he kept his eyes open for a cave. He hated to think of sleeping under a tree tonight.

He had only traveled another hundred yards when he came upon the wagon. Its tongue was broken and the canvas top ripped across. Provisions were scattered about, mingled with articles of clothing. There was no sign of a team, but crumpled near a still warm campfire were the forms of a man and woman.

"Dead." He shook his head and whistled Hawser away from the pair. He lifted the reins and rode on, regretting that he couldn't bury the two corpses, but aware that to save his own hide he'd better get out of the area in a hurry.

No cave had come in view, and darkness found Sate cold and weary, hunched in his blanket under a pine tree. He longed for the warmth of a fire but didn't dare light one. The enemy could be camped anywhere.

The next morning Sate and the dog shared a quick breakfast of cold beef and corn bread that Roth had put in his saddle bag. He gave the stallion a couple of handfuls of oats, then climbed stiffly into the saddle.

It was around noon when he spotted a rider approaching from the woods on his left. His eyes narrowed in thoughtful scrutiny. When a man shunned a well-defined trail it was good to be suspicious.

Although the man kept his face averted as he drew opposite Sate, a sudden recollection of the tall, slim figure came to him. "Chad Madison." The name was a disgusted sound. "The bastard is probably runnin' from some irate husband."

He reined Jake in, debating whether or not to ride after Madison. He had promised himself to give the man a thorough thrashing if he ever saw him again. It was a shameful thing he had done to Doxy even though she had opened herself to its possibility.

As he seesawed back and forth, trying to make up his mind, Madison disappeared behind a jumble of boulders. Sate sat a moment longer, then lifted the reins, telling himself that sooner or later that abuser of women would get his. A man like that couldn't go on forever.

The homesteads were beginning to appear more frequently, and Sate was sure he was coming to the end of his journey. Often he heard the measured whack of an axe against a tree. A little farther along he saw whole families busily collecting sap from young maples, and in the yards of the cabins he passed huge iron kettles straddled hungry licking flames. He knew they were filled to the brim with the maple's sweet juices. All day it would bubble gently, boiling down into a thin syrup.

Around sunset, in a drizzling rain that had started an hour earlier, Sate rode into Squaw Hollow. Tired, hungry, and miserably uncomfortable, his face was a mask of short-tempered impatience. Men and women, slushing through the rain and puddles, glanced up at him, and then away. "There's a mean one," one man muttered to another as they hurried on.

A sudden raucous noise emanating from a long, low building relaxed Sate's grim features. A tavern; a fire to warm his cold flesh and drink to heat his blood.

He guided Jake to the rear of the building where he found a wide, slanting overhang. He tied the horse next to another one, but beyond the reach of his stallion's sharp teeth and strong legs. Hawser was thankful to burrow down in a pile of hay, and wagged his tail as his master left him with a pat to his head.

Sate stepped up on the narrow porch. As he was about to push the door open, it suddenly flew wide and he was solidly struck in the shoulder by two straining, fighting bodies. He peered through the doorway, then grinned crookedly. Inside, there were at least a half dozen other embroiled in a smashing, swinging free-for-all. Stools and bottles flew through the air, and over the sweating, swearing din came the frightened cries of the tavern women.

A savage light of battle in his blue eyes, Sate sprang through the door right into the middle of it. As his hard fists smashed against flesh and teeth, he let loose a loud yell. He was in his element now, and the blood sang through his veins. He had tried to be what the fair Juliana had wanted, and got kicked in the teeth for his effort.

The roaring boom of a musket brought the brawlers to a faltering halt. The only sound now was the shuffling of staggering feet as swaying men caught at each other for support. Through eyes that were slowly swelling, Sate blinked in the direction in which the others were gaping drunkenly.

A heavily built man leaned calmly behind the bar, a smoking firearm cradled in his arms. When the scraping of feet died down and a medium of calm reigned once more his deep voice rang out:

"The first man who lifts his hand in anger again gets the next in the gut." He paused to let his threat sink in, then continued. "Now, one of the women is gonna pass among you with a hat. Every man who fought had better contribute freely. There's been a lot of damage done to my place and I want restitution. To save further argument I want you all to know that I have the name of every man involved."

The gun was placed on the bar and a gaunt-faced woman began to move around the room. Sate noted that those who had engaged in the ruckus good-naturedly tossed in their money. As he placed his own share in with the others he got the feeling that passing the hat was a common occurrence in the tavern, that in all probability there was an unspoken agreement between the taverner and his patrons. An understanding that said, "Look, we got to blow off steam in this manner in order to bear the monotony of idle days. When winter comes again and we can hunt and trap, we'll calm down."

Those stools and chairs which remained whole were righted by the men who had tossed them about, and an order of sorts prevailed again. Three bondswomen moved between the tables, setting drinks before the customers. The tavern whores who had huddled together before now moved swiftly to sit on a lap or sidle up to a patron at the bar.

Two of them had their eyes on Sate. When he had bought a glass of ale and was on his way to a table, the pair rushed at him simultaneously. Colliding at his back one jostled his arm and spilled his drink. Annoyed more than angry, he swung around and the women drew back fearfully at the cold contempt in his eyes. As his gaze traveled over their thin, worn bodies a small, delicate face with wide amber eyes swam before him and the hollow knot that formed in his stomach sent a flickering pain across his face.

Angry at himself for still caring, unaware that his large hands clenched and unclenched, he reached out and pulled the two slatterns toward him.

"No need to fight over me, girls. I can take care of you both." The pair tittered and ambled up to the bar, gazing eagerly at the bottle of rum in the bartendor's hand.

The creaking wheels of a wagon awakened Sate. He lay sprawled on his back, a sour taste in his mouth. He raised his head then let it drop back to a moldly-smelling pillow. "God, how much did I drink last night?" he groaned, "and where in the hell am I?" He turned his head slowly and swore under his breath.

Sleeping beside him on the rumpled bed was one of the women he remembered buying drinks for. Her thin body, in its stained nightshift, lay curled in a ball, as though seeking the warmth from inside her. His eyes swept down the length of his body and he breathed a sigh of relief. He still wore his buckskins and their front was laced tight. At least he hadn't exposed himself to disease in his drunken state.

He flipped a ragged blanket over the offending sight of the woman who made a grunting sound while, still asleep, she pulled it closely around her. He sat up slowly, and gently eased his feet to the dirt floor. While he sat quietly, waiting for the spinning in his head to cease, he searched his pockets. A breath of relief again whistled through his teeth. His money was intact.

He glanced at the supine figure and muttered, "Whore, I don't know if you're honest, of if you were too drunk to rifle my pockets." He pulled a bill from its mates and laid it on the bed, then stood up and made a careful way outside.

Sate picked his way around small and large tree stumps, noting as he went that most places of business were still closed. He prayed silently that the tavern was open, for never in his life had he needed a drink so badly. The long building came in sight and thankfulness swept through him. It was open. He'd get that drink, then tend to his animals.

He stood in the open doorway and watched for a moment the activity going on inside. The bondswomen, their sleeves rolled up and cloths tied around their heads, busily swept at the accumulation of mud, splintered wood, and broken glass. The tavern owner was hard at work, scrubbing down the rough plank bar. He looked up, called a greeting to Sate, and waved him inside.

"I see you're still with us, trapper. You're up early, considerin' the rum you put away last night."

"Yeah. Well, I need a slug of it now."

The jovial man placed a bottle and a glass before him. "Help yourself. It's on me."

"Thanks, but I only need one shot to put me in shape."

With shaking fingers Sate lifted the bottle and filled the glass with the dark liquid. Downing it in one swallow, he squinted his eyes and shook his head vigorously as it hit his empty stomach. Then he turned to leave, muttering, "I've gotta go see to my animals."

The bartender picked up the bottle and said as he replaced it on the shelf, "I've had your stallion and hound taken to my own stables. They've been taken care of."

"Say, that's right friendly of you," Sate said, surprised. "I appreciate it."

The big man waved a large hand. "Forget it. They're prime pieces, both of them. Too much of a temptation to the parasites that hang around the Hollow."

"I'll have to remember that." Sate smiled and reached a hand across the bar. "The name is Margruder. Sate Margruder."

"Glad to know you, Margruder." The two hands met. "People 'round here call me Battle."

Sate grinned as he asked, "You got anything to eat around here, Battle? I forgot to eat last night and my stomach feels like it's stickin' to my spine."

"What about some eggs, sausage, and potatoes?"

"Sounds fine. I haven't had any eggs all winter."

While one of the women prepared his breakfast, Sate moved to the fireplace. As he warmed himself front and back, a youngish man, somewhere in his thirties, Sate thought, walked into the tavern. As he talked quietly to Battle, Sate kept glancing at him. The man looked familiar, but he couldn't place him.

The early-morning visitor left just as Bessy, a young bondswoman, brought Sate his breakfast. Battle dropped into a chair across from him, telling Bessy to bring him a cup of coffee. He jerked his head toward the door. "That was John Nemeth just left here. His wife and sister bake apple pies and sells them. John comes down for my order every morning. Some of the men ain't allowed up to his place. Seems they sometimes get feisty with his sister, so I keep some on hand for the rowdy bunch."

"I think maybe I heard something about apple pies and a beautiful woman," Sate said, his tone not betraying his interest.

"Ah yes, Heller." Battle sighed. "She's a beauty all right. I'd give everything I own just to sleep with her for one night."

"Heller? That's a hard handle to hang on a woman."

"Not in this case it ain't." Battle laughed. "In most ways Heller is a perfect lady. But when a man steps out of line, she turns into a hellcat." When Sate pushed his empty plate aside, Battle said, "Why don't you go up there and sample a pie, look her over? Ain't nobody made any time with her yet. Maybe you can."

Sate reached for his tin mug of coffee. "I'm not interested in meetin' any beautiful women."

"Suit yourself"—the big man shrugged—"but you're missin' an eyeful."

"If it's all the same to you, I'll just keep on missin' it. I'll content myself with squaws and whores. The only thing they'll steal from you is your money."

Battle looked thoughtfully at the man across from him, but before he could speak, Bessy placed a steaming cup of coffee before him. She leaned heavily against his shoulder and murmured suggestively, "Will there be anything else?"

A knowing awareness glimmered in Sate's eyes as he watched the familiar way the young woman spoke to her boss. He wasn't surprised when Battle slipped a hand over a round breast and left it there while he grinned and said, "Yeah, there is. In about fifteen minutes . . . in the back room."

Bessy giggled and flounced away, and Battle sighed happily. "I tell you, friend"—he smiled broadly—"I'm one contented man. No whores or squaws for me; chancin' catchin' a disease. I've got three healthy females tendin' to my needs."

Sate's eyes searched the pleased face and he made a slight frown. "Aren't they bondswomen?"

Battle nodded ruefully. "They are, and before you say it, I know it's against the law to use them in bed. But"—his eyes flashed wickedly—"if they're willin', it's a different story. And let me tell you, them gals are willin'. There ain't no way they'll ever turn me in."

Sate mentally compared the burned-out whore he'd found himself in bed with to the plump, rosy-cheeked women at Battle's disposal. He was envious, and it showed in his eyes.

"What are you thinkin', friend?" The lucky man cocked a sly, teasing look at Sate.

"I'm thinkin', damn you," he replied pleasantly, "that you're a hoggish fellow. There ain't no way you can completely satisfy three women no matter what you claim."

He leaned forward, a rugged, impressive figure. "Why don't you hire one out to me?"

The taverner stirred sugar into his coffee in a slow, thoughtful way. "You're right, of course," he said finally. "It's gettin' harder and harder to keep up with the three of them. It's Bessy in the daytime and the two older ones at night. And though they have slowed down considerably, they each want their pleasurin' at least once." He shook his head. "I'll tell you the truth, I do worry about a time when I can't produce."

Motioning Sate closer, he said in a low voice, "If you was to have a place of your own, I could sell you the papers to one of them. That way it would be legal and all. People might suspect that you was sleepin' with her, but they couldn't prove it. You'd just have to be careful that she didn't come up big-bellied."

Caught off guard by Battle's unexpected offer, it took Sate a while to marshal his thoughts and come to a decision. Did he want the responsibility of owning a bondswoman? Could a man treat her in the same casual, offhand manner as he did a whore or a squaw?

But why not, he argued with himself. Actually, in a sense, these three women here were not much better than whores. They drained old Battle night and day of their own free will. The only difference was that he was the only man they slept with. Of course you couldn't strike one, but he'd never gone in for hitting a woman anyhow. And though he hadn't admitted it to the man who sat waiting for his answer, he was sick to death of whores and squaws.

Sate rocked his chair back on two legs and, hooking his thumbs in his waistband, looked at Battle and said, "Two questions, friend. One, do you know of a place I could get, and two, which of the women will you let go?"

Battle hitched himself closer to the table and, staring down at his clasped hands, said slowly, "To answer your first question, there's an empty homestead about a mile down the main trail. The old man died and the widow went to live with her son. She asked me to sell it for her."

The big man leaned back and scratched his head, debating which woman to get rid of to his advantage. Bessy was the best worker, being the youngest, but because of her youth she was the biggest drain of his energy. With her gone, not always pestering him to go into the back room, he could easily take care of the other two.

He looked up at the man who waited stoically and said decisively, "I will sell you the papers to Bessy. She just about wears me out."

Sate let the chair come down slowly. Was the easygoing bartender lying to him? he wondered. Would she prove worth the expense?

He dropped his eyes to hide the guile that glimmered in them. "What if I take your place in the back room? Try her out, see if you've trained her properly."

Battle looked insulted. "Don't worry on that score," he said shortly. "She's been trained properly. What I want to know is if you're serious about buyin' her, or are you just lookin' for a free fast tumble?"

"Hell, I'm serious enough, but I'll tell you straight out, I can't abide a woman who lays like a log while I do all the work."

Battle broke into a low laugh. "Fair enough. Go on back there, and if she'll let you, have at her." He put a restraining hand on Sate's arm as he stood up. "For God's sake, Margruder, don't go forcin' her. We'd both be in trouble."

Sate pushed open the door to the back room and smiled sardonically at the disappointment that flashed in Bessy's eyes as she lay waiting on the bed. She hurriedly pushed down the skirt that had been hauled up around her waist, and fumbled at her open bodice.

When he smiled at her, she said stiffly, "I thought you was Battle."

"Battle's tired."

Her eyes narrowed angrily. "It's those other two," she sniffed. "They get to sleep with him, and after layin' with them all night, he's got nothin' left for me."

"Three women are a big drain on a man."

"I guess so. When I first came here, this cot got a workout three and four times a day. Now . . ."

"Battle suggested that I take his place. Are you agreeable?"

Bessy dropped her eyes to the buckskin lacings, taking in the long length of manhood clearly outlined there. She scooted to the far side of the narrow bed and giggled. "Why don't you lay down and make yourself comfortable?"

An hour later, after Sate had experienced the bondswoman in every way he could think of, he said, as he stood up and slipped on his buckskins, "Do you think you'd like to come and work for me, Bessy?"

The buxom girl didn't take long making up her mind. This one had ten times the stamina Battle possessed. But she wouldn't tell him that, she decided. Instead she said, "I do get tired of those other two always bossin' me around."

"Maybe I'll buy your papers, then . . . if you're good, that is."

Bessy slid him a glance from the corner of her eyes and said coyly, "I don't suppose you're talkin' about cookin' and scrubbin'?"

"That's exactly what I'm talkin' about," Sate answered shortly, striding toward the door. "I'll expect a clean cabin, clean clothes, and good solid food."

He closed the door on her wide-eyed stare and confronted the foxlike grin on Battle's face.

"Well, from the look on your mug, friend, I'd say you found Bessy to your likin'."

Sate leaned an elbow on the bar. "I guess she'll do. I've had better, though."

"You have?" Battle looked doubtful.

"There was one," Sate answered bitterly.

Battle made no response, only gazed at the harsh features

and wondered what kind of woman had put that stony look in his eyes. He felt relieved a short time later when Margruder left, calling over his shoulder, "I'm gonna go look at that homestead now. I'll see you back here later."

CHAPTER 10

~~~~~~

Spring had definitely arrived in Squaw Hollow. Three weeks ago, in fact. There was a green splendor everywhere one looked; cabin doors were left open and flies buzzed in and out.

Juliana had grown nervous and irritable as time passed with still no sign of Sate. He should have been here weeks ago, she told herself for the hundredth time as she spread a thin circle of dough over a tin of apples.

For the past month she had made countless trips to the door, staring hopefully down the trail to the settlement. And every afternoon when the men made their way to the cabin she eagerly scanned the group, hoping to see the face she longed for.

Last week she had told herself to forget Sate Margruder, that he wasn't coming. If he had truly been interested in her he'd have been here already. Still, she kept hoping.

Juliana gave a start when Molly spoke at her elbow. "You haven't been looking well lately, Juliana. Even John remarked that you're lookin' kinda peaked. I hope I haven't been workin' you too hard."

Juliana rested the rolling pin on the table and smiled at Molly's concerned face. "No, Molly, not at all. I haven't been sleeping well the past week or so, and I seem to have indigestion practically all the time." She sighed. "It gets so tiresome."

"Maybe you've been thinkin' about your husband." Molly watched Juliana's face closely. "How long has he been gone, now?"

"Close to four months, I guess." Juliana sighed. "I'm ashamed to admit it, but I haven't given Tom a thought since I left Philadelphia."

Molly nodded, not really surprised at her remark. Juliana had already admitted that besides being weak in character, Tom was not the kind of man who could spark passion in a woman like Juliana. She hesitated to ask her next question. It was very personal and she wouldn't blame Juliana if the girl snapped her head off for asking it.

Keeping her eyes on the piece of dough with which she pretended to be busy, she said quietly, "It's none of my business, Juliana, but I was wonderin' if maybe you was in love with another man back there in Philadelphia."

For several seconds Juliana stared blankly at Molly. Then, amused at the frank question, she answered it in the same serious way she knew it had been asked. "It's true that I didn't love Tom, Molly, didn't even respect him, and had he lived I doubt that out marriage would have lasted. But I never once cheated on him." She raised a teasing brow. "What ever made you think that I might have?"

Molly gave a small embarrassed laugh. "I just wondered. You bein' so pretty and all, and not havin' any fun . . ."

"Having fun in bed is important to you, huh, Molly?" Juliana gave a yellow curl a playful pull.

"Yes, it is," Molly answered firmly. "As *you* know, it's very important in a marriage." After a pause, she added, "Of course, it's important to have a dependable mate, too. A man who you know will always be behind you, watching over you, protectin' you." She gave Juliana a close look. "Roth Adams is a man a woman could depend on."

Unlike Sate Margruder, Juliana thought sadly, then became aware that Molly expected a response to her statement. "He struck me that way," she said brightly. "I wonder if that Indian wife of his knows how lucky she is."

Molly gave an indelicate laugh. "I'm sure she found that out on their wedding night. You can bet that one knows how to make a woman's body sing."

Strangely Juliana didn't want to hear or think about Roth Adams making love to his Indian wife. When Molly opened the oven door to shove in another pie the escaping aroma of cinnamon and apples brought a queasiness to her stomach. Yanking off her apron, she said hurriedly, "If you don't mind,

Molly, I'm going to take a ride. Blow the cobwebs out of my brain. Maybe I don't get enough fresh air."

"That's a splendid idea," Molly agreed at once. "And take your time. I can finish up these pies in short order." She followed Juliana outside and stood on the porch until the little roan pony flashed by, its rider's long pale hair streaming back like a silver banner.

"Don't ride all the way to the Post," she called out. "There's too many scallywags around these days. They wouldn't hesitate to pull you right off that pony."

"I won't," Juliana called back lightly. "I'm only going a short piece."

Shaking her head, Molly walked back into the cabin, worrying out loud: "I pray my suspicions are wrong."

Midway to the settlement Juliana come upon a wagon road that ran alongside the trail for a short distance before turning off and disappearing into the forest. She had wondered many times where it led, and she reined the mount in, a debating gleam in her eyes. The deeply rutted way looked mysterious and inviting, and impulsively she turned the pony to walk between the ruts. Patches of wildflowers and violets grew along the trail's edge, and it seemed that under every tree mayapples lifted their umbrellalike leaves to catch the dappled sunlight.

As her gaze roved over the beauty of the woodland her eyes caught a movement several yards ahead. She peered intently to catch it again, but nothing moved save leaves in the gentle breeze.

"A deer, I expect," she said to herself, and rode on.

Going at his own pace, occasionally snatching a mouthful of tender growth from low-growing bushes, the little roan brought his rider to a narrow clearing in the forest. Juliana smiled. It would feel good to ride in the sunshine for a while.

The sun was soothing on her back and, lulled by its warmth and the singing of birds in the trees, Juliana was startled when the pony snorted and reared up, his forelegs pawing the air. Clutching the hackamore, fighting the animal down, she stared wide-eyed at the Indian standing in her path. He was short, squat, and nearly naked. His face looked fierce with red and white paint streaked down his cheeks and across his broad forehead.

She gasped, "What do you want?" and the animal, sensing

her terror, jerked his head and reared again. By the time she brought the pony under control, the brave had disappeared.

Every limb shaking, Juliana could only sit and stare at the spot where the Indian had stood so threateningly. She inhaled deeply, resisting a lightheadedness, commanding herself not to faint. Slowly the thudding of her heart resumed a more normal rate. Just as she was about to turn her pony's head and return home, a rolling nausea gripped her. She sat quietly, frowning impatiently, waiting for the weakening spasm to recede.

This time, however, nausea engulfed her entirely. Gulping rapidly, she barely had time to swing to the ground before she was overcome and dropped to her knees. When the retching was finally over, she weakly fumbled in a pocket and brought out a handkerchief, shakily wiping the clammy sweat from her forehead. This is the worse bout yet, she thought, leaning against a tree for support. Had the scare the Indian gave her brought it on? But that wouldn't explain all the other times the same queasiness had come over her in the past days.

Juliana pushed away from the tree, an uneasy thought pricking her mind. Had she contracted some sickness from eating tainted meat? She shook her head after another moment. John and Molly had consumed the same food that she had, and they were perfectly healthy.

"Let's go home, fellow," she decided finally, scrambling onto the sturdy back she rode Indian style. "I won't find an answer here."

She had just settled herself on the folded blanket when, as though someone had whispered it in her ear, she gasped hoarsely, "My God, I'm with child."

Numb, staring blindly, she tried to recall her last monthly. She couldn't believe that in almost four months she would miss the absence of something so important. But she could only recall having one the week following Tom's death, starting the day of his funeral.

Dazed at her discovery, Juliana dashed a hand across her face, telling herself that it hadn't been a true monthly, only spotting brought on by the shock of Tom's death and the loss of her home. She had heard of other women so afflicted.

Her head bent, she lifted the reins and urged the pony on. She couldn't return home yet. There was too much to think about, and foremost was the question of what Sate would think if he did come to find her. Would he still want her? Would he be willing to raise another man's child?

A well-defined path led up to the log cabin sitting on the hilltop. New grass covered the slopes around it, and the maple and mighty oaks bore young leaves. As the stallion lunged upward Sate noted the scattering of blossoming dogwood and their whiteness reminded him of the snow that must have lain here just a month ago.

He reached the level ground on which the cabin stood and turned in the saddle to look down over the valley and the settlement below. A woman's figure stepped out of the tavern and peered up toward the hill. His lips curled contemptuously. Bessy couldn't wait to get up here.

He wondered if he would make a mistake, buying up her papers, saddling himself with the responsibility of the woman. Two years could be a hellish long time, for he didn't try to fool himself that he liked the bondswoman. In truth, he *disliked* her. And that dislike had been the prime reason he had come to the decision he had. Never again would he let a woman get close to him. Tender feelings weakened a man, kept him from reaching out and taking what he wanted.

Nope—he nudged the stallion on—Bessy was in for a few surprises. She'd be treated well enough: he'd feed her, provide wood for her fire, and keep her warm at night. They'd both get out of it whatever they put in.

Sate drew rein in front of a narrow porch running the length of the cabin. He dismounted and, tying Jake to a supporting post, decided that the place looked sturdy enough. But before putting hard cash on the small farm, he intended looking it over thoroughly.

He walked slowly around the building, inspecting the windows and the caulking between the logs. The two windows were tight, and the glass in them was intact. There were spots of caulking missing but they could soon take care of that. A slow, careful scrutiny of the roof showed it weather-tight, and not too old. Nodding his satisfaction, he stepped up on the porch and lifted the latch to the heavy door.

It was dark inside, and Sate stumbled over a chair as he made his way to a window and fastened back the shutters. Once they were flung back, the large room lightened considerably.

His first act was to squat before the well-built fireplace and build a fire. If the chimney didn't pull well, a man could shiver all winter trying to keep warm. If that was the case in this building, there was no use in looking at it further.

Sate stood up and brushed off his knees when the fire crackled to life and flames licked hungrily up the chimney. Now he would look the rest of the place over.

The floor was solid, of wide oak boards fitted tightly together. There would be no drafts from below to chill feet and legs. He found the room furnished as most cabins were, except these pieces weren't crudely handmade. They were smoothly constructed and highly polished. He noted that the rocking chairs bore bright cushions on both seats and backs.

The old couple liked their comfort, he decided. He grinned, opening a door and stepping into a small bedroom just big enough to hold a large bed, a table beside it, a wardrobe, and a good-sized mirror hanging just inside the door. Barely concealed by the bright quilt spread over the feather mattress was a trundle bed. Bending over, he pulled it out, muttering dryly, "And a bed for Bessy."

Sate walked back into the main room and a sharp pain of regret stabbed him. It was just the kind of place he had planned for Juliana. Then, angry at himself for letting her slip into his mind, he kicked out at a chair, muttering savagely, "Damn her to hell."

Suddenly he could stand the room no longer. It seemed to laugh and jeer, "Crazy fool! Crazy fool!" He jerked open the door, then stopped in his tracks.

On the top step sat an old Indian, his bony shoulders draped with a bright red blanket. As Sate stared the man turned around and he looked into a proud, wrinkled, leathery face. The old man is from no scrub race, he thought. The blood of chiefs runs through his thin veins.

How should he handle this visitor, he wondered, becoming uneasy beneath the intent scrutiny. Finally, the voice of his mother whispered in his mind and made him speak first in deference to old age.

"Are you lookin' for anyone in particular, old brave?" he asked quietly.

His carriage straight and stiff, the Indian's thin lips moved after a moment's silence. "I am Nemus, and I look for no one. I sit here often, admire nature's handiwork."

Sate walked out onto the porch and sat down a few feet from the far-gazing figure. Motioning a hand toward the valley, he said, "I'm thinkin' of buyin' this place because of the view."

Nemus's expression barely changed, and neither did the wooden tone of his voice when he remarked, "We will be neighbors, then."

Masking his surprise, Sate's glance quickly scanned the surrounding area. He was suddenly all too aware that the old brave might be a bait to draw him outside while others waited in the fringe of the forest to wing an arrow into his heart.

His scalp crawled as in his mind's eye he saw his rifle lying on the table inside. Forcing himself to speak in a normal tone, he said, "I wasn't aware that there was an Indian camp in these parts."

Nemus answered in words that Sate thought sounded guarded, maybe with a double meaning: "There is no real camp . . . at the moment. I am camped on property of friend. A few of my people have joined me."

"I take it that this friend you speak of is white."

"Yes, John Nemeth he is called. He and his woman my good friends." The old brave continued to look out over the valley.

"I saw Nemeth down at the tavern this morning," Sate said, filled with a strange desire to know about the man. "His wife sells pies, I believe."

"Yes. She and Ulie bake pies."

"Ulie?" Sate lifted a questioning eyebrow. "Who is that?"

"Ulie John's sister. Also my friend." With that a warmth entered the grave tone.

Ah, yes. Sate mentally connected the two names. The one they call Heller. He turned his head and studied the wrinkled profile. "Where does your friend Nemeth come from?"

Nemus lifted his gaze from the valley and trained it on Sate, his black eyes unblinking. "He no say and I don't ask. Around here no one asks this question. He is fine man. That is all Nemus needs to know."

Sate smiled ruefully. He had been told firmly that John Nemeth wasn't to be gossiped about.

As the birds continued to sing and no attack seemed imminent from the peaceful forest beyond, Sate gradually relaxed his guard and lounged lazily against a porch post, feeling the sun on his face. There was no danger to fear from the old brave. His eyes half closed, he barely flickered them when Nemus began to speak again:

"There was a time, not too long ago, when there were many camps in valley. We planted our land, hunted our forests, a proud and brave people. Then came the white man with his long gun, his greed, his fire-water and diseases, and changed our lives. What he could not force from my people, he bought with a jug of fire-water. In six moons Indian had been pushed out of valley."

Sate made no response, for he could say nothing in defense of his own people. He knew that the old brave needed to talk and he kept quiet as Nemus continued bitterly

"Although my brothers continue to be pushed farther and farther westward, they are more and more angry at the grabbing of their land. Soon they stop and go no farther. The time is not too far off when war will again be carried on between white man and Indian."

Did the old man speak with knowledge of warring Indians, Sate wondered, or was he only hoping war would come to pass? It stood to reason that he, too, must hold grudges against those who stole his land.

His tone slightly skeptical, Sate asked, "Do you have proof of this or you merely guessin'?"

Nemus answered, an edge of irritation in his voice, "You have only to look around you as you travel to see what is in the wind. For some months there has been no evidence of braves in vicinity, and only old men, women, and children tend their camps. It is told around our campfires that the young men are up in Canada, that the British tell them attack the settlers again." A look almost of defeat settled on the stern features. "I fear before long we will see the red man wearing scalps on his belt once more."

It came to Sate in a rush of memory . . . the war that had ended only months ago, the blood-curdling cries as the Indians attacked, their unearthly war whoops. He remembered the tension of waiting, wondering where in the forest they watched, which tree concealed a half-naked body.

He sighed and stood up, no longer enjoying the sun or the scenery. "Old brave," he said, a distant look in his eyes, "I sure as hell hope you're wrong. I fought your people not long ago and I don't care to do it again."

Nemus's square chin rose a little higher. "My tribe no fight the white-eyes." Reproof was in the grunted words.

Sate grinned crookedly. "I'm sorry. I should have said,

'some Indians.'" When there was no answer to his apology, he said awkwardly, "My name is Sate Margruder." When Nemus nodded, he said, "I'm gonna go down to the settlement now and settle the deal on this place and get settled in. If ever you want to visit me, I'd be honored."

There was a slight softening of the black eyes. "Nemus will do this. You come, visit with me and John Nemeth."

The sun was low in the west when Sate drew rein in front of the tavern. It was supper time, and when he stepped into the establishment the three women were hurrying about, waiting on the men crowded into the big room. He found himself a table in a corner and sat down. Bessy spotted him and hurried across the room to ask anxiously, "Did you see the cabin?"

Sate's blue eyes reflected the displeasure he felt at her question. After looking at her for a moment he finally bit out, "Not that it's any of your business, but yes, I saw the cabin."

"Well? Did you like it?" Bessy pressed, undeterred by his sharp answer. "Are you gonna buy it?"

Sate shifted impatiently. "Again, it's none of your business, but if the price is right I might."

"I'm sure you can strike a deal." A wide smile lit Bessy's plump face. "The woman wants to get rid of it real bad."

Sate made no response to the eager claim. He dismissed the bondswoman by ordering sharply, "Go fetch me something to eat."

Bessy sniffed, then flounced away, and Sate, watching the generous hips move away, muttered sourly, "She talks an uncommon lot. I hope I won't be sorry if I buy her papers."

Of course, I won't be around all that much, he rationalized. Until trapping time, when he'd be gone all day, he'd kill time here at the tavern. He had no intention of farming his acres. Plodding along behind a horse, a pair of plow handles in his hands, was not for him.

A wish to be back in his old cabin came over him. But not with the bondswoman, he thought hastily. A man needed a strong woman for life in the woods. Wiry ones like squaws, or the silken strength of a woman like Juliana.

A look of self-disgust moved over Sate's rough, handsome features. Would that little cheat never stop slipping into his mind? He rose and walked to the bar. His old cabin and the widow were things of the past. For the time being his future was here, in Squaw Hollow, so he might as well get it started.

The price of the homestead was soon reached, but when it came to Bessy's papers a little haggling went on. Finally each man compromised a little, and Sate counted the money out on the bar. After Battle tucked it safely beneath the long counter and handed him Bessy's papers, Sate turned to look for the woman.

She stood at his elbow, smiling eagerly.

"Go pack your duds," he grunted. "I'll be leavin' in ten minutes."

"Say now, Margruder." Battle frowned at his gruff tone after Bessy hurried away. "I hope you ain't gonna be mean to the girl."

"Look, Battle," Sate said irritably, "I'm not gonna beat her, if that's what you mean, but I'm not gonna treat her like a wife either. All she has to do is keep my cabin clean, have food on the table at the proper time, and visit my bed when I want her."

"Hell"—Battle grinned—"ain't that what a wife docs?"

The trapper's narrowed eyes told Battle that he saw no humor in his remark. The taverner only grinned again, and when Bessy joined them he put an arm around her shoulders. "Got your duds, I see." He looked down at the half-filled pillowcase she clutched. "I'm gonna miss our visits to the back room." He pinched her rounded bottom.

Bessy giggled and started to reply that she would miss those times also, but without sparing her a glance Sate interrupted, "Let's go."

She stared after the retreating broad back, a let down feeling inside her. She had hoped the man would soften and become more affectionate once he owned her papers. She shrugged, kissed Battle's cheek, then rushed outside. On the porch she came to an abrupt halt. Sate was mounted and headed out of the village. He had no intentions of letting her ride.

Her eyes snapping, she dropped the bag of clothes and yelled as the stallion cantered away, "What about me? Where is my horse?"

"There isn't any," the unconcerned words floated back to her. "It won't kill a healthy woman to walk one measly mile."

"Arrogant bastard." Bessy stamped a foot. "I'm tempted not to go, teach him a lesson." A moment later she picked up

her clothes, asking herself, Who am I foolin'? It's doubtful if
any woman could teach that one anything.

After finding the reins loose on his neck, the small pony
came to a halt and, lowering his head, cropped at the lush
spring grass. Her movements trancelike, Juliana slid off his
back. Walking out on a stone ledge, she sat down and listlessly
dangled her feet. Her expression was one of silent despair as
she gazed, unseeing, out over the river that flowed below.

She raked trembling fingers through the blond hair that had
escaped its ribbon. What would John's and Molly's reaction be
when she told them about the baby? They were so cramped in
the small cabin already. Would there be room for another, even
though it be a tiny infant? And poor Molly, would she be
envious, wanting a child of her own so badly?

From across the valley floor drifted the low calls of wild
turkeys preparing to roost. With a start Juliana realized that it
was sunset, and that the forest was still; she was suddenly
lonely. As she scrambled to her feet a cool wind passed down
the hills and she shivered in her light clothing.

Her gaze swept up and down the valley, trying to pierce the
dark shadows and get her bearing. She had given the roan his
head, and God knew where he had taken her. She knew that
night was at hand and that she was some distance from home.

"John and Molly will be out of their minds with worry," she
muttered, catching up the dangling reins and swinging onto the
pony's back.

As she sat trying to decide which direction to take, she
suddenly caught something in the air—the distinctive odor of
pipe tobacco carried on the breeze. Indian or white? she
wondered. She remembered the Indian she had seen earlier and
shuddered. She would hate to meet up with him again,
especially in the dark.

The sturdy little horse moved out on his own, as though
taking over the matter. Juliana had heard that a horse always
knew its way home and, for the moment, she would let him
lead. In ten minutes a cabin loomed in front of her. But it was
not John's, she knew immediately. This one was high on a hill
and was larger than her brother's.

She saw at once the large male figure standing in the open
door, his buckskin shirt hanging open, indifferent to the chill

air. A smoking pipe was clenched between his teeth as he took a step out of the shadow and onto the porch.

Juliana's heart lurched. "Is he a figment of my mind, or is he really there!" she whispered joyfully.

Sate had watched the rider approach; noting the absence of a saddle, he wondered if he was to be visited by another Indian. He wasn't alarmed, though. The slight figure was that of a young lad. Then he stepped out onto the porch and stood paralyzed. What was Juliana Roessler doing in Squaw Hollow?

He watched her slide to the ground, and as she hurried toward the cabin, all his past mind-tearing torment rushed back on him. But the pain and hurt pride had to struggle with his need to sweep her into his arms when she stepped onto the porch and stood before him. When wordlessly, and with shining eyes, she flung her arms around his neck it took determined control for him to strike them away.

Stunned at his action, Juliana stepped back, bewilderment in her eyes as she stared up at him. "I'm . . . I'm sorry," she stammered, studying his hard and bitter face, "I thought you would be happy that you had found me."

Sate gave a short, mirthless laugh and said coldly, "I wasn't aware that I'd been lookin' for you."

He has changed, Juliana thought, pain heavy in her heart. But as he continued to look at her contemptuously, a heavy thread of anger began to spin inside her. If he had changed his mind about them, why wasn't he man enough to come right out and say so? Well, he wasn't going to get away with it. She would force him to say the words.

Her amber eyes blazing into his hard blue ones, she said heatedly, "I'm sure I don't know what you mean by that hateful remark, but you know very well that we had plans to meet again in the spring."

Sate shifted his gaze from her smoldering eyes to let it range insultingly over her body. "Yeah, well, that was a long time ago, wasn't it?" His eyes returned to her face. "Are you suddenly rememberin' it, now that your lover has grown tired of you and dumped you here in this hell-hole settlement?"

For long seconds Juliana stood in frozen silence, a pained protest locked in her throat. Finally, bewildered, she cried, "What are you talking about? I've never had a lover in my life. There has only been my husband."

Farther up in the hills a wolf yowled, but neither one heard it as each stared into the other's eyes. The amber ones begged to be believed, but there was no relenting in the blue ones. Sate's voice was like ice when he ground out, "Like hell there haven't been other men. Your sister-in-law put me wise to you. You're man-crazy and you took off with the first man you met in Trenton."

Although Juliana's face paled at his taunt, she laughed lightly with a sigh of relief. "Iva lied to you, Sate. The woman never liked me, and now that my brother has left her she would say, or do, anything that would hurt either of us. I told the maid to tell you I had come here to join my brother, never thinking that you might see Iva instead."

Sate gazed into the lovely, earnest face, wanting desperately to believe her. But, knowing that he could never bear such pain again, he willed himself to remember the sister-in-law's words, and the strength of them beat on his mind with the force of truth. Grabbing Juliana's arms, he began to shake her. "You're lyin' through your teeth. Why don't you admit that you've been left behind and don't know where to turn?"

The cruel accusation hit Juliana with sickening weight, and her brief moment of elation died. She couldn't believe that he had swallowed Iva's lies. Then, with a jolt that jabbed her heart, the thought came to her that he could be using those lies as an excuse to evade his promise to her. He had not expected to see her here—his stunned surprise when she arrived plainly told her that.

Pulling away from his loosened grip, her face was cold and emotionless. "If that's what you prefer thinking, Sate Margruder," she said calmly, "go right ahead. But for your information there's plenty of ways for me to turn. I can have any single man in this valley. Before the moon comes up tonight, I could find many willing bed partners."

The truth of her words cut straight to Sate's heart. Men would fight each other to the death to possess her, and the thought was more than he could bear. He didn't care if she'd had a hundred lovers; he loved her, wanted her. With a helpless groan his hands reached out, then were stilled. Bessy was puffing up the hill, calling his name. A smothered expletive escaped his grim lips as Juliana's head turned inquiringly.

Juliana watched the plump bondswoman come nearer, taking in the clothes that showed plainly through the thin, worn material of the pillowcase. No wonder he started right in on me, she thought dispiritedly. He wanted me away from here before she arrived.

She smiled mirthlessly. It wasn't a pleasant feeling, knowing that she had been passed over for this woman. She shot Sate a look of cold contempt. "I see everything clearly now," she said.

Before he could call forth an answer, she was down the steps, brushing past Bessy, and grabbing the pony's reins.

As Juliana swung onto the mount, Sate took a step to follow her just as a strong, concerned male voice called her name. Without a backward look, she called out, "I'm coming, John," and jabbed a shaggy flank with a hard heel.

The insulted beast sprang away, scattering mud and grass. Bessy stared after them, grumping, "Lady Heller thinks she's too good to speak to a lowly bondswoman."

Sate felt a coldness invade his heart. Snatches of conversation returned to him. Battle had mentioned the name Heller, as had Roth Adams. Was it possible that she and Juliana were the same woman? Had he made the mistake of his life? Had he accused Juliana falsely?

Bessy winced when he gripped her arm and spun her around. "Is she the one they call Heller?" he demanded, his skin pale under his deep tan.

"Yeah, that's her," Bessy sneered, rubbing her arm. "The queen of the valley."

Sate fired questions at her like bullets from a rifle. "When did she come to the valley? Did she arrive alone? Has she shown any interest in any man since she's been here?"

Bessy blinked at him, her brain having difficulty keeping up with the rapid-fire queries. Her answers came slowly as she thought out each question carefully: "She came Christmas week. She and the old Indian, Nemus, rode through the village late one afternoon. Me and Battle seen them." She slid Sate a sullen look before saying reluctantly, "I ain't heard of any man goin' up to the Nemeth place after dark."

The effect Bessy's words had on Sate were immediate. The strength drained out of his body, and he lowered himself slowly to sit on the porch step. The pain of loss in the blue eyes clashed with the harshness of his voice as he ordered, "Get on inside and make my supper."

Bessy glared at the broad back a moment. Then a satisfied smile curved her fleshy lips. The great Sate Margruder didn't look so almighty now, sitting on the step, his proud shoulders slumped dejectedly.

CHAPTER 11

Sate was unaware of his surroundings, even of his hard seat on the top step of the porch. He was only conscious of the soul-shaking pain of losing Juliana yet again. For there was no doubt that the harsh, insulting words he had hurled at her had accomplished that.

His lean tanned hands hanging between his drawn-up knees clenched and unclenched. Why had he allowed his stubborn pride to refuse to listen to her explanation? His eyes grew stormy. Because he had listened to that old witch in Trenton, that's why. He had half a mind to go back there and twist her scrawny neck.

"Oh, you have half a mind, all right," an inward voice scorned. "Sitting here feeling sorry for yourself instead of figuring some way to get her back."

For quite a while Sate blocked his mind to his own suggestion. There had been such finality in Juliana's manner when she rode away into the night.

Still the man sat on. The moon rose, exposing the poignant shadows of memories chasing across his face. Abruptly he stood up, determination etched in the line of his mouth. He would not give into this feeling of hopelessness. He had always fought for what he wanted, and never had he wanted anything as he did Juliana Roessler. He would not, could not reconcile himself to a life without her.

He stepped off the porch and into the soft evening. With the surefootedness of a hillman, he walked the hills, laying his plans. Tomorrow morning he would ride over to the Nemeth place and there he would submit to any humiliation in order to lay his love at Juliana's feet, and hopefully regain hers.

His mind made up, impatient for tomorrow to come, Sate turned around and began to retrace his steps. His half smile held self-derision. How many times he had been urged to go see the most beautiful woman in the territory, the one they called Heller?

Juliana caught sight of her brother on horseback when she gained the wagon road. Passing the back of a hand across her tear-wet eyes and forcing a cheerful note into her voice, she called, "Over here, John."

John Nemeth wheeled his mount, and the worried frown on his face as he rode toward her turned into a relieved smile. "Where have you been, girl?" He came up alongside her, his voice strained from concern. "It's after dark, and Molly said you didn't look too good when you rode out."

The fine lines reappeared between his eyes as he took in her tear-streaked face and the wary droop to her shoulders. He laid a hand on her arm. "Juliana, you've been crying. What's wrong?"

Juliana gazed down at the reins gripped in her hands. How could she begin to tell John of all that was swirling through her mind? That she was expecting a baby, that the man she loved, one he didn't even know about, had just thrown her love back in her face cruelly?

John finally broke the silence anxiously. "Aren't you happy here with me and Molly? Is the wilderness too lonesome for you? Maybe you're missing all the balls and parties you're used to."

The concern in his voice sent a wave of guilt through Juliana. He and Molly had been so kind to her, bending over backward to make her feel welcome. She folded her fingers over the hand that still lay on her arm. "John," she said earnestly, "I love being here with you and Molly. I love this wild, wonderful country, and I don't miss Philadelphia in the least."

She dropped her hand and looked away, wondering how to continue. In the next moment, however, a cramp knotted in the pit of her stomach—whether from her pregnancy, or the fact that she hadn't eaten since breakfast, she didn't know. A curious relief washed through her as she slid off the pony's back. She wouldn't have to use words to explain to John that she was expecting.

But although she retched until she was weak, it didn't once occur to John, as he held her head, that she had anything worse than a bellyache.

When he asked if she had been eating green apples, she grew impatient. "I'm with child, John."

Juliana heard John's stunned intake of breath. Lifting her head, she gazed into eyes that were wide with disbelief. His lips moved soundlessly a moment, then finally he managed, "But how can that be? You haven't been with a man since you came here . . have you?"

"Of course not, John." Juliana's eyes flashed. "What a question. I obviously conceived just before Tom was killed."

The bewildered man's eyes went to his sister's flat stomach, then looked away in embarrassment. "Then you're about four months gone?" he said awkwardly.

Juliana nodded. "I believe so. I feel foolish not realizing before that I had missed so many monthlies."

John laughed weakly. "I'd think that's something a woman would notice right away. Molly always knows, right to the day."

Juliana's returning laugh was also a little shaky. "You know me, always only half aware of anything." She waited a moment, before her next words rushed out. "I feel so badly about heaping more responsibility on your shoulders. I must feel like a yoke around your neck."

John gave her a quick hug, then helped her to remount. Looking up at her, his smile gentle, he said, "Don't give it another thought, sis. It's a yoke I enjoy wearing." When he was astride his own mount he said, "Molly will be beside herself, having a baby in the house. She wants one of her own so badly."

Riding side by side down the deeply rutted road, now brightly lit by a full moon, Juliana asked anxiously, "Do you think the Hollow will gossip about me? I doubt they even know that I've been widowed recently."

John barked a short laugh. "The folk around here aren't much to talk about anyone, Juliana. Most have too many skeletons of their own they want kept hidden." His lips curled in a crooked grin. "Anyway, you know Molly. She'll soon let everybody know your circumstances."

Juliana agreed and fell silent, her thoughts returning to the big man on the neighboring hill. She swallowed back the tears that threatened to fall. Her future looked so bleak. Rejection from the man she loved, and a baby on the way that she must raise almost completely alone. . . .

The dim candlelight through the cabin window was a warm glow in the distance. "I feel badly about going off and leaving Molly with all those men to contend with," Juliana said, urging the small roan up the hill. "They can get on your nerves sometimes."

"Molly won't mind," John said, pride in his words. "That sharp tongue of hers can handle them. There she is now."

Molly stood on the porch, waving at them. "I was gettin' worried about you," she called, walking toward them, her eyes searching Juliana's face as John helped her to dismount. "Have you been cryin', Julie?"

While Juliana fumbled with words to tell her news, John took the explaining upon himself. Placing an arm around Molly's shoulders, he said bluntly, "Julie's all right, honey. She's been fussing because she's gonna have a baby."

He had thought to shock Molly, to finally still her tongue. He was the stunned one, however, when her red lips merely curved in a smile and she quipped, "I *thought* she had something in the oven."

Juliana found her tongue first. "You knew?" she cried incredulously.

"Well, I didn't know for a fact, but everything pointed that way."

"Well, I never!" Juliana shook her head.

"Oh, yes, you did." Molly giggled, linking her arm through Juliana's as they moved across the porch and into the cabin. "When are we gonna have the pleasure of the little tad's company?"

"Sometime in August, I think."

Molly gave a speculative look to Juliana's flat stomach. "So soon?" She raised her eyes to look into the tear-swollen amber ones. "Your husband Tom's?"

"Molly!" John barked, forgetting that just a short time ago he had more or less asked the same question. "Of course it's Tom Roessler's child."

Molly shrugged, her curiosity not at all quelled by the censure in her man's tone. "I only asked because by now she should be over her queasiness. Of course there's cases where the women suffer it the whole nine months."

"Well, let's hope that won't be Juliana's case," John said, then administered a playful whack on Molly's backside. "What's for supper, woman? I'm starved."

During the meal Juliana tried to join in the couple's light chatter, but she wasn't very successful. Sate's dark face and blazing eyes as he hurled his bitter accusations at her constantly swam before her eyes. When supper was finally finished, she sighed her relief, thankful that she no longer had to feign a serenity that was almost beyond her.

When Molly said, "Juliana, you look beat. Go on to bed, I'll do up these few dishes," she agreed after only a slight hesitation. The thought of the feather mattress sounded very good. A few minutes later, curled under the sheet and light blanket, she heard John and Molly quietly talking together out on the porch. She knew they were discussing her and the coming baby.

She lay a hand gently on her stomach. This little spark of life had certainly stirred up much interest. Especially in Molly. Amusement twitched the corners of her lips. Molly wasn't completely convinced that the little one belonged to Tom.

As Sate neared his cabin, Bessy's high-pitched voice floated on the night air. "Is the girl talkin' to herself?" he muttered irritably. But when a male's laughing voice joined hers, he stopped and stepped into the shadow of a tree, listening intently. The rich timbre of the tone was familiar, one he had heard recently.

He moved from under the tree and, approaching the cabin quietly, stepped cautiously onto the porch. A man couldn't be too careful these days.

He flattened himself against the wall in time to hear the man say in suggestive tones, "So you and Margruder aren't married."

"No," Bessy tittered, "I'm only his bondswoman, if you know what I mean."

"I get your meanin'," the deep voice chuckled. "You don't have that special paper that says you can sleep with him legal-like."

Bessy's shrill titter grated on Sate's ears again before she asked coyly, "What about you? Are you married?"

There was a short pause before the deep voice answered, "No, not anymore. My Zoe left me a couple of weeks back."

Sate started with the sudden recognition. Of course—Roth Adams. The man with the Indian wife. Giving a loud whoop, he jumped into the cabin.

Startled by the warlike cry, Adams sprang to his feet, his hand whipping to the large curved knife strapped at his waist. Crouching to attack, a loud laugh of amusement held him. He stared at the big frame standing before him, then his lips spread in a wide smile.

"Margruder, you son-of-a-gun." He laughed loudly, his hand outstretched. "You damn near got my knife in your heart, you know that?"

Sate grabbed the big hand, pumping it heartily. "You humpin' wolf, how you been? What are you doin' here at the settlement? I didn't think you came in so often."

Roth resumed his seat by the fire, flashing Bessy a wide smile as he did so. When Sate had seated himself, he said, "I came in to attend to some business."

"I heard you tellin' Bessy that your wife had left you. I can't believe it. She seemed wild-hog crazy about you. What changed her mind?"

Roth stared into the flames, his eyes clouding over. "Nothin' changed her mind, Sate," he said finally. "She died lovin' me."

Shocked, Sate drew back and stared at the handsome older man. "Died! God, I'm sorry to hear that, Roth. What took her?"

There was red-hot anger in the voice that answered. "A heartless two-legged animal took her, Sate. He drove a knife between her breasts." Over the sound of Sate's sharp indrawn breath and Bessy's horrified gasp, Roth unburdened himself.

"There was no sense to her killin', no sense at all. He'd had his way with her, many times I think, but the bastard had no feelin' for her life."

Sate stared down at his knotted fists. What could he say to this man to comfort him? There was nothing, so he sat quietly, hoping that his sympathy would be assumed in his silence.

When Roth stirred, pushing away his black thoughts, Sate asked, "When did it happen? I don't suppose you know who done it."

"It happened two or three days after you left us, Sate,"

Adams said, leaning back in the rocker. "I was out huntin' fresh meat, and I was gone longer than usual because I was trackin' a young doe." He paused to rake long fingers through his thick graying hair. "I think that was the reason Zoe opened the door to the man. I'm certain she thought it was me.

"Anyhow, by the time I got the deer and returned home, it was near dark. But as I crossed the yard I could still make out the stranger's footprints, comin' and goin'. They were made by a white man's boots, and even before I saw the cabin door standing open, I knew what I'd find inside."

Roth fell silent and closed his eyes, as if to shut out the memory of what he'd found. Moved to tears by his story, Bessy laid her hand on his and asked softly, "Do you know who done it, Roth?"

Roth gave a short ugly laugh. "I know who he used to be. Zoe's people and I tracked the low-life down and, I can tell you, his death wasn't a pretty one. Chad Madison will have his way with no more women."

Sate's body jerked, and he groaned, "God, I knew I should have killed that son-of-a-bitch when I had the chance."

"You knew him?" Roth looked at him, surprised.

"Only slightly, Roth, but well enough to know that he was rotten to the core. He done a terrible thing to a young squaw I knew." He stared down at the floor in bitter regret. "Roth, I saw Madison on the trail after leavin' your place. We weren't within speakin' distance because he was off the trail, sneakin' through the woods." He got to his feet. "God, why didn't I put my knife through his heart?"

Roth shook his head. "Don't blame yourself, friend. You had no way of knowin'." He stood up and leaned against the mantel. "I've had my blamin', Sate, and put it behind me. A man has to expect, and accept, anything at anytime in this wilderness. There's a hard, fast rule in these parts: Never look back."

He reached down and tweaked Bessy's nose. "Don't you feed your visitors, Bessy? I could eat a bear."

Flushed with pleasure, Bessy gave her ready giggle and bound to her feet. "I'll put it on the table now."

The meat was tough, the roasted potatoes burned on one side, and the corn bread flat and tasteless. Sate sent Bessy a look of disgust, chewing on a piece of venison that never got any less tough in his mouth. Roth ducked his head to hide his amusement, wondering to himself if the plump woman was a better bed partner than she was a cook.

The supper was finished quickly, and the two men removed themselves to the fire. When they had their pipes going, Roth said quietly, so that Bessy, washing the dishes, wouldn't hear, "Halfway to the settlement I came across a partially burned wagon and a dead man and woman. I buried them on the spot."

"I saw them, too." Sate sighed. "But the woods were full of Indians and I didn't dare stop to bury them."

There was a short silence, then Roth said, "I hope Zoe's people didn't do it. I'd hate to have to fight them someday. Maybe kill one of her relatives."

"That would be hard," Sate agreed.

Roth slid him a glance from the corner of his eyes. "I didn't love Zoe like a wife, Sate," he said quietly, almost ashamedly. "Mostly I treated her like a pretty doll I could take to bed whenever the notion struck me." He looked back into the flames of the fire. "That was a big part of the guilt I suffered."

Sate made no response. He knew he wasn't expected to.

The two men sat in silence for a while, then Roth, nodding his head in Bessy's direction, inquiring in hushed tones, "You've no kind of feelin's for that one at all, have you?"

"Hell no. I only bought her papers this afternoon . . . and I'm sorry already."

"She sure as hell can't cook." He left the rest of his thought unsaid for the moment.

Roth looked at the big trapper then, his dark eyes twinkling. "I don't suppose you feel like sharin' her tonight?" Roth grinned. "I've been a while without my pleasurin'."

"Hell, you can have her all to yourself," Sate said indifferently. With his whole being wrapped up in thoughts of Juliana, the bondswoman held no attraction for him.

As though she had heard the agreement struck between the two men, Bessy removed her apron and joined them, sitting on the raised hearth. She made no effort to hide her pleased smile when Roth began to yawn and cast long looks at the trundle bed Sate had placed in a corner of the main room.

She rose shortly, mumbling, "I'm goin' to bed." Both pairs of male eyes watched her shed her clothes then slip between the covers. Before she was barely settled, Roth was on his feet.

"See you in the mornin', friend." He grinned unabashedly. And Sate, just as shameless, turned around in his chair and watched the man undress, then pull back the covers, baring the waiting feminine body. The heavy thighs opened invitingly, and Roth positioned himself between them. Sate's amused smile held admiration for the rigid manhood the big man held in his hand a moment before letting it disappear slowly inside Bessy.

He's damn near as big as me, he thought, watching the narrow hips lift, then drive forward. He turned back in the chair and rested his head on its back, reliving in his mind the heart-stopping moment when his body came together with Juliana's. How much easier his task would be tomorrow, he sighed, if she had been conscious of the heights they had scaled together that night in his cabin.

He sighed again as he rose and shoveled ashes over the live coals that remained in a glowing heap. Begging Juliana's forgiveness tomorrow would be the most important thing he had ever attempted in his life.

Treading softly across the floor to his bedroom, he glanced curiously at the trundle bed bathed in a shaft of moonlight. It had been quiet there for several minutes. He lifted his brows when he discovered the reason why. He was on the edge of sleep when the bedframe in the next room resumed squeaking and complaining. He turned over, muttering, "Roth sure has a lot of stayin' power."

The sun was shining through his small window when Sate awakened the next morning. He lay quietly, his thoughts directed on what lay ahead of him. What he said, and how he said it, might very well shape the rest of his life. If Juliana believed and accepted his apology, promised to be his wife, then he would be a contented man for the rest of his life.

The blue in his eyes turned steely. If he had to face the alternative, he hoped his life would be a short one. Because without her in it, he would merely exist. He had known her only a short time, but an eternity couldn't have made him feel any more convinced of his feeling for her.

He pulled his clothes on and walked into the main room. Bessy crouched in front of the fire, making breakfast. A glance at the narrow bed in the corner showed that Roth had risen also. "Where's Adams?" he asked in a sleep-gruff voice.

Bessy turned a happy, contented face to him. "He's out back

tendin' his horse." She paused, then with determination in the
curve of her full lips, asked nervously, "Margruder, if Roth
should want to buy my papers, would you sell them to him?"

Sate looked at her and shook his head slowly. "He's not
gonna want your papers, Bessy," he said, not unkindly. "Last
night didn't mean that kind of thing to him. It's Roth's way to
treat a woman nice."

The knowing look on Bessy's face said that Sate was
mistaken, that a hardened man like himself could have no idea
what she and Roth had shared last night.

A smile playing on her lips, she carried a platter of salt pork
to the table. When Sate walked past her, on his way to the dry
sink, she followed and stood beside him. "But if Roth should
ask," she persisted, "would you sell them?"

"Hell, yes," Sate growled impatiently, dipping water from a
pail and pouring it into a basin. "I'd be glad to get rid of your
chattering tongue."

A smugness settled over the round face. "Roth doesn't mind
my talkin'. You'll see."

Bessy was still smiling complacently and Sate was drying
his face when Roth returned to the cabin. As the three took
chairs at the table, Roth shot Bessy a wide smile, and she
colored brightly. Sate saw the exchange, waited a minute, then
looked across at his guest. "How long are you gonna hang
around with us, Roth? I'd be pleased to have you stay as long
as you like."

While Bessy held her breath and watched the broad-
shouldered man through her lashes, Roth answered gravely,
"Thank you, Sate, that's right friendly of you. But I'll be
gettin' on directly. Like I said last night, I came to the Hollow
on a . . ." He paused and grinned. "I was gonna say on
business, but that's not the right name to put on it."

While Sate and Bessy waited for him to go on, Roth toyed
with his coffee cup, staring into the the steaming liquid as he
chose his words. Finally he lifted his gaze to Sate.

"Sate, do you remember me tellin' you about a woman I met
here in Squaw Hollow, the one who bakes pies with her sister-
in-law?" A shock went through Sate, and his heart thudded
painfully. He remembered vividly how taken Roth had been
with the woman from Squaw Hollow. His granite-hard features
gave away none of the alarm raging inside him as Roth
continued.

"Well, like I said, I was mighty drawn to that woman. I couldn't get her out of my mind. She was even with me when I made love to Zoe." His broad shoulders lifted with a long sigh. "Zoe's gone now, and I've come here to ask that Heller woman to be my wife."

Sate didn't know if the gasp that sounded in the air was his own or Bessy's. He knew vaguely that her fist had gone to her mouth, and that tears shimmered in her eyes. As for himself, he had gone dead inside, only his mind shouting, "You can't have her. She's mine!"

Roth didn't appear to notice that his words had paralyzed the pair sitting with him, and he rose, remarking cheerfully that he'd be on his way. Sate recovered sufficiently to follow him outside and to say in a flat, expressionless voice, "Stop in again, Adams."

He leaned against the porch railing, watching the horse and rider disappear down the hill, whispering to himself, "She'll never have you. She wants another."

But even as he spoke, heavy doubts assailed him. Despite his age, Roth Adams was still a virile and handsome man. He could understand how a woman could be drawn to him. Especially if she felt lost to that other love.

From inside the cabin Bessy's sobs came softly, and Sate knew the wish to cry out his own pain and fears. He stepped off the porch and struck out walking. Roth had put a finish to his own visit to Juliana today, and all he could do now was wait and see how she received Roth's offer of marriage.

CHAPTER 12

~~~

Juliana slept late the next morning. When she opened her eyes bright sunlight was flooding through the open door. Yesterday's discoveries were waiting to claim her mind, but with firm determination she pushed them away. It was futile to waste time on happenings she couldn't change. She couldn't change the fact that she was having a baby, nor could she make Sate Margruder return her love.

No, she must now concentrate on this coming child, and the future she must build for it. It would not be easy, she knew, but she also knew that John and Molly would be solidly behind her.

The faint scratch of a hoe from back of the cabin caught Juliana's attention, and she smiled when over its sound came Molly's gay chatter, then John's low laugh. She stared up at the smoke-darkened ceiling, marveling that even so dull a thing as tending a plot of flax provided the pair with pleasure.

A tremendous amount of work had already gone into the flax field, and according to Molly an equal amount would be needed before the plant was finally turned into cloth. Altogether it took over a year from the sowing of seed to the finished product. After the harvesting there would come the rippling . . . combing to get rid of seeds . . . separating the fibers from each other then cording them to lie parallel. Finally would come the spinning of the fibers into long threads which Molly would then weave into fine linen cloth.

"And then"—Molly had beamed—"we'll have smooth sheets, tablecloths, underwear, and lightweight dresses."

"And what about the winter?" Juliana asked, glancing down at the faded homespun she now wore.

"Oh, we'll wear linsey-woolsey then," Molly explained. "I'll combine wool with the linen. John will have his first shearing before long."

"Do you think he'll be able to take the shears to his pets?" Juliana laughingly asked.

Molly grinned. "I've been wondering about that myself."

John's small herd of sheep had grown from twenty-three head to fifty, counting the lambs that had been dropped a month ago, plus the additional ones bought with the proceeds of the apple pies. He and Molly had talked it over and decided the money was better spent on a far-reaching project that would in time assure them of financial security.

"You two won't be drudges anymore when I really get the operation going," John had promised. "And you can stop wearing those things you loosely call gowns."

She had shrugged, not really regretting the fact that she had packed away all the pretty gowns she had worn in Philadelphia. Certainly they had no place in her present life. She had only smiled when John thought he was consoling her by assuring her that the time would come when she could dress like a lady again.

"In the meantime," Juliana said to the empty air, "I'd best be up and about."

After washing her face and brushing her hair and teeth, she quickly dressed, then removed the coffee pot from the hearth before sitting down at the table. Spreading butter over a still warm biscuit, she washed it down with coffee heavily laced with thick cream. She sat back then and waited for the old sickness to come upon her. But her stomach remained calm and no bile rose to her throat.

"I guess that part is over," she thought out loud as she returned the pot to the fire.

A glance at the clock on the mantel reminded her that she was late feeding the laying hens. Their care, and the gathering of the eggs, had been allotted to her since it was she who had insisted John buy them.

"They won't last out the summer," he'd warned. "The coons and foxes will make short work of them."

But she had enlisted the aid of several willing trappers in the erection of a tall, enclosure for the fowl. To make it even more effective against the critters that prowled for game in the night, there was a strong hinged cover to fit over its top. In the daylight hours it was laid back to admit fresh air and sunlight. A narrow door permitted her entrance to care for the chickens and collect the eggs that were laid every day.

Every morning, to her and Molly's amusement, John remarked, "This salt pork sure goes down better now that there's eggs to go with it." Neither bothered to point out how much he had resisted acquiring the small flock in the beginning.

The eggs will nourish my unborn baby, too, Juliana mused as she stepped inside a small shed and filled a pan with cracked corn.

It was while she was scattering the feed in the pen that the idea came to her that she should allow a couple of the brooding hens to sit on their eggs. The sole rooster among them certainly, from her observation, fertilized the eggs sufficiently. I could double the flock, she reflected and find ready buyers for any surplus eggs. And any monetary gain would go toward buying more sheep.

Juliana lifted her face to the beautiful late spring morning. As a warm breeze off the hills ruffled her hair, scattering strands across her face, she mused that it would be a small contribution, but she would be helping John in some small way.

The clanging sound of iron on stone brought her planning to an abrupt halt. Holding back her hair with her hand she stared down the trail, wondering who could be coming to visit so early in the day. It wouldn't be a pie customer, nor would it be Nemus. His little pony was unshod.

Peering intently, Juliana recognized the magnificent white stallion emerging from the forest. The big rider astride its back brought an excited cry from her throat. Roth Adams! The same strange feelings she'd had on their first meeting rushed back on her: confusion, excitement, a barely repressed joy.

Remembrance of the fact of his marriage caused Juliana's headlong rush toward him to slow down to a sedate walk. When he pulled the stallion to a halt and swung to the ground, she smiled and offered her hand. "How are you, Roth? It's good to see you again."

A tingling ran the length of her arm when her hand was

grasped by Roth's lean one, and her pulse quickened when his eyes caressed her face before he spoke in his husky voice.

"I'm fine, Juliana, and it's more than good to look on your beautiful face again."

The spirit on which Sate had trampled, almost broken, rose steadily, like smoke from a chimney on a quiet evening. "Oh, Roth," Juliana started to chide gently, then was cut short as with a sighing sound he pulled her into his arms and urgently captured her lips with his.

And she, desperate for tenderness, love, and support, responded eagerly with arms and mouth.

A roughly cleared throat brought them quickly apart under John Nemeth's dark, disapproving gaze. Juliana regained control of herself and moved to her brother's side to lay a hand on his stiffly held arm.

"It's all right, John," she coaxed. "Molly and I know Roth."

"Oh?" The single-word question was growled. "And how long have you known him?"

"We met just a few weeks ago," Juliana snapped angrily, knowing what he alluded to.

"It sure as hell didn't look that way."

Embarrassed and blushing, Juliana ignored her brother's grim look and tone and glanced at Roth instead. "Roth, this bear is actually my brother, John Nemeth," she said, frowning. "Usually he doesn't roar so loud."

Roth took a step forward and held out his hand, saying with a sheepish smile, "Nor does he usually find his sister kissing a stranger either, I'll wager."

Juliana held her breath as for a moment John ignored the offer of friendship. She let it out slowly as Roth's innate charm won John over and he grasped the lean fingers firmly.

"Come and set a while," he offered. "Have you had breakfast?"

"I ate about an hour ago," Roth answered, stepping up on the porch. "I spent the night with a friend of mine who lives over on the next hill. Name of Sate Margruder. You know him?"

Juliana felt her face blanch, and she winced at the roaring that arose in her head. As from a distance she heard John answer, "I know him to see him. He's kind of a lone wolf, according to Battle, and very handy with that knife he has strapped to his waist." Roth grinned and nodded and John added, "Battle said he bought the papers to one of his bondswomen."

"He's got one up there." Roth shifted uneasily, then glanced at Juliana's bent head. "I suppose he feels like most men; if you have a cabin, you need a woman to take care of it."

It was all Juliana could do not to strike her brother when he grinned knowingly and suggested, "Not to mention taking care of some other things."

Her hands clenched in the folds of her skirt as she followed the two men onto the porch.

The subject of Sate Margruder was dropped as Molly came through the door, the ever-ready pot of coffee in her hand. "Ah, Miz Nemeth," Roth said, smiling. "How are you this fine morning?"

"I'm fine, Roth," Molly returned amiably, unhooking a finger from the handles of four tin cups, then filling them with the aromatic brew. "What brings you in?" she asked, passing the coffee around. "I didn't expect to see you in these parts so soon."

Roth's eyes flickered briefly to Juliana. Then, speaking slowly, choosing his words carefully, he answered, "I came . . . hopefully . . . to get something that was . . . beyond my having the last time I was here."

Molly sent him a searching glance before sitting down next to John. "Well, I hope your desire is still not beyond you." She smiled.

"So do I, Miz Nemeth," Roth answered fervently, "so do I."

"What part of the country do you come from, Roth?" John asked, spooning sugar into his coffee. "Is it as settled as in these parts?"

"Hardly, John." Roth smiled wryly. "From where my cabin sits a man could travel through unbroken forest for twenty miles in any direction."

"I take it you're not afraid of the Indian trouble everyone is talking about."

"Naw, me and the Indians get along fine." Two lines appeared between Roth's eyes and he added, "At least until now."

"What is your opinion of what we hear of another uprising? Do you think it's all talk, or will they go after us again?"

"It's hard to say." Roth gazed out over the valley. "I know that the British in Canada are feedin' them whiskey and urgin' them to war on us." He glanced at Molly. "It wouldn't hurt to have your wife make you some extra bullets."

Molly turned to John. "I hefted your shot pouch yesterday, and it felt heavy enough to fight a full-fledged war."

"I may just have to do that," John said grimly.

"Would Nemus fight against us?" Juliana looked in the direction of the old Indian's camp. "He's so friendly to us."

John shook his head. "Nemus's tribe wants to live in peace, as do several others. It's the Pennacook tribe, who in my opinion have no desire to peace. It's them we must watch." He gave Juliana's hand a comforting pat. "Don't look so scared, sis, if there's an uprising Nemus will warn us in plenty of time to get down to the village with the others."

"He's right." Molly smiled reassuringly at the younger girl. "I'm not worried in the least."

"Me neither," Juliana said bravely, making herself smile. "I have complete confidence in Nemus."

"Thanks, sister." John reached behind Molly and gave Juliana's hair a tug that made her squeal. "Thanks for your faith in my ability to take care of you."

Juliana laughed at his pretended hurt. "Well, after all, you are a city fellow," she quipped, then turned to Molly. "How do you make bullets? And why do you have to make them?"

Molly shrugged. "It's always been the woman's job. I guess because it takes a delicate touch to pour the hot metal into such small round molds. When they've cooled we women seem able to file them more smoothly than the men can." She grinned at Juliana. "I'll show you how tomorrow."

The women grew silent and the men talked on. Juliana found herself watching the movement of Roth's lips and remembering their firm softness against her own. She wondered what it would be like to share with him the ultimate culmination the meeting of their lips had kindled. Would he be rough and masterful, or gentle and wholly giving of himself?

Deeply immersed in her musings, it was some time before Juliana became aware that Molly motioned to her from the door. She rose and entered the cabin, wondering guiltily if her thoughts had been read.

"Julie, you're actin' like a love-sick calf," her friend hissed, pulling her away from the door. "Have you forgotten that Roth Adams is a married man? Now don't go fallin' in love with him."

"Love, Molly?" Juliana lifted surprised eyes. "Of course I'm not falling in love with him. Caring for another woman's man is a worry I don't need right now. But"—she gave Molly a sideways glance—"I confess to being drawn to him, even though I fight it." An embarrassed flush colored her face. "He makes me think very wicked thoughts."

Molly's white teeth showed in her wide smile.

"You don't seem surprised," Juliana said.

"I'm not. That big handsome man could coax any woman into thinkin', and doin', wicked things." She pushed Juliana toward the door. "Go on back outside. I just wanted to remind you that he belongs to someone else, to save you hurt."

A part of Juliana agreed that Molly's counsel was right. Roth Adams did belong to another woman, and as such was forbidden to her. But . . . "Molly"—she moistened her lips nervously—"would it be so terribly wrong of me to snatch at a small piece of happiness even though it would be of short duration? Would I really be taking something away from his wife if she were ignorant of me doing it?"

Anxiety clouded her eyes. "What if I'm so weak I can't help myself?"

Compassion flickered in Molly's wise eyes. Here was a young woman who had never known the joys a man's body could give her. Being healthy and vibrant it was only natural that nature demand that she did. And a man of Roth Adams's caliber, handsome and fully sexed, was a lure she could very well be helpless to resist.

She answered the question in the same serious vein it had been asked. "Juliana, who am I to say what is wrong or right? I guess you could say that John and I are takin' our happiness dishonestly. Of course the Indian woman won't be hurt by somethin' she knows nothin' about. But it's you I'm thinkin' about.

"Would a night spent with Roth two or three times a year be enough for you? I think not. I believe that you're a woman who would object strongly to sharin' your man."

Juliana sighed raggedly. "You're right, of course. Still, I'm afraid that if he asks me I won't think of the tomorrows."

Molly shook her head sadly as Juliana went through the door.

Juliana no sooner returned to the porch and sat down beside Roth than John stood up. "Roth, come on out to the barn and see my new colt," he invited.

Damn you, John, she thought irritably, then relaxed in a warm glow, catching the quick look that Roth shot her. It said that he'd rather be with her, and that somehow he'd manage to do so.

But with the exception of a fast lunch, Juliana didn't see Roth the rest of the day. At the end of the meal John had laughingly remarked, "We don't want to be around here when the 'thundering herd' begins to arrive, Roth. Let's go down to the tavern and have some ale."

Again she had to be satisfied with the silent message of regret he sent her with his eyes. But that comfort wasn't complete. Many times as she rolled out dough for the pies, Sate's lean, handsome face entered her mind's eye. By the time three o'clock rolled around, she was mentally exhausted from battling her recollections.

Juliana thought that the stream of men would never stop coming through the door. Actually, there were no more customers than usual, but it seemed that each man lingered a little longer today, had excuses to talk a little more. If Molly hadn't, in a few cases, escorted some of them to the door, they would have stayed indefinitely.

Finally the last man handed in his tin in exchange for a fresh dessert and headed back toward the village. "I wonder if Roth will come back with John," Molly said as she bustled about, sliding the pie plates into a pan of hot water to be washed along with the supper dishes.

"I'm going to set a place for him just in case," Juliana said, setting the table.

Molly lifted the lid from a large dutch oven and with a long-pronged fork tested the roast steaming inside it for tenderness. "This is ready," she said, then took up a stick and raked several potatoes from beneath glowing red coals. She then stood up and walked to the window.

"Here they come." She smiled over her shoulder at Juliana. "Do you think Roth will enjoy our cooking for a change?" She walked back to the fireplace and removed a pan of corn bread left on the hearth to keep warm. "He's bound to be a little tired of wild-game stew."

Juliana moved to the window to watch the approaching men.

"I must say that whatever his Indian wife feeds him, it seems to agree with him. His body is as lean and firm as . . ." Oh, God, she had almost said "Sate's." ". . . John's," she inserted after only a moment's hesitation.

"Yes," Molly agreed, scoring the corn bread, "and that's part of his attraction, you know." She came and stood beside Juliana, and together they watched the pair enter the small patch of grass that Molly called her yard. "Have you come to a decision about him, Juliana?" she asked quietly.

"No." Juliana smiled hesitantly. "It's possible, you know, that we're putting the cart before the horse. The occasion for a decision on my part may not arise. Maybe he just enjoys the company of the Nemeth family."

"Hah!" Molly hooted. "You know better. That man's eyes eat you up every time he looks at you."

When Roth followed John into the cabin, his gray eyes going straight to Juliana, she thought with a pleasant shiver that Molly wasn't far wrong. His intense gaze did seem to devour her.

The four took seats at the table, and John beamed proudly as Roth praised Molly's roast. Molly sent her man a slumberous look, and when supper was over Juliana wasn't surprised when the yellow-haired woman suggested that Roth take her for a walk.

"John and I will clean up everything," she said when Juliana looked at the table laden with dirty dishes. "Go on." She pushed them toward the door.

Outside, Roth took Juliana's arm and, as they stepped off the porch, he remarked laughingly, "I don't think we're gonna be able to do much walkin' with night almost upon us. Molly must think that we're livin' in some big town."

Juliana smiled. "I think she's only interested in being alone with John. They're so in love, I always feel in the way." She gave Roth's arm a small tug. "Let's walk over to the spring. It's real pretty and restful there."

They walked along the banks of the swift-running stream, and followed its course to a small cave. The cold, clear water turned and twisted among large rocks and smooth boulders before disappearing into a deep cleft in the granite. Roth removed his woolen shirt and, spreading it on a flat rock, helped Juliana to sit down. The evening air was a little sharp, and when he seated himself beside her, Juliana unconsciously scooted closer to the warmth of his body. Roth's arms came naturally around her waist, snuggling her into his shoulder.

"Tell me about yourself, Roth." Juliana glanced up at him. "Where do you come from, and why it is you don't look or act like a farmer."

Roth laughed softly and laid his head on top of hers. "Well, let's see," he began. "I'm originally from Boston. My mother died giving birth to me forty years ago. When I was seventeen my father died from an Indian arrow. I was on my own then, and when I was twenty or so, I picked up with a gambler in New Orleans. He taught me all there is to know about games of chance.

"One day after a night of exceptionally good luck at cards we pooled our winnin's and bought a tavern." He paused and settled his head more firmly on hers as he gazed unseeing into the gathering darkness. "I'll pass over the next seventeen years. I'm not proud of most of it, and certainly it's not fit tellin' for your tender ears.

"At any rate, when my partner caught a bullet in the back, I took off with no particular destination in mind. I ended up here, in Kentucky territory. I built myself a cabin and took myself a wife."

He grinned down at the bright head resting lightly on his shoulder. "End of story. Now, do you want to tell me yours?"

Juliana shrugged. "Why not?" And I'll be leaving out a part of my past, too, she thought as she began.

With the exception of Sate's short appearance in her life, and her expected baby, Juliana went through her history from the death of her parents to the present time. When she had come to the part about her marriage Ruth had interrupted her.

"I wondered about the difference in your and John's last name." He bent his head and studied her face. "You still look as untouched as a young girl."

I am, practically, Juliana thought gloomily, as far as my experience in lovemaking goes. Unless my dreams count, especially the one I had that night in Sate's cabin. That one was so real I can still remember every detail of it.

They had been sitting quietly, each lost in their own thoughts, when the throaty baying of a hound drifted from a distant ridge.

"That's Sate Margruder's hound," Roth observed softly, tilting his head to listen. "He's scared himself up a coon."

So Hawser is still with him. Juliana remembered with a tug in her heart the big, deep-chested dog. *Too bad your master's affection for me wasn't as true as yours, old fellow.*

A dull, heavy throbbing began in her heart when Roth said, "I wonder if Sate and Bessy are sittin' on the porch listenin' to his song."

Juliana swallowed a few times, then said tonelessly, "Most likely."

After a moment Roth's soft voice broke into the despair that was closing in on her. "Juliana, since the first time I saw you I've dreamed of such a moment, but never in my wildest dreams did I ever think it would happen."

Juliana grew still at the tenderly spoken words. *Don't take his charming utterance too seriously,* she warned herself. *There's still that wife tucked away.*

She put some distance between them and pointed out, "What you're talking about shouldn't be happening now, Roth, you know that. I'm not going to be a part of doing your wife a cruel wrong."

Roth's arms tightened, pulling her back against him. "In my thoughts we have wronged her many times already." His lean fingers grasped her chin and turned her head to face him. Gazing into her eyes he whispered hoarsely, "Juliana, haven't you thought of me in that way just a little?"

"It wouldn't matter if I did." Juliana pulled her face free, not about to admit to the stomach-weakening thought she had harbored of his hard body pressing hers. "You are not free and that puts an end to it."

"Look, Juliana, I'm not so vain as to think that every woman who looks at me immediately wants to jump into my bed. But I did feel a pulling between us that first day, and I still feel it."

Juliana squelched the voice of reason that warned, "You're courting heartache again," when she asked herself the question she had put to Molly earlier. If she gave into what Roth was hinting at would she be taking something from his wife? And what about her unborn child? As it grew older it would look to her for guidance. It would be up to her to teach it all things pertaining to morality. How could she do that if her own morals were suspect?

Again she pulled away from Roth, clasping her hands in her

lap. She said quietly, "I'm ashamed to admit it, Roth, but yes, I have thought of you . . . us—"

"Juliana!" Roth broke in with a raspy sigh, drawing her back against him, "I have ridden two days to hear you say that."

Juliana stirred against the arm held firmly around her waist and warned, "That's as far as it goes, Roth. Only thinking."

Roth's arm held her more tightly. "If I were free, Juliana, would you marry me?"

Juliana's fast, searching glance at his face showed her that Roth was serious. Her voice held reproach when she asked, "Roth, did you leave Zoe because of me?"

"No, Juliana. As much as I love you, want you, I couldn't have done that to my wife. She would lose face with her people, and in the end would have thrown herself over a cliff." A sad bitterness clouded Roth's eyes. "Zoe is dead, Juliana."

Juliana started, and cried sincerely, "Oh, Roth, I am so sorry. What happened?"

As Roth related Zoe's fate, Juliana remembered Chad Madison and her immediate distrust of him. She shivered, wondering what cruelty he might have done the squaw, Doxy. Was she also dead?

"So"—Roth's deep voice brought her back—"I'm free, and I'm askin' you to marry me."

Juliana could only stare at Roth, even though she couldn't make out his features in the night. Marriage was the one thing she and Molly hadn't thought or talked about. Could it work between them? It was true they shared a strong attraction, but would it grow to love on her part? The image of a lean, dark face entered her mind, and she doubted it. She loved Sate too deeply, too completely.

And the baby—my God, she had forgotten the baby. She leaned away from Roth again and sighed raggedly. "Roth, there's something I must tell you. And when I have, you may want to retract your offer of marriage." Roth gave a snort, as if to say there was nothing she could tell him that would change his mind about her.

But he sat so still for so long after she explained about the baby that Juliana's shoulders sagged dispiritedly. As she thought, he didn't want to raise another man's child. Then a rough brown finger tenderly wiped away a tear that had spilled down her cheek.

"Ah, Juliana," he said softly, "for a long time I have wanted a child. Zoe couldn't have one so I had put the wish from my mind. You couldn't give me a dearer wedding gift."

"Oh, Roth," Juliana cried and threw herself in his arms. A peacefulness she hadn't known in a long time settled over her as his strong arms enfolded her.

The moon rose and they sat in its light, planning their future. They would marry as soon as possible, then Roth would take Juliana to his homestead. He picked up her hand and kissed its palm. "I want you so much, Juliana," he whispered, "but I want to wait until we're married. I know it sounds crazy, but it will make the child seem more like mine if we do it like that."

While Juliana struggled to speak over the tears choking her throat, he rose, pulling her up with him. "Let's go tell John and Molly our good news."

CHAPTER 13

~~~

The torture in Sate's mind was exquisite as he walked the hills. One moment he was sure Juliana wouldn't accept Roth's proposal of marriage. In the next breath he was just as sure she would. The older man's experience and smooth ways would sway her.

The sun sunk lower and lower and he didn't notice until the gloom of the forest made him aware. His shadow reached far ahead of him as with a sigh he began to slowly retrace his steps.

The evening meal was a silent one. One look at Sate's dark, glowering face, and Bessy quickly lapsed into silence. It was a great relief to her when he drank the last of his coffee and pushed himself away from the table. He's like a copperhead ready to strike, she thought, watching him leave the cabin. The hound stirred, sniffed the air a second, then took off after his master.

Sate arrived at the tavern, and as he tied Jake to the long hitching post the usual low rumble of voices drifted from inside. He stepped through the open door to lean against the wall, suddenly not sure he wanted to be here. The atmosphere of easy laughter and good fellowship did not match his dark mood.

He glumly watched the two bondswomen scurry from tables to bar, serving up drinks, half-heartedly and with high giggles avoiding the searching hands that reached out to them. Battle moved up and down the bar, talking constantly as he poured ale or rum.

Finally Sate pushed away from the wall and weaved his way through the tables and customers until he stood at the end of the bar. Maybe if he drank enough he could at least gain a momentary forgetfulness.

A wide grin settled over Battle's face when he spotted Sate. The first words out of his mouth when he slapped a bottle in front of him were, "Well, friend, you've waited too long. Our Heller is marryin' an outsider. Name of Roth Adams. Tom Nemeth just introduced him to me a half hour ago." Splashing rum into a mug, he added, "Seems to be a right nice feller, and mighty good-lookin'."

The bartender's words beat at Sate's mind like the measured whack of an axe against the trunk of a tree. He cursed himself bitterly for not having the courage to follow Roth and plead his own case with Juliana. His pent-up breath whistled through his lips as Battle was called to the other end of the bar. One more word out of the jovial man and he might have caught a fist in the mouth. He didn't have to be reminded that Roth Adams had his charms. Bessy was still crying over the man.

The night wore on and Sate emptied one glass after another. And though his limbs grew lax, his thoughts remained sharp and clear, intensifying his loss. It wasn't long before his dark mood turned sullen and aggressive. Those around him gradually drew away until at last he stood alone with his bottle. They remembered well the night this wild man hit Squaw Hollow. To tangle with him was like fighting a bear or a wildcat.

It was close to midnight when, unable to stand the laughter and hilarity another minute, Sate pushed himself away from the bar and stalked outside. Jake winnied a welcome, eager to return to his stall. Hawser wagged his tail, then bound away as his master climbed into the saddle and, lifting the reins, turned his back on the raucous voices coming from the tavern.

Bessy was asleep in her corner when Sate entered the cabin and made his way to the small bedroom. He sat down on the edge of the bed, then stretched out on his back. He lay staring into the darkness, hollow with longing for Juliana. What was he to do? He asked the question over and over. It would be impossible for him to stay in Squaw Hollow. To see her and Roth together as man and wife would tear him apart.

Sate never knew at what time during that long night he reached a decision, but when the first light of day came through the uncurtained window he rose stiffly from the bed, a firm resolve in his features.

In the main room, still in gray shadow, he rekindled the fire, and by its light he dug a pair of saddlebags from a chest in the corner and flopped them on the table. Bessy's light snoring choked off a moment, then resumed as he moved about, filling the bags with dried deer meet, parched corn, dried apples, and the remains of corn bread left over from the evening meal.

He sat the bags beside the door where his rifle leaned, then brought his bedroll to lie beside them. He returned to the small trunk and lifted the lid. He rummaged around inside a moment, then pulled out a sheet of paper. Straightening up he walked over to Bessy's bed and shook her shoulder. She jerked awake, gasping, "What is it?"

Sate shoved the paper at her and she leaned up on an elbow to take it. "What is it?" she asked again, peering up at him before looking down at the white square of parchment.

"It's your papers," he answered gruffly.

"But why?" Bessy gaped at him, hope flaring in her eyes.

"I have no need of them," Sate said, rising to his feet. "Get up. I want to talk to you. It's important that you're wide awake and understand fully what I have to say."

Bessy scrambled out of bed, and her trembling excitement was transmitted to her fingers as she awkwardly pulled the homespun dress over her head. She hurriedly took a seat opposite Sate and looked at him expectantly, noting the dark shadows under his eyes and the lines of strain around his mouth.

"I'm goin' away," Sate said quickly. "Into Canada, I think I don't know when I'll return . . . If ever. What I want you to do is take the stallion and hound over to Battle. He'll take good care of them."

He stood up and moved to the door. Slinging the saddlebags over his shoulder, and picking up the bedroll and rifle, he looked back at Bessy who had risen and was staring at him in dumb amazement. "You can stay here a few days while you make other arrangements."

The door closed quietly behind Sate, and while the dog whined piteously to follow his master, and even the stallion gave a shrill neigh, a ringing laugh erupted from Bessy's throat. "Shut up, hound." She nudged Hawser with a foot. "You might as well forget him. He won't never be back. And me"—she danced around the room—"my luck has changed. I've not only got my freedom, I've also got a stout cabin and farm to go with it."

Sate heard Bessy's gleeful expressions of mirth as he walked rapidly down the hill toward the river, thinking, I never did like the idea of owning a person.

The river was wide and swift this time of the year and Sate felt a rush of excitement as he hauled the canoe from its cover of brush and tall ferns. What had prompted him to buy it from the young Indian lad a few days ago? he wondered, running admiring eyes over the craft. Despite its fragile appearance it was sturdy. Constructed from the thick bark of the mighty oak, it would ride easily and lightly on the swiftest of streams.

He tossed his gear and grub into the vessel, then, giving the canoe a shove, it was adrift. He leaped nimbly over the bow to the seat spanning the middle. The craft floated a moment while he picked up the oar and dipped it into the water. With deep sweeps he edged it into the current and glided downstream, north, toward Canada.

With each dip of the oar the canoe was lifted, sending ripples along its side. Silently the vessel slipped past Nemus's small encampment situated on the wild and foggy bank. Viewing it, the lines of bitterness around Sate's lips deepened. "Watch over her for me, old man," he whispered.

The sun rose, burning off the mists, promising a hot and humid day. A couple of hours later a fine film of sweat covered Sate's skin and he allowed the canoe to drift a while with the current. But inactivity released his mind to dwell on Juliana. He was almost thankful when he rounded a bend in the river and saw a great brown bear swiping at fish in the shallows. He grimaced. The thought of tangling with that brute, especially in deep water, would take a man's mind off anything.

The broken mass of gray storm clouds that had gathered in the north opened up around noon. The rain slashed down on Sate's bare head and ran down the collar of his open shirt. He hunched his shoulders against its sting and worried about the pouch of gunpowder hanging at his waist. If it wasn't wet, it was at least damp and, consequently, worthless.

"Pray God," he muttered, "I don't run into a bunch of Indians. The weather doesn't affect their bows, arrows, and tomahawks."

The rain slackened as the day wore on, and had completely

stopped when Sate brought the canoe ashore for the night. A heavy fog was rising along the river when he crawled beneath the shelter of a large, ground-hugging cedar.

It was while munching his supper of dried meat and corn that he felt the queer tightness growing between his shoulder blades. He was being watched, he was sure.

His hand firmly grasped his knife as he rose slowly to his feet. As he waited, breath held, a great flock of teal ducks skittered from the river and flapped wildly through the trees. Even before he saw the half-naked forms rise out of the reeds and heard the first savage yell, he had known what had startled the fowl.

There were six of them and in seconds Sate was fighting desperately for his life. He ground his teeth against the pain of a blow to his head and fought on, his body acting automatically. He gripped a sinewy body and wrestled it to the ground even as warm blood dripped from the cut on his head, running into his eyes. But he had not time to react when the back of a tomahawk slammed against his head. His long body shuddered and lay in a senseless heap.

A dull throbbing in his temple and a hot, bright light on his face was Sate's first awareness of returning reality. Realization sharpened when he tried to move and found his arms bound securely to a tree.

"Damn red heathens," he grunted, blinking against the sun.

What tribe? he wondered, raising his hand, gritting his teeth against the pain the movement caused in his head. A big one, he decided, for teepees stretched beyond his vision and there had to be at least a hundred barking dogs and laughing children running about. A permanent village, he would say.

Sate's stomach rumbled loudly and saliva formed in his mouth as the aroma of roasting meat teased his nostrils. He squinted at the sun, gauging its high position in the sky, and gave a grim laugh. No wonder he had this empty feeling in his gut; he hadn't eaten since last evening. He swept his gaze over the area, searching for the source of the tantalizing odor.

Surprisingly, the cookfire was only a few yards away, slightly behind his right shoulder. Craning his head and neck he watched three squaws who tended a haunch of deer meat suspended over a bed of glowing coals. One of the women was young, the other two middle-aged.

The young one looks familiar, he thought. Although long braids covered most of her face, there was something about her movements he felt he had watched before. "By God, it's Doxy," he whispered when the girl lifted her head and looked directly at him.

Would she help him? His brow wrinkled thoughtfully. Her expression had told him nothing. He tried to remember if she was one who had showed a leaning toward him, or if she was one of those who had been interested only in food and a warm place to sleep.

As he mused on his last parting with Doxy, trying to recall its tenor, a shadow fell over his face. He raised his head and blinked at the stocky form of an Indian standing over him, a sharp-bladed knife gripped in his hand. This is it, he thought, bracing himself for the forceful plunge of the blade into his heart. Dreamlike, he saw the brave bend over him and, sighing he called Juliana's image to his mind.

The lovely mental picture evaporated as the rawhide strips fell away from his body and his arms dropped to his sides. While he struggled with his surprise, he was jerked to his feet and roughly propelled forward. He stumbled along in his weakness, a stiff finger directing his way by jabbing first one shoulder and then the other.

Sate knew his feet could not obey the impulse of his brain much longer. His steps were staggering from pain and hunger. He was clinging to consciousness with clenched teeth when he was abruptly tripped and brought to his knees.

He swayed a moment, fighting the fuzziness in his brain, then brought his eyes to focus on several Indians sitting cross-legged in a semicircle. And though it was the eagle-eyed chief that held his attention, he was still aware of the hostility radiating from the others.

Several tense moments passed, then, as though he were of no importance, the hooded eyes looked away from Sate. The conversation his arrival had interrupted was picked up and he eased himself back on his heels. The red man could talk for hours on one subject. Sometimes about something like why owls only hoot at night.

Sate's tensed again when the chief turned to him suddenly and demanded, "What brings you to Red Feather's territory? What government man sent you to spy on me and my braves?"

Taken by surprise at the sudden question, he could only stare into the cold, fierce eyes of the Indian leader. His mind asked if this was one of the tribes he traveled to fight, and if so why they were camped so close to Squaw Hollow.

But were they all that close to the village? He had been unconscious as they traveled and had no way of knowing whether his captors had gone over land or by river. Many miles could be eaten on the water.

A hard fist to Sate's face rocked his head, sending fire exploding in his brain. "I spy on no one," he managed to get out. "I was on my way home when your braves set upon me."

The words were barely out of his mouth when once again he was struck on the face. And though he took the blow across the cheek, he allowed his head to move only a little. If he should show the slightest weakness, the whole tribe would be upon him like a flock of buzzards. When Red Feather said, "You lie, you were following my braves," he stared stonily at the man, refusing to answer. From the corners of his eyes he saw the brave lift a foot, and he braced himself to receive its kick.

The blow was arrested in midair by a low, keening sound. Hope blazed in Sate's eyes as, turning his head, he saw Doxy spring to her feet and run to kneel before Red Feather. Bowing her head and clasping her hands together she began to speak rapidly in her native tongue. He listened closely, trying to hear a familiar word, but there was none. He could only wait and watch.

It was clear to him, however, that the chief did not wholly believe Doxy's words. Several times he grunted suspiciously, sending her into renewed speech, renewed urgency. And while Sate watched with held breath he was filled suddenly with self-deriding mirth. Why did he wait so hopefully? For all he knew the girl had been begging for his death all this time.

Then the chief shook his head and he knew by the satisfied grunts around him that Doxy had pleaded for his life. With an inward sigh, he squared his shoulders and set his jaw. The heathens would set about torturing him now, and he'd be damned if they drew one cry of pain from him.

Sate was so deep in gathering his courage to withstand what awaited him, it took a minute before he realized that Doxy hadn't given up. Her head bowed to the ground now, she spoke through streaming tears. Women and children had joined the men and everyone looked on with admiration. The young squaw was putting on a fine performance. Some whispered to each other that she was even better than the medicine man.

Sate, however, found nothing amusing in Doxy's action. His life depended on the strength of her argument, whatever it might be. He slid a glance at the chief's face, hoping to see a sign of hope. But the proud countenance showed only that he, too, was enjoying Doxy's artistry, her humble posture before him.

At last Red Feather leaned forward and laid a hand on her shaking shoulders. He spoke quietly for a moment, then Doxy said a word and he nodded solemnly. Smiling faintly, she rose and left the circle. A deep growl went through the braves as they stared darkly after her.

Sate also stared after her. Was he free to go? He looked back at the chief and found the man staring at him as though to read his mind. With a suddenness that startled him, Red Feather waved a dirty hand toward a nearby teepee and grunted, "Go. Smiling Waters waits for you."

Weak with relief, Sate was very conscious of the brave who stalked behind him as he made his way to the designated deerhide domicile, and wasn't surprised when the man took up a squatting position only feet away. He shrugged. He couldn't escape now, but there would come a time. . . .

He found Doxy kindling a fire in a stone-walled hole in the center of the room. He studied her face by the leaping flames and was instantly on guard. There was a smugness to the set of her lips and he was reminded of her vindictive streak. Narrowing his eyes at her, he asked coolly, "What were you sayin' to Red Feather?"

Doxy sat back on her heels and, watching him through her lashes, said, "I told him that you were my man."

Sate nodded. "That's what I figured." He smiled at her and added, "I won't forget what you've done for me. When I get out of here I'll see that you get handsomely paid."

A sly smile played on Doxy's lips as she pulled a black pot over the fire. Frowning, Sate studied her through slitted lids. The girl had her own pelt to stretch. He nudged her with a foot. "Did you hear me, Doxy?" he growled. "I said I would pay you well for helpin' me, once I get away from here."

Doxy rose and walked to a pail of water on the dirt floor. Picking up a gourd dipper and filling a basin with water, she said, "We will talk about that after you have washed the blood off your face and had something to eat."

Sate started to protest, to demand that they talk now, but he was too weak and hungry to argue about it. After he had bathed his bewhiskered face, he wolfed the stew down like the starving man he was. Doxy watched him, her expression inscrutable.

Though his knife and rifle had been taken from him, Sate's pipe and tobacco pouch still hung at his waist. When the clay bowl had been tamped full with the crumbled brown leaf and a live coal set on top it, he sat back and looked at Doxy expectantly. "Well?"

Doxy stood up and slouched over to the narrow opening in the teepee. After poking her head out and peering to either side, she dropped the flap and returned to the fire. Kneeling in front of Sate, she said flatly, "First, you are not going anywhere, not ever, unless I say so." She watched his stony face a moment, then continued, "As to payment for my good deed, I will decide what that will be, not you." Her square-fingered hand came out to stroke his thigh. "From now on, trapper," she murmured softly, "each night you will make love to me, but not as you used to. You will do it the way you loved the white bitch. You will make me call out as I lay beneath your body. You will kiss me all over, as you did her."

Sate stared at the defiant squaw so long that she stirred uncomfortably. But when he threw back his head and loud, degrading laughter rolled from his muscular throat her face turned sullen, and angry sparks gathered in her eyes. When Sate stopped for breath, she hissed, "Laugh all you want, but tonight you do as I say, or tomorrow you burn at the stake."

Without warning Sate's hand shot out and fastened in her hair. Jerking her within inches of his face he ground out, "You dumb bitch. Don't you know that you'll burn right beside me? What do you think Red Feather is gonna do when you tell him that you lied? Do you think he'll take kindly to your making a fool of him in front of his people?"

Doxy whimpered in pain and fear. Her scheming hadn't taken her that far in advance. The smile she pulled to her lips was only a grimace as she wheedled, "I was only teasing you. I don't need you to lay with me. I have a brave who does that real good."

Sate frowned. "From now on you stay away from your

buck. It would go bad for us if the chief should hear of you foolin' around with another man.'' He knew from the alarm that showed on Doxy's face he wouldn't have to warn her again. She knew better than he the cruel punishment the Indian was capable of handing out.

He stood up and began to undress. "You can sleep with me tonight. I expect your chief will check our sleeping arrangements in the mornin'; make sure that you didn't lie to him.''

CHAPTER 14

~~~~~~~~~~

Juliana's eyes opened slowly and focused on the small gray square of the window. Still drowsing, she wondered what was causing the pattering noise outside. She leaned up on an elbow, then, groaning, threw herself back down. The soft slash of rain was hitting the roof in a steady beat.

"My wedding day is ruined," she moaned.

She lay staring at the gloom of the approaching dawn, trying to convince herself that it didn't matter whether it rained or whether the sun shone brightly. The important thing was that she and Roth would become husband and wife today.

Her thoughts remained on the man she would marry that afternoon. He loved her, she knew; not only had he declared it, his every action had shown it also.

But—she drew a long breath—she couldn't say that word to him. She had tried, tried desperately. Each time, however, Sate's face had swum before her and the words stuck in her throat. If Roth had noticed the omission, he'd made no mention of it. She imagined that he probably interpreted her strong attraction to him as love.

Wasn't desire calling to desire a solid ground from which a marriage could flourish? Juliana wondered hopefully. It was a very important part at least; she had learned that from living with John and Molly. Their loving nights together seemed to last through the following day, overshadowing any little argument that might come up between them.

There was a lessening of Juliana's anxiety as she mentally numerated Roth's good qualities. He was kind and considerate, and promised to be a wonderful lover. But more important, he was giving her unborn child his name.

A pensive frown marred her forehead. Would Roth be too good to her, give in to her too readily? She hoped not. She would hate being mollified and catered to as though she were a child. Having a strong mind of her own, she expected the same of her mate; to argue heatedly if he thought the occasion merited it. Sate would have given her a good argument if he felt justified, she knew.

Juliana's eyes flashed bitterly as a small inner voice taunted, "But Sate didn't ask you to marry him. He only threw ugly accusations at you; he never even hinted that he loved you."

"Oh, shut up!" Juliana cried miserably and buried her face in the pillow.

The soft thud of bare feet hitting the floor overhead brought Juliana over onto her back. John was getting up, and Molly would soon follow. She wiped at her eyes with the heels of her hands. She must not let those two see a tear-stained face on this most important day of her life. Neither knew about Sate, and both would wonder at her tears.

I wish they were getting married today, Juliana thought as she watched her brother light a candle, then turn to building a fire in the fireplace. The image of Iva's stern face appeared before her, and she knew that only the death of the woman would ever set John free to marry his Molly.

Iva is older than him, Juliana mused. She might . . .

There were distinct voices coming from outside, and Juliana sat up, pushing her sister-in-law from her mind. Swinging her feet to the floor, padding across to the window, she peered out, then gasped. Gathered in the yard, huddled under trees, were scores of people. It appeared that the entire settlement, along with Nemus and his small tribe, had traveled through the rain to attend her wedding. Stunned, she gazed fixedly at the striking contrast of the rich colors of the Indians' robes against the homesteaders' browns and grays.

Molly and John came up behind Juliana, and after one look through the small window, Molly exclaimed, "Good Lord, John, all of Squaw Hollow is out there. What are we gonna do? They can't all fit inside here."

John ran nervous hands through his hair. "Hell, Molly, I don't know. The crazy bastards, coming out in weather like this. Nobody invited them."

"Hush up, John." Molly frowned. "They've come to show their high regard for Juliana. Somehow we've got to make them feel welcome."

"If it wasn't for this damned rain," John groused, buttoning up his pants, "there would be no problem. The wedding and merrymaking could take place outside."

Glancing at the sheet of water sliding past the window, he concentrated on recalling who had the largest place in the village. When he joined the women around the fire, and began pulling on his socks and boots, he gave his sister's worried face an uncertain glance.

"Don't fret about it, Julie," he said. "I've thought of a solution." While Juliana and Molly waited with hopeful looks, he grinned widely. "I'm gonna take them all down to the tavern. Battle will feel honored having the wedding take place there."

A disapproving frown darkened Juliana's face. She opened her mouth to object, but Molly, helping John pull his shirt over his head, was exclaiming excitedly, "That's a splendid idea, John. His place is so big; we can dance and get as wild as we want." She clasped her hands on her waist. "Oh, it's just goin' to be grand."

Whose wedding is this? Juliana asked herself, her lips firming obstinately as John and Molly took over, planning the festivities. When John left the cabin to greet their guests and lead them down the hill, she said sharply, "Molly, I'm not sure I like the idea of being married in a tavern. It isn't seemly, somehow."

Molly picked up the coffee pot, and with an impatient sigh began filling it with water. "Juliana, as I've told you before, we do many things in the wilderness that don't look seemly." She sighed. "We do the best we can with what we have. The rain is pourin' down with no let-up in sight. Battle has the only place that will shelter so many people at once. There's no disgrace in being married in a tavern," she said firmly. "Why, even the Reverend holds services there when he visits the village, you know."

As she added coffee grounds to the water and set the pot on the fire, Molly continued in a gentler tone, "The important thing is you're gettin' married. Stop a minute and give me and John a think."

Juliana felt a pang of guilt assail her. How foolish and selfish she must have sounded to Molly. If it were possible, Molly would marry John in a barn.

"Oh, Molly, I am sorry." She put her arms around the shoulders that had suddenly drooped. "I didn't mean to sound so uppity. I sometimes forget that I'm not back in Philadelphia with all its rules and regulations."

"That's all right, Juliana." Molly turned back to her with a pert grin. "You can't help it that you were raised lady-like. Right now, though, we got more important things to think about. Like preparin' the food for that horde."

She flashed Juliana a wicked grin. "I never saw a man so eager to get his ring on a woman's finger. Roth's hurry ain't hardly decent."

"Oh, Molly." Juliana blushed. "He doesn't want to stay away from his place too long. He left his livestock in the care of some Indian lads, and he says that they're not always dependable."

Molly's eyes twinkled. "I guess that's as good an excuse as any."

"Molly, stop teasing me!" Juliana stamped a foot in feigned anger. "Now, let's be serious. What in the world are we going to feed all those people?"

"Well, actually"—Molly dropped into a chair—"I don't think we'll have to cook all that much. I'm pretty sure that each woman brought plenty of food along with her. The people around here are poor where money is concerned, but they do raise a lot of food. And you can bet all the hunters have been out scroungin' for game."

She chuckled lightly. "The women were probably up half the night, roastin' and bakin', tryin' to outdo each other." Juliana smiled, and Molly stood up. "I guess we'd better get crackin'."

An hour later, when John returned, the cabin was full of mouth-watering aromas. The wild turkey he had shot the day before was roasting in the oven, while several apple pies sat on the table waiting their turn in the oven.

"It's all set, Juliana." John stood before the fire, his soaking clothes steaming as they dried, a wide grin on his face. "Battle is pleased as can be that your big to-do will take place in his establishment. He's even supplying the ale. Said it was his wedding gift to you."

"Did you see Roth?" Molly asked.

"Yeah. When I left he was buying drinks for everybody." Juliana smiled. "And how is my husband-to-be?"

"Nervous as a cat." John chuckled dryly. "He confided that his other marriage had been performed by a French priest and that he hadn't understood a word of that fancy Latin. He said that since he would understand the preacher, he hoped he wouldn't faint and shame you."

The three laughed together, but Juliana broke in nervously, "I hope the preacher shows up in spite of all this rain."

"I forgot to tell you," John exclaimed with an impatient snap of his fingers. "I met the Reverend on my way home. Poor old fellow, he looked like a drowned rabbit."

"I just hope that Battle doesn't get him drunk," Molly remarked, checking the turkey. "He'd think that was a big joke."

Seeing the shocked uneasiness in his sister's face, John hastened to say, "Battle wouldn't do that to Juliana's wedding."

The morning wore on, finding the turkey done, golden on the outside, juicy-tender inside. The pies cooling on the table mingled their spicy aroma with the fowl's.

"I wonder if we should take the food with us when we go?" Molly wiped her flushed face. "The turkey is gonna be awful hot to handle."

"It's all taken care of." John looked up from polishing his dress boots. "Would you believe that Nemus volunteered to bring the food down to the tavern?" When Molly shook her head in amazement he added, "And some of the neighbor women offered to help him."

Molly's tickled laugh rang out. "Can you imagine that—a red savage and white women working together."

"It just goes to show how well you're liked around here, Julie." John smiled at his sister. "I'll bet old Nemus wouldn't lower himself like that for anybody else."

"Unless he likes the idea of being so close to all those apple pies." Juliana passed off the compliment, although a pleased flush stole over her face.

John laughingly agreed that she might be right. He glanced at the clock and said, "I guess it's time I get out to the barn and get the team and wagon ready."

Juliana watched the door close behind her brother, a spasm

of uncertainty gripping her. Was she doing the right thing? There were so many things she hadn't had time to consider closely.

Molly glanced at her and, sensing her young friend's nervousness, went over and sat on the arm of her chair. Putting her arms around the slender shoulders, she said softly, "You're a little afraid and unsure, huh, Julie? I expect it's only natural, but I'm sure it will pass. Roth is a fine man."

"I have no doubts about that." Juliana lifted troubled eyes. "It's me I'm worried about, living so far away from people. I'm afraid I'll never get used to it."

Molly hugged her gently. "If it gets too bad you can always talk Roth into comin' back here. I don't think there's much he'd refuse you."

When Juliana made no response, only sighed and looked away, Molly took hold of her delicate jaw and urged her head around so that she could look into her eyes again. "Something else is bothering you, Juliana. What is it?"

Juliana knew there was no point in denying the accusation. Molly could spot a lie as soon as it was uttered. She sighed again. "You're right. It bothers me greatly that for the second time I'm marrying a man I don't love."

Her voice trembled, near tears. "Each time circumstance has forced me into unwanted wedlock."

Molly ran soothing hands down Juliana's back. "I know, dear, but I truly believe that this time will be different for you. You can't compare Roth with Tom Roessler. It would be like comparing a tomcat to a kitten.

"I think that in time you will love Roth. Maybe not in a wild romantic way, but a warm, contented affection." Her eyes twinkled mischievously. "Think about the nights, when he holds you in his arms and makes love to you. You'll love that part." She pulled Juliana to her feet. "Go get dressed now. Everything is gonna be just fine, you'll see."

The dress Juliana and Molly had finally settled on, after carrying several down from the loft, was a light blue voile over a shimmering satin underskirt of a darker shade. As she pulled it over her head and settled the bodice over the sheer muslin of her underclothes, it molded to her breasts and rib cage, calling attention to the waist that was still trim and tiny. The bodice was low-cut, but Molly had stitched in a piece of lace that covered the tops of her increasingly rounded breasts.

"Oh, my, you look beautiful, Juliana." Molly's face appeared beside Juliana's in the wavy mirror as she pulled a brush through her pale curls. "Roth will just about die, waiting to get you alone."

"Well, what about John when he sees you?" Juliana turned around and ran admiring eyes over the pretty, smiling woman. "Green is certainly your color."

She had given Molly the gown of figured lace over a satin underdress of the same shade of green. She had worn it only once; it was slightly too big for her. The let-out seams Molly had spent half the night doing made it fit her more buxom figure perfectly.

"I never had anything so beautiful before," Molly said shyly, fingering the smooth material.

"You'll have lots of them someday." Juliana hugged her beloved friend. "My brother will see to it."

"Oh, I'm not yearning for fancy clothes, Juliana," Molly said earnestly. "I would be perfectly content to wear homespun the rest of my life if I could only have John's name and bear his children."

"You'll have that, too, Molly . . ."

Juliana's statement trailed away as squeaking wheels drew to a stop outside the cabin door and John's loud baritone ordered, "Come on, girls. We're gonna be late."

Slipping small satin bags over their wrists, the two each took hold of a corner of a cured brown bearskin and, holding it over their heads, opened the door and dashed to the wagon.

Molly held a corner of the fur over John's head as they made the short trip to the settlement. John said nothing, but his lips curved in good humor. He was already soaked to the skin.

Bright laughter and gay voices greeted the trio when they entered the tavern and tossed the skin aside. It had served its purpose well for the pair. Only lightly shod feminine feet were wet.

Busy shaking out her skirts, Juliana wasn't aware of Roth's approach until his hands grasped her arms. Desire glittered in his eyes as she gazed up at him. "I want you so terribly, I don't know how I'll get through the next few hours," he whispered hoarsely.

Then, taking her hand, Roth led her toward the preacher. John and Molly, their witnesses, followed close behind. Juliana was surprised to discover that Roth was as nervous as John had claimed. The palm clasped against hers was damp with perspiration.

In just moments, it seemed to Juliana, she was once again a married woman, and all the single men, and half the married ones, were pushing and shoving to kiss the bride's cheek. That some tried to find her lips was not unexpected. But each time she adroitly turned her cheek to them.

Nemus and his braves were the last to congratulate the newlyweds. One by one they solemnly shook hands with Roth and gravely nodded their heads to Juliana. She longed to hug Nemus, but knew she daren't. When he grunted to his companions and they moved away, she shifted her attention to the tavern whores who stood off by themselves in a corner. She caught them darting shy looks her way, and her heart went out to those women who, often through misfortune of some kind, had been forced into such a life.

She remembered Sate saying that very few women entered this profession because they wanted to. "The squaws do it for food and whiskey, and the white woman usually because she has no one who cares about her."

When Juliana caught the eye of one of the women, she smiled and nodded at her. The woman was so surprised that she could only stare back, her mouth gaping.

Juliana turned her head away from the "painted ladies" when Molly tugged on her sleeve. "Would you look at your wedding feast?" She nodded her head toward the back of the room. Juliana looked, and gasped. All the tables in the tavern had been placed end to end and now ran the length of the long room. Many different-colored tablecloths, from many different homes, covered their rough surfaces.

Good Lord, the food! Juliana drew in a long breath as she took in the large pewter platters heavily laden with roasts of every imaginable game, the wooden bowls of vegetables, and the jellies, jams, cakes, and pies crowded in between, not to mention the tall mounds of crusty bread.

It was plain that no housewife had come empty-handed. In her mind's eye she could see them place their efforts on the table with lofty pride. She ran her eyes over the work-worn figures who had labored long hours for her. In their coarse homespun dresses, they stood shyly about, stealing wistful glances at her fancy wedding dress. She imagined that many had never seen such a garment before.

Suddenly Juliana felt like crying. She didn't want to leave these plain and simple people. They would make good friends and neighbors, something she wouldn't have when she moved to her new and isolated home. The doubts of this morning began to assail her again. But before she got too deeply embedded in them, she was drawn out of her troubled thoughts by a loud, rather coarse, laugh.

Her eyes sought the source of the laugh and she gazed at a plump, rosy-cheeked woman whose pale brown hair frizzed around her sharp-eyed face. The compact body moved among the crowd, laughing and joking and flirting familiarly with the men.

Intuitively Juliana knew that the woman's carefree display was put on either for her or Roth, or perhaps both of them. Amused, she watched her steady progress toward her and Roth. It was only when she stood by their side, a hand placed intimately on Roth's shoulder, that she recognized the bondswoman.

Her heart racing, Juliana quickly scanned the room, searching for a tall, lean frame. Had Sate come to see her married? When she failed to see him anywhere, she turned her attention back to the woman, and what she was saying. "I'm happy the lady said yes, Roth," Bessy was simpering.

But the bondswoman wasn't happy about it, Juliana saw at once. The eyes shimmered with unshed tears, and the full lips trembled slightly. I've made myself another enemy, she thought, sending a searching look at her new husband. Was he aware that this woman was in love with him?

No. Roth was oblivious to the unhappiness in the fawning eyes. He casually patted the hand on his arm. "Thank you, Bessy. Where is my friend, Sate? Didn't he come to see me get married?"

"Oh, him." Bessy swallowed hard, tossing her head. "You know how he is. He took off last night. Said he didn't know if he'd ever come back." Flashing a sly look at Juliana, she added, "I think he's hurtin' over some woman."

Roth nodded gravely. "Yeah, Margruder is carryin' a grief. I knew that the first time I met him."

Bessy shrugged indifferently, her small eyes slanting Juliana a cunning sidewise glance. "Don't waste your sympathy on the big trapper," she said. "By now he's found himself a squaw and is bedded down with her in some cave."

While Juliana almost gasped her pain at the carelessly spoken words, Bessy turned her full attention on Roth. "I wanted to tell you that I'm a free woman now." She smiled archly. "Before Margruder left he gave me my papers."

"Did he now?" Roth showed his surprise. "That was a decent thing for Sate to do." He gave the free bondswoman a teasing grin. "So, will we be goin' to another weddin' soon?"

Bessy shot a scornful look over her shoulder. With a short, belittling laugh she said loudly, "You can bet I won't end up like them sluts over there in the corner."

Juliana glanced at the group of thin, burned-out tavern women. She hid a tickled smile at the threatening looks shot their way. If Bessy was wise, she wouldn't step outside alone tonight.

When she realized that she, too, bore a look that betrayed her feelings for Bessy, she knew she had to get away from the woman, or cause a scene at her own wedding. She excused herself coolly and walked away. Roth's gaze followed her, and he knew by her stiffly held back that she was angry. He pulled away from Bessy's clinging hands and hurried after her.

Slipping an arm around Juliana's waist, he teased, "Is my beautiful wife jealous of the newly freed Bessy?"

"Oh, Roth." Juliana laughed. "You know better than that. I just didn't like the way she was insulting those poor women. In my opinion she's no better than they. Everybody knows she slept with Battle, and then with your friend."

"You're right," Roth agreed. "Actually, she's worse than most of them. In most cases you'll find that whores have a tender heart. Bessy doesn't. She wouldn't care who she stepped on or stabbed in the back to get what she wanted. She's a conniving woman. Sate couldn't stand her."

Juliana looked up at Roth in startled surprise. "But . . . but he bought her. If he disliked her so, why would he do that?"

"He told me he wanted a white woman who would cook white peoples' food, and would keep his cabin clean." After a pause, Roth added, "Squaws ain't always the best of house-keepers."

Before Juliana could ask Roth if he thought that Sate had slept with the woman, Battle interrupted by jumping upon a bench and calling for everyone's attention. "Choose your partners, ladies and gents, we're gonna dance."

• • •

It was around midnight when, exhausted from being whirled from one man to another in the high-stepping dances, Juliana signaled Roth to rescue her. His hair curled tightly from the perspiration that soaked his head and shirt, he spun his partner to another man and made his way to his bride.

"I'm exhausted," Juliana laughingly exclaimed, falling into Roth's arms. "Aren't you tired?"

He smiled wickedly and pulled her up tight against his body. "I hope you're not too exhausted," he whispered in her hair.

Juliana relaxed against him and felt his manhood grow to fullness. She blushed and whispered back, "I'm sure I'll be rested up by the time we leave here and make camp."

Roth traced a finger around her lips, his eyes smoldering with the desire that had been long weeks in building. "What with this downpour, I've made arrangements with Battle to spend the night in one of his rooms."

"Oh?" Juliana could only murmur, her pulses racing as his shimmering gaze promised delights she had never known except in dreams.

Roth nodded. "His two women have been cleaning a room for us the past half hour." His hand moved to stroke her throat. "They've finished now," he murmured, his voice thick. "Let's slip away and see what the room looks like."

Juliana smiled, signifying her willingness, and as their guests continued to dance, hopping and stomping, making the floor shake, Roth led her to a narrow door adjacent to the bar, opened it, and ushered her inside. The door closed behind them and they stood a moment, taking in the room and the fire that blazed in the fireplace.

It was spotlessly clean, the few pieces of furniture of good quality. Thank God for that, Roth sighed inwardly. He wanted his and Juliana's first night together as husband and wife to be as near perfect as possible. He knew that she was nervous as it was, and dirty quarters would have only made it worse.

I must not rush her, he cautioned himself. I have already waited for what seems an eternity, and I can wait a little longer.

"I'll bet this is Battle's own bedroom," he said, taking Juliana's arm and leading her to the fire.

"You're probably right," Juliana agreed, looking toward the big bed. "Battle doesn't strike me as the type to furnish his travelers with a feather bed."

Roth sat down in a large padded rocker and pulled Juliana into his lap. As he slowly removed the pins in her hair, letting it fall in a pale cloud around her face and shoulders, he asked softly, "Are you happy, Juliana?"

Juliana's lips curved in a gentle smile, and she ran her fingers through his crisp hair, feeling guilt that she couldn't spontaneously answer yes firmly, that her heart belonged to another man. She pushed back the image of a dark, lean face and, kissing the tip of Roth's nose, murmured, "You could make any woman happy, Roth Adams."

Roth accepted her carefully chosen words as she had hoped he would and, nuzzling her throat, he deftly undid the buttons of her bodice and shoved it down around her waist. He lifted his head and, as his mouth, warm and moist, settled over hers, his hands stroked and kneaded her breasts.

A tingling began in the pit of Juliana's stomach and she was helpless against the fiery urgency of the marauding kiss and the knowing caress of fingers gently fondled her nipples. When she moaned softly, Roth swept her up and carried her to the bed. Kneeling beside her, his experienced hands quickly finished disrobing her. Standing up, he rapidly tossed aside his own clothes.

"I have dreamed of this so many nights." Roth's voice was rough with his need as he lay down beside Juliana and began trailing kisses down her throat. "Touch me, honey," he murmured, taking her hand and sliding it down his muscular stomach, across the patch of wiry hair, and down onto his swollen manhood. "Hold it, Juliana, feel its strength; know that it's all yours, no other woman's."

For an instant, Juliana paused. She had never before touched this part of a man and was uncertain what to do. Tom would have been mortified had she ever touched him there. Then, with womanly instinct her fingers encircled his thickness and moved slowly, measuring his length.

Roth groaned his pleasure and closed his mouth over a hard, taut nipple, his tongue flicking and playing with it a moment before he began to suck hungrily.

A trembling took possession of Juliana's body and she moaned low in her throat. His head heavy on her breast, Roth smiled in anticipation. It was time to awaken the unknown fires in his bride. To render her weak and clinging, needing and wanting only him. He would take her untried flesh and teach it to respond at his touch, even at his look. He would make it hunger for him all the time. Had he not done so to Zoe?

He sat up, moved down her body, and stroked her legs apart. She opened passion-drugged eyes when he knelt between them and removed her hand from his turgid muscle. "Roth, I hurt," she whimpered. "Make me yours now."

"Soon, my love," he murmured, leaning forward, his hard body molded to her softness, his manhood pulsating against the core of her femininity. Slowly, and with purpose, he nursed each breast, drawing on the nipple until it was tender and swollen. Her breath coming in short pants, Juliana lifted a hand to press his head closer, but he eluded it by moving down her body, his tongue flicking a hot trail to the blond triangle between the valley of her hips.

"Roth!" she cried out when he gently grasped her legs below the knees and lifted them to rest on his shoulders. She raised up on her elbows as his hands slid under her bottom, lifting her as he lowered his head.

"I'm branding you, my Juliana." His words sounded almost like a threat. "When this night is over you will think of only one man—your husband."

Juliana tried to ward off the waves of overwhelming sensation that washed over her. She vaguely understood Roth's intent, and she was determined that she would not become a slave to the baser demands of her body. But she was a novice to a thrusting tongue and nibbling teeth, and moaned helplessly as liquid fire rose out of her loins and burned over her body. When Roth arched his hips and guided himself inside her, she sighed contentedly. Her response was eager as he thrust rhythmically to the center of her enflamed passion.

CHAPTER 15

~⌒~

Juliana gave the quilt of brightly colored squares a last smoothing pat, then moved to the window to look outside. A mist hung over the meadow below, following the winding river like a heavy fog.

"What a shame we don't have a cow to stake out in that lush grass," she said aloud and sighed. There had been a cow once. A cow and her calf and, in a pen back of the barn, a mother sow and her eight pigs.

She shook her head, remembering how one morning shortly after she and Roth had arrived at the homestead, Roth had returned to the cabin, his expression furious. "The animals are gone." His eyes blazed. "Only the horses are still in the stable."

"What do you mean, gone?" Juliana asked, setting his breakfast on the table. "If they've broken out of their pens, surely you can track them down."

. "Ha! That would be one hell of an undertaking." Roth threw himself down in the chair before the bacon and cornmeal mush. "They've probably been skinned and eaten by now." As her startled eyes questioned him, he explained, "The animals didn't escape on their own, Juliana. This is Red Feather's work. He's angry because I've taken myself a wife." He noted her worried look of concern, and swore inwardly at himself.

Pushing away from the table, he pulled Juliana down onto his lap. "Don't fret about it, honey. We'll have another cow by the time our son comes." He smiled at her, gently smoothing his hands over her stomach.

Juliana rubbed her head against Roth's, keeping to herself that it wasn't the loss of the cow that bothered her. She worried that Zoe's father might carry his ire further.

Her affectionate gesture didn't deceive Roth. His young wife, city-bred, was understandably frightened. His big hand stroked her smooth cheek soothingly. "The old chief won't bother us anymore, Juliana. He's satisfied that he's avenged his daughter's death."

And, thankfully, there had been no more incidents.

Juliana turned from the window, patting her now rounded stomach, thinking fondly that Roth always referred to the baby as "his" or "ours," but never "yours." She had no doubt that he'd make a good father. And a good husband, she added silently, glancing around the large room, clean and neat, everything in order. She shuddered, recalling how it had looked the first time she'd entered the cabin.

A strong, acrid odor had permeated the room, although she had admitted to herself that it seemed clean enough. It's definitely got an Indian flavor, though, she had thought later, poking among jars and gourd containers. When she took the cover off a large crock of bear grease, its rancid smell sent her running outside to retch.

Juliana remembered Roth's kindness, how he had followed her and braced her forehead with his palm while she kneeled in the dirt. When she finally raised her pale face, he took a handkerchief from his back pocket and wiped her perspiring brow and then her mouth. He led her over to the porch and helped her into a chair. "Wait here while I go clear everything out." He patted her shoulder.

She had nodded her thanks, and several minutes later watched him carry to the chip-yard the offending grease, along with an armful of miscellaneous stuff she couldn't lay a name to. When fire was set to the heap, dark clouds of smoke rose, carrying a horrible stench.

Roth's white teeth flashed as he tossed a string of bear claws, wrapped around a piece of deerhide, onto the flames. "There! I've always wanted to set fire to that thing."

"What on earth is it?" Juliana held her nose.

Roth grinned down at her. "Would you believe a love potion?"

"Oh, no!" She grimaced. "How could such an evil-smelling thing induce love?"

"I always wondered about that myself." Roth sat down beside Juliana. "How would you like to sleep with that thing under your pillow every night?"

"Good Lord, I'd gag." Juliana giggled.

"Many times I damn near did." Roth's face sobered. "Zoe was a fine woman, Juliana, and a good wife and I don't mean to poke fun at her. Putting up with some of her notions was the least I could do."

Juliana nodded solemnly, after a moment saying softly, "We both carry guilt, don't we, Roth? Not having loved our mates, I mean."

She had taken over then, making the dust fly from the loft floor strewn with strange herbs and barks to the rough pine boards below. Roth had done the heavy work; the lifting, the scrubbing, while she did the final touches.

Juliana's eyes skimmed the room. *Her* stamp was on it now. Where before the windows had been bare, now dainty curtains, made from the wide skirt of a red dress, gave them privacy in the evenings when the candles were lit. A sheet dyed pink from sassafras roots was now a tablecloth, and a bowl of wildflowers in the center of the table, flanked on each side by a candle in a pewter holder, was a bright spot in the room.

Her gaze roamed to Molly's wedding gift to her: the gay patchwork quilt and the matching braided rug spread out in front of the hearth. She sighed happily. The room had a warm, welcoming appearance, its transformation making Roth eye it proudly every time he entered the cabin.

"So," Juliana muttered, wandering aimlessly around the room, "everything is done. Now how am I going to spend the day?" It would be a long one, for Roth was out tramping the hills, and would most likely be gone the better part of the day.

A big cat had come down from the hills last night and nosed around the cabin, his tracks apparent right up to the door. Roth had grabbed up his rifle and followed the wide marks to the barn, where long gashes on the sturdy door showed that the hungry animal had tried to get to their mounts. The horses were still trembling in fear when he entered the stalls to feed them. After a fast breakfast, Roth had taken off in pursuit of the lean feline.

"*How* am I to pass the time?" Juliana asked the empty room again, as she bent to turn a chunk of venison roasting over the fire.

The meat's dripping juices sizzled on the red coals below, giving off a mouth-watering aroma, and as Juliana added more seasoning to it she wished there was more than potatoes and mush to serve with the roast. How nice it would be if their garden was old enough to provide some greens for the table.

As she turned away from the fire she remembered a small spring in the woods, and how lamb's-quarter grew abundantly around it. She grew hungry just thinking of a bowl of greens for supper. Her body was suddenly craving the blood-enriching goodness they would provide.

Juliana paused beside the table, brushing at an imaginary piece of lint. Roth had warned her not to go into the woods alone, explaining that besides the snakes and varmints she might run into, he didn't trust Red Feather's braves. "You'd be a tempting piece to those red heathens."

But the thought of the succulent greens continued to float before Juliana, and finally she tossed her head obstinately. The place was so near to the cabin that she would be in no danger, she was sure. She pulled down a basket from a shelf, picked up a small knife and tossed it inside, and closed the cabin door behind her.

Outside, she paused a moment beside a rosebush loaded with its first buds. She bent and sniffed their heavy fragrance, murmuring, "You sweet, sweet things." She straightened up and began walking, recalling how she had come in possession of the bush.

She and Roth had awakened late the morning after their wedding night, roused by voices outside. She had stretched sore muscles and settled her head more comfortably on Roth's shoulder and yawned, "What's going on out there?"

Roth had bent his head to her nearest breast and pressed his mouth to it, muttering, "Who cares?"

Juliana blushed, remembering how Roth's teasing lips had brought a warm weakness flowing through her blood, and when he rolled on top of her, she opened her legs to receive him. When Battle called, "Hey, you two love birds, when are you gettin' up?" Roth ignored the big man, continuing his slow, deep movement inside her.

Later, after their rapid breathing had returned to normal, Roth had raised up and gazed down at her. "I love you, Juliana," he said softly. "You're my whole life."

She had reached up and touched the fine lines around his

eyes, trying desperately to form the words she knew he wanted to hear. She was saved by another strident call from outside. Swearing under his breath, Roth rose and flung open the window. "We'll be right out," he shouted impatiently.

Letting her gaze travel from her husband's wide shoulders to his narrow hips, she had grown warm recalling the pleasure that body had brought her the previous night, and again that morning. Why hadn't she been about to say, "I love you, too, Roth"?

She had her answer when a hard, accusing face seemed to materialize in front of her. She had shaken her head and whispered to Sate's misty image, "I'll get over you . . . sometime."

Outside, Juliana and Roth had been quickly pulled apart. The men had dragged Roth to one side, laughing loudly, slapping him on the back. A scar-faced hunter had poked him in the ribs and snickered, "Damned if you don't look like you've been workin' all night, Adams."

Juliana, left with the women who had gathered to see her and her new husband off, had reddened in embarrassment at the coarse reference made to their wedding night. She still wasn't comfortable with the crude, and sometimes vulgar, manners of the hillmen.

While she had stood with downcast eyes, the settler women had smiled sympathetically. "Don't mind them windbags, honey," one said. "They think that's all there is to a marriage. They got pleasurin' on their minds all the time." She gave a small, wry laugh. "I guess you can tell that by all the younguns runnin' 'round." She had taken Juliana by the arm and impelled her forward. "Come over to your wagon. We brung you some weddin' gifts."

When each woman had shyly, but proudly, pointed out her contribution to the small pile in one corner of the straw-lined wagon bed—where she and Roth would sleep while traveling to her new home—tears welled up in Juliana's eyes. Holding a jar of apple butter and fingering a heavy loomed woolen blanket, she had choked out, "I don't know how I can bring myself to leave all you good women."

The care-worn faces had smiled with pleasure at Juliana's heartfelt words. They pushed forward to comfort her. "We're right sorry to see you go, Miss Juliana," a young mother of eight had said softly. "You brought some of the outside world to us . . . your pretty ways and soft skin."

An old grandmother, bent with age and puffing on a clay pipe, lay a clawlike hand on Juliana's. "If it do get too lonesome for you, child, just hint it to your big husband. He's got real feelin' for you. It's in every look he slides you. He won't want you pinin'."

Juliana had smiled and wiped at her teary cheeks with the back of a hand. Leaning forward, she'd kissed the wrinkled face, murmuring, "Thank you, granny."

Roth then came up and stood beside her, and the women stepped back shyly, their expressions saying how lucky she was to have such a handsome and caring husband. Each knew wistfully that he would be thoughtful of his young wife's welfare, that he would be careful of planting his seed. Roth Adams would not ruin her youth and beauty by getting her with child every winter.

Roth's wide, friendly smile took all the women in as he said softly, "It's time to say good-bye, Juliana. We've got a piece to go."

Juliana had embraced and kissed each woman before Roth swung her onto the high wagon seat. When he had climbed up beside her and taken up the reins, Juliana laid a restraining hand on his arm. "Can't we wait a moment longer?" she had implored, her gaze on the trail that led to her brother's cabin. "John and Molly haven't come down yet. I want to tell them good-bye."

Roth's rough palm had covered her small hand. "They're not comin', honey. They left you a message with Battle last night. They said to tell you that it would be too hard to see you go I guess Molly is pretty upset about your leavin'."

While Juliana's eyes grew watery, he had run nervous fingers over his knees. "I feel like a skunk takin' you away from your friends and family."

He truly does feel bad, Juliana had thought, darting Roth a quick look, and if I should ask him to remain in Squaw Hollow he'd do it for me, put my wishes before his own. Dear Roth, she sighed guiltily. The least I can do for you is hide my reluctance to leave civilization so far behind.

She squeezed his tense arm. "Roth," she scolded gently, "stop feeling guilty. If I didn't want to go with you, I wouldn't. So let's get going."

Relief spread over Roth's face, and he gave his wife a quick hug. "Thank you, honey. I was gettin' some worried. What with the tears and all." He snapped the reins over the team's backs and they rolled out, the stallion and Juliana's little roan hitched to the tailgate. Juliana turned and waved to the women until the forest hid them from view.

She had just turned around when Roth pulled in the matched pair of grays. Standing in the middle of the road, defiant and yet self-conscious, were the whores from the tavern. Her eyes were drawn to the woman who nervously clutched a spindly, thorny bush, its roots wrapped in a piece of homspun.

Roth, ever the gentleman to women, no matter their station in life, had flashed his teeth in a wide smile as he removed his hat. "Good mornin', ladies. Where are you off to on such a fine day?"

The gaunt faces broke into pleased smiles. Giggling like young girls, the bush-bearing woman was pushed forward with the hissing command, "Give it to her."

While Juliana and Roth watched with hidden curiosity, the woman approached the wagon diffidently, the sun striking fire to her red hair. To ease the shyness that clearly enveloped her, Roth asked kindly, "What you got there, Red?"

Her eyes losing the battle to look into Juliana's, looking at a spot past her shoulder instead, "Red" lifted the plant to her. Speaking in a low voice she said, "We brought you a slip from our rosebush. My mother gave me a start when I left Virginia. I've had it a long time, in many places, and it never fails to bloom. We hope it will bring you joy when you see its red blossoms."

"And it smells so sweet, Miss Juliana," another from the group offered, when Red stopped for breath.

Juliana held the plant carefully in both hands, her eyes luminous with unshed tears. "A rosebush, Roth," she murmured. "Can you imagine . . . in the wilderness."

She had gazed down into the tired eyes, eyes that had seen too much in their harsh world, and said softly, "Roth will plant it right outside our door. Every time I pick a blossom I'll think of you ladies. It is my dearest gift."

Pink pleasure had suffused the upturned faces that smiled at her widely. Roth spoke to the team, and when she could no long see the small group behind them, she had laid her head on Roth's shoulder and wept bitterly for the women whose only prized possession was a rose that bloomed only once a year.

Now stepping off toward the forest, Juliana wondered how Red and the girls were faring. Theirs was a hard profession, a long life not expected by any of them . . . and usually not wanted.

In a short time she had walked across the clearing in front of the cabin, and entered the cool shade of the woods. The forest floor was damp and heavy from the rain of two days ago. She breathed deeply, enjoying the odor of wet earth and decaying leaves.

Soon, as Juliana followed a faint path, she heard the tinkle of the spring as it flowed among smooth rocks, them disappeared into a deep sinkhole. As she had expected, the delicate plant she sought grew thick beneath the lacy pattern of the sun that penetrated the canopy of leaves above, and her basket was soon filled.

Thirsty from the sun that had grown steadily warmer, Juliana knelt beside the spring and cupped its cold fresh water to her mouth. Sitting back on her heels when her thirst was quenched, she mused that the spring that ran beneath the cabin was equally cold and pure. So cold, Roth had told her, that moisture had formed on the crocks of milk and butter Zoe had once kept there. He had added that eggs remained fresh for a long time when placed on the stone ledge that cropped out over the slow-running stream.

She stood and stretched, then bent and picked up the basket of greens. The murmur of the nearby river coaxed her to come and watch its flowing path a moment. Reluctant to return to the cabin to hours of idleness, Juliana cut across the woods, humming under her breath, the basket swinging on her arm.

The distance was greater than Juliana had thought, and when she finally stood on the gravelly banks of the Ohio, perspiration dotted her brow and upper lip.

The water was smooth, and moved so slowly it seemed to invite her to journey along with it. "I could," she thought out loud. "If I keep to its banks I can't get lost."

The way was free of weeds and ferns as Juliana walked, timing her steps to the musical flow of the water. There was only one spot where she had to swing wide of the stream to avoid the heavy growth of reeds that grew several feet out onto the bank. As she studied the tall, slender, hardy plant, she recalled Roth saying that in the summer the squaws gathered the reeds and wove them into baskets. Then, when winter set in, they traded them to the settlers for food and grain. She glanced down at the one on her arm and wondered if Zoe had made it.

When Juliana came to a large muddy place at a shallow edge of the river, recognizing it as a bear-wallow, she decided it was time to retrace her steps. She had no desire to run into one of those mean-tempered brutes. Especially a mother with a cub.

The midday sun glared white with its heat, and Juliana soon grew uncomfortably warm. When she arrived back at the spot she had started from, she knelt on the bank and cupped the cool water to her face and throat. She was patting her cheeks dry with her handkerchief when she had the sudden feeling she was being watched. She could feel hostile eyes boring into her back.

She rose slowly to her feet and turned around. Her breath caught in her throat. Only feet away stood a wild, shaggy pony, an Indian woman astride its bare back. She lifted a hand to shield her eyes against the bright rays of the sun, and stared into a face filled with sparking malice.

"Doxy!" she gasped.

The young squaw made no answer, only continued to scowl at her. Annoyance firmed Juliana's lips and she asked sharply, "What do you mean by sneaking up on me? What are you doing in these parts?"

She was glowered at a moment longer, then, in a voice thick with hostility, Doxy answered; "This is my area. I live here. What are *you* doing in these parts?"

Was the girl of Zoe's tribe, Juliana wondered, maybe even a relative? She lifted her chin and, with an edge of irritation in her voice, said, "I live here, too."

Doxy stiffened. Staring suspiciously into Juliana's face, she asked shortly, "Where?"

It's none of your business, Juliana thought angrily, but I've a feeling you'll only follow me to satisfy your curiosity. Picking up the basket she had put down before kneeling to wash her face, she answered coolly, "If it's any of your business, I live in that cabin back of you."

Doxy turned her head to look over her shoulder, and when she swung back to face Juliana her black eyes were narrowed to glimmering slits.

"So you're Roth Adam's new wife."

Juliana simply nodded.

The silence grew tense as Doxy gave Juliana's thickened body a slow study. She started when the girl asked abruptly, "When do you go to your birthing bed?"

Juliana glared back at the stony face a long moment before snapping, "In August."

"Whose is it?"

You insufferable bitch . . . Juliana's fingers tightened on the handles of the basket at the insult in the lazily spoken question. She is intentionally needling me, she fumed, and I shouldn't even answer her. But she will only come to her own conclusion, and it won't be the right one.

In a voice that was as calm as she could make it, Juliana answered, "My husband's, of course."

"Roth Adams."

"No! My dead husband's."

Juliana strove for utterance but could not speak when Doxy, a smile, faint and suggestive, on her lips, said bluntly, "You lie."

"What?" she finally managed, taking a step toward the pony, her eyes blazing. "You'd better explain that remark." Her voice was low and measured.

Undisturbed by Juliana's anger, Doxy sat the little mount loosely, scanning her figure closely. Then, as though talking to herself, she said, "From the size and shape, the whelp will be delivered in September, not August.

Her black eyes moved up to Juliana's flushed face. "If I recall rightly," she jeered, "that leaves your dead husband out."

Juliana stood rooted to the ground, fighting for composure. How she'd like to slap, to scratch that hateful sneer off the red face. She opened her mouth to refute the squaw, but the question was sharp and quick

"How long did you sleep with Adams before his wife died?"

Stunned, Juliana stared into the hooded eyes in disbelief. Her pulse raced so a blackness seemed to surround her. "I never slept with Roth before we were married," she finally managed.

Doxy stared down into the irate face, knowing suddenly that the white woman spoke the truth. Her eyes narrowed at the final truth. Sate Margruder! Why hadn't she thought of that before? Her black eyes flickered. This fragile pale-face didn't know it, though. How she ached to throw the knowledge in her face, to take away the contemptuous look in the strangely colored eyes.

Although the telling would give her much pleasure, Doxy knew she must bide her time. If Margruder should learn that she had told this woman his secret, he would beat her with his fists.

Yes, she must wait. But when the time was right she would tell them both. Tell them in a manner that would rip them apart. In the meantime she would mention to the chief only that Adams's new wife was already with child. He could draw his own conclusions and she was pretty sure she knew what they would be.

Bringing her attention back to Juliana, she began her charade. "You knew Roth Adams before you married him," she said flatly. "Chief Red Feather will be interested in this bit of news."

Before Juliana could deny the charge, Doxy kicked the pony in the flanks and sprinted away. But just before she was hidden by a bend in the river she pulled in the mount and called back, "It might interest you to know that Margruder is sharing my blankets again. He lives with me now . . . in my people's camp."

Feeling as though she had been hit in the chest Juliana stared at the spot where the squaw and pony had disappeared. The reason for the girl's animosity was clear now. She, too, was in love with Sate. Juliana's appearance near their camp represented a threat Doxy would rather not confront.

With a low wail Juliana gave in to the jealous ache that gripped her. Throwing herself onto the ground, she wept bitterly. Sate had lied about the girl all along, just as he had lied to her about so many things.

Her tears fell faster, then a pair of gentle hands gripped her shoulders. "Julie girl, what's wrong? Why are you cryin'?" Roth asked anxiously, drawing her up, his arms enfolding her.

"Oh, Roth." Her arms went around his waist. "I'm so glad you're home."

He held her trembling body and smoothed the hair away from her face. "It's all right, honey," his voice soothed her. When she quieted a bit, he said gently, "Tell me what has upset you so."

Haltingly, her voice husky from her tears, and remembering in time not to mention Doxy by name, Juliana told Roth of her meeting with a young squaw, and the girl's accusation that her baby belonged to him. Fresh tears ran down her cheeks when she finished with, "She said that her chief would be very interested in the news."

Roth turned Juliana's head into his shoulder so that she couldn't see the worried frown that marred his forehead. The tribe would be against him now and from here on he must stick close to the cabin and keep an eye on his back trail.

His arm around Juliana's waist, Roth turned their steps toward the cabin. "Let's get you out of this heat." When she nodded, he said soberly, "You realize, don't you, Juliana, that you must be more careful about straying too far away from the cabin."

"You can rest your mind easy on that, Roth," Juliana said firmly. "After today's event I won't be venturing far from the cabin again."

Roth smiled and planted a kiss on top of her head. "I'm glad to hear that."

They had walked in silence a while when Juliana asked, "Is it safe for us to stay here now, Roth? Maybe we should go to John and Molly's until the baby comes."

Roth had known this question would be voiced, that it was only natural Juliana would be worried, fearful. However, she didn't know Red Feather, that he was more bluff than action.

"We're safe enough, honey." His arm tightened around her waist. Red Feather stews about things for a long time before he makes a move. By the time he gets around to botherin' us, winter will be here.

"Once the cold and snow sets in Red Feather won't give us another thought. His tribe is a lazy bunch and never lay in anything for the cold months. He and his braves will be so busy tryin' to keep food in the camp, he'll not think of anything else," Roth said reassuringly to her.

They stepped up on the small porch and Roth pushed the door open, saying, "So don't worry about the old savage. Everything will be fine."

CHAPTER 16

Sate smiled smugly as he stroked the broad blade of his knife over a small whetstone. His patience, his pretense of satisfaction, in living with the tribe and sharing Doxy's teepee had paid off. He was fully accepted by Red Feather now, even allowed to go on short hunts alone.

And today he had done Doxy's father proud. His accuracy with the rifle that Red Feather had returned to him had brought down more game than the others put together. He glanced over at the group of braves sitting before the chief's lodge and grinned sardonically at the black looks cast his way. It still gnawed at them that they had been outdone by a pale-face.

"They got no love for me," he muttered and, returning the stone to his pocket, leaned back against a tree and closed his eyes. He might as well catch a nap while supper was being prepared.

When an hour or so later Doxy shook Sate awake, for a moment he could only stare at her. He had been deep in a dream; a dream where Juliana dwelled. When full awareness came, bitter disappointment darkened his eyes. Doxy stared back at him, a sullen pout sliding over her face as though she read his mind. She got to her feet and returned to the cooking fire. As she helped the other squaws fill the stacked wooden bowls with stew, she shot Sate glances of pure malice.

Ignoring her black looks, but wondering what sly trick she would try next, Sate rose and took his designated spot at the fire.

He was not surprised to be the last one served, figuring that
would be the squaw's revenge for letting her see his revulsion
for her in his eyes. But when he looked into his bowl he
discovered that the sly squaw had paid him back in harder coin.
He saw only thin, greasy gravy with one or two pieces of fatty
meat floating around.

So the bitch is testing me, he thought grimly. All right, I'll
test the chief and her father.

He held the bowl silently, waiting for the right moment.
When Doxy, a sly, pleased look on her face, came and sat down
beside him he turned and smiled at her. A glimmer of gloating
shone in her black eyes. She had won her first battle with the
trapper.

Sate let her enjoy her moment of false victory until she
dipped her fingers into her own bowl which was generously
filled with big chunks of meat. With a sudden loud curse, he
dashed his bowl to the ground. When Doxy gasped her surprise
he swung the back of his hand hard across her cheek. She
sprawled on her back, crying out her pain and shock.

Everyone stared at them. As Sate had expected, Half Step,
her father, rose to his feet and stalked over to them. Sate met
the threatening gaze directed at him unflinchingly. Doxy
remained where she lay, fearfully watching her father's face.
She had not expected things to go so far.

"Why you strike your squaw, Margruder?" the old man
asked gravely.

Sate stabbed a finger at the two paltry pieces of meat lying in
the dust. Half Step's gaze came back to him when he demanded
in an injured voice, "Can a brave exist on such after walking
the forest floor all day? Is my fare to be so little after bringing
in so much?"

Black anger mixed with shame slowly spread over the old
man's face. He turned and bent a dark, disapproving look at his
daughter and, in a voice that shook, demanded, "What kind of
daughter are you to bring such disgrace to your father? What
kind of squaw are you to do such a thing to your brave?"

Her lips twitching nervously, Doxy could only stare up at her
enraged father. She had indeed gone too far. When Half Step
turned on his heel and walked purposefully to a slender maple,
dread grew in her eyes. She was to be punished either by him
or Margruder.

Drawing his knife, the older brave moved around the tree,

scanning its branches as though looking for a special one. He was watched with tight interest by everyone, the squaws grinning in anticipation. Doxy's sly ways and sharp tongue had made her few friends among the women.

In the bated silence Half Step grunted; reaching up, he grasped a slender whip about three feet long. The sharp blade of his knife sliced through the half-inch thickness. Methodically he trimmed off the twigs and leaves that lined it, then flayed the air a couple of times with the sturdy, supple limb.

Trembling now, Doxy watched her father return to the fire and toss the whip at Sate's feet. She whimpered when he said stonily, "Your squaw has shamed you. Beat her."

Sate hid his triumphant smile. With a deceptive calm, he picked up the swtich and stood over the shrinking squaw. Speaking low, so that only she could hear, he grated, "Try your rotten tricks on me, will you? I thought you had more sense."

Yet, as his arm rose and fell, Doxy making low cries that caught in her throat, Sate had no taste for flaying the squaw. She was the first female he had ever struck in his life. He wouldn't do it now if it wasn't so important to keep the chief's full trust.

He saw to it, however, that the switch lost most of its sting in the folds of the doeskin skirt, and on the eighth smarting cut to the copper-colored legs he let his arm drop. He must punish the squaw only enough to redress the wrong she had done him in the Indians' eyes.

Sneaking a look at Red Feather's pleased countenance as he resumed his seat, he could almost read what the chief was thinking: he had showed appropriate behavior to the squaw, had showed that he thought enough of her to punish her for a wrong-doing. And this time when Doxy hurried to bring him a fresh bowl of stew, the gravy was thick with meat and vegetables.

Taking it from her, he grunted, "You can sit now." As she settled herself beside him he smiled grinly. He could feel the rage that burned inside her. The vindictive girl would be after his hide; scoring tonight, tomorrow, or maybe a month from now.

The meal was finished, and as the women gathered up the bowls the men lit their pipes. "She's up to something," Sate muttered inwardly, watching Doxy narrowly as she moved among the women. There was a smugness on her face that spelled trouble: her devious mind had hatched some kind of mischief. Perhaps she was going to seek her revenge tonight.

He stretched his long legs to the fire and made his back comfortable against a tree. When she was ready she'd hit him with it.

Twenty minutes later a tingling warning sounded inside Sate's head and he swept his gaze around the camp, stopping when it fell on Doxy. She had edged herself inside the circle of braves and was making her way toward the chief. While everyone watched with interest she knelt in front of Red Feather. Folding her hands and bowing her head, her voice was low.

"If I may speak, Great Chief?"

Sate sat forward. He knew that tone of hers. She used it when she was plotting some deviltry.

Red Feather puffed on the long-stemmed clay pipe, studying the young squaw through the clouds of smoke curling around his head. Finally he nodded. "You may speak."

Doxy leaned back on her heels, indicating that what she had to say wouldn't be brief. When she began, her voice remained low, but was still heard clearly around the now tight circle of both men and women.

"Today I took a long ride. A ride that brought me near Roth Adams's place."

Sate's heart jumped, then raced madly. Intuitively he knew that she was going to reveal something that would twist his guts. She had waited all evening in anticipation of this moment.

The chief's voice, now perceptively hardened, broke the suspenseful silence Doxy had purposefully invoked. "What did you see at my former son-in-law's place?"

Doxy dropped her lids to hide the elation in her eyes. The arrogant white trapper would feel his pain now. Not the physical kind he had meted her, but the sort that would eat at his mind and heart.

Her voice rose a trifle as she said dramatically, "I saw his wife. In fact, I talked with her."

Intensely curious now, the chief leaned forward; unconsciously so did Sate. He knew the time had come. Doxy would put her knife to him now.

"What did you and Adams's new wife talk about?" Red Feather grunted, his black eyes boring into the kneeling girl.

Doxy darted a gloating look at Sate. "We talked of the child she is carrying."

A pain so sharp it took his breath away shot through Sate's chest. His fists clenched and his eyes closed. Already she carried Roth's seed. As from a great distance he heard Red Feather remark scornfully, "That does not surprise me. Adams is like a stallion. He could service many mares. No doubt his seed took on their marriage night."

"Oh, but his lady hasn't so recently been serviced," Doxy put in, her eyes darting slyly at Sate. "She is quite big. She will deliver in another couple of months."

Sate's eyes flew open. The little demon had to be lying. How could the child be Roths's? Swiftly he counted back the months. Impossible. She was lying through her teeth to hurt him.

He started when Red Feather, his face twisted with rage, roared, "What kind of insolence is this that Adams shows me; rubs my nose in his unfaithfulness. Must he tell the whole red nation that he slept with another while my Zoe still lived?"

Doxy, always eager to slash with her sharp tongue, forgot to whom she spoke as her jealously of the dead girl spilled out. "Perhaps he did it because Zoe couldn't give him children herself."

Her eyes widened in dread as her last word prompted a tense silence. Too late she realized she had bit the wrong one this time. She had taken the chief's beloved daughter as her target.

She did not move fast enough to elude the moccasined foot that shot out, landing with force between her breasts. As she went over backward, dangerously close to the fire, the enraged man jumped to his feet. His long finger pointing at her, he shouted furiously, "Margruder, take your squaw from my sight. Take her to your teepee and teach her a lesson she will never forget."

Sate grabbed Doxy by an elbow and pulled her to her feet, shoving her roughly forward. Losing her balance, she staggered through a group of sitting squaws who took the advantage of her proximity to reach out with angry hands. With painful squeals she sped for the doubtful safety of the teepee, tripping and falling through its opening.

Sate stepped in behind her and dropped the door flap, leaving the room lit only by the small fire burning in its central pit. Standing over the sprawled figure, he demanded, "What devil's work are you up to now?"

Doxy scrambled to her feet, ready to dodge out of his reach if neccessary. "Your beautiful white woman is big with child," she hissed. "She has carried the seed for many months."

Sate took a threatening step toward her. "You lie, you damnable slut."

The girl backed away, but her eyes gleamed with satisfaction. There was uncertainty in Margruder's eyes even as he denied her claim. Keeping a wary eye on him, she asked, "Why should I lie about something that can easily be proved?"

Sate stared at her another minute, then began to pace the floor. Doxy flinched when he turned on her and asked abruptly, "When did you say the baby is due?"

"She says in August," Doxy sneered.

Sate studied the amusement on her face. "You think otherwise?"

"Ha! I know otherwise. Her body hasn't thickened enough yet. She, of course, thinks she's very large, and vainly tries to hide her growing belly in loose gowns."

"I'm sure Juliana would know when her child was due." Sate impatiently dismissed Doxy's jeering remark. "She's smart enough to know that."

Black eyes flashed maliciously. The white woman was perfect in Margruder's eyes. She had thought to wait, to savor the anticipation of bringing this proud man to his knees, but the sudden scalding rage inside her insisted she had waited long enough.

Watching Sate closely, not to miss one spasm of pain that would grip his hard features as he tasted a bit of hell, Doxy began to talk silkily.

"She says August because she honestly believes the baby belongs to her dead husband. But she will go to her birthing bed in mid-September."

Sate stared blankly at the squaw. From her tone he knew that he had been sent a cutting barb, but what was the girl trying to say?

He caught his breath when the truth hit him. He wanted to shout joyously, to proclaim to the world that he was to become a father. Then an icy cold seized his heart. The baby's mother was married to another man, and dear God, she doesn't even know it's mine.

He lifted the tent flap and walked blindly outside. Looking neither left, or right, he moved across the campground and into the forest. There he paced among the trees, black despair overwhelming him. Finally, exhausted, he threw himself onto the ground. His fingers dug into the loam and pine needles as he bitterly reflected what his foolish pride had robbed him of. A little daughter, perhaps, with blond curls and amber eyes like her mother.

The slashed grooves alongside his mouth deepened. No, Juliana would have a boy. A picture of a straight little back and sturdy little legs moved through his mind. A son in his own image. A son to teach and to love.

Cold reasoning made Sate's fists clench. It would not be him guiding and teaching a son through those tender years; Roth Adams would do that.

A ragged, defeated sigh moved his wide shoulders. It would be his secret. Over the years he would skulk around, trying to catch a glimpse of his son or daughter, watch Roth play the father, gradually grow to hate the man.

Sate was halfway back to camp when he remembered that Doxy also knew his secret. With sickening clarity he knew that someday she would tell Juliana. The animosity she carried in her heart for the white woman would never be satisfied until she did. Setting Red Feather on the warpath against Roth was but part of her revenge.

What would the old war chief do? In his desolation Sate had forgotten the rage that had swept across the man's face. If he firmly believed that Roth had dishonored his daughter, the man could be cruel and unforgiving. He frowned thoughtfully. His plans for leaving the Pennacook tribe at the end of the week had to be abandoned, at least for the time being. For Juliana's sake, and the baby she carried, he must watch and listen, learn if Red Feather meant to move against his former son-in-law.

Doxy was still asleep, lying naked on the pallet of furs, when Sate entered the teepee. He threw her a dark look and yanked half the furs from beneath her. She sat up and watched him spread them on the other side of the fire. When he disrobed and stretched out on his back, she crawled over beside him. After gazing down at him a moment, she boldly traced a finger down his flat stomach. When he neither stirred nor swore at her, she took courage and slid her hand down to the thick mat of hair below his belly. When he still made no movement, her fingers closed around him and stroked.

"Is my man weary?" she purred. "Would he not like to lay in my arms, and together take pleasure from each other?"

The reaction she expected did not come. Giving an exclamation of disgust, Sate roughly swept her hand away. Sitting up, he fastened his fingers in her hair. "You think to force me into layin' with you?" His fingers tightened on her scalp until the skin drew taut. "Never will it happen. I don't care what lies you carry to the chief, what tricks you may use. Never again will you share my bed."

Her black eyes shooting a mixture of hate and desire, Doxy hissed, "You will, or I'll visit your lovely Juliana and inform her of a few things."

"Do you think that I don't already know that?" Sate shoved her away with a force that sent her tumbling. "But remember well one thing. The day you speak your poison may be your last."

Doxy crawled back to her pile of furs, and it was a long time before either fell asleep.

CHAPTER 17

The late July sun beat down mercilessly. The dust Juliana's feet kicked up seemed to coat everything. Plodding along she brought an arm across her sweating forehead. Would August never come, bringing the arrival of her baby, letting her walk lightly again?

A few yards ahead Roth stopped. Watching Juliana's approach, he thought she had never looked lovelier. He, too, wished August would come, the baby born. He burned to hold his wife up tightly against his body again, to feel her long, silken length pressed along him.

He sighed. Two weeks ago was the last time they had made love. He had once overheard an Indian woman say that the husband must control himself six weeks before the birthing, and six weeks after. He had carefully counted, then stuck religiously to the rule. Juliana would never come to harm through him.

A rueful smile curved his lips, remembering how he had teased Juliana about his forced abstention, remarking that he'd have to find himself a squaw for those twelve untouchable weeks. She had snuggled her head closer on his shoulder and murmured sleepily, "You wouldn't. You'll just suffer along with me."

Roth smiled and shook his head. How well his wife knew him. She was fully aware that no other woman would hold any interest for him, that one could parade naked in front of him and he would take no notice of her.

Were his feelings of total devotion returned by Juliana? he

wondered wistfully. Sometimes, in the early evenings when the two of them sat on the porch to catch a cool breeze from the hills, he would sense her thoughts leaving him, her mind wandering away from the present. What did she think about then? Who did she think of? A man from her past? It was not her husband, he knew; she hadn't loved him.

Jealous of her secret thoughts, he'd sometimes call her attention back to himself. She would turn her amber eyes upon him, and far back in their golden depths he would catch a pensive yearning. Then she would smile and he'd convince himself that he had imagined it all.

Panting slightly, Juliana reached Roth and slipped an arm around him. "Roth, you walk too fast." She smiled up at him. "I'm all out of breath."

Immediate concern furrowed Roth's brow. "I shouldn't have brought you out in this heat." Leading her to the shade of a large maple, he eased her down on the grass. "We'll rest a while."

"It's a good thing you did bring me out." Juliana leaned back against the trunk. "I was so tired of being cooped up in the cabin I was ready to go out of my mind."

Smoothing away the damp wisps of hair clinging to her forehead, Roth said sympathetically, "I know it's hard on you, this heat and not being able to take your walks, but it will soon be over. Red Feather is doing just what I said he would. His anger at me is beginning to cool by now, and before long you can be out and around in absolute safety."

"I hope you're right," Juliana murmured, remembering with a shiver Doxy's warning.

They rested for some minutes, then Roth rose and helped Juliana to her feet. "Come on, missus," he teased, "them fish are hungry. Let's get down to the river. There's always a cool breeze there and you can lay in the grass and watch me catch those speckled trout that hide among the rocks."

An hour later, back at the cabin, after Roth had cleaned the long string of fish he'd caught, Juliana floured them and was dropping them in hot grease when Roth called from the porch, "Juliana, isn't this your friend Nemus comin' our way?"

Excitement sparkled in Juliana's eyes. Someone from home? She pulled the skillet off the fire and hurried outside to stand beside Roth. Shading her eyes against the setting sun, she peered at the two figures coming toward the house.

"It is Nemus!" She smiled broadly, recognizing the erect carriage and proud stride. "He has one of his squaws with him." She turned to Roth, her eyes big. "Roth, he has never brought any of his womenfolk around the family before."

Roth hugged her shoulders. "Then you should be honored."

"Oh, I am. I am indeed."

As the pair drew nearer, Juliana wanted to rush to meet them, to ask a hundred questions; how brother John and Molly were and the people of the settlement. She forced herself to remain where she was, however. The staid, proud Indian would frown on such a display of emotion.

When Nemus and his companion stood at the foot of the porch, she walked sedately down the steps and grasped the old Indian's bony hand between hers. "Welcome to our home, Nemus. It is good to see you."

A soft glimmering in his eyes was the only indication Nemus gave that he was pleased to see her. After he shook hands with Roth, he turned to the woman at his side.

"This is Snow Bird. She is of my tribe. She help women in birth bed. John's woman say you will need her soon."

Snow Bird was short, stout, her movements slow, her manner placid. Her age Juliana could not determine, but it was quite advanced, she thought. When she reached both hands to grip the old squaw's, the stern lines on the weathered face softened, and the features became kindly.

"How nice of you to come, Snow Bird. I confess I'm a little nervous; I didn't know whether Roth could handle the delivering of a baby."

"When baby come?" Snow Bird inquired, her sharp eyes studying Juliana's body closely.

When Juliana said August the black eyes searched her face. After a probing stare, the Indian midwife shook her head. "No August. Baby come in mid-September."

"Oh, no, Snow Bird, you are mistaken. It is due in August," Juliana assured her.

The old squaw glanced at her stomach again, then shrugged her shoulders, muttering, "We see."

Juliana led the pair onto the porch, inviting, "Come on into the cabin. I was just frying some fish. It will soon be ready. I hope that you're both hungry."

Following behind her, Roth bringing up the rear, Nemus

announced that he and Snow Bird would be pleased to share their supper.

As Roth pulled seats forward for their guests, Juliana hurried to replace the fish over the fire, and check the corn bread browning in the oven. She added two more plates and forks to the table, then raked out the four potatoes that had roasted slowly all day in the hot ashes. She and Roth would have to do with one each tonight.

As Juliana moved from fire to table she was unaware that Snow Bird's black eyes followed her every move. She hoped that the fish was crusty enough, that the corn bread wouldn't fall, that the potatoes wouldn't be raw in the middle. If the meal was lacking in some way Nemus would take her aside and sternly tell her so.

She grinned crookedly to herself. Ever since the old brave rescued her from the two bullies in the Trenton tavern, she had constantly striven to meet his approval.

What ever the outcome, the meal was finally on the table. Juliana took a deep breath and announced that supper was ready.

Sitting across from Nemus, she didn't breathe as he bit into his fish, chewed a moment, then swallowed. His solemn black eyes raised to look at her, the barest deepening of the wrinkles around his eyes apparent. But it was enough for the cook. Her lips spread in a wide smile as she picked up her fork.

Very little was said as supper was consumed. To the Indian, conversation had no place in the partaking of nourishment. Later, over pipes, the talking would be done.

Juliana missed the gay chatter she and Roth always indulged in. Between laughing and teasing their meals often lasted over an hour. This time it seemed they had barely sat down before everyone was finished. She had just swallowed her last bite when Roth and Nemus rose to walk outside.

She stood up and began to clear the table. Snow Bird came and stood beside her, laying a restraining hand on her arm. "Snow Bird do this," she said. "You join men. Talk to Nemus. Ask about your brother and his woman. Nemus leave early tomorrow."

Juliana gazed at her in surprise. How had the old woman known she was eager to do just that? She smiled gratefully. "If you don't mind, then, Snow Bird, I would like to to talk to Nemus."

She stepped out to the porch and Roth patted the floor beside him. "Sit down, honey, and catch up on the news. Nemus was just tellin' me somethin' that you'll be interested in hearin'."

"Oh? And what is that?" Juliana made herself comfortable between the two men.

Nemus took the long-stemmed pipe from between his lips and, cupping the clay bowl in his hand, announced unemotionally, "John's woman in Trenton, she dead." In the stunned silence he puffed on his pipe again. When he felt that the air was suspenseful enough, he continued, "Skinny woman had mad fit, broke the blood vessel in her head. She die two weeks ago."

Juliana fought the glad smile that wanted to spring to her lips. It was unchristian to be happy about a person's death. She wondered what had brought on the fatal attack of violent temper. Probably one of the maids had broken a cup, or spilled a pitcher of cream.

She could not suppress the joyful smile that curved her lips when she realized that now John and Molly could marry. She turned to Roth to express her thought, but Nemus was talking again.

"John in Trenton now. Sell house and take care of business." He looked significantly at Juliana's stomach. "After baby come, they will quietly seek preacher. John and Molly say you both come, bring baby."

Juliana squeezed Roth's arm, her nails biting into his skin in her excitement. "Oh, Roth, isn't that wonderful of them; waiting so that I can see them get married."

Roth patted her hand and agreed that it was very thoughtful of John and Molly. "You know," Juliana mused out loud, "I'm not surprised that Iva died the way she did. She was always going into a rage over the slightest thing. I always felt so sorry for John. Thank God he got up the nerve to leave her. She was destroying him."

Juliana grew quiet, remembering the damage the vicious, vengeful woman had caused in her own life. If Iva hadn't lied to Sate, she might be married to him today. Roth stirred beside her, and she was ashamed. She had a good and wonderful husband who loved her very much. And Sate? She wondered if he would have accepted her pregnancy the way Roth had.

She gave herself a mental shake of impatience and turned to Nemus, touching his sleeve. "Is there any other news from Squaw Hollow? Is Molly still baking pies?"

Nemus shook his white head. "John say no bake pies while he's gone. He don't trust men when he not there. He say maybe no more bake pies, ever; maybe he be back with plenty money."

Juliana nodded her agreement. "Iva had money all right, and she clung to it fiercely. She even served short rations at her own table. Many times I went to bed still hungry. And the poor servants, I don't know how they managed on the scraps she allowed them."

She looked out across the twilight-shrouded clearing, recalling the tight rein Iva had kept on her purse strings. "Isn't it ironic," she said thoughtfully, "that Iva wouldn't give John a divorce, and now because of her spite her estate goes to him."

"Justice, I guess," Roth said. "It's a shame how some people can become so greedy."

Nemus grunted. "There is one like that in settlement now. She bake pies, too. No good at it, though. Pies too thin, too sour. Molly say she cut corners. She say woman charge too much for such mess."

Juliana smiled. She could just hear her soon-to-be sister-in-law. Her round little chin would jut out, and her eyes would snap in indignation. "Who is this woman that has riled Molly so, Nemus?"

"Sate Margruder's bondswoman." Nemus's words dropped like rocks on Juliana's heart. In her mind she saw the brash young woman sidling up to Roth at the wedding party. The hot glimmer in her small eyes had spoken loudly of a passionate nature, of a physical hunger that needed regular feeding. Why had Sate gone off with Doxy, leaving such a willing bedmate behind? Was he the type of man who needed variety? When he tired of the red woman, did he return to the white one?

Suddenly she was swept with painful humiliation. She couldn't believe that for almost a year she had given her love to such a man—a man who sought his pleasure from Indian squaws and tavern sluts. Her face tightened. She had been too ladylike for him; he had believed that she would fail as a lover.

Roth's deep voice shattered Juliana's self-mocking thoughts, bringing her back to the present. "Are rumors still going around that war will break out between the Indians and whites again?"

"Talk still go. Some say English in Canada now offer money to Indian for settler's scalp. People say English eager for fight between white and red man, that the Redcoats tell the red man the white militiamen can't be relied upon to fight, that it will be easy to whip them. That after a few battles white man's thoughts turn to homesteads and families, and that settlers will turn their backs on the fighting, walk away."

Roth nodded gravely. "In a sense that is true. But most of our settlers are expert marksmen, and they fight to the finish when it comes to defendin' their homes and countryside."

Nemus shook his head. "The British think poor of American fighters. Claim that they unruly and untrustworthy."

Anger flushed Roth's face. "Yeah, and by God that's where the bastards made their mistake," he retorted hotly, "when they thought they could lick us before. If we have to beat hell out of them again, then we will. But it's damned underhanded for them to deliberately turn the Indians on us again."

Nemus knocked his pipe out against a rock. Slipping it into a pocket, he looked at Roth and asked quietly, "Do you know your friend Margruder is prisoner in Chief Red Feather's camp?"

Roth's surprised "The hell you say?" eclipsed Juliana's small distressed cry. While Roth was demanding, "When did this happen?" she was agonizing over the possibility that Sate was being tortured. She had heard such horrible stories of Indians' cruelty to white captives. She made herself listen to Nemus's answer to Roth's question.

"Six braves take Margruder on day you do marriage dance."

Roth's brow wrinkled in surprise. "He's been there that long? I know Margruder pretty well, and I'm thinkin' he could have been gone from there a long time ago if he wanted to."

The Indian's hooded eyes rested briefly on Juliana's white face. Then, looking off toward the forest, he said, "Margruder have reason to stay. He watch and listen in camp. If Red Feather plans mischief he will manage to know it. Then he slip away to warn his friend and his woman."

Juliana shot the old brave a quizzical look. How exactly had he meant "his woman"? Was he referring to her as Roth's woman, or had he meant she was Sate's? When she felt Nemus's eyes on her again, she nervously looked away. His sharp penetrating eyes were able to see and understand things that were hidden from ordinary people. She slapped at a mosquito that had drawn blood from her bare ankle, and Roth stood up, drawing her with him.

"I'd better get you inside before the pesky little devils carry you away."

"I don't know which is worse," she muttered peevishly, entering the cabin, "the mosquitoes at night, or the flies by day. Either is enough to drive you crazy."

Nemus's leathery face stirred in a semblance of a grin as he watched Juliana scratch at a large welt on her arm. Ulie's skin was tender, not tough like the Indian squaw, nor covered with bear grease whose odor repelled any insect that came around.

Snow Bird had put everything straight in the cabin, and had retired to her pallet in the corner. Hearing her gentle snoring, Juliana smiled. It was a great relief to have the old squaw here.

"The old one is tired," Nemus said as he stood beside her. "I was day longer on the trail because of her age. But when your time come, her age will benefit you. She has helped many babies into world."

He picked up his bedroll of furs from beside the door and held out a hand to Roth. "I leave at daybreak, so will sleep outside, not to awaken you when I leave."

Roth shook his head, thanked him for bringing the squaw, and urged him to visit again. Nemus nodded and turned to Juliana. Laying a hand on her shoulder, his black eyes gazed into hers. "May your white god look down on you with favor when your birthing time comes. May your pain be not too great, and may your son be strong and healthy."

Juliana lifted her hand to cover the red wrinkled one and smiled warmly. "Thank you, Nemus, for bringing Snow Bird to me. Give John and Molly my love, and tell them that I miss them terribly. Tell them the baby and I should be ready to attend their wedding by the last of November, just before the first snowfall."

Nemus did not voice his doubt, but the quick glance he slid over Juliana said that it would be more like December before she could travel. Without further words, he turned and walked through the door. When Juliana moved to the window to watch him, he had already disappeared into the darkness.

She slumped against the door frame, a melancholy settling over her. It seemed as though Nemus had taken all civilization with him. He had been a touch of family, of home. A single yowl of a wolf drifted down from the hills, its plaintive sound making her shiver. She had tried, but she could not make herself like it here. Roth was a wonderful man, but . . .

She stood gazing into the darkness until Roth called her to bed. She carried her unrest with her, and she was a long time falling asleep. She could not get Sate out of her mind. Was he suffering in that Indian camp, or was Doxy consoling him? Although Nemus said that he was a captive, maybe Doxy had told her a half truth. Maybe Sate stayed there because of the young squaw. Roth had said that he was the sort of man who didn't stay anywhere he didn't want to.

When Juliana finally drifted off, the old dreams of Sate returned to fill her sleep. Once again he held her in his arms. A moan and happy sigh escaped her lips, and then all was silent.

CHAPTER 18

The sun was hot and the scent of dark green cedar filled the humid air as Juliana sat listlessly on the small porch. Occasionally she set the rocker in motion, but more often she sat quietly, staring out at the autumn forest, every so often dabbing with a handkerchief at the fine film of prespiration that gathered on her upper lip.

Her body was quite cumbersome now, and she eased her back against the chair, seeking a comfortable position, while inwardly praying that a breeze would find its way to her. She sighed softly. Would this heat never break? Roth had said this morning that it was an unusually hot September, the first he'd ever experienced. Snow Bird had agreed, adding that the last one like this she could remember was about fifty years ago.

Juliana glanced down at her clasped fingers resting lightly on her protruding stomach. The baby should have been here a month ago, and she was quite worried about its being overdue. And Roth was worried also, she knew. Several times a day she caught him watching her, concern in his eyes as he asked her how she felt, if the baby was kicking much.

The infant's vigorous movement was the only reason she wasn't more upset at its reluctance to enter the world, although for the life of her she couldn't figure out why it was taking a month longer than she had figured. Over and over she had counted back to the time of Tom's death and always came up with the same date; it could not otherwise.

Juliana slowly rubbed her stomach, telling herself that the baby had to be all right in order to move about so much. And, too, Snow Bird wasn't in the least worried that she was so late. She only muttered brusquely when asked about it, "He come when time is right."

A long sigh escaped her lips as she leaned her head back. She hoped the time would soon be right. She was tired of lumbering around, looking like a waddling duck, even though Roth claimed she had never looked more beautiful. She smiled ruefully. She doubted his claim; how could she possibly look beautiful with that huge stomach and her ankles all swollen? Dear Roth, so kind and gentle.

Inside, she heard Snow Bird moving about, the rattle of a pan, a scrape of the dipper against the wooden pail. Her lips curved softly. A bond of affection had developed between them as she learned from the old woman.

She and the squaw had formed the habit of sitting together in the shade of the porch every afternoon, she sewing on tiny garments and Snow Bird chewing on a piece of doeskin which would be made into baby moccasins when sufficiently soft. The old woman's teeth were well worn down from years of chewing hides, and she paused often to rest her gums. It was then that she spoke of herbs, barks, and roots, and how if properly mixed together they would cure various ailments.

Yes, the elderly squaw had imparted to her knowledge that was priceless; living in a wilderness, her nearest neighbor thirty miles away, she had no one to talk to, and equally important to her, Snow Bird had helped her lose a fear that had been born the day of her coach ride from Trenton, the terrifying fear of being lost. If she was to be lost in a blizzard today, she knew to burrow herself in snow bank and wait until it had blown itself out.

Recalling that frightening experience in the snowstorm brought Sate to mind. Was he still in the Indian camp? she wondered. And would he, as Roth and Nemus claimed, be able to warn them if danger should arise? Her eyes grew soft with the assurance of her mind that he would. He was the sort of man who would find a way to look after a friend.

Believing Sate to be nearby had calmed most of Juliana's fears the past two months. As for the winter ahead, she had a secret plan. When she and Roth returned to the settlement for John's wedding, she was going to insist on remaining. She knew that John and Molly would add their encouragement, and that between the three of them Roth would surely agree.

Lulled by the confidence that she would soon escape the loneliness of the small cabin and its lonelier surroundings, she closed her eyes and rocked slowly, trying to ignore the boiling heat of the sun.

Juliana was half asleep when suddenly she clutched the arms of the chair, her breath catching in her throat. A pain such as she had never experienced before had ripped through her lower body like lightning cutting through a black cloud. As she sat rigidly still, her face drained white, the pain gradually eased, and she could breathe again. As she struggled to her feet, calling out to Snow Bird, she knew the baby was on its way and, crazily, she half wished it wasn't so. Suddenly, after waiting all this time, cold fear had struck her.

The squaw was immediately at her side, leading her into the cabin. "He ready to come now." She grinned through her stubby teeth. When Juliana would have headed toward the bed, a bony hand on her arm directed her away from it. "No lay down. Better you move about. Next pain may not come for hours. First baby take long time, maybe."

When half an hour of walking around the small room had ticked by and no more cramps attacked her, Juliana decided that the old woman was right. She felt fine now; there was only a small nagging ache in her lower back. She looked around for something to occupy her mind, to pass the time.

She spotted the dough she had put on the hearth to rise earlier in the morning and glanced at the clock. Would she have time to form it into loaves and bake it? When she put the question to Snow Bird the old woman smiled indulgently: "You have plenty time."

Her second pain came as she kneaded the dough, bending her over and stilling her hands. Snow Bird glanced at her in surprise, then grinned. "He come sooner than I think."

The loaves were in the oven and almost baked when the next jolt hit Juliana. But she was used to it now, and the spasms of fear did not grip her so badly. It would last but a minute, then go away. When she could move again she walked to the door and gazed at the western horizon.

Brushing a strand of damp hair from her forehead, she was startled to see that dark rolling clouds had gathered, dimming somewhat the heat of the sun as it sank behind the hills. Roth should be coming home now, she thought, and she wished he'd hurry. She needed the comfort of his presence.

Snow Bird's soft step sounded behind her. "When your man come home, don't tell him at once. Men get nervous and in the way. Let him eat and have pipe first."

Juliana turned and stared belligerently at the dark, leathery face. What was the woman thinking of? Didn't the old squaw know that she desperately needed Roth's arms about her, assuring her that everything would be all right?

She became aware then of the watching look in the black eyes, and knew that she would be judged by her actions tonight. The old woman would think poorly of her if she cried and clung to Roth. Her back stiffened proudly, and she answered loftily, "I had no intention of telling him."

The corners of Snow Bird's lips lifted slightly in amusement, but as she padded back to the fire she said softly, "You would make fine Indian squaw, Ulie."

Juliana's body was gripped one more time before Roth returned home, his shirt hanging damp on his body, his sweaty hair curling tightly over his head. Giving Juliana a hurried peck on the cheek, he took clean clothes from a peg in the wall and grabbed up a towel and bar of yellow soap. "I'm gonna take a dip in the creek before supper," he said as he went through the door. "I smell like a boar hog."

When the three sat down to eat a short time later, the night was black and heavy with humidity. Mosquitoes buzzed in and out through the open door and Juliana and Roth swatted at them impatiently.

"We're gonna have one hell of a storm," Roth grunted. Wiping his wet brow, he added, "And it wouldn't surprise me to see it snow soon after."

"Surely not." Juliana looked at him in surprise. "I don't see how it's possible."

"It happens," Snow Bird agreed with Roth. "I see it often. One week so hot the skin scorches, the next week walk in snow."

When Roth drained his coffee cup and pushed away from the table, Juliana rose and began to clear away the dishes. When she reached for his plate she was brought to her knees by a searing hot flash that tore through her whole frame. Roth's chair went over backward as he jumped up and knelt beside her contorted figure. "What is it, Juliana?" Anxiety clouded his eyes as he swept her up in his arms.

"Baby. He come pretty quick," Snow Bird explained,

leading the way to the bed. "Lay Ulie down, I examine her."
When Roth had stretched Juliana out on the feather mattress
the old woman added with a wave of her hand, "You go
outside, smoke pipe."

The big man stood a moment, looking down at Juliana
helplessly, then at her encouraging smile moved through the
door, around the back to the chip-yard where he sat down on
the weathered chopping block. He reached for his tobacco
pouch, unaware of the lightning zigzagging through the sky,
the distant rumble of thunder rolling through the hills.

Two hours and three pipes later Roth was arrested by a sharp
sound, as though two palms had been slapped together. Relief
smoothed his features when on the hot, heavy air an angry wail
rang out.

"Thank, God, it's finally here."

Juliana lay spent, thankful for the cessation of the convul-
sions that had gripped her body relentlessly the past hours. Her
eyelids drooped, then opened expectantly when Snow Bird,
smiling so proudly she thought the thin old lips would surely
split, lay a tiny bundle in her arms.

"Your son, Ulie."

Juliana was sure her heart couldn't bear the joy that washed
through her as she gazed in awe at the small head resting in the
crook of her arm. She ran loving fingers over the cap of silky
hair. "My goodness, baby," she said softly. "Where did all
that black hair come from? As far as I know, neither of your
parents have any black-haired relatives."

She glanced up at the old squaw and frowned. The Indian
woman watched her and the baby, a strange, knowing
amusement flickering over her features. As her eyes searched
the wrinkled face, trying to analyze what she had glimpsed, the
baby fussed, his rosebud mouth working eagerly.

Snow Bird, her face once again wearing its usual stony
expression, leaned over Juliana, saying, "He hungry," as she
untied the ribbons at the throat of the muslin gown. "You feed
now."

The squaw's disturbing, enigmatic look forgotten in her first
role of motherhood, Juliana guided a nipple into the little
mouth as though she had done it a hundred times before.

The newborn nursed greedily and, still bemused by her son's
plentiful supply of black hair, his mother touched it tenderly.
"That extra month certainly gave you a cap of hair, baby," she
murmured softly.

Snow Bird shook her white head. "No late baby," she grunted. "He full term."

Lord, I'm tired of hearing how I miscalculated my child's arrival. Juliana's lips tightened grimly. There was irritation in the words she snapped out: "Snow Bird, that's just not possible. I should know, after all."

The old woman shook her head stubbornly, muttering, "Baby full term."

Juliana's eyes bored into the stiff retreating back. She opened her mouth to refute, then, shrugging, snapped it shut. "Senile old woman," she muttered, then turned an adoring look on her son. "What does she know, huh, baby?"

The sound of familiar footsteps lifted Juliana's gaze from the nursing baby. She held out a hand to Roth as he sat down on the edge of the bed. His eyes searched her tired face and, running a caressing hand over her hair, he asked huskily, "How are you feeling, honey?"

Juliana lifted a hand to his sun-weathered cheek. "Tired a bit, but happy." She looked back down at the baby. "How do you like your son?"

Roth watched the baby a moment, then ran a finger around the small pursed lips tugging at his mother's breast. Letting his hand linger on the same breast, he mused out loud, "He's so little. Do you suppose he'll ever make a big man?"

Juliana frowned. Was Roth finding fault with her perfect baby? Her arms tightened around the warm bundle and she said reproachfully, "Of course he will."

Roth grinned at the sharp tone. "What shall we call him, this big boy?" he asked teasingly.

Juliana relaxed at the soft, bantering words. "I would like to name him Nathan, after my father. That is"—she lifted her eyes to Roth—"if you don't mind."

"That's an awfully big name for such a little tyke," Roth continued to tease.

Juliana kissed the top of the downy head. "He'll grow up to it, my big boy."

Roth continued to gaze down at Juliana, his fingers now toying with the open edges of her gown. Slowly he pulled them apart, revealing both breasts. Looking into her eyes, he slid a hand over the free one and slowly caressed it. Laughing lightly, he joked, "I'm jealous of the little fellow. He's got my spot there."

Seeing the dark desire in his eyes, Juliana drew his head down to lie on her breast. "Oh, Roth dear," she murmured, "I know it's been hard on you, but try to be patient a little longer."

Roth pulled the pink nipple between his lips and muttered around it, "I will, honey, but, damn, it's gonna be hard."

"It looks to me as if it is now," Juliana teased, nodding significantly at the bulge pushing at the front of his trousers.

Roth raised his head and, giving her a mock glower, promised, "I'll fix you, lady, when the time comes. I'm gonna keep you in bed for a week."

"Only a week?" Juliana pouted, feigning disappointment.

"I'd better get out of here," Roth growled, kissing her cheek and standing up. He smoothed out the covers where he had sat, then, leaning over and kissing Juliana lightly on the lips, said, "Get a good night's sleep, honey. You, too, Nathan." He gently touched the baby's head.

Across the room, on her blanket, Snow Bird was fast asleep, and as Roth blew out the candle on the small table beside the bed, he noted that Juliana, too, had drifted off. He quietly pulled the seldom-used bedroll from under the bed and unrolled it in front of the door. If there was a breath of air he wanted to feel it. Thirsty, he moved silently across the floor to the water pail kept in the dry sink. As he lifted the gourd dipper to his lips, a flash of lightning revealed a movement right outside the window. Slipping the dipper back into the pail he dashed to the door in time to see the shadowy figure of an Indian woman sprint away in the darkness. Rushing onto the porch, he stood listening.

In the still, close darkness the sound of running feet was loud at first, then gradually faded away down the path that led to the river. Roth swore under his breath. He could never catch her in this darkness. She could elude him a dozen different ways.

But as he returned inside, Roth had no doubts about why the young squaw—and she had to be young to run so fast—had come to spy on them. Red Feather must have sent her to see if the baby had arrived yet. How long, he wondered, had some squaw or other waited and watched outside the cabin?

Gooseflesh broke out on his arms and he shivered in the heat. How careless he had been of their lives. How easy it would have been for a brave to sneak into the cabin while they slept.

When he finally stretched out on the blankets, two things had been done. The door and two windows were closed and barred, and he had decided that as soon as possible he was going to face the old chief and tell him to keep his braves away from his cabin.

Sometime during the night Juliana roused to hear vaguely the roll of thunder and the slash of rain across the window-panes. The air had cooled and, sleepily, she pulled the light quilt up around her shoulders and snuggled Nathan up against her side.

CHAPTER 19

Out of habit, Sate awoke at dawn. In the early morning hours, while it was still cool, he hunted game with the braves; they were hours that he looked forward to.

As much as he enjoyed walking the forest again, however, the short time of relative freedom had its drawback. Many times his heart was set afire with the desire to make it permanent. Only the dark threat of danger hanging over Juliana and Roth kept him staying on.

Stretching his long, bare limbs on the roughly woven blanket tucked around a pallet of cedar boughs, he wondered why Red Feather hadn't acted against his friend yet. His time spent in the chief's camp had taught him that he wasn't a man to make fast decisions, nor on the other hand was he one to forget a grudge. Sooner or later he would move against his son-in-law.

A frightening thought hit Sate. It would be like the cunning old devil to await the birth of the child, give Roth time to love and cherish it, *then* cut him down in one brutal stroke.

"Never!" The single word came so loudly, so forcefully, that Doxy stirred and complained in her sleep. In an inward whisper, Sate continued, "I will tighten my watch, keep my ears attuned. Nothing he does or says will escape me."

He stared up at the hole in the teepee's roof through which smoke from the fire escaped, his eyes narrowed contemplatively. It shouldn't be too difficult an undertaking, for more and more the chief seemed to trust him. He hadn't been invited to sit in on council meetings yet, but it hadn't appeared to bother the old man that his prisoner had sat only feet away clearly hearing every word, although he hadn't understood everything. Even the night plans to start raiding the whites come spring had been freely discussed in his hearing.

It had been a relief to learn that at least for several months there would be a respite of sorts for the settlers. He would have plenty of time to get word to Roth, send him to warn them. And through the winter months they could mold their bullets and lay in a plentiful supply of gunpowder in readiness for the savages when they swept through the village. And those living in isolated cabins and lone outposts could move into the settlement and fight their battles there.

Would full daylight never come? Sate moved restlessly, anxious to leave the confines of the small tent where the hot, humid air was stifling. But to walk about alone in the night would be pushing his luck.

He turned on his side. Maybe he could lull himself back to sleep, reenter the dream he had awakened from. A dream where Juliana had lain in his arms, her lips and hands caressing him.

Minutes passed and sleep would not come. Thoughts of Juliana only tensed his body, tightened it with a driving need for her. Sighing heavily, he ran a hand down his flat stomach and slowly rubbed his hard arousal. Lord, how he ached for her softness beneath him, her arms holding him close, reaching eagerly to meet the thrusts of his hips.

He turned his head and looked in the direction of Doxy's blankets. He had kept his word about never laying with her again, but . . . His eyes skimmed over her curled form. She could at least give him relief, if not fulfillment and contentment.

No, he thought contemptuously; never. Besides, Doxy had recently found a source of satisfying her own needs and he didn't want to encourage her in thinking that he wanted her back. His lips twitched slightly, remembering how he accidentally stumbled onto the squaw and her new lover.

One afternoon, a few weeks back, right after a light shower, he and another brave had gone squirrel hunting. Once in the woods they had gone off in different directions, and the damp leaves had given off no rustle as he trod softly, eyes searching the forest. Then a sudden snap of wood, a small branch or twig, had halted him behind a tree. He let his eyes slowly scan the vicinity, waiting for a glimpse of an animal or perhaps human form. He smiled when he caught sight of two half-grown squirrels rolling around in play, much as a couple of pups would do.

He decided that they were too small to waste gunpowder on. He was ready to step from behind his concealment when the muted sounds of lovemaking came from his right. Amusement glimmered in his eyes as he followed the sound, wondering which of the braves had found a willing squaw so early in the day.

Sate came upon the pair in a small shaded patch of tall fern. He recognized immediately the naked back of the brave, rising and falling rhythmically as he drove at the female body wrapped around him. The crisscrossing scars on the copper skin could only belong to one brave. "The Silent One," his people called him.

As a young man, in his late teens, he had been captured by an enemy tribe and beaten with knotted strips of wet rawhide. But worse, as a last act of cruelty, his tongue had been cut out. Ever since then the young women of the tribe had shied away from the mute brave.

Which of the young maids, Sate wondered, as he watched the couple, had agreed to lay with the Silent One? For certainly she wasn't being forced. She was working feverishly beneath the red body, reared up on her heels, panting like an animal.

Straining to see over the brave's back, to catch a view of the female face hidden beneath the scarred shoulders, Sate almost laughed aloud when he recognized Doxy, her face contorted with pleasure.

I'll be damned, he thought, easing himself to the ground and leaning back against a tree. The poor devil must be in a hard way indeed.

His grin was almost fiendish as he continued to watch Doxy and her new lover. He had her where he wanted her now. One word to the chief of his discovery and it could be all over for her. In Red Feather's camp, death was the punishment for unfaithfulness.

Following an exceptionally loud grunt and a high squeal, signs that the crest of pleasure had been reached, Sate rose and went to stand beside the pair. The Silent One sprawled tiredly over the squaw, his breathing fast and hard; her eyes were closed, an arm flung over her head. It wasn't until the spent brave was crawling to his knees that they became aware of his presence.

Doxy saw him first. Her eyes widened, and with a whimpering cry she tried to roll from beneath the body that still straddled her hips. The stricken fear in her eyes caused the brave's head to turn quickly. As he stared up at Sate, shame and alarm flooded his black eyes. Resignedly he rolled off the now tense body and sat waiting to receive a knife in his heart.

The trapper gazed down at the bowed head, pity for the mute stirring inside him. What a shame this proud young man was reduced to chancing his life, finding release with another man's woman.

Doxy touched Sate's arm timidly. "What are you going to do, Margruder?" Fear laced her voice.

Sate looked at her, his eyes narrowed slits. "What do you think I'm gonna do?"

Doxy dropped her eyes, swallowed nervously, but made no answer. "You know *what* I could do," Sate prodded. When she nodded dumbly he pulled her to her feet. "I'm not sure that you do. Suppose you tell me what you're thinking I'll do."

She licked her dry, trembling lips. "You have . . . you have the right to . . . to kill us."

"That's right. Do you have a good argument as to why I shouldn't? In the eyes of the tribe you have shamed me."

Her fingers twisting and torturing each other, sweat breaking out on her forehead, Doxy choked out, "No one but you knows about me and the Silent One. If you will forget what you saw I swear that from now on I'll be a good squaw, not give you any trouble at all."

Sate studied the repentant expression on the copper-colored face, not entirely fooled by it. He had discovered that she had a habit of quickly forgetting promises made. So, to add emphasis to the dangerous predicament she had placed herself in, he grabbed her wrist and tightened his fingers around it. "I'll think on your words, but I'll tell you this—one more threat, one more dirty trick, and I'll go straight to the chief." He scowled down at her. "Do you believe that?"

Doxy nodded her head vigorously, nudging the Silent One to do the same. "I will be the perfect squaw." Sate turned to the mute. The brave made no motion of his head, but relief and promise shone in his black eyes.

A grimace of satisfaction flickered across Sate's lips. To save his own hide, Doxy's lover would be ever watchful that she behaved herself.

And so far she has kept her word, Sate mused now as noises outside the teepee hinted that the village was coming alive. She was careful to do his every bidding, bringing him the biggest and tenderest pieces of meat when the braves gathered for the evening meal.

But that could change in the blink of an eye, he reminded himself, sitting up and reaching for his clothes. Time might dull the fear he had implanted in her and he would do well to continue his close vigilance of the cunning girl.

Sate and his three hunting companions came to a shady glade and flopped down beside a swift-running stream that sparkled through it. They drank deeply of the cool, clear water, then chewed industriously on strips of pemmican.

They had seen no game since leaving the village early this morning, and it was now well past noon. The heat was keeping the animals in the coolness of their lairs, and the heavy atmosphere was now affecting the hunters in the same manner. After a few desultory remarks between them, they stretched out and dozed.

The sun was well to the west when Sate and the braves awakened and resumed the hunt.

It was beginning to look as though they would return home empty-handed when from a timbered ridge there came the whistle of a buck deer. Sate moved stealthily toward the sound, slipping behind a tree when he spotted the animal. He stood a moment, gazing with admiration at the magnificent antlered head, the nostrils delicately quivering, sniffing at the air. Almost reluctantly he raised the rifle to his shoulder. Then, his breath eager in his breast, his finger tightened on the trigger. The deer dropped, the ball taking him in the heart. His companions, who had stopped and waited at a distance, let out a whoop and ran toward the fallen prey. As they pulled knives from their waistbands and began swiftly to dress down the large game, Sate sighed wearily. Night was close at hand, and they were still some distance from camp.

Heat lightning flashed in the north as Sate walked behind the two braves carrying the deer between them. He prayed a full-fledged storm would develop and cool the stifling heat. It was fully dark when the welcome smell of wood smoke and cooking brought a tired smile to his face. Soon his gnawing hunger would be sated.

Red Feather and his braves sat around a fire, wild, picturesque figures, lean, ragged, and disheveled. A rag-tag bunch. Sate's lips curved. Had they always been so slovenly, or were they just giving up as the whites pushed them farther and farther away from their territory?

He turned his gaze to the cooking fires some yards away, quickly scanning the women who moved about, preparing supper. He could not spot Doxy. He stared out through the woods, a dark uneasiness in his mind. Where was she? His apprehension growing, he strode toward their teepee. She was probably sleeping instead of helping the other squaws.

The tent was empty. Sate stared down at the grass-mat floor a moment, then walked back outside, scanning the camp, searching for the Silent One. Maybe Doxy had taken him into the forest for a quick tumble.

But the brave sat with the others, a noticeable tension in his posture. Now why, Sate wondered as he walked toward the man, does he look away from me, almost with guilt? He banished the thought when he glimpsed Doxy's father approaching the fire and hurried to intercept him.

"Half Step, do you know where your daughter is?"

The middle-aged Indian nodded, his breast visibly puffing up with pride. "Chief Red Feather has sent her to the cabin of Roth Adams. It has come to his attention that the new white wife has gone to her birthing bed. He say watch and see what baby is; boy or girl." Half Step paused, then added importantly, "Our chief tell me that if baby is man-child, Adams will soon pay for the wrong he did the gentle Zoe."

The dark threat of the words took Sate aback. He thanked God for the darkness that hid the anger and alarm that most surely showed in his eyes. He did not have to be told what would happen if Juliana gave birth to a son. Red Feather would surely steal the child, and what he'd do to it he couldn't bear to think.

The image of the Indian's hands on the body of his son ripped through Sate's mind, leaving a trail of unbelievable anguish in its wake. "Never!" his mind shouted. "Never in my lifetime."

He turned abruptly and left the older man who still talked on. He had to get to Doxy before she made her report to the chief. If Juliana had given birth to a boy Red Feather must be told it was a girl. With winter coming on it would be several months before the lie was discovered. In the meantime Roth would have plenty of time to move his family to safety. As he moved into the darker blackness of the forest, he silently asked the question he had asked himself many times before: Why had Roth brought Juliana here in the first place, exposed her to certain danger? The damn fool.

Sate strained his eyes for the path that led to Roth's cabin, a path worn smooth by the late Zoe's daily visits to her parents. Finally, guided by the flares of lightning which grew in brilliance, he spotted the beaten way. A short time later he forded a shallow spot in the river, and hurried on. When the wavering candlelight in the Adamses' window appeared he halted and hunkered down beneath a tree within feet of where Doxy would pass on her return to the Indian village. He took his pipe from a shirt pocket, tamped it with tobacco, then struck his flint over it. Leaning back, he prepared himself for a long wait.

Two hours passed as Sate sat in the close darkness, slapping at mosquitoes and listening to the gathering force of the storm as it drew nearer. What was taking so long? He got to his feet and began pacing the forest floor. Was Juliana having a difficult time? She was so delicately slender. His hands clenched in his desire to be with her.

He judged it to be well after ten o'clock when the humidity that had smothered the land like a blanket for three days met the cool northern breeze and exploded. He swore through gritted teeth as the constant zigzag of lightning and pouring rain blinded him, and the crackling and rumbling thunder deafened him to any other sound. Quickly soaked in the deluge, he wavered, wondering what to do. There were caves nearby. Should he take cover in one? A tree was no place to seek shelter at a time like this. Besides, it was becoming damnably cold.

When a bolt of lightning splintered a tall oak only yards away, his mind was made up. With the exploding light seemingly chasing at his heels, he turned off the path and dove into the first cave he found. It was tall enough for him to sit upright, and was in sight of the narrow trail. Shivering in his wet clothing, he wrapped his arms around his knees and waited.

In the half hour that passed the rain slackened, the thunder became a distant rumble, and the air became miserably cold. When only a fine drizzle pattered on the leaves, Sate returned to the path and stared in the direction of the Adamses' cabin. The windows were black now, signifying that everyone was in bed, and that everything must have gone well.

His lips firmed grimly. Where was Doxy, then? Had she slipped past him in the storm? He suddenly had the strong, sure feeling that he should be back at camp. Giving in to its insistence, he struck out running, an inner voice urging, "Faster, faster."

Sate slackened his pace only when firelight shone through the darkness, caution warning him not to be seen. The chief would become suspicious and would ask many questions. Now was not the time to raise doubts in the old devil's mind.

Only one fire burned, that just inside the door of the council house. Slipping beneath a low-spreading cedar and peering into the long, low building, he was not surprised to see it crowded with braves. Everyone was anxious for Doxy's report.

He scanned the dark heads, and hope stirred in his breast. There was no sign of the young squaw. Maybe he could still head her off. Crouched on the balls of his feet, ready to slip away, he smothered an oath. A brave had shifted position, revealing Doxy kneeling in front of Red Feather. His eyes frozen on the woman who grasped her side and struggled to catch her breath, he knew she had been mere seconds ahead of him. When the chief stirred impatiently, she gasped out:

"The baby is here. A healthy man-child."

Sate slumped against the tree, two emotions warring inside him: wild elation that he had a son, although it would never know its real father, and a fear such as he had never known before. He waited with held breath for the chief's response to the news.

Red Feather's stern red features betrayed no emotion, not even by the blinking of an eye. After a moment he glanced at Doxy and grunted, "You may go now."

A muscle knotted and twitched at Sate's jaw when he caught the disappointment that slid over Doxy's face. "You sneaky, vengeful bitch," he ground out. "You want to hear all the details of what is planned for my son; hang on to every word, drain them to their last vengeful dregs."

When the squaw reluctantly rose and left the lodge, he slipped from his hiding place and hurried after her. Inside their teepee he found her squatted beside the fire, a smug, knowing look on her face. It was too much for him to bear. In two strides he was beside her, his hand lashing out, catching her across the cheek. She fell back and lay cowering at his feet. He stood over her, his eyes flashing a deep hatred.

"You'd better look afraid, you sorry squaw." He snarled. "I know about Red Feather's plans for my son." He came down on one knee and grabbed Doxy's chin, forcing her head up to look at him. "You listen carefully to what I'm gonna tell you. The day he attempts to steal the child is the day he dies . . . taking you with him."

Sate released his punishing grip and Doxy shrank back, her face ashen. "Please, Margruder," she begged frantically, "it will be no fault of mine if Red Feather raids Adams's place, takes your son. It would not be fair for you to blame me—"

"Don't give me that innocent noise," he interrupted her with an unpleasant twist of his lips. "You know everything that goes on in this camp. And you'll know when Red Feather plans to make his move. So, if you want to live to be an old squaw, you'll give me plenty of warnin'."

He was not completely satisfied with Doxy's eager nod and assurance that she would let him know the minute she heard anything. This one had a sly and devious mind. As he pulled the soaked shirt over his head and tossed it on the floor he caught her watching eyes with his own.

"To be on the safe side I'm gonna have a word with the Silent One. If he thinks that you're puttin' him in danger he'll drop you like a piece of fly-blown meat . . . and where will you get your pleasurin' then?"

A flash of defeat crossed Doxy's face and Sate was more at rest as he finished undressing and crawled between the blankets. The dread of losing the mute's attentions to her body appeared greater than the squaw's fear of death.

I'm not surprised, he thought, remembering the day he'd come upon the pair. While the Silent One had stared at him, stunned, he had dropped his gaze to where the brave's breechcloth had been pulled to one side. The size of the manhood resting against the squaw's stomach had been a spectacular sight indeed.

Sate turned several times, trying to get comfortable so that sleep would come. But excitement still gripped him and his mind wouldn't slow down. Juliana and his new son had taken firm hold on it. He had the overwhelming desire to see them.

He had tossed and turned for close to an hour before a small inner voice whispered, "Why not visit them? It would be so simple. As Roth's friend it would only be natural to go see the child. You have to see Adams anyhow; tell him how things stand with Red Feather, the danger he and his family are in."

Sate began to relax, now that a decision had been made. He lay quietly, formulating his plans. After discarding several ideas, he came up with what he thought the perfect one. Tomorrow afternoon, in front of all the others, he would invite Doxy to come fishing with him. Red Feather would understand that he wanted to be alone with his squaw and would not have them followed. Then, while Doxy fished, he would go on to the little cabin across the river.

His last conscious thought as he drifted off to sleep, was that soon he would see Juliana, and the child they had made together.

CHAPTER 20

It was still raining when Juliana awakened the next morning, although it was not the hard, slashing drive of last night. This rain was a comforting, steady wash on the cabin's roof. Nathan, snuggled warmly by her side, made sniffling noises and, smiling, she hastened to untie the ribbons at her throat and pull him closer to her. As the small mouth tugged hungrily at her breast, Juliana burrowed deeper into the covers. Warm and cozy she listened to the slow beat of the rain, thinking that she hadn't been so content in a long time. Tom Roessler had finally brought her fulfillment.

A series of grunts came from Snow Bird's corner, and soon the old squaw came shuffling toward the bed. Juliana smiled sleepily at her and the wrinkled face smiled back. "My son has a good appetite," she remarked softly. "He's a greedy little boy."

The elderly woman frowned. "Time you change him to other breast. Suck too long, nipple get sore."

She helped the new mother turn to her other side, then lay the infant back in her arms. She watched the drowsy pair a minute, then, satisfied that milk was flowing freely into the tiny pink mouth, she moved to the fireplace and stirred up the fire before starting breakfast.

The rustle of bed clothing drew Juliana's glance to where Roth had spread his bedroll last night. As she watched her husband, he sat up, stretched, and yawned, then, finding her eyes on him, rose and hurried to the bed.

"How's the beautiful new mother this morning?" He smiled, leaning over and kissing her forehead.

"Sore." She grimaced with a smile, adding quickly as she dropped her gaze to her son, "But worth every pain he caused me."

Roth ran a gentle finger down the infant's velvet smooth cheek, a slight frown marring his forehead. "I still think he's awfully small."

"Roth!" Juliana widened her eyes indignantly. She looked back down at the baby. "His father was a tall man, although not overly large. However, on my side, his grandfather was a large man, as is his uncle John."

"Well, maybe," Roth agreed, studying the small bundle in his wife's arms. "It just doesn't seem like he'll ever get big right now." He smoothed the child's dark head. "Does all this black hair come from his father?"

"No," Juliana answered, running her own hand over the silky black cap. "Tom was very fair. Nathan's dark coloring must come from some very distant relative, probably generations back."

She grinned mischievously. "Maybe some maiden relative, years ago, was indiscreet and it's just now coming out in my son."

Roth's eyes sparkled humorously. "No doubt the indiscretion was on his father's side."

"Of course," Juliana smilingly agreed as Roth stood up.

"I'm glad he doesn't look like his father," Roth said, walking toward the door. "It makes me feel all the more as if he's mine."

Juliana watched the big-framed man disappear outside, a tender, musing smile on her lips. What a wonderfully kind man he is.

A few minutes later she heard the spluttering noise Roth always made when washing up, and at the same time she became aware of the cool air seeping under the window frame. She sighed softly. Soon it would also be too cold to sit on the porch in her rocker.

She gazed down at the sleeping baby, and anxiety gripped her. What if they didn't get away from here before the snows started? And what if Nathan should become ill and they became snowbound? The thought was intolerable. Her arm tightened around her son as her delicate features set with determination. She would make sure they returned to Squaw Hollow before that happened. As soon as her strength returned it would be good-bye to this lonely little cabin.

Her thoughts were interrupted when Roth hurried back inside, going straight to the fire. "Man!" he said through chattering teeth. "It feels like winter out there."

Snow Bird nodded solemnly. "Soon Nemus come for me," she said, picking up a plate filled with eggs, salt pork, and fried potatoes and carrying it to Juliana.

I'll never be able to eat all that, Juliana thought as she eyed the steaming food. But when a little later Roth took a seat beside the bed, balancing his own breakfast on his lap, her plate was wiped clean. "I'm as greedy as the baby." She laughed when Roth raised a surprised eyebrow.

From her seat at the table Snow Bird grunted and remarked, "You eat for the papoose, too, now. Everyday you must eat much red meat. Make you, and your man-child, grow strong."

Juliana nodded. The old woman, and her husband, were going to be amazed at how fast she grew strong.

While Roth went to tend the stock, Snow Bird brought a basin of warm water, a bar of soap, a soft cloth, and Juliana's hairbrush to the bed. "While you wash, I bathe papoose." She laid a clean gown at the foot of the bed, then settled down with Nathan in front of the crackling fire in the fireplace. As she soaped his sturdy little body, she crooned an Indian lullaby in her gentle, cracked voice.

Shortly after lunch the rain stopped and rays of sun broke sporadically through the clouds. The wind dropped and, with it, the temperature. "Damned if it don't feel like we're about to go into winter," Roth speculated, placing a large log on the fire.

Snow Bird, sitting close to the heat and grinding corn for supper's pone, nodded wisely. "We have early winter this year. The bats fly low, and the bark on the trees is heavy. It will be long, cold one, with many blizzards."

Juliana shivered at the old woman's ominous prediction. She almost cried out when a loud rap on the door resounded through the cabin. Her fear-filled eyes looked to Roth, and her voice was tight as she whispered hoarsely, "Who could it be?"

"Don't be frightened, honey." Roth smiled reassuringly at her, but nevertheless took down the long rifle from over the mantel as he added, "It's probably some traveler looking for a bite to eat and a chance to warm his bones."

He moved to the door and, standing to one side, jerked it open. Juliana, propped up on an elbow, gazed at the tall figure leaning loosely against a porch support, then with a low gasp fell back on the pillows. "Sate Margruder!"

What is he doing here? She gaped at the two men greeting each other enthusiastically. Forgetting the presence of her husband, oblivious to Snow Bird's narrowed scrutiny of her face, her eyes devoured the man she still loved so desperately.

She forced herself back to a semblance of lucidity when Sate's lips curved in a rare smile and he said, "Well, friend, I see you're still wearing your scalp."

Roth laughed and ran his fingers through his heavy hair. "Yeah, but I'm surprised that you still are. I heard you've been old Red Feather's prisoner for the past few months. What's keepin' you there?" He teased, "Me, or a pretty young squaw?"

Sate's eyes darted toward the bed in the corner, his face flushing a dark red. For a moment he wanted to strike Roth's grinning face.

But Roth hadn't waited for an answer. Instead, he asked another question as he took Sate's arm and steered him across the floor. "Did you know that I've got myself a fine, healthy son?"

Managing to hide the tearing pain ripping through him, Sate muttered, "Yes, I heard. Nothing is missed in Red Feather's camp."

There was no emotion in the words, yet Roth caught the undertone of warning. When they stood looking down at Juliana, however, his face still wore a carefree smile as he said proudly, "Sate, this is Juliana, the woman I bent your ear about." Transferring his gaze to his wife, he added, "Honey, meet my friend, Sate Margruder."

Her voice husky, her lips trembling, Juliana said, "How are you, Sate Margruder?" she held her breath, wondering if he would betray what they both knew.

Sate stared down at the reality of the vision that had ruined his nights and teased his days. The small oval face and pale cloud of hair spread over the pillow brought a longing that threatened to bring him to his knees. For a long moment he fought the urge to grab her up and flee the cabin.

None of what he felt showed as he said quietly, "I'm tolerable, ma'am."

Unaware of the emotion that charged the air between his wife and friend, Roth pulled aside the blanket, revealing the little black head resting in the crook of its mother's arm. Without looking up he urged, "Bend down here, Sate, and take a look at my son."

Sate's eyes swept over Juliana and the infant and for a split second they grew reckless, dangerous, as he fought the desire to claim his son. It passed, but frustration shuddered through his body as he forced himself to say:

"You have a fine-looking boy there, Roth."

"Thank you, Sate." Roth smiled, then walked over to the fireplace to lay another log on the fire. Left alone, a silence grew between Juliana and Sate, neither knowing what to say to the other, but both remembering how it had been the last time they'd seen each other—hurled accusations from one, sobbing protestations from the other.

Sate lifted a hand as if to touch Juliana's cheek, then quickly dropped it. It was a little late to let his love show now. He'd had his chance and thrown it away.

Both gave a startled jerk when Roth called, "Come warm yourself, Sate, while you fill me in on what's goin' on in that old buzzard's camp."

"I can't stay too long," Sate answered with one last lingering look at Juliana and his son. "I'm supposed to be fishin'. I bought along a squaw who's waitin' for me at the river."

Roth looked uneasy. "Is that wise, lettin' her know where you are?"

Sate smiled thinly. "I don't have to worry about this one. She knows what will be in store for her if she opens her mouth about it."

He's talking about Doxy. Juliana blinked back hot tears, raw jealousy inside her. She knew she was posing a foolish question when she asked herself silently if he shared the young squaw's bed. He did, of course. Sate was a healthy, virile man.

She watched him take a seat beside her husband and heard Roth ask, "Well, how do things stand across the river? I'm sure Red Feather has his nose out of joint about me."

The trapper stretched his long legs to the fire, crossing them at the ankles. As his wet moccasins began to steam he grinned across at Roth. "He thinks that you took your present wife to bed while still married to his daughter."

Roth stared into the flames, shaking his head. "Of course I could never convince him that I didn't touch Juliana until we were married. With the child coming so soon he'll never believe that it belongs to her first husband."

Sate lowered his lids to hide the impatience in his eyes. Good Lord, couldn't the man count? It was a simple matter of arithmetic that the child couldn't be Tom Roessler's.

But then, he sighed inwardly, Juliana believed it, so why not Roth? He'd believe it was dead summer outside if she told him that it was. He stared bitterly into the flames, envying his friend's blind faith in his young wife, and wishing that he had had the same faith in her several months back.

Roth broke in on Sate's wishful thinking. "Is the old devil plannin' any devilment for me?"

Sate sent a warning inclination of his head toward the bed. Then, lowering his voice to a whisper, he asked, "Could we talk outside?"

Roth gave a silent nod at the grim tone, and they chatted about the weather for a while, predicting an early winter; plenty of snow. Then, after a short silence, Roth asked in innocent tones, "Would you like to take a look at my new stallion, Sate?"

Sate stood up. "It'll be good to look at real horseflesh for a change. I'm sick to death of thin, half-wild Indian ponies." There was a wistful note in his voice when he added, "I sure miss my own stallion . . . and Hawser. I hope Battle is takin' good care of them."

"The man seemed a responsible sort to me," Roth said, shrugging into his coat, then heading outside.

Sate followed him, but he stopped at the door and looked across the room at Juliana. She was sitting up, gazing at him. The sight of her hair hanging in disarray about her face and down her shoulders twisted his heart. She had looked like that the night he made love to her and started the life of his son.

Not daring to go near her again, he said gravely, "It was good to see you . . ."

Unshed tears glimmered in Juliana's eyes and she could make no response over the lump in her throat. She could only wonder dully how she was to rid herself of the emptiness in her heart after he walked through that door.

Before Sate followed Roth outside he walked back to where Snow Bird sat, and spoke to her in Shawnee. She nodded, and answered him in the same. When he closed the door behind him, Juliana looked at the old woman questioningly. "What did the trapper say to you, Snow Bird?"

Several long moments passed while piercing black eyes studied Juliana's flushed face. She was beginning to feel uncomfortable when finally the old squaw said quietly, "He say to make sure I watch over baby carefully. He say little one is special love baby."

Juliana stared at the white-haired old woman, bafflement in her expression. "What a strange thing for him to say," she puzzled out loud.

Snow Bird rose stiffly from the hearth and approached the bed. Uncovering the baby's face, she stared intently at the tiny features for a number of seconds. Then, while Juliana watched wonderingly, she put the cover back over the infant and stood up. Fixing the wide-eyed girl with her black eyes she stated, not questioned, "You know trapper before."

Taken by surprise, Juliana blushed guiltily. Her first thought was to deny the assertion, but she knew at the same time it would be useless. The wise old eyes would see straight through her.

Drawing a deep breath, she nodded. "You're right. Today isn't the first time I met Sate Margruder. I met him a few months before I became acquainted with Roth." She lifted anxious eyes to the watchful woman. "I'd appreciate it if you didn't tell Roth. He might feel hurt that I never mentioned it before, and though nothing happened between me and the trapper he might find it hard to believe."

Again there was a long silence before Snow Bird grunted, "Your secret safe with me, Ulie." But just as Juliana was relaxing, she asked bluntly, "When exactly you meet Margruder?"

Juliana shrugged. "Around mid-December."

It looked as though the old woman would speak again, but after a while she merely grunted and returned to her spot in front of the fire. Juliana sighed in relief, not really knowing why. But the simple questions had made her uneasy somehow, as though they were more meaningful that they seemed.

I'm being fanciful, she told herself impatiently after deep

thought proved no weighty significance to Snow Bird's curiosity.

A good twenty minutes passed before Roth pushed open the door, remarking, "It's colder than a whore's heart out there." As he stoked the fire and held his hands out to it, Snow Bird grunted agreement and put their supper on the table.

All through the meal, Roth talked and joked in his usual manner, but Juliana, who watched him closely, knew that he camouflaged what he was truly thinking. What had Sate said to him, she wondered, to bring the concern that lay in his eyes?

It wasn't until the fire was dying, the candles snuffed out, and he lay quietly beside her that Juliana received a hint of what was on her husband's mind. Sliding an arm beneath her head and bringing it to rest on his shoulder, he mused out loud, "It might not be a bad idea for us to head back to the settlement before long."

Sate Margruder walked swiftly toward the stand of maples where he had left Doxy with her fishing line. "Pray God," he muttered, "Roth gets her out of here soon. Otherwise, he's lost her . . . and I'm not thinking of Red Feather." His hands clenched into tight fists. It had taken all his willpower not to sweep Juliana and the baby up in his arms and carry them away. He knew as certainly as the wind would blow this winter that if she remained in that cabin much longer, he'd go after her.

CHAPTER 21

The first snowfall came a few days after Sate's visit to the Adamses' cabin.

Juliana awakened to the hushed silence outside and knew what it meant. "It's only a squall, quickly gone," she whispered hopefully. She heard Snow Bird stirring on her thick pallet of fragant cedar boughs, and turned her head to watch the old woman rise stiffly and walk across the floor to the window. She smiled sympathetically when the gnarled hands pulled aside the curtain and the thin lips grumbled in their native tongue.

The old soul hasn't many winters left, she thought, and it's only natural that she would want to spend them with her own people, not waste one snowbound winter with a pale-face family . . . although I know she likes us, she added thoughtfully as the wizened figure shuffled across the floor to the fireplace and knelt in front of it to rekindle the fire.

The aroma of meat cooking that Snow Bird later prepared in the iron skillet awakened Roth. He stretched and yawned, then lay still, listening. His deep sigh said that he, too, knew what the silence meant. The fact that he made no mention of the turn in the weather was proof to Juliana that he wasn't pleased with it.

He must be concerned about getting us back to the settlement, Juliana realized, since generally the men are jubilant at an early snowfall. The earlier it came, the longer the trapping season, and the larger the profit.

Juliana had more proof of Roth's preoccupation with nature's cold white gift when he left the bed without first tormenting himself by running his hands up her gown and caressing her body while kissing her breasts, carefully avoiding the nipples. They were exclusively Nathan's. This morning when Snow Bird would slyly glance down at his trousers she would see no hard arousal thrusting against it.

No, her poor husband had more serious things on his mind today, she thought, watching him wash up at the dry sink, then take a seat at the table. A wife and a new baby in an untamed wilderness was a big responsibility for a man.

Suddenly Juliana decided that she would join Roth at the table; have breakfast with him. She would show him that his mate was no useless weakling who would cling like a burden around his shoulders.

Snow Bird watched her slow progress across the floor and grunted approvingly. Roth's eyes lit up with pleasure, which was then quickly replaced by alarm.

"Are you sure you should be up, honey?" He jumped to his feet and helped her to sit down. "It's awfully soon after Nathan."

Juliana smiled up at him. "I feel fine, Roth. Only a little weak in the legs."

"She get stronger faster. It weakens woman to stay in bed long time," Snow Bird remarked, placing breakfast on the table. "After eat, Roth, go kill deer. I make good strong broth for Ulie to drink. Soon she be her old self."

But as the meal progressed Juliana knew by the way her husband's eyes kept straying to the window where the snow still fell like a white curtain that the old woman's encouraging words, and her own gay chatter, hadn't lessened his anxiety. And later, when he drew on his great fur coat and picked up the rifle, the kiss he dropped on top of her head before leaving was only an automatic gesture.

She rose and moved to the window to watch him disappear into the forest. She lingered a while, hating the drifting flakes, desperately wanting them to stop falling. When she turned her back to the window and surveyed the small room, an almost frantic expression was in her eyes. To be cooped up within these four walls for months would be more than she could endure. In the end she feared her feelings for Roth might turn against him, straining their marriage beyond repair.

Juliana moved purposefully to the table and began helping

Snow Bird clear it. She must regain her strength rapidly. From now on she would eat and drink any concoction the old woman prepared for her. The sooner she recovered her health, the sooner they could leave here.

The October snow had finally stopped, and the end of November was nearing. Although there had been no more of the white stuff, dark, threatening clouds hung often in the north as though warning they could expect more of the same at any time.

The weather, however, had turned so cold that Juliana and Roth now slept between feather ticks, Nathan snuggled between them, and a cured bearskin had been added to Snow Bird's blankets. And she padded a dozen times a day to the window, watching for Nemus to arrive.

Juliana and Roth continued to make plans for the trip back to Squaw Hollow, although it was always she who brought up the subject. Roth said very little, as though reluctant to discuss it. When Juliana would press him for a specific date his usual rejoinder was "There's no great hurry. The weather is holdin', and Red Feather is sittin' tight. Let's wait a while longer until you're really on your feet."

She could have pointed out that she had regained her strength weeks back and was now as healthy as ever. She held her tongue, though, not wishing to quarrel with Roth, even as she knew he didn't really want to return to the settlement. He had mentioned once that he disliked having a lot of people around him, that basically he guessed he was a wilderness man. Sometimes she almost wished that Red Feather would do something that would break Roth's belief that the old chief had forgiven him and would leave them alone.

Juliana pushed her unhappy, troubled thoughts away and lifted Nathan's slippery, wet body from the wooden tub and hurriedly enveloped him in the large towel that Snow Bird had warmed before the fire and now held up for her. Like his mother, the baby was healthy and alert, his round eyes moving solemnly around the room, full of curiosity.

As the infant grew and became more dear to Juliana, he also brought much puzzlement to her. Sometimes as she watched him she'd catch an expression on his small features that unaccountably sent her heart racing. The tiny face held a striking resemblance to someone familiar to her, but as hard as

she pressed her mind, the other face always eluded her. She
continued, however, to watch that fleet crinkling of the eyes,
the gentle curving of the small mouth. It would come to her
someday.

Sate knelt in front of a piece of cloudy mirror attached to the
teepee wall. Steam rose from the basin sitting on the floor
beside him as he screwed up his face, tightening the skin so
that he could scrape away the lather and black stubble on his
firm jaw.

I'm fixin' to do a fool thing, he thought as he swished the
straight razor in the water, then wiped it dry. He knew
to the very marrow of his bones that he was begging for
trouble . . . more heartache.

But since seeing Juliana again, her beautiful face haunted
him constantly. He couldn't put his mind to anything, couldn't
sleep at night. If Roth was wise he'd be taking his small family
back to Squaw Hollow any day, and this morning could very
well be the last chance he'd ever have to see her again. For
once she and his son were safely away, he was striking new
trail away from the vicinity.

Doxy lay stretched out on a fur next to the fire, her head
propped on the heel of her palm, her black eyes not missing a
move the trapper made. She watched him slip into clean
buckskins, lace on the tough deerhide leggings that would let
him run silently, then shove his feet into double-soled moccasins. Standing up, he shoved a broad-bladed knife into a sheath
on his right hip, then a tomahawk went into a sheath under his
left arm. The last to be placed on his person was a flintlock
horse pistol which he shoved into his waistband. She didn't
speak until he was striding toward the teepee entrance.

"So, you're off to visit Adams's woman."

Her sneering words hung in the air as the big man paused,
then turned around. Ice tinkled in the deep voice. "Where I'm
goin' is none of your affair . . . nor anybody else's . . . am
I right?"

Doxy dropped her eyes from the harsh face and, picking at
the bearskin, answered sullenly, "That is true."

"And if anybody else should ask where I am, tell them that
I've gone huntin'."

The squaw nodded shortly and he undid the teepee's laced
flap and stepped outside.

The river bore a thin crust of ice and the little pony snorted his displeasure as Sate forced him to ford it. Five minutes later horse and rider were approaching the Adamses' cabin.

Juliana swung the pot hook away from the flames and lifted the heavy lid off the kettle. With a long-handled spoon she stirred the bubbling stew. Her lips firmed in a grimace of distaste. She was getting mighty sick of venison and hoped that Roth would return with a couple rabbits for a change.

To kill some time she stretched out on the bed beside Nathan. While he played happily with the fingers she held out to him, her thoughts turned to the journey that must surely take place soon. Suddenly, her musings were abruptly interrupted by the sound of rapid hooves clip-clopping toward the cabin.

Alarm sparked in her eyes, as well as in Snow Bird's; they were two women alone. She slid off the bed and hurried to the window, then caught her breath sharply as Sate pulled his mount to a halt and dismounted.

"It's all right." She smiled at Snow Bird and rushed to open the door.

Sate looked at her soberly for a moment, then his harshly chiseled mouth softened with a smile. "How are you, Juliana?"

Juliana's slender hand jumped to her throat, her pulse beating rapidly against her palm. Oh, God, why do I have to love this man? she cried inwardly as an ache for him burgeoned within her.

It was only by making herself remember how this same man had once amused himself with her, falsely leading her to believe that he wanted marriage between them, that she was able to say coolly, "Well, you seem to come and go as you please. Does Red Feather trust you so completely?"

Sate lifted a contemptuous shoulder as he stepped past Juliana into the cabin. "The chief is an easy man to fool."

Especially if you're sleeping with a Pennacook squaw, Juliana thought with pain and bitterness, following behind him as he walked over to the fire and greeted Snow Bird. "Is Roth around?" The chair squeaked protestingly as he lowered his weight into it.

"No." Juliana took the remaining seat that was placed uncomfortably close to his. "He's out hunting." After a short pause she asked, "Would you like a cup of coffee?"

Sate shook his head. "I had some just before I left for here."

Jealousy, deep and alive, swept over Juliana. Doxy had made it for him.

A strained silence gathered, neither knowing how to break it. Snow Bird put an end to it temporarily when she rose and shifted the sleeping Nathan from the bed to the cradle that Roth had finished making the day before. Straightening up after tucking a soft blanket around the little body, she said stonily, "I need fresh air. Do not worry if I gone a couple hours."

As the old woman wrapped a heavy shawl around her head and shoulders, half of Juliana wanted to beg her not to go, while the other half wanted to hurry her out the door.

The door closed softly and Juliana and Sate were alone, the silence between them returning, heavier than ever. When the clock began to strike with a noisy whir of loosened cogs, they both jumped.

"Why do you suppose the old woman left us alone?" Sate asked hurriedly, as if to head off another spell of taciturnity between them.

"Probably for the reason she gave," Juliana answered rather sharply, the image of Doxy serving Sate coffee still eating at her. "I have always found her to be utterly guileless."

"Maybe." Sate nodded. Then, fixing her with ice-shot eyes, he made a statement that sent Juliana's blood racing. "You didn't waste much time gettin' married, did you?"

When her stunned mind regained composure, anger flooded in a dark wave across Juliana's face. "Can you blame me, a baby on the way and no husband to father it?"

Sate's quickly lowered lids hid pain and regret. "You could have—"

Juliana jumped to her feet, cutting him off, and with a rustle of skirts moved to the fireplace. She stared into the flames, a single tear sliding down her cheek. She was thinking, "God, the callousness of men," when she heard the squeak of a floorboard behind her. When she spun around, Sate stood only inches away.

Raw desire flamed in his eyes, demanding her response. She stared back at him, her heart thumping heavily as she thought, "I should move away from him, say something to break his hold on me," but her legs refused to move, her lips to utter a sound. After what seemed forever, Sate reached for her, gathering her into his arms. As he pressed her hips to his, the sinewy body enlivening every nerve in hers, he muttered thickly before searing her lips with his, "Ah, Juliana, you tear at my very soul."

The blood coursing wildly through her veins, the remembrance of his prior rejection of her gone as though it had never been, Juliana groaned and arched her back as desire mounted inside her. When Sate released her lips at last, tilted her chin so that she could see the haggard appeal in his eyes, she nodded eagerly.

In seconds they undressed each other, Juliana sighing at the sight of Sate's broad chest, the masculine grace of his flat muscled hips. Sate, eyeing hungrily the jutting firmness of Juliana's breasts, remembered how they had filled his caressing hands almost a year ago.

Juliana drew a long shuddering breath, and with a choked groan Sate swept her up and carried her to the bed. Laying her down gently, he came down beside her, one muscular leg thrown possessively across her hips. Tenderly, he kissed her forehead, her eyes, murmuring thickly before he took her lips, "God, the nights I've dreamed of this."

The minutes passed as they feverishly caressed each other with hands and lips, Juliana amazed that the real thing was so like the dream she'd had in Sate's cabin. Her body quivering in a passion too long denied, her need clouding her brain, for a moment she didn't understand when Sate whispered:

"Exactly how old is Nathan?"

She smiled then and whispered back, "Five and half weeks. Just short of the prescribed six."

"I won't hurt you, then?"

Her arms tightened around his broad shoulders. "No, darling, you won't hurt me."

For another moment the velvet tip of his stiff manhood worked deliciously against her stomach as his tongue laved her taut nipples, then he moved slowly between her thighs. And despite his urgency, he entered her gently, taking care not to hurt her.

When she had accepted all of him, gloriously filled with his largeness, his single long drawn breath said more to her than any words could have.

Sate began to move in long smooth strokes, becoming lost in an ecstasy greater than he had ever experienced, giving no thought to its possible consequences as he let his life-giving force flow into her.

Juliana eagerly accepted the demands of the powerful body as, glistening with sweat, it moved rhythmically over her.

They lay beside each other finally, breathing heavily, exhaustion enveloping Juliana, Sate's skin sweat-beaded.

Sate stared up at the smoke-stained ceiling, a deep sense of guilt washing over him as a vision of Roth Adams's face swam before him. God, what had he done; to his friend, to Juliana, to himself? Especially to Roth. The man was his friend, a good man, one who didn't deserve to have his wife taken away from him.

And Juliana, the other half of himself. Had he given her hope that the two of them would have a future together? He closed his eyes in a gesture of despairing resignation. He must hurt her now, hurt her cruelly, bring sorrow to those beautiful amber eyes.

With lines of bitterness around his mouth, Sate sat up and reached for his clothes.

Juliana watched him drag on his buckskins, lace up his moccasins, her soft, contented smile slowly fading. The old aloof, hard look was back on his face. Her eyes swam with tears, gathering on her lashes as he stood up and, neither looking at her nor speaking, he walked across the floor and squatted down beside Nathan's cradle. She blinked, startled, when he asked suddenly, "When is Roth takin' you and the child away from here? Snow will be fallin' again soon."

Juliana bit her bottom lip so hard that pain shot through her. He had asked "When is Roth taking you away?" not "When are you going away with me?"

Her voice was toneless when she answered, "I intend to see that we leave here as soon as possible."

During the heavy silence that ensued Juliana held her breath, waiting for some word that would give her hope. But the words that finally came were so hard and cold she winced at them.

"The sooner, the better," Sate said shortly, shrugging into his coat and striding toward the door.

The latch was in his hand when he paused, stood a moment, then turned his head to look into Juliana's bewildered eyes. Then, with a soft curse, he crossed the room and swept her off the bed and into his arms.

"Ah, Juliana." His big body trembled as he buried his face

in her hair. "If only I could go back to that evening in Squaw Hollow and do it all differently."

"But Sate . . ." Juliana's pleading words choked off. The cabin door was closing softly behind Sate. She ran to the window to watch him leave, sobbing, "Oh, Sate, surely this past hour isn't all we're to have."

As Sate climbed onto the shaggy pony, his face haggard with the emotions tearing through him, two pairs of black eyes watched him ride away. The old eyes were curious, the young ones filled with malice.

Juliana sobbed out her grief for her lost love until her eyes were dry of tears. With their end there also died her hope of a life with Sate. Clearly it was not to be. From the very beginning fate had worked against them. It appeared that Sate had bowed to destiny, and so must she.

The young mother was nursing Nathan when Snow Bird returned to the cabin. She did not look at the old woman. Her heart was now full of shame and self-contempt. Not once in the past hour had she given a thought to her husband; a man who loved her dearly. "Oh, dear God," she whispered, "forgive me, but I can't help whom I love. I would probably do the same thing tomorrow if I were given the chance."

The baby's body relaxed in sleep and Juliana tucked him back into the cradle, then she hurried to swing the pot hook away from the flames. She glanced at the clock. Roth should be coming home soon. Were there remnants of passion still in her eyes? she worried.

She started across the floor to where her mirror hung on the wall to check her eyes and face, then paused at the sound of hooves once again approaching the cabin. Her heart raced. Was Sate coming back? Coming to tell her that he loved her, that they must go away together?

Halfway to the door she halted her hurried footsteps. She shouldn't act so anxious. She would wait until he knocked.

Seconds passed, the only sound breaking the silence, Snow Bird's gentle snores where she lay sleeping after her walk in the fresh air. Juliana cocked her head, listening intently for sounds outside. All was quiet, and after several tense moments unease settled over her, gripping her with an awful thought. What if the rider wasn't Sate? What if a red man lurked outside the door?

Her eyes flew to the pole used to bar the door and her heart almost stopped: it lay propped against the wall! Cold sweat dampened her entire body. How many times Roth had warned her to drop it in place while he was away? Zoe had been killed while he was out hunting.

Petrified with fear, Juliana's mouth opened soundlessly, trying to call Snow Bird's name. Her voice was loosened in a sudden cry when a dark face peered through the window. When her gaze froze on two long black braids framing female features, an irritated sigh whistled through her teeth. "Damn you, Doxy. Always slinking around."

She jerked the door open, demanding, "Why are you snooping around out here? Why don't you knock on the door like everyone else?"

Doxy's stony gaze slipped past Juliana to the cabin's interior. "I did knock—no one answered," she muttered sullenly.

"You must have knocked very softly," Juliana retorted. "I didn't hear anything." When the squaw only stared down at the porch floor, Juliana said impatiently, "Do you want to come in or not? The cold air is pouring in."

For a split second the young squaw's black eyes flashed hatred, then wordlessly she pushed past Juliana and walked to the fire. Juliana ran her gaze over the well-curved figure and her stomach knotted as she pictured Sate holding that body in his arms every night. When Doxy turned to warm her backside their glances locked, and as though Doxy read the white woman's mind, her lips smirked smugly.

Forcing back the urge to slap the taunting face, Juliana snapped, "Did you come here with a purpose? Maybe on Red Feather's order?"

An uncomfortable look flickered in Doxy's eyes before she answered, "No one know I come." Her eyes slid to the cradle. "I come to see the child."

Juliana raised a doubtful eyebrow. "I find it hard to believe that you're interested in my child."

Conscious of Juliana's probing stare, the squaw shifted uncomfortably, then, shrugging indifferently, remarked, "I'm only curious about it."

The ticking of the clock was loud in the tight silence as Juliana debated the truth of the offhand statement. Was the sullen-faced girl still of the opinion that Roth was Nathan's father? Maybe, but she couldn't help thinking the girl was here for another reason.

From the corners of her eyes she saw Snow Bird quietly sit up, and some of the tension left her body. The old woman's puny strength would not help her a good deal if Doxy was bent on some mischief, but she might make the girl hesitate at the presence of a witness.

Forcing herself to speak calmly, she said, "He just woke up," and led the way to the cradle.

When Doxy stood beside her, gazing down at Nathan, Juliana's nose wrinkled. The girl smelled of rank bear grease mixed with some odious root or other. And when she leaned over the cradle, her swinging braids caught Nathan's attention, and Juliana held her breath when his chubby hands reached for them. Don't touch them, honey, she gasped silently.

To her relief the hanging hair was kept just out of Nathan's reach as Doxy stared at him intently. When she finally looked up and said slyly, "I see the child resembles his father, especially the eyes and mouth, and his dark coloring," Juliana knew that it wasn't her son the girl wanted to hurt, but rather his mother, not in a physical way, but so that her emotions would feel a lasting sting.

Well, let her try. Juliana's eyes narrowed. She can mouth all the insinuations she pleases, but the troublemaking bitch is not going to get under my skin. Shooting a withering look at the squaw who watched her closely, she snapped, "How utterly ridiculous. Nathan looks nothing like his father." She eyed Doxy suspiciously. "When did you ever see my dead husband?"

"Your dead husband?" Doxy looked from the child, mock surprise on her broad face. "I've never seen him."

"But you just said that Nath—"

"I never said he looks like your dead husband," Doxy cut in. "I said he looks like his father."

Juliana stared back into the baleful black eyes. The wretched girl was still trying to say that Roth was her child's father. "Look," she said coldly, "even you can see that my son looks nothing like Roth Adams."

Doxy dropped her gaze back to the infant. "Nor did I say he looks like Adams."

Juliana's patience was gone. "Who, then, for God's sake?" she demanded tightly.

Her eyes dark and secretive, the Indian stared at Juliana to the accompaniment of the crackling fire. Finally she spoke: "Is the white squaw strong enough to hear the truth?"

Startled by the vehemence in the question's tone, Juliana could only nod dumbly as her spine stiffened apprehensively.

It looked for a minute that Doxy had changed her mind, a slight dilation in the pupils hinting that a sudden thought had warned her to hold her tongue. Then, as though she could not hold back the words, she began with a question.

"Do you recall your arrival in Sate Margruder's camp last winter?"

Juliana nodded, confused by the strange turn in the conversation. "I remember, vaguely. I was unconscious most of the time. Why?"

Her question was ignored and the interrogation continued. "That night, did you have dreams that the trapper made love to you?"

Juliana felt the blood rushing to her face, staining it red. How did this hateful squaw know about her dream?

A gloating, satisfied smile curved Doxy's thin lips. "I can see from your face that you did."

A roaring in her ears, Juliana groped for a chair and sat down. "What exactly are you trying to say, Doxy?" she whispered hoarsely. "I wish you'd say it and be done."

Hate and spite filled the squaw's eyes. Her voice heavy from months of suppressed enmity, she half snarled, "I'm saying, white bitch, that it was no dream you had. Sate Margruder did make love to you that night." She leaned over Juliana, her eyes venomous. "And you loved it. You were like the worst kind of whore. You drove the trapper out of his mind with wanting you."

Straightening up, she glared down at Juliana's white, stricken face. "You took his seed that night," she hissed, "and there in that cradle is the fruit."

Her limbs paralyzed, only her mind able to cry out in denial, Juliana was vaguely aware that Doxy left, closing the door behind her with a quiet click of accomplishment. "No wonder it was all so real," she whispered. "No wonder that when I see him I know exactly how he looks and feels beneath his buckskins."

Did Sate know that Nathan was his son? The thought popped into her mind. Would Doxy tell him that he was a father? No, she decided, the girl would not. She loved the man herself and would take no chance of him leaving her on learning that he had a son.

Nathan made a small noise in his sleep, and Juliana gathered him into her arms, a tender smile on her lips as she explored the miniature features one by one. She shook her head. How could she have been so blind to what was so clearly a small replica of Sate?

Rocking slowly and crooning softly to the little one, Juliana stared dreamily into the flames. No matter what, from now on she had a piece of Sate. A living, breathing piece of him.

"So"—Snow Bird's cracked voice broke into her thoughts—"now you know who papoose looks like."

Juliana didn't pretend ignorance at the quiet statement. She looked into the wrinkled face and sighed raggedly. "What am I going to do, Snow Bird? It would hurt Roth so if he should find out."

The old woman's words were quiet and positive when she answered, "You must see that many miles are put between husband and trapper. If Adams don't see baby and father together he may never know. But they are like two pebbles in a clear pool and, if they stay in same territory, one day your husband will see."

Juliana nodded agreement, then said, "You know the first time you saw Sate, didn't you, Snow Bird?"

"Even before he told me baby was special," the old woman agreed. She rose stiffly, warning, "Adams comes now. Straighten your face."

Later, as Juliana helped Snow Bird put supper on the table, her mind worked out ways of getting Roth started for the settlement. When they sat down at the table she was unaware that her husband had sent her several curious glances.

It seemed to Juliana that the meal would never end. Roth's spirits were high, and he was full of talk; going into detail about places he'd been, amusing events of the war. She squirmed impatiently, but feigned an interest in his long discourses.

When he finally ran down, drained the rest of his coffee, and took a seat by the fire, his wife gave the old squaw a look that said "Wish me luck" and followed him. Curling herself in his lap, Roth smiled and stroked her hair. "Come on, Juliana," he teased. "Out with it. You've been about to bust ever since I walked through the door."

Juliana raised her head from his shoulder, looked seriously into his eyes, and didn't pretend otherwise. "Roth, I want to start for Squaw Hollow tomorrow. Snow Bird says that if we put it off much longer we'll run into bad weather."

A slight frown marred Roth's forehead. "Tomorrow? That don't give us much time to get ready. It takes a little plannin', you know."

"We've been planning for weeks." An undertone of irritation sounded in Juliana's voice. "Anyway, what is there in getting ready? We have only to throw some food into a sack and gather up some blankets and robes."

Roth studied her eager face in thoughtful silence. He had known that his strong-willed wife wouldn't be put off much longer, and in truth she was right in wanting to leave. Red Feather was a cagey old devil, capable of leading a man to feel safe, then striking when least expected.

But, Lord, he hated the thought of returning to that squalid settlement, leaving his clean wilderness. None of this, however, showed in his eyes or voice when he asked, "Are you sure you and Nathan are strong enough for such a cold and long trip?"

Juliana's eyes danced. "I've never felt better in my life, and Nathan is as healthy as one of the bobcats up in the hills."

Roth pulled at an ear, doubt entering his eyes. Then, dropping a kiss on her nose, he nodded. "I guess tomorrow is as good a time as any."

Snow Bird's lips spread in a toothless grin, and Juliana squealed and threw her arms around Roth's neck. "Thank you, Roth, thank you so much."

But later, in bed, in the quiet darkness, when Roth reached for her, asking softly if they really had to wait out a few more days, Juliana's gratefulness at finally escaping the small cabin did not extend to lovemaking. The memory of Sate's hard body loving hers was still too strong in her mind. And hating herself for doing it, she put Roth off, explaining gently, "Snow Bird says it's very important to wait the full six weeks."

CHAPTER 22

It was barely daylight when Roth and the two women finished eating the large breakfast that Snow Bird had prepared. Then, while Juliana nursed Nathan and then dressed him, the old woman packed the grub sack while Roth went to the barn to hitch up the team.

After the first snowfall he had removed the wagon bed and attached it to runners. The previous snow was well packed now and the runners would glide easily over its frozen surface. The foot-high board sides would block most of the wind and, filled with hay, the women and child could burrow themselves in it and be warm and cozy.

Before leading the team through the big double doors Roth took a look around at the large building which had taken him three months to build, and sighed. There was a sadness on his features as he wondered if he'd ever see it again. Something told him that he would not.

Juliana, as she made the bed and tidied the cabin, hoped she would never see the place again. She had spent too many lonely hours inside its four walls.

She hid her thoughts from Roth when he stepped inside the cabin, bringing the cold air with him. He was proud of his little home, and rightly so. She had seen very few that could compare with it.

Outside, the team stamped their hooves against the morning's icy chill, and Roth hurried the women along. As he closed the door for the last time he thought bitterly to himself that before nightfall the cabin would be thoroughly ransacked.

Repressing another sigh, he lifted Juliana into the sled, and after she had worked herself into the hay, Nathan warm in her lap, he pulled a big buffalo robe over them. Turning to Snow Bird he swung her in beside his wife and pulled a matching robe over her slight body. She looked startled a moment, then smiled. Never in her many years had a man, red or white, shown her such kindness.

Roth returned the smile, giving half his attention to tying his stallion's lead rope to the back of the sled, the other half to the dark clouds building up behind them.

"I don't know if it's a good idea to start out, Juliana." His brow was furrowed. "It looks like bad weather is on its way."

A look almost of panic jumped into Juliana's eyes. Nothing must stop them from leaving. "Those clouds are miles behind us, Roth," she pointed out, a sharp tone to the words. "I'm sure we'll out-travel them."

"Only if the wind lies still," Roth answered, climbing into the sled and slapping the reins over the horses' backs. "If it picks up, we're in for it."

Good time was made in the morning hours, the sled gliding over the frozen snow, putting little strain on the team. The baby slept, warm and secure in his mother's arms.

When the pale white sun was straight overhead they stopped in a sheltered stand of cedar for their noon meal, munching on pemmican and parched corn, washing it down with draughts from a jug of sweet cider. After Juliana nursed and changed Nathan, the journey continued on.

It was a couple of hours later that Juliana first became aware of the moaning in the top of the cedars they were passing beneath. Before long her hair was whipping from the edges of her head scarf and the sky was overcast, the sun barely in evidence. She turned her head to look behind her and frowned. The clouds were definitely darker, and much closer. Glancing at Roth, looking back over his shoulder, she caught the worried look on his face.

"We'll be all right," she called reassuringly. "If it does come down, we'll be camped by then."

"I don't know, Juliana." Roth continued to anxiously study the roiling clouds. "I've seen blizzards come up real fast in this country."

Juliana voiced no response, but thought irritably as she

scrunched deeper into the hay, if he'd whip up the team, they could out-run the storm.

The sky continued to darken steadily, becoming a gun-metal black. The storm broke just as they approached a long stretch of burned-out timber. Almost blinded by the driving pellets of snow, Roth used his whip now, keeping them in the right direction by instinct alone. Behind him Juliana had pulled the robe up over her and Nathan's heads, but Snow Bird, her eyes shielded with an arm, peered ahead.

After what seemed forever, they were finally back in the forest with Roth's harried eyes searching frantically for shelter. Here in this particular area there were no huge cedars to protect them, only leafless oak and maple, growing so thick the sled and team could not penetrate them. If they were forced to stop in the middle of this wilderness road, all would be lost. If the horses didn't freeze to death, the wolves would attack, and they would never make it to the settlement.

Even as the thought went through Roth's mind, an eerie howl drifted over the wail of the wind. His hands gripped the reins more tightly. Had the varmints caught their scent already? He swiveled his head slowly, searching. In that jumble of boulders to his right there must be a cave. The area was over-run with them, some shallow, some going for miles beneath the earth's surface.

He pulled the team to a halt and jumped to the ground, surprised that the snow reached to his knees. Snow Bird peered at him questioningly and he shouted over the wind, "I'm gonna investigate that bunch of rocks over there through the trees. Maybe there's a cave. Do you think you could handle the reins a minute?"

The old woman nodded and scrambled through the hay and took up Roth's seat. He was handing her the reins when the wind stopped so suddenly the stillness rang in their ears. They exchanged pleased grins even as Roth's attention was taken by the distant, muffled roar of rapids, and the yawning black opening of a cave just yards away.

Two emotions ran through him. One was distress that he had strayed off the rutted road to Squaw Hollow and was now on a ridge with a several-hundred-foot drop. A cold shiver ran through him. He had probably stopped the team just in time. But off-setting the chilly realization of what had nearly happened to them all was the elation of finding shelter. They were fortunate indeed.

Roth's sigh of relief was interrupted by the crack of a rifle. It came from behind him, echoing between the hills, the bullet striking a tree only inches from the stallion's head. The startled animal screamed, reared up, and snapped the rope holding him to the sled. Roth grabbed for the trailing end, but too late. His prize mount was plunging blindly through the forest.

"Damn! He's some wolf pack's supper," Roth grunted grimly and hurried to the sled where Juliana stared at him, wildeyed. "Come on, honey." He swung her and Nathan down beside him. "I'm afraid Red Feather's braves are after us. There's a cave over there." Hurrying Juliana along, he called over his shoulder, "I'll be right back for you, Snow Bird."

The cave was several yards deep and tall enough for Roth to stand upright. He steered Juliana to the farthest wall and helped her to sit down. Laying the provisions he'd grabbed up beside her, he whispered, "Hang on to the grubsacks, and no matter what, you stay in here. I'm gonna bring Snow Bird in, then try to divert the Indians' attention."

Juliana watched his broad shoulders fade into the gray darkness of the approaching twilight, and snow falling straight down now, wanting to call him back. She was filled with a terrible lost feeling, a sense of emptiness.

The feeling intensified when seconds later a volley of rifle shots rang out again. "Oh, God," she whispered, depositing the sleeping Nathan on the furs and stumbling to the mouth of the cave. She was in time to see, dimly, Roth jump into the sled and take the reins from Snow Bird. As he whipped up the team, from the corners of her eyes she caught a movement back in the forest. Peering through narrowed eyes, she made out the form of an Indian, half sheltered by a tree, a rifle held to his shoulder. She cried a warning to Roth, but abject fear allowed only a croak to escape her throat.

In mute helplessness she watched the brave take careful aim, then heard the crack of the rifle. Her eyes flew to the fleeing sled and its occupants. Before her stricken gaze she saw Roth give a sharp jerk and slump forward as the straining team and sled dropped from sight. As she sank to the ground, her hands over her face, she heard the loud splash of water below. Shudders rippled through her slender body. Just like the old driver out of Trenton, in a matter of seconds, Roth was gone forever.

Desolate sobs shook her shoulders as she fell to her knees. Never again would she hear Roth's spontaneous laughter, never again look into his dear face. She had not loved him in that desperate way she did Sate, but she had loved him.

Finally Nathan's small cries penetrated her grief and she struggled to her feet and felt her way to him. Sitting down, she lifted him into her lap and pulled the robe up around them. All was quiet outside. She wondered if the savages were still around. Did they think that everyone had gone down with the sled?

A ragged sigh escaped her as she stared ahead in the darkness. Aside from the Indians, what was she to do? How long would the storm last? When it stopped, what then? She had no horse . . . wouldn't know in what direction to go even if she did.

She hefted the grub sack; it wasn't very heavy. If help didn't come soon . . .

Sate was out when the first snowflakes fell. He paused on the edge of a timbered ridge and gazed across the valley floor from where drifted the last low calls of the wild turkeys preparing to roost.

Damn! Roth had waited too long to get Juliana out. Winter had come with a vengeance and they would be snowbound until spring. His slim fingers clenched in tight fists. Why had the damn fool brought her here in the first place; dangers all around, she delicate, expecting?

As was in his custom, he had stood across the river at dawn and watched the Adams' cabin. Smoke had curled from the chimney and Roth had moved around outside. Why hadn't he obeyed the urge to go to the man and demand that he take Juliana away?

Slowly the big man's throat emitted a long breath. He was some distance from camp and had better head in. He remained standing a moment, breathing deeply of the fresh, sharp air, lifting his face to the bit of the snow. He always dreaded returning to the teepee.

But I'll endure it until Roth gets Juliana and my son out of here," he muttered, striking across country, heading for the valley. A few of those turkeys would help fill out the stew kettle tonight.

Until recently, Sate recalled as he fought a bitterly cold

headwind, the kettle hadn't been too well filled. Red Feather's lazy braves had lain around the campfires, letting the white man provide the food. He hadn't minded, had welcomed the change to get away from camp.

Then one evening, after he and the men had eaten supper, he'd happened to glance into the kettle whose remaining contents would feed the women and children. He had blinked, then stared in astonishment at the meager amount of meat remaining there. Not nearly enough to still the hunger pangs of growing children, to keep up the strength of the squaws. No wonder they sold themselves to white men every winter. To remain in this camp meant starvation.

With an anger such as he seldom had boiling inside him, he marched into the chief's lodge, not bothering to ask permission. In the face of the man's startled stare, he stated bluntly, firmly, "I will no longer bring in game for the men to eat. Starting tomorrow I provide only for the squaws and children."

Watching his stiff back retreating, Red Feather knew that the trapper made no idle threat, and that it would be useless to try and force this man to hunt for them all. He stared into the fire, pondering the softness that ruined an otherwise perfect brave.

"Such is the white man," he grunted, and rose to have a word with his braves.

The next morning, with grunts and groans, the braves had reluctantly pulled themselves away from the fire and headed into the forest. Later in the day Sate glimpsed through the trees a young buck swinging between two red hunters.

From that day, everyone ate well, even Doxy grudgingly admitting that this was the first winter she could remember in which the women and children hadn't gone hungry.

Sate walked into camp just as the blizzard came roaring down the valley, carried by a howling wind. The squaws were waiting eagerly for his kill, stoically ignoring the snow that was fast covering their heads and shoulders, making hissing sounds in the fire. With loud grunts they seized the four turkeys he held out and immediately began plucking them. The feathers were thrown into the fire, creating a nose-twitching stench, and the entrails were tossed to the rib-thin dogs to fight over.

One woman, a tomahawk gripped in her hand, chopped the

fowl into small pieces and dropped them into a waiting kettle of boiling water. Herbs and dried roots were added, and a savory stew was begun.

Sate sat close to the fire, stretching his wet moccasins to the flames. The cooking fire was the squaw's domain, taboo to the men, but this hard-faced man who kept their stomachs filled was always welcome.

The weariness and chill was finally leaving Sate's bones when Doxy rushed into the circle of light, visibly upset, her face ashen, her eyes fearful. Apprehension crept over him when she whispered hoarsely, "I must speak to you; in the teepee."

As soon as the tent flap closed behind them, Sate grabbed Doxy's wrist, demanding, "What is it? What has happened?"

Swallowing hard, the girl begged fearfully, "Please, Margruder, you mustn't blame me."

Sate's fingers tightened on her flesh. "Blame you for what, woman? Out with it."

Avoiding the eyes that stabbed at her, Doxy answered nervously, "I just found out that Red Feather has sent some braves after Adams. He loaded his family on a sled this morning and left for Squaw Hollow. The chief wants him stopped, and killed.'

"Juliana and the baby?" Sate's tone was icy. "What about them?"

"I don't know. They, too, I guess."

Sate's drawn features made him look ten years older. Death was in the threat he hurled at Doxy as he dropped her wrist: "If you leave this teepee tonight, talk to one soul, I swear I'll cut your heart out."

Her eyes wide with the certainty that the trapper would do exactly that, the young squaw nodded dumbly, and Sate grabbed up his coat and rifle and slipped outside.

He stood in the teepee's shadow a moment, his first glance discerning only the squaws around the cooking fire. The men and children had sought shelter from the weather. He retreated behind the skin covered abode and, dropping to his hands and knees, crawled to where the Indian horses were tethered at the fringe of the forest. Standing up slowly, not to startle them, he whistled softly for the little pony Doxy's father had given him. Its pointed ears pricked, then it trotted toward him.

Sate cupped its flaring nostrils, cutting off its welcoming

whinny, and swung onto its back. Guiding it with his knees, he kept the mount at a walk until they were well out of hearing distance. Then, with a quick look over his shoulder, he whacked his hand on the round rump and the startled animal lunged into a racing gait, heading in the direction of Squaw Hollow.

His thoughts only on the woman he loved more than life, and on his tiny, helpless son, Sate was oblivious to the bite of the wind, the sting of the snow. "Please, God," he prayed, "let me catch up with them before the Indians do."

In no time, it seemed, drifts began to gather and obscure the sled tracks, and the spirited little animal began to tire since in many places the drifts almost reached his chest. From time to time Sate dismounted and broke through them. When the storm worsened an hour later, he remained afoot, leading the animal, and now very conscious of the howling of the wolves up in the hills.

The pony's nose stayed constantly at Sate's shoulder, almost treading his heels, nervous from the hungry yowls drifting on the wind. Man and animal were thankful when they hit a long stretch of wind-swept, burned-out clearing. The runner tracks were now clearly visible, sharp and recently made. Sate quickly remounted and urged the mount on. He should come upon them any time now.

But in what condition? he wondered with dread in his heart. He pushed the images from his mind. They weren't bearable to think about.

It was nearly dark when Sate spotted the mass of boulders looming half as big as houses. "If Roth is smart, he's holed up in there," he whispered hopefully.

He had only two short warnings that the Indians had arrived ahead of him: the crack of a rifle echoing hollowly in the otherwise silent air, and the dark figure of a riderless horse thundering past him. He wheeled his pony around, peering after the animal. "Dear Lord," he groaned, "that's Roth's stallion."

Sate slid to the ground and, keeping behind the screen of tangled bush, crept forward, wondering at the quietness. Had the single shot killed Roth? If so, why didn't he hear Juliana's cries?

Several minutes passed as Sate remained crouched, his eyes scanning the area. Nothing moved. Flattening himself in the snow, he wiggled another three yards, almost immediately spotting the faint figures of six braves sitting their mounts on a nearby ridge. They looked northward, and he turned his gaze in that direction. His breath stopped short. Through the curtain of snow he saw the sled and team, a slight figure holding the reins.

"Ah, God, Juliana," he groaned, "why hasn't he hidden you somewhere?"

He stood up, his firm jaw determined. He would get Juliana and the baby out of there himself.

He took one step and six spurts of flame erupted from the distant hill. Twigs and needles showered down on his head and shoulders as bullets bit through bare limbs and green fir. He whipped his gaze back to the sled and saw Roth appear out of the snow, jump into the sled, and take the reins from Juliana.

The team was galloping wildly when a single shot rang out. As Sate watched, holding his breath, he saw his friend jerk, then slump forward. As in a nightmare, he saw the team and sled shoot into space, then drop out of sight. A trailing scream was cut short, then there was nothing.

He sank slowly to his knees, his arms crossed over his stomach, a mournful singsong intoning inside him, "They are gone, they are gone. Everything dear to you is gone."

Sate didn't know how long he knelt in the snow, his heart and soul ravaged. It was a stealthy scraping of feet that brought him back to awareness. Raising his head, his grief-filled eyes fell on the back of an Indian poised on the edge of the ravine, peering downward. A red film of madness dropped across his eyes. Here was the one who had fired the fatal shot.

His teeth bared in a low snarl, Sate whipped his knife from its sheath and, as if released from a spring, his lithe body shot across the snow-covered ground and landed behind the unsuspecting brave. His arm came up, then swiftly down again. The red man gave a gentle sigh, bent forward, then went tumbling down, joining his victims in the water below.

Panting slightly, Sate dropped to the ground and began to carefully crawl up the ridge. There were five others to take care of. Reaching the top, he crouched behind the dead foliage of a huckleberry thicket and peered around its dry branches. Four Indians were mounted while the fifth stood looking down at the boulders below.

Gathering himself to stand up, his foot dislodged a stone,

and he held his breath as it rattled down the rocky hill. The standing brave spun around, a guttural cry rushing through his teeth. His eyes flashing joyfully, Sate raised the rifle to his shoulder and squeezed the trigger. The brave landed on his back and lay motionless.

The others were off their mounts now, moving quickly for him. Sate dropped his firearm. Tomahawk in one hand, knife in the other, and a cold, frightening fire burning in his eyes, he darted among them, terrible vengeance on his face.

In a furious flash, three braves were down, never to rise again. Sate spun around to meet the charge of the fourth and found only emptiness. The sound of churning hoofbeats came faintly on the still air.

"Run, you bastard, run," he yelled through cupped hands before dropping to his knees, his fingers nursing a long gash on his left arm. The snow fell gently on his bowed head. The little pony trotted up to him, whinnying softly. Sate pulled himself up and, resting his arms across its back, buried his head between them as dry, harsh sobs racked his lean body.

Raising his contorted face to the sky, he called wildly, "God! What am I goin' to do now?"

When the echo of his grief died away into the hills, he swung onto the pony's back to ride off, his chin sunk onto his chest.

CHAPTER 23

Utterly fatigued from grief and weariness, Juliana's chin dropped, and she dozed.

But her light sleep was not restful. It was filled with fitful dreams, where again Roth was hurrying her to a cave, where again she watched him climb into a sled, bullets flying around him. And, as before, only in slow motion, he took the reins from Snow Bird's hands. Despair descended. Her vision caught the brave with the rifle to his shoulder.

The shot rang out and she jerked awake. Her heart racing, she stared at the lighter shade of black at the cave's opening. Had that been a real shot? It had sounded so clearly.

She carefully transferred Nathan to the furs and pulled them around his small body. Then, moving as quietly as possible, she slipped toward the patch of night.

It was deadly quiet outside, almost eerie. The shot must have been in her dream after all. Pulling the scarf tighter around her head and throat she turned back inside. She took but three steps before she spun around. Not many yards away from where she stood there had exploded such a clamor of raucous shouts and yells that her spine had tingled. Fearful, but helpless not to do so, she stood just inside the cave and listened with growing terror. A terrible fight raged outside.

She slumped against the wall. The braves hadn't left after all. Why were they fighting among themselves? What would happen if they were still here when daylight came and they discovered her hiding place?

Suddenly, as swiftly as it had begun, the fighting had

stopped, only the fading sound of drumming hoofbeats breaking the silence. While she mused on the possibility that one brave had killed the others, heart-stopping alarm shot through Juliana. Nathan had awakened, and his loud, angry cries filled the small stone-walled room. If there was an Indian within a mile he would hear the wailing.

She stumbled in her hurry to get to the infant, falling to the ground, scraping her knees. Then she had the baby in her arms, rocking him back and forth, trying to soothe him without success.

Juliana was about to place her fingers across the tiny lips when a scuffing sound outside froze her limbs. A tall form loomed against the night and she choked back a terrified cry. All was lost. She lay the screaming child down and rose on trembling legs. She would not be easy prey for this heathen.

Hugging the wall, she began edging toward the blanketed shape standing so silently. When she drew opposite the shadowy form it began to move. When it took a step past her, she leaped, letting out a screech that rivaled the screams of a wildcat, landing on the intruder's back. She fastened her fingers in the long hair, pulling with all her strength.

All the fight went out of her when strong fingers caught her wrists and a familiar voice hissed, "Ulie, it's me, Nemus."

"Oh, Nemus," she wailed, and the old brave turned around in time to catch her before she fell to the ground.

Nathan's loud cries and several sharp slaps to her face brought Juliana out of her faint. She moaned softly, then murmured, "I'm all right, Nemus."

"Good," he grunted, pulling her to her feet. "We got to get out of here. One brave got away from trapper. He'll be back with others. Margruder killed four of their brothers. They'll be wild for revenge."

Juliana's heart slowed, then raced. Sate had been so near and she hadn't known it. "I wonder if he knows he was too late to help his friend and Snow Bird," she said softly.

"Margruder knows. He thinks you all went down with sled. He in deep grief when he ride away."

"He has gone?" She wheeled and sprinted toward the mouth of the cave.

Nemus caught her arm, holding her fast. "You not go after him. You not even know what direction he go. He no go back to Pennacook village."

"But, Nemus, he thinks me dead."

"He learn different if it meant to be."

Juliana sighed resignedly at Nemus's seemingly callous remark. But he was right in his first observation. There was no possible way she could follow Sate. She squeezed her eyes tight and prayed silently, "Please, God, let him learn that Nathan and I still live."

Nemus touched her elbow. "Can you get papoose to be still? We must be very quiet."

Juliana picked Nathan up and held him close. "He's only crying because he feels my fear. See," she said as the cries dwindled to soft sobs. "He'll be all right now."

Nemus grunted and began rolling up the fur robes. "You ready?" he asked, picking up the grub sack. "Red Feather's braves be back any moment."

Juliana nodded and pulled the blanket over Nathan's face. "Are we going to travel through the storm all night?"

"Only to old cabin couple miles away. It is well hidden in trees, and if we in favor with Great Father, snow hide tracks and we be safe there. There a fireplace for warmth to wait out storm."

A frown creased Juliana's forehead. "Will your pony be up to carrying all three of us?"

"I have another pony hidden in woods. I come to take Snow Bird home." He gave her arm an impatient shake. "Come, we must ride now."

Juliana thought it was the longest two miles she had ever ridden, Nathan clasped to her breast, the freezing cold making her teeth ache, sending tears running down her cheeks. For the most part Nemus walked, sometimes to break through a tall drift, other times to get his bearing, recognizing a certain ridge, a special lone tree. It wasn't until Juliana had become so numb with the cold, fearful that her lifeless arms would drop Nathan, that the old cabin loomed in front of them.

Half falling into Nemus's arms, he helped her to the small building, and while she leaned against its rough log walls he kicked the snow away from the door then led her inside.

"I have fire going in minute," he promised, easing her down on a stool. Squatting in front of the small fireplace, he fumbled in the dark, scraping away an accumulation of ashes. There was the sound of kindling being snapped, then the scrape of his flint. Slowly he coaxed a bright, leaping fire to life.

As Nemus lay a log on the flames, he remarked, "Someone put wood here recently. It was work of trapper just for this."

The old man stood up. "Move close to fire and warm feet." He walked toward the door. "I bring in ponies now. Wolves get them otherwise."

When he was gone Juliana ran her eyes around the small room. A haversack fastened over the sole window billowed in and out with the force of the increasing wind. From a dozen different places large chinks between the logs let in a rush of cold air. How different it is from Roth's tight little place, she thought, tears gathering in her eyes. Before they could fall, Nathan stirred, then fussed hungrily. She bared a breast to him, and rocked back and forth as he nursed contentedly.

She had just changed the baby's wet clothing when Nemus pushed open the door and led in the ponies. The room had grown warm enough for her to remove her coat, and while the two animals were tied in a far corner, she laid out half the food in the grub sack.

It was after they had eaten and Nemus smoked his pipe that Juliana brought up Snow Bird. "I'm sorry about Snow Bird, Nemus. I hope you don't blame Roth for her death."

Nemus shook his white head. "The old one was tired, nearly done. Soon she would fall into deep sleep anyway."

"She seemed quite content to be with Roth and me, although she was anxious to get back to the settlement."

Nemus shook his head again. "Snow Bird foolish old woman. She got no family left, no one care for her." He puffed clouds of smoke from the long-stemmed pipe a moment before he said, "It is better she go into river than die slow from starvation."

Juliana's shocked face lifted to the old man. "But wouldn't someone have looked after her? Surely her people wouldn't just sit by and watch her die."

"It is our custom. Squaw must look after herself if she outlive family."

"That's terrible. You speak as though she was being punished for outliving her family. It was no fault of hers."

Nemus shrugged his shoulders and repeated, "It is our custom."

Juliana's short snort told what she thought of the Indian custom. Arching a skeptical eyebrow at Nemus she said, "And I suppose that practice extends to old braves also?"

She wasn't sure she saw the thin lips stir as though in amusement, but she was sure that she'd give anything to be able to withdraw the question. "I'm sorry, Nemus." She laid a hand on his arm. "I shouldn't have said that."

"It only natural for white woman to wonder," Nemus said after a while. "And, yes, Ulie, when old brave got no one and can no more hunt food, he, too, must go off alone, meet the Great Father."

The fire snapped and the wind howled around the corners of the old cabin. "Do you have family still living, Nemus?"

The noise outside almost drowned out the blunt "No."

"Yes, you do." Juliana smiled widely. "You have me and Nathan . . . as well as John and Molly. When you grow to be a hundred, you will sit by our fire, and I will bake you an apple pie every day."

For the first time she saw the thin lips spread in a full grin.

The next morning when Nemus forced open the door, the snow had stopped and the sun shone brightly. Eager to end the cold journey, he and Juliana hurriedly breakfasted on the remaining food in the grub sack, and set out on the trail, Nathan taking his meal as the ponies struggled through the snow.

About three miles had been covered when they heard the guttural tones of Indians somewhere nearby. Nemus motioned to Juliana that they should take cover behind a large cedar. He slid to the ground into snow up to his knees, and cupped a palm over each mount's nose. Several minutes passed before the voices faded away.

"Red Feather's braves," Nemus muttered, climbing back on the pony. "Very angry they lose Margruder's trail."

Hope flickered in Juliana's eyes. "Do you think we'll find Sate in the settlement?"

"No. I think trapper head for Canada. He talk to me one time about Canada."

Canada! Juliana slumped in the saddle. It was so far away. Would Sate ever come back?

She could not bring herself to talk for some time. She was afraid if she opened her mouth she would bawl like a baby. When Nemus began to slip her curious looks, she said the first thing that came to her mind: "What date have John and Molly set for their wedding?"

Nemus dug a heel into his pony's flank, urging him through

a white drift. "Your papoose came so late, John and Molly not think you come to Hollow. They wed three weeks ago."

Happiness and sadness gripped Juliana simultaneously. At long last the couple most dear to her was married, but she was disappointed that she hadn't been there to witness it.

The sun was well westward when, tired and hungry, Nemus led Juliana into Squaw Hollow. As they rode along the winding, snow-packed street, curious faces appeared at doors and windows. Juliana smiled. Rumors would fly as to why she had returned alone. Some would speculate that, accustomed to the easy life of Philadelphia, the wilderness had proved too much for her, that she had left her husband. Others would only think that she had come to visit her brother.

She and Nemus had gone almost past the post when one woman, prompted by a curiosity she could not resist, ran out her door and up to Juliana's mount. "Miz Adams, I do hope nothin' is wrong with your husband. You bein' alone and all."

Since the woman seemed genuinely concerned, Juliana reined the pony in. Speaking softly, she answered, "On our way here, we were set upon by Indians. My husband, and an old squaw, were killed."

"Oh, ma'am, I am sorry to hear that!" the shocked woman exclaimed. "Such a shame. And you with a new baby."

When Juliana's eyes misted at the caring tone, the woman patted her knee. "Don't worry, dearie. You bein' so young and beautiful, it won't be no time afore the men will be knockin' on your door."

A sharp rebuke sprang to Juliana's lips. Did this simple woman think that a man, any man, was the answer to all problems? She bit back her words. The honest, homely woman staring up at her meant only to console. In her hard, cruel world maybe a man was her salvation, no matter what kind of life he chose to hand her.

She smiled kindly at the woman. "Thank you for caring, but I'll get along fine." She kicked the pony lightly, hurrying to catch up with Nemus.

"Nosey white squaw." He grunted as she rode alongside him.

Juliana laughed lightly. "She meant well, Nemus. At least everyone will know now why Roth isn't with me." The last was said sadly.

The riders reached the outskirts of the village and Juliana noted that many new cabins dotted the hillsides and valley. She mentioned the fact to Nemus. After a discontented grunt, he said, "All summer and fall, new settlers come. My people be pushed and pushed until we all fall off end of world."

Juliana nodded sympathetically. "I know I shouldn't, since they killed Roth and Snow Bird, but I do feel sorry for your people. We whites don't have the right to push in on them the way we do."

No more was said between them as they began to climb to John's cabin.

John's dog spotted them first. Then a loud "Hallo" brought Juliana's gaze flying to the small porch. John and Molly stood there, waving wildly. Happy tears smarted her eyes. How dear they looked. She goaded her mount into a gallop. Fatigue, sadness, and worry slipped from her shoulders as Molly reached for the baby and she tumbled into John's arms.

After much hugging and kissing between them all, John and Molly chorused, "Where's Roth?"

Juliana started to explain, choked on the words, and Nemus related what had happened. John and Molly stood in stunned silence. Molly finally managed to utter, "Oh, Juliana, I'm so sorry." Her free arm hugged her sister-in-law tightly. "But thank God you and the baby are safe. . . ." She urged Juliana inside the cabin, a still shocked John and tired Nemus following them.

"I can't wait to see this baby," Molly said, breaking the spell of low spirits as she laid Nathan on the bed. As she unwound the blanket swathing him, she glanced brightly at Juliana. "By the way, do we have a niece, or a nephew?"

Before Juliana could speak, Nemus answered proudly, "Papoose big man-child. He named Nathan."

While amused laughter sounded softly, John squeezed Juliana's shoulder. "It was nice of you to name him after Pa. He'd be very proud."

"I think so," Juliana said softly.

While Nathan's aunt and uncle made a fuss over him, Juliana looked around the cozy, familiar room and smiled. It was good to be back. Her eyes lingered on the long table on whose surface she and Molly had rolled out so many pies. It seemed a lifetime ago; so much had happened to her since.

She sighed, then looked at the bed when Molly laughed. "Look at the little scutter smile at us."

"Who does he look like?" John inquired as he glanced at Juliana. "Where'd he get that dark hair and skin? I don't recall anyone on our side with that coloring."

Juliana had known the question would be asked, had dreaded it all the time on the trail. How should she answer? she wondered as she sat down in the rocker in front of the fireplace. Should she simply say "I don't know" or should she tell them the truth and be done with it?

The image of Doxy flashing before her made up her mind. There would always be that squaw to worry about. It would be like her to show up one day and spread the story of Nathan's parentage all over the settlement. She didn't want John and Molly finding out through vicious gossip.

She would tell them a half truth, she decided, leaving out the fact that the baby was conceived without her knowledge. If John should ever meet Sate, she wanted him to have nothing but respect for Nathan's father.

Taking a deep breath, she eased into what would shock the pair again. "Nathan has his father's looks."

"He looks like Tom?" John snorted. "You're crazy, Juliana. Tom was as fair as we are."

"I know how fair Tom was, John."

"But you just said—"

"I said that Nathan has the looks of his father."

John came and sat down on the hearth facing Juliana. As Molly watched, the baby forgotten, he asked quietly, "Who is Nathan's father, sis? Certainly not Roth."

Juliana stared at John, swallowing, groping for words that might somewhat soften the blow she was about to give him.

There were none, she knew, and, dropping her eyes to her tightly clasped hands, she blurted out, "The trapper, Sate Margruder, is Nathan's father."

There was absolute silence for several long moments. Then the air bristled as John jumped to his feet and almost shouted, "Sate Margruder! That wild man! How in the world did you ever get mixed up with him?"

Juliana darted a glance at her brother's dazed expression, then looked away. "Give me a minute, John, and I'll tell you the whole story."

With Molly's eyes gleaming excitedly, and John's flashing,

she told of the coach accident in the storm, and how Sate had found her, near death. She moved lightly over how she and Sate had fallen in love, and of their plans to meet in Trenton, come spring.

"But when Sate arrived at Iva's, she told him that I had gone off with another man." She paused a moment while Molly interjected her thoughts about John's dead ex-wife, then resumed.

"Sate believed her. And then, he had no idea where I was." Juliana paused again to lay her hand on John's knee. "When I discovered I was in a family way, I truly thought it was by Tom."

John patted her hand. "Have you seen Margruder since that first time?" he asked, his voice back to normal.

Juliana nodded, but it was Nemus who told of Sate's abduction by the Indians, how he had kept watch over Roth and Juliana, but unhappily hadn't arrived in time to save Roth and the old woman.

"Sate thinks that Nathan and I are dead, too." Tears flooded Juliana's eyes. "Nemus believes that he's gone into Canada, and I'll probably never see him again."

Her soft sobs brought Molly's comforting arms around her shoulders. "You'll see him again, honey. After all that has happened to you two, I know that someday you'll be together again."

"Those are my thoughts, too, Juliana," John said firmly. "Hunters and trappers are always going into Canada. Sooner or later Margruder will hear the story of Roth Adams's beautiful widow living in Squaw Hollow."

Juliana's eyes brightened. "I never thought of that."

"Well, you just think about it, and in the meantime go about the business of raising little Nat. Before you know it, his father will show up."

Juliana smiled wanly. "You give me hope, John, but it could be years before Sate hears any news of me and Nathan. Meanwhile, here I am again, a burden around your neck. It looks like you'll never be rid of me."

"Don't talk nonsense, Julie," Molly said sternly. "You know we're happy to have you and the babe here. Now I don't want to hear any more such talk."

But later in bed, Nathan cuddled close to her, Juliana lay staring into the darkness. Only on two short occasions had

John been free of caring for her. Before long he'd have children of his own to tend, and he wouldn't need the load of his sister and nephew. And there was no need for this extra weight. She was a grown woman now. Birth, death, and grief had turned her into a strong, able-minded person. She felt she could meet and overcome almost any obstacle—at least she'd like the chance.

Her last thought before falling asleep was that she wanted a home of her own. A place just for her and Nathan . . . while they waited for his father to return. For Sate would return when he learned that she and Nathan still lived, she was confident of that. She had felt his love like a warm blanket enveloping her body the last time he'd held her in his arms.

CHAPTER 24

The wiry mount, the wind at his back, struggled through drifts often higher than its knees. The man astride his back paid the animal no heed. The trapper wasn't even aware of his whereabouts as the pony fought along. He dwelled on the events that had taken the love of life from him.

The pony, exhausted, stopped with head hanging. Sate sat for several seconds before realizing he was no longer in motion. Then, desolately raising his head, he gazed about indifferently. The fact that the snow had stopped made no impact on him as he gazed dully at the small cabin squatting in the gloom, only a few feet away.

Suddenly, weary and mentally drained, he craved sleep. Sliding to the ground, he plowed through the snow and pushed at the rough plank door. With a creaking of rusty hinges, it swung open and he woodenly moved inside, the pony at his heels. There was a sound of tiny scurrying feet as he rolled himself in his blanket and immediately fell asleep.

Sate's sleep was dreamless as he lay still as death. When the pony's low whinny awakened him the next morning he frowned into the partial gloom, having no remembrance of the long ride that had brought him to this place.

But as he leaned up on an elbow, yesterday's events came rushing back. He groaned and slumped back on the blanket, an arm flung across his face, the soft doeskin sleeve soaking up his bitter tears.

For five days Sate remained in the deserted cabin, hunting his food and feeding the pony on tender bark he stripped from young maples. Pain and despair still gripped him, but, resolute, he learned to accept the hurt for it would be with him the rest of his days.

Gradually he could think of Juliana without succumbing to grief, and on the sixth morning, upon rising, he rolled up his blankets. It was time he got on with an imitation of living. He packed the remains of last night's supper in his saddlebag and led the pony out.

One day followed the next, with Sate guiding the mount in northerly direction. The stubble on his face became a beard, and his hair hung to his shoulders in tangled strands. His eyes were mere slits in his wind-burned face as a result of squinting against the white glare of the snow. When several times he came upon small parties of Indians, after one look at his cold, still face, they turned their mounts away from him. The braves began to say around their campfires that the trapper was a man who walked with death, that even bears and great cats avoided his trail, that only the wolf, who was his brother, would keep him company.

Sate had been on the trail for four days. As the sturdy pony slipped his way across snow-slick rocks on a seldom-used path hunters and trappers called "trace," he pulled his collar up around his ears, blocking the cold wind that had picked up. When the image of a warm cabin slipped into his mind, he hurriedly pushed it away. Thoughts of Juliana were sure to follow.

Night was coming and the tired pony was beginning to limp. Sate sighed heavily. It looked like he and the animal would be spending another night outdoors. He hadn't seen one cabin in his travels, and in this dense wilderness he doubted that he would.

He was keeping his eyes peeled for a likely place to camp when he spotted movement several yards down the trail. Peering narrowly, he made out the stooped figure of an old man leading a mule. He reined the pony in and waited the few minutes it took the man to reach him.

A friendliness looked out of a face that was wrinkled with age, hardship, and privation. Faded blue eyes studied him from under shaggy brows that matched the silvery white hair that grew to his shoulders.

"Howdy, stranger."

"How are you, old-timer?" Sate grinned.

"Sure is a cold one, huh?"

"It is that. My feet and hands are so cold I can hardly feel them. I don't suppose there's any place around here to warm them up . . . maybe a fire to sleep in front of?"

The old man shoved gnarled fingers beneath his coonskin cap and scratched his head in thought. His twinkling eyes gave away the lack of seriousness in the action.

"Wal now, I got myself a cabin a couple miles from here. It ain't fancy, but you're welcome to come home with me."

"I'm much obliged to you, grandpa. I sure am tired of sleepin' in the snow." He held out a hand. "The name is Margruder, Sate Margruder."

The old man let loose a cackle as he shook the offered hand. "You're that hellion the Indians talk about, huh? You can call me Grandpa Watkins. Everyone else around here does."

Sate kneed the pony out of the way, let the old man pass, then followed him down the snowy path. "This sure is pretty country," he said to the slow-moving old man. "A man could live out his days here."

"It's a fine land, all right. Plenty of good water, lots of green grass in the warm season for the deer and moose to feed on."

"What other kind of animals are around here?"

"Wal, there's bears, cats, beaver, mink, wild turkeys. Just about any kind you can mention."

"Good trappin', then?"

"The best. If a man don't make money here, he's just plain lazy."

The sun had set and the air cooled sharply by the time they reached old Watkins's place. The building was low and sturdy, its back a scant foot from the bluff towering over it. Time and the elements had weathered the logs to a silvery gray and it was hard to believe that there had been a time when it was raw and new.

Watkins pushed the door open, stepped aside, and motioned Sate inside. The trapper waited while his host fumbled for a candle in the darkness. After a few raspy scratches of a flint, the wick caught fire. Carrying it across the floor, the old man placed it in a holder on the mantel of a stone fireplace. As he knelt to coax a fire from the glowing coals there, Sate's gaze scanned the room.

It was clean, the dirt floor neatly swept. But the small quarters were in total disorder. Every corner was littered with furs, broken traps, remnants of gear, broken jugs, snowshoes, and some articles he could not name.

Double bunk beds, piled high with fragrant cedar-bough mattresses took up most of one wall. Only the lower one was made up. A long bench flanked the hearth, and in the center of the room stood a table and three chairs. Two pegs fastened in the wall next to the door held the owner's clothing.

The old man stood up and, dusting off his hands, invited, "Hang your hat and coat over there with my duds, then help yourself to the jug on the mantel. I'll get us a bite to eat."

The fiery raw whiskey burned down Sate's throat and exploded in his stomach. Watkins grinned as he gasped for breath.

"That's strong stuff, young feller, but it will sure warm you up. Makes you forget why you come to this country in the first place."

When Sate's throat returned to a semblance of normalcy, he asked, "Is that the only reason men come here—to forget something in their past?"

"Most do. 'Course, there's some who come for the money to be made in furs."

Both men grew silent, each with his own thoughts. Then the old man asked, "Why did you come here, Margruder? I see sufferin' in your eyes, lad . . . recent sufferin'."

When Sate made no response and kept staring into the red heart of the fire, Watkins turned back to dishing stew out of a black iron kettle. "The Indians say that the soul is purified by sufferin'. You reckon that's true?"

When silence greeted him again, the old man took the dented coffee pot off the coals, saying, "Come on, let's eat."

"This is about the best stew I've ever eaten, grandpa," Sate said a few minutes later, chewing the tender pieces of meat and washing it down with hot black coffee.

Pride blushed the old man's cheeks. "I shot a young moose calf down by the spring yesterday mornin'. He must have been born late in the season. That happens sometimes, you know."

"Who taught you to cook? You ever been married?"

"Naw, I never took the plunge. Had me a good squaw, though. Ugly as all get out, but clean and honest. She saved my life. That's how I met her."

"Tell me about it." Sate pulled a pipe and tobacco pouch from his shirt pocket. "How did you meet this squaw?"

"Wal"—Watkins reached for his own "smokins"—"I was in my mid-twenties and full of myself. Pennsylvania was like Kaintuck then, mostly wilderness, and I built myself a three-sided hut and laid my first trapline."

The old man puffed a moment, then with a derisive snort went on: "Within a week I had pneumony and was burnin' up with fever. I was skin and bones from not eatin', too sick to make me anything, and the water had froze in the pail. I had decided that the end had come for me when this young squaw lifted the flap of my hut and walked in.

"I learned later that she had just lost her two-week-old infant and was about out of her head with grief. Wal, in my half delirium, I watched her build up the fire, then walk toward my pallet, freeing one of her breasts from her shift. Rich, warm milk was oozing out of it, and nothing ever tasted so good when she lay down beside me and stuck that nipple in my mouth. I emptied both the breasts within ten minutes."

There was a pause in which the old man stared broodingly before him. "I sucked her the rest of the winter, even after I was up and around. But I didn't force her." He looked earnestly at Sate. "She liked it, wanted me to." He grinned slyly. "She liked doin' the same to me, if you get my meanin'."

Sate grinned his understanding, and Watkins added, "She's the one who taught me to cook."

"What happened to her? Did you get tired of her and send her on her way?"

"Naw. She lived with me for almost nine years. Then the pox swept through her village and she caught it. She was dead in three days."

Watkins sensed the stiffening of Sate's body and, when he saw the bleakness that settled over the rough features, smoothly changed the subject.

"You aimin' for anyplace in particular, Margruder?"

"I been thinkin' to go to the Champlain Valley up in Canada. I hear tell there's real good trappin' around Lake Champlain. Then, maybe later, cross over to Valcour Island."

Watkins puffed his pipe, eyeing Sate speculatively through the clouds of smoke. "You couldn't find better trappin' than 'round here. Why don't you string your line in these parts?" You could stay right here with me; save the trouble of buildin' your own place."

Sate leaned back in the chair, staring up at the ceiling. It was a tempting offer, but would it work out? He had always been a lone wolf.

He turned a dubious eye on the old man. "You think we could get along?"

"I don't know why not," he was answered eagerly. "We'd mostly go our separate ways during the day . . . runnin' our traps and all. In the evenin's if my talkin' gets on your nerves, there's a post of sorts a couple miles down the river. It's a combination fur post and tavern. Trappers and hunters meet there a lot."

The old man grinned crookedly. "And if you get a hankerin', there's some female flesh around. 'Course, I have to caution you, they're probably none too healthy." He waited, then offered, "I could put out the word that you're in the market for a good, clean squaw."

The corners of Sate's lips lifted a fraction. "Thanks, old-timer, but we'll just batch it."

Watkins grinned, pleased. When the clock struck eight, he leaned over and knocked his pipe out against a stone. "I think I'll turn in. I ain't as young as I used to be, and runnin' the traps tires me some.

"You can spread your blankets on the top bunk. If you ain't got enough covers, help yourself to a bearskin from that pile in the corner."

He removed his moccasins and disrobed down to his long underwear. As he crawled into bed and pulled up the furs, Sate asked, "Will I be able to buy some traps down at that post?"

"Yeah. The keeper carries a pretty good line of what the men in these parts need. He's higher than hell, though. Knows there ain't no other place a man can go to."

Sate made up the top bunk, then went to check on his pony. The old man had stabled him, but he had grown fond of the stout-hearted little animal and wanted to make sure he was well out of the cold.

The pony was contentedly munching hay, occasionally aiming a kick at the mule who had been wisely tied a safe distance away. The slant-roofed shed, like the cabin was well built. Neither wind nor wolf would get to the two animals.

After an affectionate pat on the pony's rump, Sate left the building and stood a moment staring up at the sky. Nothing in life had changed for him. He was right back to his same lonely

existence. His one slim chance at happiness hadn't lasted even
a year. He had been a damn fool to think it would ever be any
other way.

It was almost dawn when Sate awakened to old Watkins's
grunts and groans as he laboriously struggled out of bed. He
opened his eyes to watch the elderly man renew the fire, then
stand with his back to the flames, idly scratching his backside.

When the aroma of frying bacon and brewing coffee filled
the room, Sate rose and dressed.

Both Sate and Watkins were taciturn men in the mornings,
with nothing said between them until they had each drunk a
cup of coffee. Then, breakfast eaten, the rising sun casting a
pink glow on the glittering snow outside, the old man rose and
reached for his coat.

"I'll be back before dark. I'm gettin' too old to stay out after
the sun goes down."

Sate nodded. "I'm gonna visit that post today and get some
traps. But I'll be back in time to have supper ready when you
get home."

The door closed and Sate cleared the table, then melted
snow over the fire to wash the two plates, tin cups, and coffee
pot. There were no knives; trappers used their own sharp
hunting knives to do all their cutting. He washed the iron
skillet last, setting it close to the fire to dry to prevent rust.

By the times he had smoothed out the beds and brought in
wood from the ample supply stacked against the cabin, the sun
was nearing its zenith. Sate picked up his rifle and headed for
the post.

CHAPTER 25

~~~~~~~~~

It was still dark out when Juliana awakened, Nathan warm in her arms, his soft hair brushing her chin. She turned her head to look at the gray square of window. Daylight would be coming soon, for overhead came the rustling of covers, the occasional squeak of the floorboards as John and Molly began their predawn lovemaking.

The intimate noises awakened longings and sensations of Juliana's own. Although she had never initiated the lovemaking between Roth and herself, it took only a few caressing strokes of his hands and she was melting against him.

As she lay in the soft darkness, musing to the background of rhythmical sounds, Juliana admitted to strong passions and wondered how she'd handle these yearnings if they should come over her. She could only pray that Sate returned before she was faced with overwhelming desire.

Where was he? she wondered. Not in the Pennacook village, for that village no longer existed. The news of Roth's death at the hands of the Pennacooks had outraged the settlement and, within an hour, fifty men had gathered in front of Battle's place, swearing vengeance. The Shawnees were equally irate that one of their own had also been killed, and thirty braves, their faces fierce with warpaint, silently joined the whites and marched with them the two days and nights it took to arrive at the Indian village.

Two days later all returned, proudly bursting with the news that the Canadian tribe was no longer a threat to their settlement. They had hit the village in the dead of night, and without firing a shot had taken every brave prisoner.

John and Nemus had saved the captured men's lives, John pointing out that the women and children would surely starve to death without their menfolk to hunt for them, and Nemus convincing his people that to kill the Pennacooks might only start a war between the two tribes. "We will have our hands full keeping an eagle eye open that the white man doesn't overcome us. We do not need to fight our red brothers at this time. Snow Bird, after all, was in her last winter," he explained in their native tongue.

So the entire tribe was directed northward, and their village set afire. "They'll be in Canada in about a week," one man said.

That had been three months ago, and there were no more rumors of invasion. Along with this relief, winter was gasping its last cold breath. A week ago, with loud reports and deep rumbling, the river had began to break up, rough immense pieces of ice floating in the water.

All things are following their normal course, Juliana thought bleakly. Only I am different. Her monthly cycle had been broken. For two months now she had known she was in a family way again; again by Sate Margruder. And for two months she had struggled for a way in which to tell John and Molly.

I could let them make the natural assumption that Roth is the father, but what if it, too, should be the spitting image of Sate? John might hate her for the deception. There had always been honesty between them.

Juliana flung an arm across her face, the action of dejected hopelessness. Somehow she must create a home for her growing family.

All sound ceased above her head, and she quickly pulled her arm down under the covers and pretended to be asleep when John descended the ladder and started a fire in the fireplace.

The room began to warm up, and when Molly's feet sounded softly on the rungs of the loft ladder, Nathan roused and fussed for his breakfast. Juliana freed a breast for his hungry mouth.

The first meal of the day was always a leisurely one in the Nemeth household, with much laughing and teasing going on between eating and passing the coffee pot. This morning, however, Juliana said little, her mind firm on the decision she had arrived at earlier: a home of her own. She was unaware that John had finished eating and was studying her frowning, pensive visage. When he spoke, she gave a start.

"Well, sister, you seem to have the weight of the world on your shoulders this morning. What's troubling you?"

Juliana toyed with her cup, her brother's unexpected query throwing her for a moment. "I want a place of my own, John," she said finally, lifting earnest eyes to him.

John frowned at his sister, his expression saying that was the last thing he had expected her to say. "That's plain crazy." His tilted-back chair came down with a loud thump. "How could a lone woman with a baby get along on her own?"

"I'm sure Nemus will come with me if I ask him to."

"Ha!" John snorted. "A lot of good one old brave would be if your cabin was attacked by a bunch of Indians, or some drunk from Battle's place was bent on getting into bed with you."

"I'm not helpless, brother," Juliana snapped back. "Papa taught me how to shoot, too, remember. I can shoot as accurately as you can."

"I agree. At a target you're fine, but I think when it's a man you aim at, you wouldn't have the nerve to take bead on his heart."

"Yes, I could." Storm signals began to flash in Juliana's eyes. "If he meant me harm, I could."

John jerked to his feet and stamped over to the brightly burning fire. "Reasoning with you, Julie, is like the deaf trying to teach harmony. It's impossible."

"I need a home of my own, John," Juliana urged softly, joining him by the hearth.

Until now Molly had remained silent as brother and sister argued back and forth. Now she rose and, coming to stand beside her husband, laid a hand on his arm. "John, dear, any woman is happier in her own home, with her own fixin's."

John gazed down into the urgent eyes. "Perhaps," he conceded finally. "But where will she find this place?" He looked at Juliana. "This place of your own. Around here, with new people coming in all the time, a cabin doesn't stay empty more than one night."

"I'll find something," Juliana insisted doggedly.

"Look." John gave in, scratching his head irritably. "There's no hurry. If you'll wait until I finish building Molly's

new house, you can have this one. I can keep an eye on you
then."

Hope flared in Juliana's eyes. "How long will it take you to
build the new place?"

"I don't know. With spring here and the crops to be put in,
I'd say about ten months to a year."

"I can't wait that long!" Juliana wailed, throwing herself
into a chair.

"For God's sake, why not?" John almost shouted, his eyes
snapping angrily. "Are Molly and me that hard to live with?
We're trying our damnedest to make you feel welcome."

"Oh, John." Juliana's eyes pleaded with him, "If it was just
me I'd never want to leave you and Molly. But now there's
Nathan and . . ." She paused, then, taking a long breath,
blurted out what had caused her so much anguished turmoil.
"This coming September there will be a new baby."

Molly caught her breath in the heavy, stunned silence that
descended, and John stared at his sister in disbelief. Juliana's
hands nervously twisted the folds of her gown, refusing to
meet his eyes.

After a long sigh, John muttered, as though to himself,
"Sate Margruder's, of course."

Juliana nodded silently, her vision blurred with tears.

"I'm gonna kill that bastard," John said grimly, his fists
clenching and unclenching. But when he saw the wide-eyed
fear in his sister's eyes, he dropped a comforting hand on her
shoulder. "Only half kill him."

"Oh, John, I'm so sorry." Juliana threw her arms around his
lean waist. "If Sate knew I was alive he'd be here. I'm sure he
loves me."

John smoothed the silkly blond hair, his lips still grim. "I
hope so, honey, but trappers aren't well known as family men.
They'd rather run the woods."

"Sate will make a fine family man." Juliana's eyes shone
with deep belief. "If he ever learns that he's got one," she
added on a sad note. Twisting around to look at Molly, she
asked breathlessly, "Will you watch Nathan while I run into the
village to see if I can hear of an empty cabin?"

The door slammed behind Juliana and John grunted, "She'll
never find anything."

But Molly wasn't so sure. "Don't be surprised if she does.
She looked awfully determined when she sailed out of here."

• • •

The little horse seemed attuned to Juliana's mood as it nimbly, almost jauntily, picked its way over the rock-strewn trail to the Post. As Juliana tied the reins to a well-worn hitching rail, a babble of feminine voices drifted through the open door. She smiled. If anyone knew of a cabin, one of these ladies would.

When Juliana had first returned to the Hollow she had worried what attitude the women would take toward her son, he so obviously looked like his father, but it hadn't seemed to matter in the least. It was quite common for her to hear such remarks as "My, my, that boy looks more like his father every day," or "Wouldn't Margruder be proud if he saw his son." Word had spread that the trapper thought Juliana and his son were dead.

She had remarked one day how nicely everyone accepted Nathan's parentage. Molly answered that the trapper was well liked and respected in the settlement, and John had grumped that it was probably more like fear of his ability with the broad-bladed knife than respect.

"John, you know that's not true," Molly scolded. "The people just naturally admire the man. That's why they refer to Nathan as Margruder's youngun and Juliana as Margruder's lady."

Juliana had blushed with pleasure at this revelation, and now, because of it, was quite relaxed when she entered the dim post and greeted the women cheefully. She was answered with genial warmth . . . except from one woman.

The former bondswoman, Bessy Oates, leaned against the rough counter staring at her, a malicious look in her small eyes. Juliana's skin prickled. This was the first time she'd seen Bessy up close since her return, and she knew she was up to something.

The two women stared at each other, matching glare for glare in silent conflict. Then Bessy's fleshly lips pulled into an ugly leer.

"So, Miss High and Mighty Heller, you've finally fallen off your pedestal."

"Oh?" Juliana said softly, dangerously, as she planted herself in front of the florid-faced woman. "It's news to me that I was ever placed so high. But if in your mind that's the case, maybe you'll tell me in what way I fell off."

"I should think you'd know." Bessy's voice took on a sanctimonious tone as she sent a glance to the women who had stopped their activity and were listening attentively to the exchange. "You come back here, bold as brass, flauntin' your bas—"

"You'd better back off," Juliana broke in softly with dangerously narrowed eyes. "If you ever call my son a bastard I'll see to it that a whip is laid on your back."

"Hah!" Bessy blurted, her eyes sliding away from Juliana's penetrating glare. "I suppose you mean Margruder."

"That's right. He wouldn't take kindly to Nathan being called names."

It was while Juliana waited for another retort from Bessy that, unbidden, a small inward voice began to speak. "Why not tell them now about the new baby on its way? Get it over and done with. You can't hide the fact much longer?"

I'll do it, she thought, and before she could lose her nerve, she rushed on, only a slight nervous tremor in her voice, "And that goes for the one I'll give birth to in September."

A sharp intake of breath came in unison from the gathered women, but Bessy's surprised gasp was the loudest.

There wasn't a sound in the room as all eyes looked to Bessy, waiting avidly to see how she'd respond to this latest piece of news.

The woman finally managed to splutter, "You've got no shame, Juliana Adams, bringin' another bas— child into the world and no place to raise it. How can you add another burden to your brother?"

While Juliana fought back the desire to slap the fat, painted cheeks, she was hit with a thought that stunned her. She laughed out loud. Why hadn't she thought of it before?

Raking her eyes over Bessy in a way that made the woman flinch, she began: "You're a regular damn fool, Bessy, you know that? My children will have a home of their own. They'll live in their father's home." She waited until the last indrawn breath behind her was released, then went on, "I want you out of his cabin before sunset."

Bessy tried to laugh scoffingly, but it died in her throat. "You can't order me out of there. Sate . . ."

"If you're not out," Juliana continued as though the other woman hadn't opened her mouth, "I'll send the tavern women up to set you out. You've made enemies of them, and they'll be quick to lay hands on you, and it won't be in a gentle way.

"And don't take anything but your clothes," Juliana shot over her shoulder as she left the silent room filled with open-mouthed women.

Molly had sneaked quizzical looks at her sister-in-law ever since Juliana returned from the Post. The dispirited girl who had left that morning had returned in a state that could only be described as giddy. But every time she tried to lead the conversation to its source, Juliana detoured her to another subject.

It wasn't until after supper when they were having dessert, dried apple pie, that the puzzle began to unravel slowly. "Nemus tells me that Bessy woman is now baking pies and selling them," Juliana said, popping a last bite of flaky crust into her mouth.

"Yeah," Molly answered in a voice that betrayed her dislike for the woman. "They're so sour they pucker your mouth."

"It sounds like you don't like her, sister." Juliana's eyes twinkled.

"I can't stand the woman." Molly's eyes snapped. "And not because she made up to John one time. It's the airs she puts on. It's enough to make a person sick. You ought to see how she lords it over them poor whores at the tavern."

John helped himself to another piece of pie. "Ole Bessy acts real respectful these days. Anyone with half an eye can see she's out to land a husband."

"And she'll do it, too," Molly interposed with grim lips. "A lot of men would marry her just to get their hands on that piece of property. They'll overlook the fact that she used to be nothin' but a whore herself."

As John and Molly continued to discuss the character and desires of Bessy Oates, Juliana only smiled thinly. But when Molly made motions as if to start clearing the table, she spoke, shattering the small silence with her words.

"If Bessy thought Sate's property was going to get her a husband, I hope she's changed her mind."

"Why do you say that, Juliana?" Molly looked at her curiously.

"Because this morning while I was at the Post, I told her to clear out of Sate's cabin before sunset; that I was taking it over for my children."

She waited out the dazed silence, patiently waited for the

questions that were sure to come. She wasn't surprised when Molly regained speech first.

Casting the younger woman a pitying look, she scoffed, "And just like that, she agreed?" Molly shook her head. "No, honey, the trapper gave her the cabin, and that one will hang on to it like death."

"Hold on a minute, Molly," John said, a look in his eyes as though he had just remembered something. "I recall something that Battle said a few months back. He remarked that Margruder would be madder than hell if he knew Bessy was still occupying his cabin. That he'd given Bessy permission to stay there only until she could find another place."

"Well, that's not what she spread all over the Hollow." Molly's face flushed with indignation. "I'll bet she thought that Margruder would never come back, and that she was set for life." Her excited eyes turned to Juliana.

"What did the sneak have to say when you told her to get?"

"Oh, she put up a howl at first. Then I told her I'd set the women from the tavern on her and she settled right down."

Molly's eyes sparkled gleefully. "Oh, I'd love to have been there and heard it." Her lips curved in a tickled smile. "Juliana, if you start sellin' pies again, there ain't a man around who'll buy Bessy Oates's old sour things. The girl will have to start peddin' herself again." The pretty little woman roared in laughter, and after a moment John and Juliana joined in.

The mirth subsided and, as the kitchen area was put to order, plans for Juliana's move on the morrow were made.

"You must take one of the milk cows," Molly decided out loud. "You'll be takin' the breast away from Nathan before long. And the chickens too. They are, after all, yours."

The women hadn't been aware that John had left them sometime back, and when he reentered the cabin, they looked up, startled. "Where have you been?" Molly asked in surprise.

"Down by the river, talking to Nemus. I mentioned your plans to him, Juliana; that you'd like him to come with you."

"And?" Juliana asked impatiently when he didn't take the information further.

"Oh. He agreed."

"That's all? He just said yes?"

"Well, he did say that the trapper's son belonged under his father's roof."

"I hope you didn't exhaust yourself too much, John, telling me all that." Juliana grabbed a handful of hair and tugged as she went past her brother.

John reached for his sister's own flowing mane and muttered "Little hellion" when he missed.

Juliana showed him the tip of her tongue, than yawned widely. "I'm going to bed. I have a long, important day ahead of me, and I might still have to wrassle with Bessy." She said good night, and was half asleep as she pulled the covers up around her shoulders, holding Nathan close to her side.

The sun was an hour high when the two men, two women, and infant started out the next morning. John led the way along the narrow trail, his wife and Juliana with Nathan followed, and Nemus brought up the rear, leading a pack mule and the cow.

The draft animal strained under the load of provisions, crate of cackling hens, and bedding and pillows that Molly had insisted upon. "I got a feelin' that Bessy woman isn't all that clean," she'd said with a sniff, "and you're gonna want to change the bed the first thing."

By the time reins were pulled in front of the sturdy cabin, the sun had burned off the mists and the air had warmed up. There was no sign of life in or around the building, and no smoke curled from the chimney.

Juliana sat quietly, slowly taking in her first daytime look at the cabin and outbuildings that comprised her new home. She recalled with a sharp pang the one glimpse she'd had the night Sate had rebuffed her, sent her into Roth's arms.

That's in the past, she scolded herself, calling a smile to her lips as John reached out for Nathan. "It looks like you scared her off, sis." He smiled, using his free hand to help her dismount.

Juliana's cheeks dimpled. "I don't think it was me as much as it was the threat of Battle's girls." Her eyes shone triumphantly when from the barn several yards away there drifted a loud whinny. "I was afraid she'd take Sate's stallion despite my warning. It must have griped her to leave him behind."

"She never did have the stallion or hound," John said as, en masse, the four stepped up on the porch. "Battle has been taking care of them. Nemus went down to the tavern last night and brought them up here.''

He pushed open the door and Juliana exclaimed, "Hawser!" as the big dog lunged at her. Nemus's leathery face stirred in a pleased grin as he saw her greeted with wagging tail and lapping tongue.

"Trapper's hound good dog," he grunted. "We sleep easy. Man nor beast will slip up on us when him here."

While the men brought in the provisions and staked out room for the animals, Molly and Juliana attacked the inside of the cabin.

Molly was right. Bessy was no housekeeper; a film of grease and dust covered everything. While Molly heated water for scrubbing, Juliana changed the bed, then positioned Nathan in its center. She took time to tie a scarf around her hair before grabbing the broom.

Everyone stopped at noon for a cold lunch, then resumed setting things to order. Darkness had closed in by the time John and Molly felt that Juliana was settled in.

She stood on the porch watching husband and wife until they were out of sight, then turned her head to watch Nemus make his way to the barn, a lantern swinging from his hand. She leaned against a supporting pole, relaxing and listening. The woods were full of mysterious noises at night. As usual, especially at this hour of the day, thoughts of Sate came to her. Where was he tonight, she wondered, and what was he doing? She yearned with body and mind to see him; to feel the touch of his hand and hear the sound of his voice.

"Please don't be too long, Sate," she whispered. Then she straightened her back and walked into the cabin.

CHAPTER 26

Sate Margruder found himself uneasily watching his back trail, for several times the muddy, well-defined path was bisected by fresh wolf tracks.

"Keep a sharp look-out today," old Watkins had warned as he prepared to leave the cabin. "There's a pack of wolves working over the ridge somewhere. I heard them growlin' last night."

Sate hoped that the old man's eyesight was keen enough to spot one if it should creep up on him. The devils were hungry this time of year, and grandpa would be no match for one.

His eyes took on a somberness as his thoughts remained with his elderly friend, so gnarled and shrunken. He had aged this past winter, tiring easily, finding it more difficult to crawl out of bed in the mornings. It had been a good idea he'd had, running their traps together. The old fellow hadn't objected to the suggestion, and they laid the line in a wide circle around the cabin, a total distance of nearly sixteen miles. Every morning each started at a different end of the line and met somewhere in the middle. As the season neared its end, he had found himself working more and more traps.

He's tiring, and he knows it, Sate thought morosely, remembering a remark the old fellow had made one night, phrasing the words as an Indian would: "The winter of death is not too far off for me, Sate." The simple statement had left him with the impression that Watkins didn't care, that he regarded death with indifference. Did age do that to a man? he wondered now.

"At any rate we've made it through the winter," Sate mused out loud. "The snow is mostly gone except on the north slopes, and a good rain will take care of that."

Their catch had been a good one, with prime furs bringing top price. His share of the profits was substantial, cached away in the bottom of the flour barrel. Watkins had his hidden beneath a loose hearthstone.

During the long winter, Sate had healed to some degree. He no longer walked the forest floor in abject misery, although there were some nights when he lay in bed, hollow inside with thoughts of Juliana. A deep sigh escaped him. He would never fully forget her.

A sudden burst of laughter and the smell of wood smoke brought Sate out of his somber reverie. He was nearing the post; it was just another bend in the trail away.

The long building stood before him, built close to the ground, giving the appearance of having been hastily thrown together. It boasted two windows, one on each side of a rough, heavy door. Several horses were tied to a well-worn hitching post, switching their tails at the large horseflies the warmer weather had brought out.

Sate paused on the narrow porch, half wishing he hadn't made the two-mile trip. That bunch in there was basically an obscene and filthy lot, spending their evenings drinking, playing cards, and bedding down with the post sluts. Old Watkins had remarked once that during the summer season, when all the trappers came down from the hills, the place really became a hell-hole.

Taking a long breath and shrugging his shoulders slightly, Sate pushed the door open, entered swiftly, and stepped to one side. In these parts it was not wise to stand silhouetted against the light. Too many about were running from something, or someone.

When his eyes became accustomed to the dimness, he closed the door. The place was full of backwoodsmen, and a sprinkling of mountain men. These heavily built individuals stood out sharply against the slimness of the woodsmen who kept trim and lean from hunting and trapping. A fast glance showed several new faces as he walked toward the bar in the room. He felt all eyes flicker to the knife at his waist before scanning his face. A quick look from the corners of his eyes

showed curiosity in their faces, but he caught no sign of antag-
onism.

Several nodded their heads in greeting as he walked past
them, their eyes measuring him quietly as he ordered whiskey.

Sate took the glass of spirits to the far end of the bar, where
its side was left open so that the heavyset barkeep could
squeeze through when necessary, and leaned back on his
elbows, his indifferent gaze wandering over the sundry items
on the dusty shelves opposite him.

Bright gaudy beads and other cheap trinkets, displayed to
catch the eye of squaws, shared space with various dry staples,
while colorful Indian blankets vied gaily with coarse, gray
horse blankets. His eyes moved to a wall where traps,
snowshoes, and boots hung on pegs, and then to the corner
where, piled to the rafters, were fur pelts of every description.
His nose twitched; they made an ungodly smell.

He let his gaze survey the patrons again, this time more
slowly. Beside the dozen or so men bellied up to the bar, there
were two poker tables, each with four men. His eyes flicked
briefly over the painted faces of the whores who lurked in the
dim background. Their lackluster eyes swept over his face,
then dismissed him, as if to say: "He's not for the likes of
us . . . yet. But give him more time and we'll look different
to him."

Sate smiled grimly and turned his back on the slatterns.
"God, I hope not," he muttered grimly, taking a long sip of the
amber liquid. Several times this past month he had awakened
in the middle of the night to find his hand on a hard arousal. It
told him that nature was demanding he pay it heed, but he was
damned if he'd answer it with whores like those creatures.

When the outside door was abruptly thrown open, Sate
turned with the others to stare at the fat man standing there, a
bone-thin woman at his side. It was obvious the woman was
quite ill, a red flush on her cheeks contrasting harshly with the
paller on the rest of her face. The eyes were lifeless yet burned
brightly with fever. She was coatless, and the shoes on her feet
were badly broken.

The man, on the other hand, was warmly dressed against the
cold, spring wind, and sported heavy ankle-high boots. His
deep-set beady eyes shot a quick glance around the room
before he spoke in a high, nasal voice.

"Men," he began, "I'll get right down to it. I'm here to do a
little business. For one dollar you can spend twenty minutes

with the girl here. She's prime and knows her business. She can please a man in every way there is.

"Now. Who's first?"

He had hardly finished talking when a dry cough racked the girl. She quickly tried to smother it with a soiled rag she clenched in her fist, while gazing fearfully at her companion. Enraged, the man glared back at her.

The patrons, even the whores, looked pityingly at the sick woman, then looked away, one man muttering, "She looks more dead than alive."

The irate man waited impatiently for the thin shoulders of the girl to stop shaking, then spoke jovially to a huge mountain man: "What about you, mister? You want to go first?"

A set stare was his answer, and an angry flush swept over the fat face. Grabbing the woman by a thin arm, he jerked the girl over to the nearest card table, hissing in her ear, "Get them tits to showin', Myrt."

With fingers that fumbled, Myrt began to unbutton the worn, soiled blouse. Finally she pulled the edges apart, and the men looked away from the sagging breasts laying against her rib cage. The averted eyes caused the girl to be spun around so that she faced Sate, who still stared at the oddly matched pair.

"What do *you* think, mister?" The words were whined ingratingly. "Don't she look good to you?"

Sate ran an eye over the wretched-looking creature, then raised an eyebrow in contemptuous amusement before deliberately turning back to the bar.

The trapper's insulting action was too much for the already enraged man to bear. His fat fingers gripped Sate's shoulder. "Can't you answer a man when he speaks to you?"

There was not a sound in the room as everyone watched the two men. The regular hangers-on had wondered for a long time how this hard-faced trapper would handle himself in just such a situation.

Sate's rock-hard muscles bunched beneath the gripping fingers, sending a silent warning to their owner. Too late, the stranger realized he'd laid hands on the wrong man. His arm dropped to his side, and he furtively touched dry lips with the tip of his tongue when the dark head swiveled around and he stared at death in cold, threatening eyes.

"Sorry, mister, I meant no harm," his thick lips muttered as he backed away. "I thought maybe you was lookin' down on the girl."

"You thought right," came the icy acknowledgment. "She's a perfect misery. And if you don't want my knife in your gut, you'll stay the hell away from me."

Pent-up breaths were released throughout the room, and the fat stranger, thankful to escape the mean-eyed trapper with only a warning, took the girl by the arm and steered her toward the door. A thick hand was on the latch when a voice spoke from the bar.

"I'll give you fifty cents for however long it takes."

All eyes swung to the speaker, a tall, thin man with a cadaverous face. Stained homespun hung loosely on his angular frame and a dribble of tobacco juice stained the corner of his thin lips.

"Lousy farmer," Sate muttered to himself. "Probably has a dozen younguns at home with no mother. He's the type who buries wives regularly from overwork and childbearing."

It looked at first that the insulting offer would be refused. But while everyone waited and watched, the man shrugged his heavy shoulders and muttered, "Go ahead. I can see there ain't no money in this bunch." His small eyes narrowed. "You'll have to pay for the room at this cheap price."

The farmer already had his hand on his trouser buttons and, taking Myrt by the arm, he led her toward a dark corner, remarking slyly, "Don't need no room. I take my pleasure standin' up."

The girl began to struggle weakly, whimpering, "I'm too sick, Ike."

Ike lifted a hand as though to slap it across the sunken cheeks, then his gaze fell on Margruder. The trapper had unsheathed his knife, and now stared menacingly at Ike as he toyed with the blade.

The fat man shuddered as again he received a silent warning. He quickly took the girl from the farmer's grip and said in a loud voice, "I think I'd better take a room for Myrtie. It looks like she's took a cold. A few days rest and she'll be fine." He looked over his shoulder at Sate and saw him shoving the knife back into its sheath. Wiping the cold sweat off his forehead, he silently handed the bartender the price of a room. Then, muttering that he had to step outside a minute, he left.

The men watched him go, amusement on their faces. "By God, Margruder." One man laughed. "You scared the water out of the bastard."

Sate shrugged, tired of the whole shoddy affair, feeling no pride in being a part of it. He lingered at the bar, however, until Myrt entered the room pointed to by the bartender and closed the door behind her. At the rasp of the latch being lowered, he finished his whiskey and stood up. The sun had traveled over the building and was now almost obscured by the western treeline. It was time he headed home.

Outside, he stood a minute, breathing deeply of the fresh air. Then, as he was about to step off the porch, whistling lead whacked into the wall behind him only inches from his head. As he went sideways over the end of the porch, he heard the report of a rifle. He jumped to his feet in time to see a horse disappearing down the trail. He was not surprised when he recognized Ike's fat figure in the saddle.

"You lousy bastard!" he yelled furiously after the drumming hooves. "You'd better run, and far. If I ever see you again I'll shoot you!"

A night wind was sighing through the trees when Sate walked into the small clearing and saw the light old Watkins had put in the window for him. He stepped up his pace. Inside it would be warm, with a hot meal waiting for him.

Grandpa is a fine man, he thought, pausing to scrape the mud off his boots before entering the cabin. A little too talkative sometimes, always brimming with stories to tell. "But hell," he muttered, "all he has left is memories, and anyway, I barely listen to him." He pushed the door open and walked in.

"What took you so long, boy?" Watkins looked up from the pot of stew he was stirring. "I was about to go out lookin' for you. Thought maybe a wolf had got you."

"I was followed by a couple of the devils," Sate said, leaning his rifle beside the door, then hanging his cap and jacket on a peg. "And I tangled with a two-legged one at the post," he added, placing the powder horn and shot pouch on the mantel.

"Oh? And which of that bunch was brave enough to go up against you? I figured by now they was all afraid of your knife and fists." The old man waited expectantly.

Sate sat down close to the fire, stretching his feet toward the heat. "He was a stranger," he said, then related what had happened.

"I've seen that polecat," Watkins growled a few minutes later as he ladled out stew. "Ike Dunn is his full name. Came through here last spring with a young squaw. Peddled her to the men until she was wore out, then took off, leavin' her behind."

He placed a pan of corn bread on the table and motioned Sate to take his seat. "He's a mean cuss, son, and he won't take kindly to your shamin' him today. You walk careful, and keep your eye peeled on your back trail."

"Don't worry about it, grandpa." Sate grinned at his friend. "I've dealt with his kind before. I can handle him."

"Yeah, I expect you can." Watkins grinned back, then lapsed into silence.

It didn't occur to Sate until several minutes after they had left the table and were sitting in front of the fire that the old man wasn't jabbering in his usual fashion, and that he squirmed about in his chair a lot, crossing and uncrossing his legs. When he rose and poked at the fire unnecessarily, Sate quirked a questioning eyebrow at him.

"Grandpa, do you have somethin' on your mind? If you do, I wish you'd stop fidgetin' and spit it out. You're makin' me nervous as hell."

The old man grinned sheepishly and sat back down. "Well, son, maybe you're gonna be madder than hell at me, but I guess you wouldn't hit an old man."

"I've never been known to strike an elder . . . 'course, there's always the first time. What have you been up to?"

Watkins stole a look at Sate, hesitated, swallowed, then burst out, "While I was out huntin' today, I run across a squaw."

Sate waited for the old man to go on, and when it looked like he didn't intend to, he asked, "And what's so surprisin' about that? You can find one behind every bush around here."

"This one is different. You see, her husband died a week ago, and her not havin' no children or kin, the tribe made her leave their village. She's still youngish, and she swears she ain't been with no man but her husband."

Understanding began to show in Sate's eyes. But his face was blank of knowledge when he said, "So? Why would that make me mad?"

"Of course that wouldn't make you mad." Watkins sent him a sour look. "But I've been noticin' lately you've been kinda restless. I figured that since it's been a long time since you've had any pleasurin', maybe that was the reason."

When Sate gave him a lowering look, careful to hide his amusement, the old man said stubbornly, "It ain't natural for a young, healthy man not to have it once in a while." The faded blue eyes glared at Sate defiantly. "Anyway, I brung her home with me. If you don't want her, I'll send her packin'."

"She's here?" Sate ran a surprised look around the room. "Where?"

"Out in the barn, buried in the hay." Watkins scooted to the edge of the chair. "Want me to bring 'er in?"

"Hell, grandpa, I don't know," Sate answered, an image of the last woman he'd made love to rising in front of him; her face achingly beautiful, her body slender and delicate. He didn't know if he could bring himself to bed another woman.

"Drat it, Sate!" The words were impatiently angry. "You don't have to feel anything for the squaw. Just imagine to yourself that you and her are swappin' goods of some kind; a business deal. You'll provide her food and bed, and she'll take care of your itch when you get one."

When Sate made no response Watkins pointed out, "You'd be doin' her a favor. If you don't give her your protection, she'll end up down at the post. You know what will happen to her there."

"All right, all right, I'll take a look at her." Sate got to his feet, remembering the empty-eyed squaws at the post.

Cackling gleefully, the old man was out the door, and back, within five minutes. "Well, what do you think?" His lips spread in a toothless grin as he pushed the Indian woman ahead of him. "She's clean, just like I said."

The squaw stood in front of Sate, her eyes downcast. He swept a cursory glance over her, noting that her face was still unwrinkled; probably around his own age, he thought. Her face was too broad and her cheekbones too high to lend her any beauty, but her hair was neatly braided, and her body hadn't gone to fat.

"What are you called?" he asked, not unkindly.

The black eyes lifted to his. "Morning Dew."

After a short pause, Sate said as he indicated the pot with a nod of his head, "Eat your supper, Morning Dew."

He watched the woman try not to bolt the food in her hunger, and wondered when she had eaten last. When the pot was

scraped clean and the last piece of corn bread eaten, Morning
Dew moved about, washing the dishes and tiding the room. He
watched the swing of her hips beneath the soft doeskin of the
short shift and felt his loins stir.

Sate did not fight the lust that was growing inside him, for
suddenly he understood that it had no kinship to the love desire
that had kindled his blood when he held Juliana in his arms. He
felt his ears grow warm under the old man's grinning, knowing
look when Morning Dew came and sat down beside him, silent
and waiting.

"Look, you old reprobate," he said gruffly, standing up and
pulling his shirt over his head, "I don't want an audience
tonight, so make sure you face the wall."

"That was my intention right along, boy." The old man's
eyes sparkled mischievously. "Do I have to cover my ears,
too?"

"And your damn mouth."

Sate stepped out of his buckskins and climbed into bed with
the waiting squaw.

CHAPTER 27

Juliana stood outside the cabin, breathing in all the scents of the hill country; the strong odor of cedar, the pungent aroma of earth and rotting leaves. She had been thus for several minutes, her gown gathered up above the damp grass with one hand, a cup of coffee in the other.

Her gaze ranged slowly around the wilderness she loved so. There were signs of autumn. Sumac flamed crimson on the ridges and along the bluffs, and the air was taking on a crispness now that the days were growing shorter.

She slid a caressing hand over her proturding stomach. Two more weeks and she's be rid of this awkward, unyielding belly. She sighed softly. She had thought, hoped, that Sate would have returned to the Hollow by now, with her when this child was born. All summer she'd had Nemus and John questioning every stranger who came through; did they know a trapper called Sate Margruder and, if so, did they know of his whereabouts?

None so far had ever heard of him.

A bleakness shadowed Juliana's eyes. A trip to the Post last week had caused her to face the possibility she had so far refused to consider: Sate Margruder wasn't coming back, simply because he didn't want to.

In the group of women gathered in the Post when Juliana had arrived that day was Bessy Oates. The overly plump woman stood at the counter, handing over money for a small package lying in front of her. On seeing Juliana enter, her eyes sparkled maliciously and she nudged the woman beside her and said in confiding tones, though loud enough for all to hear; "I don't know what makes her think Margruder would want her. She's too soft. She don't know nothin' 'bout woods runnin'. And that's the only kind that devil wants. One who can live like an animal with him. That's why he's always got some squaw or other in his blankets."

Juliana felt her face blanch at the intended bite of the words even as she felt the baby kick inside her. In the silence that hung close and heavy, the women looked everywhere but at her.

She was about to wheel and run when a big, raw-boned woman swung on Bessy, her ham-sized fists planted on broad hips. "Bessy Oates." Her eyes glared at the smirking, painted face. "I recall that you spent a night or two with the trapper. So I guess he likes whores, too."

Bessy's face turned beet red as giggles and snorts of laughter greeted the large woman's remark. Shaking with rage, her small eyes shooting hatred at Juliana, she grabbed up her package and, chin in the air, stomped out of the room.

Juliana had been grateful for her neighbor's championship, but as she walked home later she gave Bessy's spiteful words close consideration. There was the possibility that although Sate loved her—and she refused to believe that he didn't—he could be one of those men who valued his freedom above everything else. That being the case, he might, to avoid becoming tied down, stay away from her.

"Damn you, Bessy Oates!" Juliana's eyes blazed as she suddenly set down her empty cup. "Putting doubts in my mind. In my heart I know that someday Sate is going to come riding up this hill, and he'll stay here with me. And I'm *not* soft!"

She examined her callused palms. All spring and summer she had spent in arduous labor, working like a slave from sunrise to sunset. At dawn, before anyone else was up, she had baked her pies, milked the cow, and fed and watered her chickens. Then, after a quick breakfast, it was out to the garden to chop weeds and tote water to the thirsty plants, all the time feeling as though her back might break in two.

Still in thought, Juliana sat down on the porch step. Nemus had been a tremendous help, of course, but if not for Aggie's tending Nathan and doing the household chores, she doubted there would have been a garden.

Aggie, she thought with a tender smile. She hadn't wanted to take the woman in that day Battle approached her about it, for Aggie was a whore. The one, in fact, who had given her the rose slip on her wedding day.

"She's not diseased, Juliana," Battle had said earnestly. "I'd never expose you and Nathan to anything like that. Aggie's just worn out. She needs rest and some good food, then she'll be fit as a fiddle."

Battle had drawn a gentle finger down her cheek. "She could be a big help to you, once she got on her feet. You're killin' yourself on this piece of land; just you and the old brave to take care of things."

The big man had returned that night with Aggie, a woman thin and gaunt, her few possessions stuffed into a haversack. But she was immaculately clean, from her fingernails to her red hair. Juliana wondered if the woman had attended to her appearance on her own, or at Battle's insistence. When a short time later the taverner was leaving, and she followed him to the door, he said in a quiet voice, as though he had read her mind, "Aggie scrubbed up on her own. She has great respect for you, Juliana."

He motioned to a bare-rooted bush lying beside the door. "That's her beloved rosebush. She dug up the whole thing for you."

She watched the big, soft-hearted man ride away through tear-blurred eyes. Then, walking briskly to the tool shed, she returned with a spade and planted the bush beneath the kitchen window.

Juliana looked at it now, smiling to see how it had responded to love and gentle care. Just like Aggie had done. The former prostitute had absolutely bloomed, and within two weeks had taken over the care of Nathan and the housework, including the cooking.

Yes, it had been a good day when she took in Aggie, Juliana mused, thinking of all the work the woman had freed her to do. The harvesting of the garden, storage of its fruits for the winter months ahead, the hay she had helped Nemus to cut and spread out in the barn to dry. And the countless pies she'd rolled out and baked.

This past summer she had surprised and pleased her customers with fresh fruit pies. First had come dewberry, then rhubarb, and in August had come juicy blackberry.

But before long they'd be back to dried apple. Her gaze traveled to the three apple trees a few yards away, planted there by previous owners. They were heavy with fruit, ready to be picked. She and Aggie would spend many evenings peeling and slicing the apples, then spreading them out on the attic floor to dry.

Juliana turned her head and sniffed the air, smiling as she recognized a mixture of tobacco leaves and bark. *Kinnikenick,* Nemus called it. "Today good day to gather bark and roots," the old brave said, coming and sitting beside her, clouds of smoke puffing from a long-stemmed pipe. "I see your herb supply. You have enough. Now you gather those things that go with them."

All spring and summer, off and on, when there was time to spare, Nemus had walked in the woods with her, pointing out mayapple, ginseng, the sassafras bush, the sweet birch, explaining what each would cure when mixed with certain barks and herbs. There was no doctor in Squaw Hollow, leaving the settlers to do their own healing when necessary. With Nemus's help she had compiled a long list of what would heal cuts and bruises, what would make the best tea for stomach disorders.

It had been Molly, though, who in the early spring had taught her how to recognize and find the green plant life that the body craved after a long winter of meat and dried foods. How delicious were the salads of dandelions, meadow onions, ramps, lamb's-quarter, pepper grass, and brook lettuce. Later there had been the bigger plants of poke, dock, sorrel, and Indian mustard, cooked together in a pot, a chunk of salt pork added to it.

Juliana glanced at Nemus who watched her, waiting. "Will you be coming with me?" she asked.

"Not necessary. You know what to gather. Today I go pay visit to my people."

"I've kept you away from them, haven't I, Nemus? I'm sorry."

"No importance." Nemus waved away Juliana's apology. "Young bucks soon make me nervous with bragging and boasting. I not unhappy when it come time to leave them."

Juliana nodded understandingly. Nemus was happiest sitting quietly under a tree, smoking his pipe, dreaming of the days when he was a young man, and not bedeviled by the pale-faces.

"I'll get a basket and go right now," she said.

The old man nodded, then warned, "Watch out for deadfalls I dig for bears. You no want to fall on top one."

Juliana's response was a deep shudder.

Juliana walked slowly along the river, the basket swinging on her arm. So clear and fast-running, she thought, watching autumn leaves rush by. She sighed gently. Soon these waters would be frozen tight, sometimes even where the current was at its most rapid and powerful.

A gloominess settled over her. She dreaded the thought of winter, of being at the mercy of the cold that went straight to the bone, forced you to stay indoors for days on end . . . too many long hours in which to simply think. Of course this winter she would have the added company of Aggie and the new baby. And this year it would be different with Nathan. He was walking now and learning to say a few words.

Her heart twisted painfully. Every day the little fellow looked more and more like his father.

A sudden crackling of brush brought Juliana wheeling around, all thoughts fled. Her body froze. Only yards away stood the biggest bear she'd ever seen. His small, mean eyes stared at her while his huge head wagged from side to side.

"Dear God," she prayed, "make him remain on his hind legs," recalling what Roth told her about the imminent danger of attack when a bear was on all fours.

Her heart raced and her eyes were full of terror when the grizzly let out an enraged roar. She cried out again and again at the top of her voice. But no answer came. Only the echo of her own words rang in the valley. She was alone, utterly, absolutely alone.

She whimpered when the bear suddenly dropped to all fours and lumbered toward her. In desperation and panic, she wheeled and started running, letting out a gasp of pain when her feet slipped on the dew-wet grass and she fell headlong to the ground. She clamped her teeth togther against the pain that ripped through her lower body.

"Dear Lord," she whispered, her eyes darkening with despair, "the labor." Tears ran down her cheeks. She would never see this baby's face, never know whether she carried a son or daughter.

The bear was only feet away. Giddy with the pain that tore at her insides, Juliana was fighting off oblivion when a cracked voice whispered behind her, "Don't move, Ulie."

Moving only her stricken eyes, Juliana saw Nemus kneeling, an elbow resting on a knee, his long rifle leveled. She gave a startled jerk when a streak of fire and a heavy report exploded beside her.

Her eyes shifted to the bear when the animal gave another enraged roar and reared up on his hind legs. He had only been grazed. Then Nemus's gun boomed again, and this time she heard the lead find its mark. The bear went down with a heavy thud, one big paw resting on her foot.

With one sweep of his eyes Nemus took in Juliana's pain-contorted face. He hurried to squat over her, frowning with concern. She moaned and he picked her up in his wiry arms. "Must get you to cabin, help papoose to come."

Juliana looked at him in pain and surprise. "Do you know how, Nemus?"

"Have helped mares," he muttered, settling her on the pony's back, then climbing up behind her. "No different with squaw."

The last thing Juliana clearly remembered was a tearing pain, and the devoted Aggie standing at the foot of the bed helplessly wringing her hands.

It was near morning when she roused sufficiently to realize that she had been delivered of her baby. The bedding was clean and smooth, and she wore a gown. But what of the child—where was it? Her heart contracted as if it had been squeezed. She rose painfully on an elbow and let her dread-filled eyes search the room.

She saw Nemus almost at once. He sat in the rocker, in front of a low fire, a tiny bundle in his arms. Joyfully she called his name and he rose and came toward the bed. He laid the small blanketed form in her arms and then straightened up.

"Girl-child," he grunted, as if the little female was of no significance. But Juliana's quick glance at his face caught a look of pure pride in the black eyes.

She pulled a corner of the blanket off the baby's face, then laughed delightedly. Again she looked on Sate's face i miniature. Nemus's lips stirred with a hint of amusement. "Trapper put strong stamp on what is his."

"He does indeed," Juliana murmured quietly, wondering if Sate would ever see his daughter, would ever know of her existence.

"What you call papoose?" Nemus roused her from her dark musing.

She gazed down at the little black head, the tiny features. She had planned on Elisabeth if she had a girl, but . . . She lifted affectionate eyes to her old friend and said softly, "Her name will be Nema. After the bravest man I've ever known."

CHAPTER 28

~~~~

The wind shifted during the night. It came out of the north, bringing dark clouds heavy with snow. The storm howled through the hills, enveloping them in a blinding blizzard.

Sate Margruder awakened to the moan of the wind coming down the chimney and knew what it meant. His traps would be covered with snow, an extra hour at least to run them.

The bed was warm, and he tried to coax himself back to sleep, to regain the dream in which he'd been making passionate love to Juliana. But the somnolence he sought eluded him. His loins were too tight, his arousal too insistent.

He turned reluctant eyes to the cedar pallet alongside his bed where Morning Dew slept. He didn't use her often, even though he knew she would be willing if he called her to his bed every night. But taking her was only a momentary relief, and guilt followed on its heels. Always when he lay replete, his heart resuming its regular beat, Juliana's image would swim before him, her amber eyes sad and accusing.

He groaned as a painful throbbing sent a shudder through his body. The small sound had barely died away when a naked copper-colored body slid in beside him. He raised up to crawl between Morning Dew's thighs, but she sat up, stopping him with a hand on his chest.

"Trapper lay back down and relax," she whispered. "A hard day ahead of you tomorrow." She took his tumescence in both hands and added as she bent her head toward it, "Morning Dew soothe you the way a man likes best."

Not necessarily, Sate thought as her moist mouth settled over

312

him, remembering the slide and thrust of his body into Juliana's. There was no pleasure on earth to rival that.

But that would never happen again. His eyes were bleak as he stretched out and relinquished himself to Morning Dew's ministrations.

The next morning heavy drifts of snow covered the cabin's small window, extending to the low shingled roof. When Sate forced open the door he gazed upon a white, even world. Barely a foot of the shed showed, and huge cedar boughs drooped to the ground under their white burden.

Where had the summer gone so swiftly? he asked himself, hurrying back inside and slamming the door behind him.

"Where do you think you're goin' today?" he asked Watkins, who sat on the edge of his bed, laboriously lacing up a double-soled moccasin, his lips flinching in pain. Rheumatism rarely left the old man free of pain in his hands and knees.

"Now where in the blazes do you think I'm goin'?" Watkins's faded eyes tried to glare at the younger man. "I'm gonna run my traps, as usual."

"Come on, grandpa, that snow out there is up past your rump in spots. Stay inside today. I'll make your run."

"I might as well lay down and die if I'm past fightin' a little snow." Watkins stood up and moved to the table where Morning Dew had breakfast waiting. "And I'm not ready to do that yet," he added as he helped himself to fried salt pork and potatoes.

"You stubborn mule-head," Sate muttered, taking a chair across from him. "If you should run into trouble, will you at least let off a shot so that I can come lookin' for you?"

The old man grinned. "That I'll do, Sate. I ain't lost all my senses, you know."

"I wonder about that sometimes," Sate growled, stirring sugar into his coffee.

"Me, too," Morning Dew said softly, then clapped a hand over her mouth when both men looked at her in surprise.

The squaw never said more than a dozen words a day, and that only when questioned about something. Sate had remarked to Watkins once that he hadn't known there were women who knew how to keep their mouths shut. The old man had snorted. "Find one who has been married to a buck and you'll find one who is mighty silent. Indians don't let their women talk overly much."

Watkins patted Morning Dew's hand as she poured him a cup of coffee. "Don't you go worryin' about me, too," he said kindly. "Sate's worse than an old woman."

"Why you no ride pony today?" The squaw looked at him hopefully.

"I wish you would," Sate broke in earnestly before the older man could answer.

Watkins washed down the last of his breakfast with a long drink of coffee, then pushed his chair back. "All right," he conceded. "Anything to keep you two from yakkin' at me."

The squaw's anxious eyes followed him as he stomped out of the cabin, closing the door noisily behind him. "Old man should stay by fire today," she said to herself. "I feel it here." She tapped her breast. .

"Yeah, the proud old fool," Sate muttered, shrugging into a fur jacket. Picking up his rifle, he followed his partner outside.

The crunching of his footsteps in the snow and the soughing in the trees was the only sound around Sate, except for the occasional distant howl of a wolf, sounding sad and wild at the same time.

Of all the animals in the hills, he liked the wolf best. When asked why, he'd answer, "He kills clean, he's a fighter, and he dies game." Many had whispered to each other that if he only knew it, the trapper was describing himself.

After a couple of hours of plowing through snow drifts past his knees, Sate was beginning to tire. He knew that grandpa was not nearly as vigorous as he was, and he worried about how the old man fared. The catch wasn't all that good. The storm had driven the animals to hole up in their winter quarters until hunger drove them out.

He plodded on. The traps had to be uncovered regardless. As he moved doggedly on, his thoughts drifted back to the night he'd found Juliana in that blizzard. He had fought through snow drifts that time, too.

A ragged sigh softly escaped his lips. Recently she had been on his mind almost constantly . . . as though she still lived. God! His eyes beseeched the sky. Would he never get over her?

Sate had worked another two hours when he heard the blast of the Kentucky rifle. Grandpa—he's in trouble. He turned southward toward the sound of the shot, trying to hurry but too impeded by the heavy snow to make any rapid progress. When he felt that his lungs were on fire he stopped and squatted down at the base of a lightning-blasted oak to catch his breath. He had been there but a moment when a startled flock of pigeons came whirring over his head.

What had frightened them? His eyes made a quick survey of the area. When he saw nothing but trees and snow he lifted a shoulder. Pigeons were strange birds. They panicked easily. The movement of a dry leaf on a tree could have set them in flight.

Sate was about to rise and continue on when, suddenly, soil, gravel, and snow exploded at his feet, showering his face and shoulders.

"What the hell!" He jumped to his feet, rubbing his eyes, at the same time looking for the telltale smoke. About fifty feet to his right he spotted it drifting slowly from the top of a rock-strewn limestone bluff. Almost at the same time he glimpsed a figure darting off through the trees. Swinging the long rifle to his shoulder he took quick aim, and the barrel belched smoke and flame.

"Did I hit the bastard?" He swore angrily, rapidly pouring lead and powder into the rifle, then ramming it home. Grasping the firearm, he loped to where the sniper had disappeared.

Savage joy leaped into Sate when he found the tracks. They were deep and sprinkled liberally with glaring red. His bullet had hit home with good force. He smiled grimly. Now to find out who the skunk was that wanted to see him dead.

His eyes glued to the bloody trail, he moved out.

The time he spent in the Pennacook village had taught Sate to think Indian, to assume an animal instinct to move quietly through the woods, to step behind a tree occasionally and look around. It was at such a time that he spotted his prey. The man was hunkered down behind a boulder, intently scanning the forest. Recognition stirred in Sate as he studied the back of the man's head, his heavy bulk. When the broad, florid face turned to search his back trail, Sate could only stare and hiss, "Ike Dunn!"

Why has that no-good come back? He swore darkly. How did he have the nerve? That girl he'd run off and left had died two days later. Her shallow grave lay behind the tavern.

Revenge. Sate remembered grandpa's warning. As with most weak men, there was a stubborn hardness in Dunn. In his eyes he had been shamed, and retribution would be uppermost

in his mind. Well, by God—Sate braced the rifle on a bent knee
and took careful aim—he has brutalized his last woman.

He was ready to squeeze the tripper when four riders
appeared at the fringe of the forest. Dunn immediately stood
up, waving at them wildly. Now what? he wondered, sitting
back on his heels as he watched the newcomers rein in and
dismount. The bastard knows them, he muttered inwardly as
all four spoke familiarly to the fat man.

"Hey!" one exclaimed, spotting the dark patch near Dunn's
right armpit. "You're bleedin' like a stuck pig."

"I know it, damn it," Dunn swore loudly, his paralyzing
fear leaving him now that he had company. He knew the
trapper wasn't about to take on all five of them. He eased his
coat over his arm and one of the men bent over to examine the
wound.

"You're only creased," he said carelessly. "The bullet got
the fleshy part of your shoulder."

A bearded man guffawed loudly. "There's a lot of flesh on
you to hit, Ike."

Dunn snarled an inaudible answer.

"Who done it, Ike?" a man asked.

"That damned trapper, Margruder. Came at me from
nowhere."

"You mean he shot at you for no reason?" There was doubt
in the question.

"That's right." Dunn made a big to-do of pressing a dirty
handkerchief over his wound. "Just up and fired at me."

"I don't know. He's mean, I grant you, but I don't peg him
as the type who would fire at a man for no reason." The
speaker studied the sullen face through slitted eyes. "What'd
you do to him? Cheat him at cards, sell him a diseased
squaw?"

"I ain't never had no dealin's with the man," Ike blustered,
heaving his great bult up. "And I want you fellers to help me
get him."

There was a long silence in which no one spoke, and Sate
remembered old Watkins saying: "None of the men have any
use for Ike Dunn, not even the bad ones. They only let him
hang around when he's got a woman with him so's they can
pass her back and forth."

It seems the old man knows what he's talking about, Sate
thought when the bearded man asked, "Where you got you

woman hid this time, Ike? Back in some cave? Naked, so she can't run away from you?"

Dunn's face darkened at the thick sarcasm in the words, but he let it pass. "I won't have her for a couple weeks. But she's worth waitin' for. She's a looker, the likes of which you fellers have never seen."

The men abruptly started throwing gear, making camp. The bearded one cleared away a patch of snow, and as he coaxed a fire out of damp wood, said coolly, "There ain't no hurry to go after Margruder, Ike. We know where he lives. We'll just dig in and let him stew for a couple of weeks. In the meantime you can go and fetch that pretty little gal you're braggin' about."

Dunn's a bigger fool than I thought if he believes that hogwash. Sate's lips curled. He couldn't help knowing that the men's only interest lay in the appearance of the woman. He rose slowly, his muscles stiff from squatting so long. He couldn't beard five of them, not that he thought the men would defend Dunn. The thing was, one of them might admire the bearskin jacket Morning Dew had made him, or maybe his rifle, and wouldn't hesitate to kill him for it.

No, he could wait. Sate's face took on a hardness of stone, but Dunn's day wasn't far off.

Night had almost fallen when Sate arrived back at the cabin, lines of fatigue on his face. Morning Dew jerked open the door as he stepped heavily onto the porch, anxiety in her black eyes.

"Old Watkins no come home yet."

Sate stared at the squaw as there echoed in his mind the shot which had sent him looking for the old man. His hands clenched into white-knuckled fists. His anger at Dunn had made him forget. An awful thought hit him. Had Dunn shot the old man?

His voice was tight as he ordered, "Fix me a quick cup of coffee, then light the lantern. I'll go after him."

The coffee scalded his throat, but Sate didn't feel it. He felt only his guilt. "I should have tied him in bed." He stared into the dark, steaming liquid.

He was ready to pick up the lantern when Morning Dew exclaimed from the window, "I think I see horse outside." Instantly Sate was peering over her shoulder. He drew a sharp breath.

There was a horse in the shadows of the trees. It stood on

braced feet, its head hanging. No—Sate shook his head—not
hanging; the horse was nudging at a figure that lay face down
in the snow, so lax that it could mean only death, or near it.

He knew that it had taken him only seconds to reach the
silent figure, scoop it up, and carry it to the cabin, but it
seemed like an eternity to him. Morning Dew was waiting, a
basin of water in one hand, a candle in the other as he laid his
burden on the bed that had received it for many years. They
both gasped at the sight of blood streaking the white hair.

His fingers working with desperate swiftness. Sate parted
the silken strands of hair and found the deep, ragged tear just
above the right ear. He swore harshly, but his touch was as
gentle as a woman's as he began to bathe the gunshot wound.
In seconds the basin of water was red with the blood that
refused to stop.

Sate sat back on his heels with a resigned sigh. He was going
to lose his old friend. His chin sunk to his chest; his eyes
squeezed tight. Then Morning Dew nudged him and when he
raised his head he found the old man staring at him. The faded
blue eyes were filled with complete knowledge and resignation. Sate took the cold, bony hands in his and Watkins
whispered, "I'm about done for, I reckon, son." He paused
for breath, then added slowly, "It was . . . was . . . Ike
Dunn . . ."

With a long sigh the aged body went limp, and Sate rose
stiffly. "He's gone," he said to the squaw standing at the foot
of the bed, and walked outside. He leaned against a post,
staring into the darkness. A terrible look came into his eyes and
his words had a wild sound.

"I'll avenge you, old man. That's a promise on my dead
Juliana . . . and our son."

CHAPTER 29

After grinding out his promise to old Watkins, Sate reentered the cabin and picked up the lantern. A muscle twitched in his jaw as he noted Morning Dew bathing their friend's wizened body, preparing it for burial. His eyes flickered over the clean buckskins in which she would dress him.

He closed the cabin door softly behind him and walked to a stand of cedars several yards behind the shed housing the two small ponies. Grandpa had always liked it here, saying once that the constant whispering of the wind in the green branches had often been his only companion.

How ironic, he thought as he stepped off the gravesite, that grandpa had been the one who had told him how to dig a grave in frozen ground.

"What you do, son, is clear away the snow, then start a hot fire over the entire cleared area. You have to keep the fire fed, sometimes for hours, once in a while, all day. Depends on how far down the ground is frozen. You see, you burn a while, then you dig out the thawed soil, then fire it again. You do this until you come to where it ain't froze anymore."

Sate picked up the shovel he had taken from the porch and bent his back to the first operation. Five minutes later he made his first trip to the pile of logs stacked against the shed. In half an hour there was a six-foot framework of glowing red coals. He stared down at the snapping pieces of wood, thankful for the chore that kept him outside. For inside the cabin Morning Dew had started intoning a low death chant. It sent shivers down his spine.

After a while Sate wrapped a blanket around his shoulders and sat down on a rock close to the fire. The squaw's chant rose to a shrill keening. Pulling up his collar to deaden the sound, he pondered his future.

Would he want to stay on here now that grandpa was gone? It was a perfect set-up. A sturdy cabin, good trapping, a silent, willing squaw. Still . . .

A wolf howled in the distance and he sighed heavily. Was he to spend the rest of his life like that wild, shaggy animal? Tramping the forest, howling his loneliness?

For he was lonely, God knew. Even grandpa's constant chattering hadn't always penetrated that sense of desolation. Maybe it was time he moved on. After he'd taken care of Ike Dunn, maybe he'd seek out some settlement and spend some time around people. Civilized people.

It was nearing dawn, and Sate was letting the fire die out. The grave was half dug, the remaining three feet untouched by frost. Another hour would see it finished.

He picked up the coffee pot Morning Dew had brought him some time back, then set it back down. In the muted silence of snow and darkness he had heard the muffled sound of hooves. He reached for the rifle, a chill rippling down his spine. Was Dunn out there, anxious to finish what he had set out to do?

His finger had slowly lifted the hammer on the long rifle, the one that had seen him through the war, when a horse and rider emerged from the forest. Keeping his hands well in sight, the man's deep voice called out, "I saw your fire and thought there might be a cup of coffee around. Can I come in?"

Sate peered through the gloom of first light and decided he had never seen the tall, lean man before. He stood up, the rifle cradled in his arms. "Come on in."

The rider lifted the reins and the horse moved forward. In the red glow of the coals, Sate studied the thin face, figuring him to be somewhere in his fifties. And, from the open frankness of the brown eyes that met his steadily, a cut above average compared to the men who lived around the hills.

The stranger swung stiffly to the ground, then paused, staring down into the half-finished grave. "I see you've had a death. I'll move on."

"No, it's all right," Sate said quickly. "I'll be glad of some company." He reached for the blackened pot again. "And I've got coffee."

"Thanks. That will sure hit the spot." The older man took the tin cup of steaming liquid. "It's damned cold in the woods." He took a long drink, then asked quickly, "A member of your family?"

Sate shook his head. "No, but he was the best friend I ever had."

"What took him—an accident, pneumony?"

Sate's jaws clenched. "A low-life buzzard took him. Snook up behind the old fellow and shot him in the head."

"A sneakin' coward," the stranger muttered. "I don't suppose you know who done it?"

"I know. A varmint by the name, Ike Dunn."

"Say, I know that man." Coffee slopped over the cup as the man started. "That is to say, I don't know him to speak to, but I know who he is. He was down at the fur post last night. He was goin' on about some trapper called Margruder. Said he was gonna put a bullet in him." The man nodded toward the grave. "Is that Margruder?"

"No." Sate smiled grimly. "I'm Margruder. He killed my old partner."

The newcomer's eyes narrowed in angry disbelief. "You're not speakin' of Grandpa Watkins, are you?" At Sate's brief nod, an explosion of swearing ensued. "Why, that miserable bastard. The men at the post warned him to leave the old man alone. Said they warn't worried about you takin' care of yourself, said you could fight off the devil if necessary."

He shook his head. "The bastard said he had no intention of botherin' the old man. In fact, he went on to say that he wasn't sure yet that he'd shoot you, that he had a better way of makin' you suffer." He finished off the coffee. "You have any idea what he was talkin' about?"

Sate shook his head. "There's no tellin' what goes on in the head of a man like that."

"I reckon," the man agreed, then offered his hand. "My name is Perkins. Abe Perkins." When Sate returned the firm grip of the cold fingers, Perkins said, "I'll spell you a while with the diggin'."

The eastern sky was turning pink as Sate stood looking down at the raw earth of the grave. It was finished, ready to receive his old friend. He turned away when the aroma of frying meat and brewing coffee drifted on the cold air. Perkins shot him a surprised look.

"You got another partner?" His lips curved in a broad grin. "Or maybe a squaw?"

Sate smiled briefly. "There is a squaw. A decent woman. She was mighty fond of the old man."

"You don't mean . . ." Perkins looked startled.

"Naw, not that way. More in a fatherly way. She's takin' his death hard." Sate picked up the rifle and spade. "Take the lantern and let's go see what she's cooked up for breakfast."

In her silent way, Morning Dew merely nodded when Sate made her known to Abe Perkins. But she had known he was outside, for the table was set for two. She, in Indian fashion, had never taken her meals with Sate and grandpa. She had taken her plate to the raised hearth and eaten alone.

Sate motioned Abe to sit down, his eyes avoiding the still form laid out on the bed in the corner. "Help yourself." He pushed a platter of fried rabbit and potatoes toward his guest.

There was silence as the pair took the edge off their hunger.

"When do you think Dunn will come gunnin' for you?" Abe asked midway through the meal.

"He already has." Sate helped himself to another piece of meat. "Yesterday afternoon."

"Oh? Well, it looks like he missed you."

Sate grunted. "I didn't miss him, though. He's packin' my bullet in his shoulder."

"Maybe he'll get lead poisonin' and rid the world of his presence," Perkins said, eyeing Morning Dew appreciatively as she poured him a cup of coffee.

Sate changed the subject. "Where do you hail from, Perkins, if you don't mind my askin'?"

"Actually, I'm from all over." Perkins sipped the hot brew. "But recently I'm from Sqaw Hollow."

"The hell you say?" Sate's head jerked up. "I spent some time there once. How is everything in that hell-hole?"

Wry amusement twisted Perkins's lips. "It's still a hell-hole, I reckon. But the place is growin'. Before winter set in there was new cabins goin' up all over."

"I expect you met Battle."

"Yeah, the big feller that owns the tavern. We got to be pretty good friends. He can sure handle them hellions that come in his place."

"Did you ever run into a woman called Bessy? I don't recall her last name."

Perkins laughed. "Everybody knows Bessy Oates. For a while there she thought she was big cheese. She had a cabin some trapper had give her. For a time she baked apple pies for a livin'." Not noting the angry, hard look that had came over Sate's face, the man continued, "They was the awfulest tastin' things I ever stuck in my mouth. I don't think she put a grain of sugar in them.

"Anyway, old Bessy put on airs that would make a person sick. Everybody knowed she was lookin' for a husband, that she was actin' prim and proper, thinkin' that the men would forget that she used to be Battle's whore."

When a long silence ensued, Sate pressed, "Well, did she land a husband?"

"Nope." There was no doubting the satisfaction in the single word. "You see, one day a young widder woman with a baby showed up in Squaw Hollow. The next thing the village knows, she's ordered Bessy out of the cabin, said that the place belonged to her baby's father and that she needed it."

Sate stared in stunned disbelief as the man talked on, hearing not a word as he went over the gossip that had occupied the villagers for over a week. Was it possible? Hope made his heart race. Could Juliana and his son have survived that plunge over the cliff?

A weakening excitement gripped him, and in a harsh voice that trembled he interrupted the stranger's gleeful narration.

"Describe the widow to me."

Perkins paused midsentence, startled at the abrupt order. When he saw the half-wild look in the trappers eyes, he hurried to comply.

"Well, she's the most beautiful woman I've ever seen. Her hair is like a pale cloud hangin' 'round her shoulders, and her whiskey-colored eyes make a man purely melt when she looks at him. And her body . . ." Perkins rolled his eyes to the ceiling. "Even through her clothes a man can—"

"All right! I've got the picture." Sate glared across the table.

It grew quiet in the room as Sate stared into his coffee. The only sound was sap running out of the burning logs and hissing as it hit the red coals below. When finally he lifted his eyes, the

man sitting opposite him blinked at the radiance shining out at
him.

"After I've buried grandpa I'll be headin' for Squaw
Hollow."

Perkins studied the lean, glowing face. "I take it you know
this woman."

Sate smiled. "I better. I'm her son's father."

"The hell you say. Well, I'll be damned. Some men are sure
lucky."

I certainly hope so, Sate thought, suddenly unsure what
Juliana's reception of him might be. She had suffered a lot at
his hands. There was every possibility she would slam the door
in his face.

These uneasy thoughts were banished when Perkins sat
forward, a frown wrinkling his forehead. "Margruder, Ike
Dunn said that he was goin' to Sqaw Hollow. Do you think
there's any connection with your woman?"

Sate's blood ran cold as once again he heard Ike Dunn's
boast to his companions: "I'll have her here in a couple of
weeks. And she's the prettiest thing you fellers ever laid eyes
on."

He jumped to his feet, the chair scraping across the floor.
"It's connected all right, Abe. The bastard knows I couldn't
bear knowing that Juliana was being sold to any man who had
the price."

"What are you gonna do?" Perkins stood up also. "He's got
a good day's start on you."

"I know." Bleakness clouded Sate's eyes. "I've got to start
after him as soon as possible." His eyes traveled for the first
time to the stiff figure of his old friend. When he looked back
to the man at his side his face expressed how hard was the
decision he had arrived at.

"Perkins, I hate to ask this of you, pratically a stranger, but
would you see to grandpa's burial? You know how important it
is that I leave immediately."

"Say no more," Abe said. "The livin' must come ahead of
the dead. I'll see that the old feller is buried proper."

Sate nodded his thanks, then turned around to confront
Morning Dew who had come up behind him. Her face reflected
stunned disappointment. He sighed. He had forgotten about
her. His gaze looked beyond her as his mind raced. What was
he to do with this squaw who had faithfully tended his every
need? She deserved better than to be left alone.

His eyes sought Perkins again. "Abe, what are your future plans? Are you plannin' to move on?"

"Hell, I don't know, Sate. To tell the truth I'm gettin' a little tired of always movin' on. I'm past fifty and beginnin' to slow down."

"I know the feelin', and I'm not forty yet." Sate stared reflectively at the floor. When a gust of wind rattled the windows he looked up, fixing Perkins with grave eyes.

"I want to put a proposition to you, Abe." The older man nodded and he went on, "Morning Dew is too decent a woman to just go off and leave. That bunch at the tavern would be after her in no time. She'd be used and abused and end up like them other women at the post.

"Now you strike me as a decent sort with no cruelty in you. I'm wonderin' if you would like to take her over, along with grandpa's cabin and traps."

At first Abe Perkins could only stare stupidly. Eventually Sate's steady regard convinced him that the offer was sincere. His hand shot out, and was received. "You go on to Squaw Hollow, friend, and don't worry about a thing back here. I'll do right by the squaw." He put a comforting arm around Morning Dew's slumped shoulders. "Me and her will settle in and live out the rest of our days together."

As Sate rode along, the Kentucky flintlock across the saddle pommel, he kept a ceaseless vigilance on the area around him. But in the three hours he'd been traveling he'd seen nothing except once when off through the trees he'd spotted a buck deer pawing at the cover of snow for some tufts of dry grass.

He was not surprised, for an hour back he had taken the advice Abe Perkins had given him on leaving: "When you come to the river don't follow it, even though Dunn is. Veer to your left, cuttin' cross country. It's a little rough, but you'll save yourself a full day's ride and maybe beat that buzzard to the village."

And he's right about it bein' rough, Sate muttered inwardly, guiding the pony around boulders half as big as cabins, through trees standing so close together their trunks sometimes scraped the little animal on both sides.

He shifted in the saddle, trying to relax his long body as the pony fought for footing on the steep, rocky hill. He swore under his breath, knowing from experience that Dunn was following an easier route along the river.

"I sure as hell hope Perkins knows what he's talkin' about." Sate patted the laboring mount as he plunged through a two-foot drift. "I'd sure hate to be lost in this country."

It was coming on dark, and horse and rider had just reached the bottom of a hill, when the sturdy little horse gave a protesting snort and began to struggle. Sate's lips were grim when he swung out of the saddle. He had a pretty good idea of what had happened.

His surmise was right. The animal's left foreleg was caught between two rocks. If he should move the wrong way, the thin fetlock joint would snap.

Two uncomfortable thoughts hit Sate as he bent over the trembling animal. To put a bullet in its brain would be the hardest thing he had ever done, and to be stranded in this wolf-infested wilderness was equally daunting. He took a careful hold of the delicate foreleg in both hands and, keeping up a gentle flow of words, slowly and firmly pulled. The leg came free and he let out the breath he had been holding.

The pony limped a bit, however, and Sate walked alongside him. The spunky little beast needed a rest anyway, he told himself. A frown marred his forehead. He was losing precious time.

Dusk came quickly in the thick forest, and as soon as Sate came across a large rock shelf of about three feet he stopped for the night. Camp was quickly made, involving only the unsaddling of the pony, spreading a tarpaulin on the snow, tossing the bedroll on it, then digging into the grub sack. It would be cold meals while he traveled.

A short time later, pemmican and parched corn consumed, he rolled up in his blankets, the mount tied close by, his nose in a feed bag. Then, his hand on the flintlock, Sate had one last thought before falling asleep: Will I get to Juliana first?

His senses always alert, the next three days more or less followed the same pattern for Sate. On the fourth day he began to recognize familiar landmarks. That day the sky became overcast, the wind picked up, and the temperature dropped. He knew that the area was honeycombed with caves, but he didn't like the idea of entering one at this time of year. They made good homes for any manner of wild animal.

His lips pressed grimly. No beast could be worse than the icy cold beating at his back. As he kept his eyes peeled for shelter, the wind began to howl like a wild demon and the air grew colder, threatening to suck his breath away.

There was only one comfort for Sate. If he could not push on, neither could Ike Dunn.

But ten minutes later Sate was pulling the weary mount in and knuckling a mittened hand across wind-blurred eyes. Had he seen a light at the bottom of the hill from where he sat? Shielding his eyes and peering through the gloom, his blood began to pump faster as he watched other lights spring to life. Squaw Hollow! He hadn't dreamed it was so near. And now, pray God, had he arrived before Ike Dunn? The tired little pony turned reproachful eyes on him as he lifted the reins and urged it downward.

The first thing to catch Sate's notice as he cautiously approached the cabin he had lived in such a short time was the restive movement of a saddled horse tied nearby in a stand of cedar. He swung to the ground and walked a few yards to the nervous animal. A sweep of his hand down its rump brought a smile of grim satisfaction to his lips. It has been ridden hard; its shaggy, unkempt hide was still wet with sweat and lather. Dunn hadn't beaten him by much, maybe just minutes.

His mouth compressed into a tight line, Sate quietly climbed the two steps to the porch, then, testing each board for a squeak before puttin his weight upon it, his thumb finally came to rest on the latch.

CHAPTER 30

Eighteen-month-old Nathan lurked crossly around the bedroom door. Mama was with that ole baby again.

Juliana glanced up from nursing her three-month-old daughter and spotting the pouting face, a somberness flickered in her eyes. Even when he was displeased the boy looked like his father, the same pulled-in lips, the same lowering brow.

She reached a hand toward him. "Come here, Nat, and say hello to your little sister. She's through eating for the time being."

"Her eats a lot," Nathan grumbled, although he was fascinated by the dainty, doll-like features he studied closely. Everybody said she looked like him and her daddy. He shook his mother's arm and asked gravely, "Where our daddy? He come home soon?"

Juliana sighed. She had dreaded this question. Nathan was a bright little boy and was bound to wonder about this man people were always saying he resembled.

But what was she to tell him? She picked up the sturdy little body and held him in her free arm. "Your daddy, Nathan, is a trapper. You know what a trapper is, don't you?" Nathan bobbed his head up and down, proud of his knowledge, and Juliana continued. "Well, trappers have to go far into the forest to set their traps in order to catch their furs. Sometimes they have to stay away for a long time."

She kissed the top of the black curly head beneath her chin. "We'll just have to be patient until he comes home." She lifted the round little chin and gazed into the blue eyes. "Do you understand?"

"I spect so," Nathan answered, a bit doubtful.

Of course you don't understand, darling. Juliana breathed a long sigh, setting her son on the floor, then rising to place the sleeping Nema in her cradle. As she buttoned her blouse, she walked into the main room, stood in its center a moment, then, to break the dreary gloom settling around her, moved to the window and gazed out.

"Where are you, Sate?" she whispered. "Are you dead as my brother thinks?"

John had mentioned that possibility one day after hinting that her children needed a father. She had set her chin stubbornly and refused to comment. John had muttered that she was a foolish woman who waited for a man who, considering the wild life he led, could easily be dead.

But Sate wasn't dead. She'd feel it in her heart if he were.

Juliana sighed as she lifted her eyes upward. A wintery sun strove to pierce the grayness of the leaden sky. We're in for a change in the weather, she thought as she turned back to the cheerful fire that cast a ruddy glow on the windowpanes. At least it's nice and cozy in here, she thought, sitting down in the rocker and picking up the half-finished sweater she was knitting for Nathan.

She was startled when Aggie spoke behind her: "Miz Molly just rode up. I'd better push the coffee pot a little closer to the fire."

But Molly wasn't staying, she explained. She had ridden over to borrow Nema for a while. "To get in the practice of taking care of a baby." She patted her thickening waist. Her own baby would arrive in another five months.

"She's just had her lunch, and should be good for another three hours." Juliana smiled, rising and going into the bedroom.

"Me go, too." Nathan pulled at his aunt's skirt.

"Why, honey." Molly hunkered down beside the small boy. "I'm takin' Nema away for a while so that you can have Mama all to yourself. Don't that suit you?"

The way the large eyes lit up and twinkled was answer enough. When a few moments later Molly took the well-wrapped bundle from Juliana, she was told by her nephew, very seriously, that she could keep Nema all night, too.

"When's he gonna get over this jealousy of his?" Molly grinned as she opened the door. "I think that youngster needs a father."

"Molly Nemeth, don't you start on me, too," Juliana wailed laughingly, then closed the door. She stood a moment, shaking her head, a small smile on her lips, then began to roll up her sleeves. It was time to start the round of baking pies. The men would be climbing the hill around six o'clock.

Giving Nathan his own piece of dough and a corner of the table, she immersed herself in the job at hand. Aggie sat next to the fire, taking a turn at the knitting needles. There was a comfortable silence between them with no need for idle chatter.

"Well, that's done." Juliana smiled her satisfaction as she pushed the last pie into the brick oven. The clock struck four and she added, "Just in time to get the milking done."

Aggie quickly laid the knitting aside and started to rise. "I'll do it. I know you're tired."

"I'm not tired in the least, Aggie." Juliana swung a shawl around her shoulders and picked up the milk pail. "Besides, your lungs are still weak, and I don't want you catching pneumonia."

The air was cold and sharp when Juliana stepped outside. She lifted her eyes to the cloudy gray sky hovering ominously over the timberline. "We're in for another blizzard," she muttered, stepping off onto the path Nemus had cleared to the barn. "I hope Molly gets Nema back before it breaks."

By the time Juliana had milked the cow, fed the stock, and headed back to the cabin, the wind had built to gale force, bringing heavy snow with it. The wind whipped strands of hair across her face as she peered through the gathering darkness in the direction of her brother's place.

"Please, God," she whispered, "don't let Molly and Nema be on their way here now."

Juliana's worry was pushed from her mind when she opened the door and saw Aggie. The woman stood in front of the fire, her eyes full of terror, her arms clamped across her stomach. Juliana set down the pail of milk and took a step toward the obviously frightened woman, exclaiming, "Aggie, what's wrong? You look ready to faint."

Aggie's mouth opened and closed, but no sound came out.

Then a jarring laugh, like a flint on stone, brought Juliana swinging around. She froze, her eyes growing wider. Leaning against the wall, in line with the door, was the most evil-looking person she had ever seen. A hand fluttered to her throat.

"Who are you? What do you want? My husband is in the barn and will be here any minute."

Again that harsh laugh grated on her nerves. "You ain't got no husband, missy." Fat lips twisted in a leer as Ike Dunn pushed away from the wall and walked toward her. Juliana darted a glance at Aggie, silently asking about Nathan, and received a barely discernible nod toward the bedroom door. She closed her eyes a moment in relief. Thank God her son was sleeping.

"Don't look to the whore to help you." Dunn's interception of the silent communication led him to misunderstand.

"Don't call her a whore, you tub of bear grease," Juliana snapped as a small inner voice counseled her to keep him talking, get him between her and Aggie.

"She is a whore." Dunn leered as Juliana slowly backed away from him, inching her way opposite the ashen-faced woman who seemed incapable of moving. "It ain't been more than six months ago I rode hell out of her one night."

His small eyes glinted at Aggie. "It only took a little rough persuasion to get her to do anything I wanted her to do." He licked his smirking lips. "You couldn't hardly speak above a whisper the next day, could you, whore?"

While Juliana was thinking hotly, "So you're the one who caused Aggie to be brought to me," abject shame and fierce hate transfigured the former prostitute's features. She sprang at Ike Dunn, the nails of both hands tearing at his face. He let out a bellow of pain and rage, and before Juliana could move to help the frail woman, he sent a large fist cracking against Aggie's jaw.

Juliana uttered a low cry as Aggie's fragile body folded to the floor, her head hitting the corner of the hearth with a sickening crunch. She ran and knelt beside the lifeless body. Blood trickled from the ears, out of the nostrils, and the pale brown eyes unseeing at the ceiling.

Juliana stared up at Dunn, her eyes wide with loathing. "You animal! You've killed her!"

Fat shoulders shrugged indifferently. "So what? She's only a whore. No one will miss her."

"Damn your soul to hell, I'll miss her," Juliana cried, struggling to her feet and putting the table between them. "She was my friend."

Anger flickered in Dunn's eyes at Juliana's maneuver, but kept the feeling out of his voice as he wheedled, "It was an accident. Now come on and be nice to old Ike. You been a widow for a long time. You know you're needin' a man."

"And you call yourself a man?" Juliana sneered, disgust plain in her voice and on her face. "You're nothing but a low, crawling snake."

The enraged man lunged across the table so swiftly that Juliana jumped back without looking. She gasped her dismay as she stumbled and fell over a chair. As she lay on her back, stunned for a moment, she heard Dunn's lumbering tread approach her. At the same time there came the faint baying of a hound. "Oh, Hawser," she cried inwardly, "what a time for you to go hunting. And you too, Nemus, to pick this day of all days to visit your people."

She was kicking her feet from under the chair, trying to rise, when thick, stubby fingers reached for the neck of her bodice. And though she grabbed at the grimy hand, it was too late. Buttons popped and scattered over the floor.

"You're gonna be nice to Ike now." Dunn's lips pulled back from yellowed teeth. "Just like the whore was."

Juliana's blood was a frantic pounding in her ears as the man reared up on his knees, unbuckled the wide belt, then fumbled with the fastening of a frayed, soiled fly. She pushed back a threatening blackness, knowing what would happen to her if she should faint. She called on her failing senses, compelling them to rally, to help her.

She did not waste her breath in futile cries, but used all the strength that hard labor had given her to fight off her tormentor as she flung an arm across the protruding stomach, its force wringing a painful grunt. And while Dunn was caught off guard she began to crawl away, desperately scrabbling toward the door.

But her ankle was caught and held. Dunn flung himself at her. Telling herself that she was no Aggie who would give in at the first threat of pain, she pitted her agile body against that of the stronger, though slower, opponent.

They rolled back and forth on the floor, knocking over chairs and bumping against the table. But even as Juliana scratched and clawed, and pulled the greasy hair, she felt the strength draining out of her.

Through terror-glazed eyes she saw the doubled-up fist coming toward her face and knew she couldn't evade it. Her mouth flew open and one piercing scream rang out.

The fist landed. As Juliana began to lose consciousness, she was dizzily aware that the cabin door had crashed open. Her last thought was that, thank God, someone had come.

When Sate rushed headlong through the door his wild eyes first fell on Juliana's limp body, then flew to the panting man hanging over her. From his peripheral vision he noted another female shape crumpled against the hearth. This one, he knew, was dead.

But what about Juliana? Had the life been struck from her also?

His body bathed in a cold sweat, afraid that he had arrived too late, he pinned Ike Dunn with eyes that made the man's face contort with terror. There was no doubting the deadly intent in the icy glare of the cold eyes.

Dunn began to heave himself upright, but never made it. A hard body with catlike swiftness brought him crashing to the floor. With a supple twist of his body, Sate landed on top of the man he hated with every fiber of his being.

Straddling the great paunch, he began to systematically land hard, punishing blows to each vital feature of the fat-creased face. Blood flew from the wide flaring nostrils, then the thick lips became a bloody smear.

It was some minutes before Dunn's agonized whimpering penetrated the raging roar in Sate's ears. He let his upraised fist fall, swearing viciously. Why hadn't he killed the man as soon as he entered the cabin? he asked himself, doubting that now he could do it in cold blood. And while he waited, undecided, a frightened wail came from the bedroom. Caught off-guard at his son's distress, he turned his head toward the door separating them.

Ike Dunn took advantage of the distraction. His hand moved stealthily to the handle of the knife sheathed at his waist. Sate straightened up, ready to climb to his feet, and saw the knife coming toward him. His reflexes swift as ever, he caught Dunn's wrist and, straining every last ounce of muscle, slowly and surely turned the broad blade toward its owner.

Ike Dunn gasped as the sharp point plunged through his heavy coat and into his chest. His heels beat a tattoo on the floor for a moment, then his huge body relaxed forever.

Sate drew a sleeve across his sweating face, then rose to his feet. As he leaned against the table, steadying himself, the cabin door swung open and Molly stepped inside, the bundled-up Nema in her arms.

The sound of a crackling fire brought Juliana back to consciousness. She lay on her bed, a light blanket covering her from the waist down. She stared blankly at the ceiling. What was she doing in bed?

Everything came rolling back as she heard Nathan's pleased chuckle mingling with a man's low laugh. That dreadful Ike Dunn, and poor little Aggie. And someone had banged open the door just as everything went black for her.

Who had answered her scream? she wondered, leaning up on her elbows.

Her heart thundered, stopped, then thudded anew. Sate had returned. For there he sat on the floor, playing with his son. His face glowed with a mixture of love, pride, and satisfaction. Joyful tears sprang to her eyes. *I knew he'd hear of us someday and come find us.* Her eyes drank in the whip-lean body that had given her such incredible pleasure. *And he's very pleased with Nathan, thank God. I couldn't bear it if he treated his son lightly.*

Juliana also noted that the little boy was equally pleased with the big man when he gravely offered him something he had refused to share with anyone else. "Would you like to play with my puppy?" Nathan pushed a furry, wiggly body toward his father.

Soft feminine laughter joined Sate's, and Juliana became aware for the first time of Molly's presence. She turned her head to where her sister-in-law sat with baby Nema on her lap.

What does he think of his daughter? she wondered, sitting up and attracting both their attention.

Sate stood up slowly, and in the sudden silence he and Juliana gazed at each other across the room. He has aged, she thought. Deep furrows that hadn't been there before now creased his cheeks, and on his features was a strange stillness . . . as though he waited for something.

She instinctively sensed that he was uncertain about her; wondering if she would accept him in her life, wondering if she blamed him for fathering two children on her without benefit of marriage.

Nerves were fluttering in her stomach as she smiled at him waveringly.

Hope flared in Sate's eyes at that encouragement, and he walked toward her, stopping at the foot of the bed. "How are you feelin'?" he asked softly, awkwardly, his eyes caressing her, making the old excitement wash through her.

Juliana fingered her sore jaw. "I feel like I've been kicked by a mule."

"That woman-killin' bastard." Sate's eyes grew flinty hard.

Tears blurred Juliana's eyes. "I was very fond of Aggie. She and I became very close in the months she spent with us."

"Yes, Molly told me." Sate paused a moment, then said, "I've put both bodies in the barn for the time being. I figured Nathan isn't old enough to see Aggie . . . like that."

"You said 'both.'" Juliana leaned forward. "Are you saying that awful man . . . ?"

Sate's eyes glinted. "That bastard won't bother no more women, nor kill any more helpless old men," he grated out.

Nema's fussy whimper had turned into an outraged crying, and Sate relaxed his tense face and turned his head to look at Molly and the baby.

He grinned. "Your daughter has a healthy pair of lungs, Mis Adams."

"Yes, she has," Molly agreed as she stood up. "The poor little thing is hungry."

Sate nodded his understanding, then looked like he'd been kicked in the stomach when Molly moved to the bed and laid Nema in Juliana's arms. He gaped, his eyes widened, as Juliana freed a breast and guided a pink nipple into the waiting pink mouth. He drew in a sharp breath when he noted that the tiny face was a replica of Nathan's . . . his own.

His shock was unmistakable as his face turned almost gray

and a muscle in his firm jaw twitched spasmodically. He directed a muttered string of blistering words at himself, and as the two women gaped at him in wide-eyed surprise, he wheeled and almost ran from the cabin.

"Sate!" Juliana cried as the door slammed shut, alarmed tears welling in her eyes. Molly rushed to put her arms around her shoulders and to speak comforting words.

"He'll be back, honey. He needs to be alone for a while." She picked up one of Nema's tiny hands and held it gently. "This little one gave him quite a shock."

"Yes, I suppose she did," Juliana agreed. "Nathan alone could have jolted him, but to learn that he'd fathered another child . . ."

"Do you think he'll stay with us?" There was longing in Juliana's question.

"Yes, I do," Molly answered after a thoughtful pause. "But you'll never smooth off all his rough edges, Juliana. You'll never make a farmer out of him. You're gonna have to accept that fact."

"I know that, Molly." Juliana's eyes sparkled wickedly. "I wouldn't even try. I like him just the way he is; wild and disreputable."

"Well." Molly grinned, picking her coat up from a chair where she had tossed it and sliding her arms into the sleeves. "Don't let that wildness of his land you with another baby before he stands in front of a preacher with you."

Juliana chuckled as the door closed behind her sister-in-law. She rose and laid the now replete Nema in her cradle, then buttoned up the front of her dress. The men would soon start arriving for their pies.

As she lined her baking efforts up on the table, Juliana's thoughts were of Sate. Would he return? And if he did, would it only be a fervent coming together, and then would he ride off again? Was Bessy right; was Sate not a family man?

But there was such a look of love on his face when he played with Nathan, she reminded herself. He is capable of being a good father.

A knock on the door alerted Juliana that the men had arrived for their pies. She forced a pleasant smile to her face and opened the door.

• • •

It had stopped snowing, and a full moon shone from a cloudless sky, while Sate tramped the forest, describing himself in all manner of derogatory terms. What an uncaring brute she must think me. He struck out at a tree in frustration. Carelessly fostering two children on her without benefit of marriage. And had she suffered mean gossip because of it? Some women could be very cruel; Bessy Oates, for instance.

And what about the men? Had they lowered their respect for Juliana? Did they make rude remarks to her? Seek to share her bed?

"I'll kill them," he muttered, then walked blindly into Molly on her way home.

The pleasant-natured woman looked into his haggard face and pity stirred inside her. The man was hurting. None of her compassion sounded in her voice, however, when she said coolly, "I don't think Juliana should be left alone tonight." She paused to fix him with a hard look. "Neither do I think she should be left with a third baby to raise on her own."

Sate cringed visibly at the accusation in the curtly spoken words. There was a tremor in his voice when he said, "I'll marry her tomorrow, Miz Nemeth, if she'll have me."

If he thought Molly would give him encouragement, he was disappointed. For, after giving him a long, searching look, she turned and continued down the trail toward home. Sate watched her until she was out of sight, then turned homeward himself.

Twenty mintues later he stepped from the fringe of the forest only to stop short. A dozen or so men milled around his yard, some going into the cabin, others coming out.

"What the hell," he muttered, and started forward, his face resembling a storm cloud. But when he caught a whiff of spicy apples, he stopped short, ashamed of what had passed through his mind. He had forgotten that Juliana had once earned her living through the sale of pies.

At first Sate decided he'd remain hidden among the trees until all the men had gone. But to hide wasn't his way, and after all, that was his cabin. His woman . . . ? His children at any rate. No one could deny him that.

Sate strode boldly up to the cabin, receiving many strange looks, some agreeable, others downright hostile. His face darkened uncomfortably as some glances shot his way said clearly that he had a nerve, showing his face.

Righteous anger brought his chin up. He could not be blamed for something he knew nothing about. He'd had no idea that Juliana still lived, that she had given him a daughter.

His movements were a little rough as he shouldered his way through the press of people crowded around the cabin door. Once inside, he avoided Juliana's eyes as he strode to the fireplace and wordlessly took Nathan from the arms of a young trapper.

The youngster was happy to go with his father, and when Sate sat down with him, he wound his arms around his neck and chattered away.

Sate didn't hear a word his son said; his emotions were swinging like a pendulum. The shining welcome in Juliana's eyes every time she glanced at him made his heartbeat quicken, his breathing become heavier. But he was also gripped with a black jealousy as the men laughed and joked with Juliana, some of them stealing quick glances at her full, shapely breasts. He's soon put a stop to this pie backing, he promised himself through gritted teeth.

Finally the last man was gone. Nathan slid off his father's lap and joined his mother who stood, uncertain, at the dry sink. "Mama, Nathan hungry." The little boy tugged at her skirt. "When can I have my supper?"

"In just a few minutes, Nathan," Juliana answered distractedly as she returned the smoldering gaze of the lean-faced man who looked at her as though he'd never get his fill.

Her son pulled at her skirt again. "Will him eat with us?"

Before Juliana could answer, Sate swept the boy up in his arms. "I'd like to, son." His eyes sought Juliana's, love in their blue depths.

Juliana suddenly felt shy, very conscious of what other things those eyes were saying; promises of what would come later.

Her mind and emotions in turmoil, she set about preparing the evening meal. As she bustled about, mixing a pan of corn bread, basting the venison roast spitted and hanging over a bed of blowing coals, she watched Sate play with his son. She smiled at the deep contentment on his lean face each time he looked at the miniature of himself.

Sate caught her gaze once and smiled sheepishly. "He does look like me, huh?"

Juliana started to answer that he could never deny that Nathan was his, then stopped. She would not force him, shame him into saying something he wasn't ready to say. If he ever mentioned the word marriage it had to come from him without any prompting from her.

However, her pride would never allow her to go to bed with him again unless the words she yearned to hear were spoken.

And while those thoughts tumbled in Juliana's mind, Sate continued to watch her, his eyes lingering on her breasts, remembering with a weakness in his loins how they filled the cups of his hands, how hard the nipples became when he caressed them. And each time his eyes traveled downward he shuddered, remembering how sweetly her smooth hips had received him, cradled his body while eagerly taking his thrusts.

Supper was on the table at last, although Juliana couldn't remember putting it there. Of the three who sat down, only Nathan tasted and enjoyed what he spooned into his mouth. His parents were too aware of each other to know what they automatically chewed and swallowed.

Finally the hour came when the kitchen area was put to order and Nema was nursed and, along with her brother, put to bed for the night. Juliana came from the kitchen and sat down in the chair next to Sate. He stood up to lay a log on the fire and as she watched the powerful muscles of his back rippling under the supple buckskin shirt, red-hot desire scorched through her body.

She leaned her head back and closed her eyes against the sweet pain of it. Silent moments passed, then a log hissed and collapsed onto the bed of coals, showering sparks onto the hearth. Her eyes flew open and she met Sate's gaze from where he had come and hunkered down beside her. Their gazes locked, each telling the other of desolate days and lonely nights.

"Ah, Juliana," Sate half whispered in a low and broken voice, "I almost went out of my mind when I thought you went over into that ravine." His lean fingers stroked her cheek. "I still can't believe you're here, alive and more beautiful than ever."

"I'm sorry you had to suffer so, darling." Juliana covered

his hand with hers, keeping it on her cheek. "Roth and an old squaw were the ones in the sled."

"Your sister-in-law told me." Sate's eyes became somber. "I grieved for Roth, too. He was a good man; a good friend. That fact alone kept me from snatching you up and carrying you away that day in the cabin."

Juliana's lips curved gently as she remembered that day, how Sate had tried to act cold and uncaring.

As though Sate also was experiencing thoughts of that day, he tilted her face up and searched her eyes. "Did you ever hate me for . . . Nema? The past months must have been dreadfully hard on you in every way."

"Oh, darling." Love shone in Juliana's eyes. "How could I hate you for such a wonderful gift as Nema? And John and Nemus helped me with the outside work, and with a few exceptions my friends stood staunchly beside me."

"Still, it couldn't have been easy for you." Sate stood up, drawing Juliana up with him. "But that's in the past. You'll never have to stand alone again. Tomorrow we find a preacher. I'm not taking any chances of ever losing you again."

His arms tightened possessively around Juliana, and she could feel the beating of his heart against her breasts. Unable to speak for her happiness, she wound her arms around his neck and lifted her lips.

Whispering, "My lovely Juliana," Sate took them hungrily.

A hurt began to grow in the pit of Juliana's stomach and when his lean fingers began to undo the buttons of her bodice, then moved to knead and caress her breasts, she moaned and arched her body into his.

Sate shuddered at the desire-filled sound, and in seconds he disrobed her, and discarded his own clothes. The bearskin in front of the fire received their bare bodies.

Juliana lay on her back and Sate knelt at her side. Her eyes moved slowly over his wide shoulders and across the dark pelt on his chest, then followed the thin line of hair down to where his hard arousal thrust out proudly between his legs.

She trailed a hand across his flat stomach, then let her fingers circle his thickness and measure his length. She peeked up at his passionate expression and murmured huskily, "I'd forgotten how large you are."

"I won't hurt you," Sate whispered against a breast before

drawing the puckered nipple into his mouth, gently nibbling it, but not drawing. "I'll see to it that you'll be ready to take it without discomfort."

Conscious thought became impossible for Juliana as Sate's mouth and tongue worked their magic on her breasts. Her thinking didn't improve as his dark head moved down her body, his hot tongue laving her flesh, his teeth gently nipping. When he moved lower yet and flicked his tongue across the valley of her hips, her control shattered.

"Please, Sate," she whimpered, "I hurt."

"I know you do, honey," Sate soothed. "It's comin' to an end soon."

And while she watched through desire-drugged eyes his tanned hands gently parted her legs, making room for him to kneel between them. Then, a hand on each bent knee, he spread them wide and slowly moved his mouth over the silky smoothness of her inner thighs. He paused occasionally to take the soft flesh between his teeth, then he gently licked his tongue across the slight mark they made.

By now, almost weeping from the maddening pulse at her core, Juliana gave a strangled sob when Sate parted the triangle of blond hair that guarded the damp core of her desperate need.

"Oh, Sate," she gasped in sweet agony when his tongue invaded the special territory. Her fists clenched and she moved her head back and forth, sure that she could not bear the waves of ecstasy that grew and pulsated inside her.

She bore it, sustained the wave that snatched her up, carrying her to a crest that made her narrow hips buck gently. She gave a great shudder, called Sate's name, then slid into soothing waters.

Later, when the tremors released their grip on her body and her breathing subsided to normal, Juliana smiled lazily into the blue eyes watching her face intently. "Oh, darling," she whispered huskily, "I never knew . . . had no idea that anything could—"

Sate interrupted wickedly. "I could tell."

"But what about you?" Juliana glanced down at the manhood that still stood rigid and throbbing.

"You're gonna take care of that right now," Sate growled, then braced a hand on either side of her shoulders. "Take me in your soft hands and sheath me inside your warmth."

The purring order brought desire blazing through Juliana again. Lovingly she took the long, hard thickness in both hands and guided it to where she burned to feel its power. Sate carefully and slowly entered her, filling her until the blond hair meshed with the black.

Sate waited a moment, watching her face, looking for any flicker of pain. When there was none he slipped his hands under her small buttocks and, lifting her so that she fit snugly into the cradle of his hips, took up a firm rhythm.

His name a constant sound on Juliana's lips sent waves of passion sweeping over Sate, and it took all of his control to wait until weakening spasms began to shake her slender frame.

They collapsed together, their bodies slick with sweat.

Sate rolled over on his back, bringing Juliana with him, still buried deeply inside her. When she would have lifted herself off the still trembling member, he grasped her hips, keeping her in place.

"Don't think I'm finished with you." His hands tightened possessively, his eyes slumberous in the aftermath of their love. "I've waited too long, hungered too long. It will take most of the night to appease me."

He reached a hand to circle a finger around a pink nipple, then raised up on his elbows. "Come closer. Give them to me, Juliana."

She hung over him, a hand on each of his shoulders, and teasingly slid each nipple across his parted lips. She gasped her pleasure when his white teeth quickly closed on one, biting gently.

As he kissed and teased the pink-tipped mounds, Juliana felt him growing inside her. In seconds she was filled completely and he was rolling her back beneath him.

This time it was a slow, sensual riding, with Sate whispering frank words in Juliana's ears, making her blush fiercely.

"Ah, Sate," she whispered when at last they lay side by side, trembling and panting for breath, "each time it gets better."

Sate chuckled and drew her head onto his shoulder. "Just think how it's gonna be fifty years from now."

"I'm thinking, I'm thinking." Juliana snuggled up to him.

Sate stroked Juliana's hair, contentment on his face as he felt her relax in sleep. On a distant hill a gaunt timber wolf raised his head, and his wild howl echoed through the hills. This time Sate only smiled sleepily and drew Juliana closer. He no longer had anything in common with the lonely howler. He had come home.